I0546250

SPLITTER

A NOVEL BY STU CROSKELL

SEVERED**PRESS**

SPLITTER

ISBN: 978-1-923165-44-1

For my parents, June & Ernie. Fair Winds.

CHAPTER 1

USS *Bloomington* – Independence Class
Tuesday, 0234 hoursWest of Andros Island, Bahamas (24°46'45.6"N
77°38'12.4"W)

Seaman Apprentice Dusty Rhodes flicked his cigarette butt into the sea, enjoying the way its tracer-like arc disappeared into the ocean's blue-green bioluminescence. Under his feet, the steady throb of *Bloomington's* turbines vibrated through his steaming boots. He drank in the ship-ripe mix of paint, diesel, and ocean.

Bloomington. Three thousand five hundred tons of sleek and deadly warship. She could crack up to fifty knots, and her shallow-draft trimaran hull meant she could get close up and personal with coastal targets. Dusty had been thrilled to be drafted onto such a cool-looking ship. A thrill factor that had – due to his own damn stupidity - waned over the last few weeks. And here he was yet again on the ass-end of the ship doing after lookout on his own for four middle-of-the-night hours. It was *his* turn on the bridge. This was the third time in a row he'd been given the balls o' clock life buoy watch. No doubt, it was the fucking shits. If ever there was an ultimate bag of dicks, this was it. In fact, another fine Navy day.

The eerie sea glow, he knew, was due to the light released by a squillion-squillion tiny sea creatures, their light's intensity increased by *Bloomington's* churning props. Pawpaw had told him some such years ago, on one of their occasional fishing expeditions off the coast of Cape Elizabeth, back in Maine. How he wished to God he was there now. Trouble was, Pawpaw had told him a whole bunch of stuff—most of it Dusty should have kept to himself.

Standing up from the guardrail, he patted his shirt pocket for another cancer stick. Froze.

A wave of nausea shuddered through his body, and sweat broke out on his forehead, rolling down his face. He leaned back on the guardrail to steady himself, aware of a vibration existing alongside the engine's regular pulse. It was weird. He could feel it in his knees, his hands. He could even feel it in his damn eyes. Dusty gripped the guardrail tighter, convinced he was about to pass out.

As he did so, something changed. It'd gotten darker. As if someone had switched off a light. But there were no lights on this part of the ship at night – any illumination would compromise the watchman's night vision. So why did there seem to be more ... night?

And then he understood. The squillions of glowy plankton and itsy-bitsy crustaceans had disappeared. They weren't doing their light show anymore. Odd. As a seething mass of light-emitting creatures, they'd just stopped ... emitting. Shut down at the same time as if they had a hive brain, acting as one organism. Well, he'd never seen that before. It was something he'd want to share with his messmates, but he knew he wouldn't. He'd sit on it, keep it to himself. Dusty didn't want to seal the deal with the crazy-man stuff.

The horrible queasiness reduced in intensity simultaneously with the eyeball wobble-inducing vibrations. As Dusty gathered his wits, he became aware of another strange sensation. This time, it was a low-bass rumble, slowly gaining in volume until it was masking, even, *Bloomington's* screw turbulence. And then it, too, ceased.

Dusty knew he should contact the Officer of the Watch. Tell him about the vanishing bioluminescence, the creepy noises, his unnerving body shakes. Again, he decided against it, imagining them up there laughing behind his back. There goes dillhole Dusty, up to his old tricks again. Go figure. Nope – he had no desire to upgrade his crackpot creds.

Because of Pawpaw's stupid-ass stories, Dusty had morphed into the ship's designated fruit loop, the go-to wackadoo. And now he had the reputation as a believer of tall tales, a dyed-in-the-wool woo-woo boy. His buddies and the rest of the ship's crew wouldn't let it go. It was kind of okay initially, and he mostly laughed it off. But then, when they wouldn't let up with the sea monster jokes, it got old. Fast. And then something changed. People avoided sitting next to him in the chow hall. Liberty pals drifted off ashore without him.

It was the weird way things worked on a ship – you did one dumb thing, and because of that one dumb thing, you were forever tarred with its brush. When he started telling the guys Pawpaw's sea stories, he'd thought they'd been genuinely interested; how was he to know that with every yarn he told, they were all laughing behind his back? And then he'd told the sea monster story, Pawpaw's most famous story, which got in the newspapers, even on TV. For a while, way back in 1959, young Dirch Gustavsen and his first mate had been the toast of the town with their sea serpent sighting. A couple of miles off Cape Elizabeth, Pawpaw Gustavsen had been shocked to see a massive shape moving toward their tiny craft. According to Pawpaw and his crewman, they'd first assumed it was a submarine or at least some kind of submersible. However, when it got within thirty yards or so, they realized it was a living creature. They were about to cut the nets and get the hell out of there when the beast suddenly submerged. When it emerged after three or four minutes, it was swimming away. The way Pawpaw told it, it was a similar color to a cusk fish, sort of browny-yellow. One other thing that Pawpaw noticed was that every time the Portland Light Ship sounded its foghorn, the creature turned its head toward it. Only years later did young Dusty realize the significance of that detail. If the foghorn had been sounding, it must have been foggy. Therefore, how could Pawpaw have been so sure what he saw? Yet, despite the admission, he always stuck to his story. Pawpaw had been a big man, a broad-shouldered chunk of Norwegian brawn, Viking vintage. When Pawpaw told his monster story, folks listened respectfully.

Weighing in at one hundred and thirty beanpole pounds, the berserker gene – much to his annoyance - had bypassed Dusty. At twenty years old, Dusty reckoned, you'd think he'd put some meat on the scrawn.

Bloomington was Dusty's second sea draft. As a Seaman Recruit, he'd taken all the newbie sailor BS on his first temporary draft, a San Diego destroyer. Now, he was a fully made-up hardass Seaman Apprentice, no longer a baby sailor. So when would all the dissing stop?

Dusty's training had always been to report anything anomalous, anything out of the ordinary. Of course, the main job of the aft life-buoy spook was to be alert to a man overboard. Yet when they patrolled over TOTO, the Tongue of the Ocean, they were always alert to anything anomalous, the out of place. They were, after all, about twenty miles east of AUTEC, jokingly referred to as the Navy's Area 51. When you were out on the Tongue, all the jokes about AUTEC stopped being funny. The Tongue was six thousand feet deep, almost a sheer drop from Andros Island to the west and Nassau to the east. Dusty had noticed that it always unsettled the crew when they sailed over the Tongue. It was a small, subtle thing, but there was always an odd quiet about the ship when she plied these parts. Instead of a ship in regular one-in-four sea watches, it felt like she was closed up at defense stations, readying to go to battle. Only ever got this feeling out on the Tongue. Dusty theorized it was his dumb stories that had holed his shipmates' hard-won composure whenever they voyaged over the Tongue. And he'd stupidly walked right into it with Pawpaw's yarns. In this modern Navy, there was no room for sailors' quaint yarns and superstitions. *Bloomington*, after all, was a littoral combat ship. Her role was to stay in and protect coastal waters. The guys on this ship were mostly committed brown-water mariners, not for them the depths of the blue-water ships; they liked rivers, the coast, messing around in the shallow depths of Caribbean islands. The Tongue gave them the heebies *and* the jeebies.

Dusty knew that most sailors didn't like to think about what was beneath them – going over the Tongue, there was over a mile of water to think about. It was why sailors wilfully knew nothing about marine life, about what lived down there. They didn't want to be reminded that the only thing keeping them from being down with Davy Jones, swimming among the fish and God knew what else, was a thin membrane of marine steel.

He pinched the bridge of his nose, breathing in slowly, trying to clear his head and get his thinking chops back on track. Was the plankton's odd behavior possibly connected to climate change and the sea's warming? Something like that? These days, everything seemed linked-up with what was happening to the warming planet. Truth be told, it kind of scared him. He wished he knew more about the science of the sea and not just all the crap his grandfather had told him.

He leaned over the guardrail, hungry for his next smoke. From now on, he would keep his big fat pie hole shut. He was going to hunker down, do his goddamn job. Not do anything to disabuse his shipmates that he was nothing but a regular guy. Not some enlisted puke with a liking for fantastical stories.

The ship slowed down. He waited for the bridge to contact him on his radio and tell him why. But no one did. Should I ask, he thought? But again, no. Keep a low profile, don't get involved in any funny stuff, keep your head down, and get your credibility back. He looked longingly over at the internal comm sound-powered telephone. The old-school red batphone was connected to all five lookout stations, including the pilot house and the Combat Information Center. If Dusty used it instead of his radio, he'd practically alert the whole ship to his concerns. At least with the radio, he'd only be talking to the OOW.

Suddenly, a resounding, resonant splash accompanied a whoosh of water about twenty yards off the starboard beam. More water then hit the ocean with a series of loud rhythmic splashes. Something big had emerged. Dusty whipped his NVGs from his watch night pack, peering into the lens. Immediately, the sea took on an eerie green glow. He checked the starboard quarter, guessing that nothing would be there now unless it - whatever it was – kept up. Another splash, again on the starboard beam. This time, the splashing sounds were partnered with an unbelievable eyewatering stench—an evil ammoniac get-together of rotting seaweed and decomposing shellfish.

Maybe Pawpaw's stories weren't the complete crock after all.

Gagging on the stink, Dusty tried to focus the goggles on where he thought the splash occurred, but again, nothing. And then, right underneath him, along the side of the ship, just below the water level, something scraped. It sounded like metal on metal or rock on metal. But it couldn't be rock; they were over the Tongue, and there were no rocks. Had they run over a sub, some experimental vessel from AUTEC? But no – the noise wasn't coming from the hull; it was on the ship's side, almost above sea level. If *Bloomington* were a merchantman, it'd be just below the plimsoll mark. And then something splashed again, again about twenty yards off the stern. Was it the same … creature? Or was there more than one?

The scraping continued until it reached the aft end and then stopped. Whatever was doing the scraping had run out of ship. What the hell was it?

The scraping now transferred to *Bloomington's* portside. Dusty crossed the afterdeck and used the NVGs to scan the ocean again. Nothing. At least the hideous smell had returned to wherever it came from, and Dusty inhaled a big, clean gulp of air.

Again, the scraping switched sides, now back to starboard. It was as if whatever was responsible was deliberately trying to freak Dusty the hell out.

Well, pal. Whatever you are, it's working. Color me freaked.

What would Pawpaw do? Dirch Gustavsen would shout it out. Tell the world. To hell with the consequences. Demand his grandson grow a big hairy pair.

Dusty grabbed the big red phone before he could chicken out, feeling a little like Commissioner Gordon.

He might not be a Viking, but he was no coward.

CHAPTER 2

Conanicut Island
Wednesday, 1115 hours
Narragansett Bay, RI (41°54'46.4"N 71°36'62.8"W)

John 'Jack' Tarr had been judged and found wanting. Loading his backpack carefully, methodically, one item at a time, mentally checking a box for each piece of kit, he could feel the laser-like focus of his soulmate's scrutiny. She stood in the bedroom doorway, leaning on its frame, arms folded, next to the highboy, its antique walnut solidity somehow emphasizing her vulnerability. Her ash-blond hair was tied in a tight bun, her expression the business end of righteous injustice, and not one square millimeter's worth of facial real estate was left for anything remotely agreeable. No doubt about it, Jack was in the doghouse. That Erin Lansky was mightily pissed off was a no-brainer.

'I'm not okay with this, John,' she said. They'd been together for five years, and she only ever used his birth name when she was royally hacked off. It didn't happen often, but when it did, it cut through. Jack hated falling out with her. During these post-Navy SEAL days, he avoided any falling out or conflict. It didn't sit easily with him anymore. Even relatively minor unpleasantness could trigger recollections of a more brutal form of hostility; not an actual PTSD episode as such, but shitty, hateful memories he did not care to engage with. Far as he was concerned, these memories could stay in their damned box. They were the other man's, and Jack Tarr wasn't that man anymore. He'd worked hard to extract himself from his past life. Not because he was ashamed but because he'd had enough of it. And while he was aware that he was a part of all he'd ever connected with, he didn't want his whole existence defined by what he'd done as a young man. Few men managed to leave the SEALs behind, even when they'd left the SEALs behind. The Life imprinted on your DNA.

Jack stopped packing. He looked straight at her and smiled.

She said, 'Got nothing to say, huh?' Erin's accent dipped into its New York origins. Her parents might live in Riverdale now, but her grandfather had clawed his way out of the South Bronx. Truly, Erin's *zayada* was no slouch. And Erin, if she was anything, she was her grandfather's daughter. Old Joe Lansky, a Soviet Jewish émigré, still had a formidable presence even at eighty-nine.

Before he knew what he was doing, Jack shrugged. It was a bad move. He'd just lit the touchpaper.

'I know you,' Erin said, her voice low. 'You're thinking, "Just keep shtum, and pretty soon she'll run out of steam."'

Jack sneaked a peek at his watch. It was an unconscious, unnecessary reflexive action. But, too late, the damage was done.

'Holy moly, I saw that. I honestly saw that.' She put her hand on her hips. 'You looked at your watch. God*damn*.'

'I don't know what to say,' Jack said. 'I get that it pisses you off, but -'

'Just … just don't say anything,' Erin raised her hands, palms facing out, shaking her head. 'Right now, I actually hate the sound of your voice.' Tears of white-hot anger rolled silently down her cheeks, her breathing ragged. She was trying to calm down enough to speak without breaking up.

Jack had misjudged this whole situation. He moved toward her, intending to draw her to him, hold her, and ride the storm. Be with her. But she was having none of it. Instead, she backed away from him, her hands up again, palms out, shaking them side to side. *No, no, stay away from me.*

'I just wasn't there, was I?' she said.

Jack clenched his jaw, wary of Erin's curveball. 'There? *Where?*'

'In your calculations. I wasn't factored in.'

'Factored into what?'

She searched his eyes and held his gaze, looking for what? Understanding? Empathy? Compassion? 'I had things planned. *We* had things planned.'

'I - '

'No, Jack. Don't even try. There's nothing you can say can make this right.'

'What? *Ever?*'

'Don't make it worse, Jack.'

He stood there, frozen in the glare of her implacable suffering. He knew he should do something, say something, anything, but he couldn't; he was paralyzed, his feet rooted to the floor. And deep down in the depths of his psyche, he felt the old rage, the old anger. Felt it circling, swimming upwards, wanting to surface and come back into the world. He could not let that happen. Not if he wanted to stay with Erin, not if he wanted to live with himself. Breaking eye contact with her, he hung his head and focused on his packing.

Three pairs of socks. Boxers.

From a great distance, the bedroom door slammed shut.

When Jack was sure he was fully in control again, he let himself sit down on the bed—his and Erin's bed. Downstairs, she clattered around, slamming doors and stomping in and out of rooms, the old swaybacked floorboards amplifying her every move. In a way, it was comforting. At least she was still in the house. She hadn't totally given up on him—not yet, at any rate.

In moments like these, Jack missed the sage advice of his old SEAL chief, Skeeter. His sea daddy. Skeeter had always been able to straighten Jack out. But since Jack had left the Navy ten years ago to get in the marine biologist game, his old buddy had given him the big kiss-off. Not once had he been in contact. And whenever Jack had reached out – radio silence, nada. He wondered if Skeeter knew that Jack was now a fully tenured professor, one of the world's top five crustacean guys.

Jack remembered Skeeter's love of old-time Delta blues singers and how Skeeter had pretty much adopted his life's philosophy from those long-dead blues men and women: Jackson Dupree, Mississippi Harry Jones, and his constant favorite, Deelie Thomas. This philosophy fit perfectly with the unofficial SEAL creed— the only easy day was yesterday.

Miserably, Jack stared out the bay window across the house's extensive lawns, which sloped gently right down to Hull Cove, just above Beavertail State Park, south of Conanicut Island. The massive Queen Anne Victorian house, with its ancient fieldstone fences and killer views, made Jack fairly sure that Erin's grandfather was—or had been—mobbed up. How else could he gift such a place to his only granddaughter? Joe Lansky was a successful businessman, no doubt about it. But surely not five million dollars-worth of house successful. Joe had made his fortune in retail, but what that retail was, Erin was always studiedly vague.

Jack had decided he didn't care. He had his skeleton closet, Erin hers.

He sighed, unconsciously touching the metal tags resting under his T. They were a set of dog tags bearing his and Erin's names that Erin had half-ironically given Jack as a gift. To Jack, they'd morphed into a kind of rosary, a talisman. He often touched, even kissed, them in those moments when he required a little grounding, something to remind him of where he was now and how blessed he was to have Erin in his life.

He let out a slow stream of air. On a clear day, you could see right out onto the vast Atlantic. Jack loved it here, this house, the bay.

Erin. He already missed her full-wattage smile.

Jack had never had a woman go all in on him, willing to do the hard yards. He supposed it was because, in the past, he'd never been around long enough. With Erin, Jack suspected that at the beginning of their relationship, he'd been something of a project and that she'd taken him on as a challenge. It was, he realized later, a significant characteristic of her personality. She was nothing if not persistent. And she stood by him, even when he had the bad days, the nightmares. Not nightmares, really. Bad dreams. Dreams about being in the Navy again and not knowing how he got there or how to get back out. Dreams about losing Erin. Being someplace with her, then literally losing her, and not being able to find her. Funny, he never had flashbacks or nightmares about specific incidents, just dreams accompanied by a pervasive sense of dread, the imminence of something unpleasant slouching toward him, taking its sweet, awful time. He often wondered what was coming and what shape it would take. And then, almost immediately, he would think, *What a stupid thought.*

Nowadays, when he slipped into the occasional bout of pathological gloom, Erin was always there to dig him out. And now, when she'd needed him to do the right thing by her, he'd been AWOL. Jerk.

A couple of days ago, the renowned Zassenhaus Institute of Oceanography contacted him. Dr. Zassenhaus himself had called Jack to see if he would be interested in a berth on R/V *Lemuria*, the institute's flagship research vessel. Their carcinologist—a crustacean guy—had fallen ill, and they needed a replacement; they were sailing in days, shipping out to the Hawaiian Archipelago, one of the best places on the planet to study crustaceans. Without thinking it through, Jack agreed.

Though initially dubious about the short notice and arranging teaching cover for Jack, his boss understood the potential importance of the trip – to the department. Without a doubt, his boss was thinking about all the original research papers Jack would contribute to the Faculty's output. It was too good an opportunity to turn down. This would up the department profile. And so Jack's absence was greenlit.

Agreeing to the trip without consulting Erin was his first stupid mistake. Idiot. And then he'd compounded the first stupid mistake with another – worse, really – like a white-feather coward, he'd not told her until the last minute. And now he was reaping what he'd sowed. But it was when Erin found out that Jack had told his boss at the Oceanographic Department at Matunuck University before he'd told her that she really lost it. And rightly so.

His judgment call, such as it was, was unconscionable. But it had revealed how much he needed to do this, to get away, not from Erin, not from anything, but to … to what?

He stood up from the bed and moved over to the bay window, once more gazing out to the Atlantic. He loved that Erin's house was about as far away from California as you could get and still be in continental North America. California brought all the old memories back. Especially San Diego, where he'd completed his training. He didn't think he'd ever have to go back there. Too many triggers, too many mental souvenirs. *Lemuria* was sailing out of San Pedro, a hundred miles north of San Diego, close to his old stomping grounds. Close enough to give him pause for thought.

But it was an offer – as they say – he couldn't refuse.

Later that night, Jack slunk into their bed like an old errant tom cat. Erin stiffened, but she didn't kick him out. Didn't say anything either. In fact, she hadn't said anything to him since she stormed out earlier. Jack lay there on his back in the dark. Wary of speaking, of touching her.

'I'm sorry,' he said, feeling desolate, alone. There was no way he could leave Erin like this, as things were. He had to make it right.

Long minutes ticked by, and then Erin turned over to face him. 'I know,' she said. 'But you hurt me. All this keeping me out of the loop; it can't be a thing. It's got to stop.'

'It will. It has.'

Silence. 'Alright, Jack,' she whispered.

But she kept the distance between them. To Jack, it might as well have been a thousand miles. He didn't have the courage to make the journey.

CHAPTER 3

RV *Lemuria*
Friday, 1130 hours
North Pacific Ocean (33°14'03.0"N 131°10'01.8"W)

'Hey, Green Face, how much do you want today?' Lead Deckhand Gruber jibed.

'Just fill her up, Gruber,' Jack said. 'Same as you did yesterday, the day before, and the day before that.' Jack was not in the mood. He'd woken up on the wrong side of his rack. Last night, his sleep was hounded by the recurring dream of losing Erin, rendered even more potent by their recent falling out. The dream had pursued him into his waking day, later morphing into that all too familiar feeling of impending doom. Something bad was going to happen.

'Aye, aye, Froggy,' Gruber replied, giving a quarter-assed Navy salute, his greasy work shirt straining against his belly. Sweat popped on Gruber's face, rolling into the valleys of several unshaven chins. That Gruber had gone to rack and ruin was underplaying it.

Jack's luck to get the honor of working beside the Ship's Asshole every morning. It was only half an hour or so, but the ritual felt much longer. Gruber had been on his case since he'd laid eyes on Jack's Navy ink. Jack's forearm bone frog was what gave the game away. Ex-US Navy Gruber knew the frog's significance straight away.

Jack waited for Gruber to pump up his first seawater sample of the day. Despite Gruber's grubby, depressing presence, *Lemuria* seemed to be a happy ship. There wasn't that curious, edgy, ragged atmosphere that some ships had. It was always tricky to pin down what it was that made a ship unhappy. However, in Jack's experience, the crew always fell out of love with their ship first, and then *she* returned the favor. Ships were like dogs or children – treat them badly, and they'd eventually snap back. He'd never bought into the idea that some ships were just plain trouble, jinxed from the day they launched. It was – in his view – always the crew. Of course, he'd heard the stories about ships doomed from the get-go. But Jack attached no credence to it. But even on a happy ship, there was always an asshole or two. It was an ineluctable law of social physics - at sea, on a ship this size, you could never be further than twenty yards away from an example of world-class assholery. It was Jack's fate that his designated slurp hose operator was also the research vessel's mandatory douche.

Jack's muscles tightened, and he took a deep breath, counting down from five in his head, slowly emptying his lungs. Keep the beast in its cage.

Gruber flipped a couple of switches on the pump control panel. 'Were you even in the SEALs? Lot a guys have SEAL tatts. Trident, scary skeleton frog, all that shit. Guys that've never been near a rebreather, let alone sucked on one. Impress the chicks, you know? You one of them guys? Big freaking phony?'

Jack breathed in again. Five, four, three, two, one.

Gruber continued. 'All the perks, none of the hard yards. That your thing, frogman?'

'You a good swimmer, Gruber?' Jack said, voice level, standing up to his full height.

Gruber squinted into the early morning sun before turning to Jack.

'I'm okay,' Gruber said. 'Why're you interested?'

'Gruber, I'm not interested. I couldn't give two shits whether you sink or manage to swim back to San Pedro.'

'Hell you saying?' Wary now.

Jack smiled. 'Work it out, swabbie. You're a clever guy. Deck ape at the age of - what? Thirty-five? And advanced broom handler to boot. No holding you back.'

Gruber tried to stare out Jack but failed, muttering, 'Screw you.' But there was no vim in it, and Jack let it go.

Jack leaned over the portside guardrail of the fo'c'sle, *Lemuria* plowing through the near-flat seas. He breathed in deeply, senses invigorated, sucking the ozone-rich air way down into the depths of his lungs. My kind of oxygen, he thought – sharp and salt-tanged. Just the way I like it. They'd been at sea for three days, and Jack's muscle memory of ocean-going ship life – unconsciously rolling with the rhythm of the ship – had reasserted itself. Like riding a bike, once learned, never forgotten. Only thing he missed was watch-keeping. As a guest onboard, he didn't have to stand a watch, which was okay with him, but not being part of the crew and, therefore, partaking in crew responsibilities had disadvantages. Being a mere passenger made it harder to get to know the ship and ease into a relationship with her. And Jack always liked to get intimate, so to speak, with whatever ship he served on. If you worked a ship, you eventually became part of her. It was a strange intimacy that only sailors understood. Sure, airmen and their aircraft, petrolheads and their cars, had an inkling of that special relationship. But theirs was a mere skimming of the surface when it came to human-machine alliances. For sailors, a ship was not a place of employment. She was their home. It was why many sailors returning from a long voyage to their land-based digs felt oddly bereft. Jack had seen grown men weep when a ship they'd served on years ago was taken to the scrapyard.

As for *Lemuria*, he still needed to get her measure. He liked her. And he was pretty sure she liked him. But the status of their current connection was that of flirtation rather than the real deal. He doubted that would come; after all, he would only be on her for a month, and then he'd be flying back from Hawaii to be with Erin once more, where he belonged. He'd get it right this time. He'd fight to win back her trust. He'd hurt her, and he was frustrated and disgusted with himself for the doing of it. It made him feel like a monster, like one of the bad guys, a feeling he was unused to. He'd spent his whole life trying to be one of the good ones, even if being a good guy meant he had to do bad things.

Their Zoom conversations since he'd shipped out had been amicable and civil enough, but there was none of the old ease of communication. She was pale and polite, with no makeup and vulnerable-looking, while he felt like the proverbial bull in a China shop, lumpen, awkward, and desperately trying not to knock off the fragile things that precariously lined the shelves of his and Erin's relationship. But he was going to put things right. He wasn't going to lose her. It would be like losing himself.

Jack's days so far had followed a routine of taking ocean samples to check on the presence or absence of any crustacean animal, comparing the data with similar statistics from past studies. He mostly looked for the smaller crustaceans, krill, brine shrimp, copepods, and ostracods. While most big crustaceans – crabs and lobsters – lived on the ocean floor, some swam – the portunidae crab family - around at various depths. It was always possible that he'd sweep up something substantial. So, his mornings consisted of collecting the specimens into the two tanks below deck sample hold. The afternoons were spent collating his finds. The evenings were the most exciting part – the most creative. This was where he would make certain extrapolations, looking for trends. To do this, he needed a lot of samples. While Jack's specialism was carcinology, it was also in the larger environmental impact and conservation context. Crustaceans were a good measure of what was happening in the ocean if you wanted a bigger picture of climate change and its effects on marine life.

'Should do it,' Gruber said, breaking into Jack's thoughts. 'Your below-decks tanks'll be nicely topped up,' he added, pressing his palm onto the console's big red button before turning off the pump's engine.

'Why thank you, Gruber,' Jack said. 'Always a chore, never a pleasure.'

Gruber looked about to say something but then thought better of it. His swagger had crumpled. Instead, he proceeded to fit the pump's tarp back on. Jack left him to it and strolled to the starboard entrance to the lower decks.

*   *   *

Jack's lab was underneath the afterdeck next to the winch house. It was a tight space dominated by two recirculating tanks, both of which held one thousand liters of fresh Pacific Ocean. The lab was hot, too, regardless of the loud rattle of the air conditioning unit. Adding to his discomfort, the sense of something rotten winging his way had gotten worse. It had followed him below decks.

Come on, Jack. Get a damned grip. Erin issues notwithstanding, his life was in pretty good shape. He was on the ocean doing what he loved. What's more, no one was trying to kill him. He cast back to the reasons he was drawn to marine biology. Yes, it was a desire for a new challenge. Yes, he had a passion for the ocean. Yes, he wanted to do something about protecting marine ecosystems. Yes, there were transferable skills: powers of meticulous observation, data analysis, and innovative problem-solving were all grist to the mill in the SEAL day-to-day. Blah blah blah. But, really, when it came down to it, Jack had wanted to become a crustacean man because he simply loved the little guys. Crabs, lobsters, shrimps, for as long as he could remember, they'd fascinated him. With their armored suits and mighty claws, they were nothing less than ocean-going warriors.

Jack exhaled slowly. *Five, four, three, two, one.*

Right.

Today, he was going to check out the density and presence of phytoplankton, a staple of the crustacean diet. The ship's position was in an area traditionally rich in this food source, and Jack wanted to see if there was any correlation between the diminishing crustacean population and the availability of this particular microalgae. Warming waters were not good for phytoplankton, and alarmingly, loss rates were now greater than growth rates in many. Next to the tanks, Jack's personal water analysis kit lay on the dull surface of an aluminum workbench. This morning, he decided he would focus on finding out just how much biomass was in his sample. As he reached for the chlorophyll meter, he couldn't help thinking how it reminded him of the shape of an automatic pistol with its narrow hand grip and barrel-like sensor.

Despite the heat, Jack shuddered.

CHAPTER 4

Patrol Boat *Gacrux* - Defiant-Class - Dominican Navy
Saturday, 2343 hours
Greater Antilles, Caribbean (22°02'25.2"N 74°59'57.9")

Lieutenant Teniente Dex Medina scanned the night-time horizon from the bridge with his NVGs. The sky was a deep, inky blue, dotted with a scattering of twinkling stars. The full moon hung high, casting a luminous silver glow that danced upon gentle waves. The sea, a smooth expanse of dark sapphire, reflected the moon's light, creating a shimmering pathway that stretched to the horizon. He cursed his brother for the thousandth time that night. No doubt about it, his little bro was a stupid cocksucker - *mamagüevo*. This whole nasty situation was Saul's mess, his brother's doing. As always, it would be up to Dex to pick up the pieces and try to undo what had been done. Except this time, Dex didn't know what to do. There were, it seemed to him, two options. Both options came with risk, the kind of risk that got somebody killed.

At twenty-nine years old, Dex was the elder sibling by only one year, but Saul's reckless antics belonged to a teenage kid, not a fully grown man nearing his thirties. It was the way it had always been, ever since their father's life had been cut short by cancer. At age sixteen, Dex had given up college and got a job. The Navy was recruiting, and he joined up. The Navy fed him and gave him a bunk, allowing him to send almost all his wages to his mother. Best thing he ever did. And now, fifteen years later, he had his own command. The *Gacrux* may only have a complement of ten men and be just eighty-five feet long, but she was his, his baby. And he'd worked like a mother to get this far. And now Saul had screwed everything up. The dumbdick had clearly made some weird internal mental computation, figuring that if Big Bro was taking all the family responsibility, being the big man, then that gave him, Saul, a de facto license to be completely irresponsible.

The *Gacrux* was running dark, and the sea was calm enough to turn the engines off. The auxiliary power source kept the radar and communication systems alive. Only Dex and Ronny stood on the bridge.

Dex still held the hardcopy priority message from the Naval Communications Station in Puerto Rico.

TWSY
DE BFR NR 115

P 202312Z JUN
AUTEC

CLAS. RELAY ANOMOLOUS UNIDENTIFIED PHENOMENA –
SURFACE, UNDERWATER. VISUAL, SONAR, RADAR,
ACOUSTIC.

END MESSAGE.

Using the bridge-to-bridge radio, Dex had ordered *Alnitak* and
Fomolhaut to prioritize the P message. When asked what the message
meant, Dex had told his lieutenants that their guess was as good as his.
Just be vigilant and run anything past him first before contacting
AUTEC. The mysterious message went a little way – not far enough, of
course – to ease his problem. He could now claim that his bosses had
legitimately hierarchized the narcos into second place. No matter what
bullshit the narcos were blackmailing him with, orders were orders. It
wasn't much, but it gave him some breathing space.

He scoped the sea again, this time with his regular binoculars. It
was a bright, moonlit night, rendering night vision goggles next to
useless, the ones they'd been issued with anyway. Dex knew that NVGs
were not created equal, and he suspected that theirs sat at the low end of
the tech. Budgets were tight, and the Navy always cut corners.
Technically, even the *Gacrux* herself wasn't one hundred percent
Dominican Navy, having been gifted by the Americans to help fight the
good fight, aka the war on drugs, just like the two Defiant-Class – the
Alnitak and the *Fomolhaut* – they were patrolling with. It was why the
three patrol boats were doing picket duty between the north of Cuba and
the south of the Bahamas. Being the lead ship, the *Gacrux* sat plumb in
the middle of the picket line, with the *Alnitak* ten miles north of *Gacrux*
and the *Fomolhaut* ten to the south. It still left an awful lot of ocean
unaccounted for and easy for the drug runners to slip through. But that
wasn't the problem. The problem was that Dex had been ordered to let
the drugs through on their way to Mexico. The gang - the *nacione* - his
brother had gotten mixed up in had let it be known that if Dex and his
small squadron of ships didn't turn the other way, Saul would pay the
price.

So. Get his brother killed or put his ship and crew in the pay of the
gangs.

He was almost glad that his mother had passed on and that the
gang couldn't use her as leverage – which they would. They wouldn't
think twice about torturing and murdering an old woman. A lot of

psychos gravitated towards the gangs, guys that were beyond human. Depraved.

The drugs had come from Venezuela to the Dominican Republic, and now they were on the second of a three-leg journey to the States by way of Mexico. The gang was using two narco boats, customized go-fast vessels. They were low and streamlined, hard to detect by radar. But that didn't matter because Dex had given Saul the position of the *Gacrux*, and the go-fast boats right at this moment were headed their way. It was unlikely that *Alnitak* and *Fomolhaut* would pick up the go-fasts - they sat too low in the water. At least he wouldn't have to explain to the other two skippers why he'd failed to interdict the narcos when they'd sped right on by him. No, the problem was how he explained to his crew that he'd failed to take action. They'd know he'd been bought off, that he was dirty. Dex hated that thought. His crew were his boys. They looked up to him to do the right thing. How was he going to play this? Saul had said that the narcos intended to stop, board the *Gacrux*, and pay Dex – right in front of the crew - for turning a blind eye.

Though less than a hundred feet long, the *Gacrux* could stay at sea for extended periods, periods that seemed to be getting more extended. It was pissing the crew off. They had wives and families. Like him, they didn't join the Navy for the travel opportunities and sightseeing; they joined because of the wage packet. His guys looked to him to get them a fair deal. So how the hell could he now tell them that, alongside spending more time at sea, they were now the *naciones'* bitch?

Dex knew that it was all a performance. The narcos didn't need to pay off the Navy, least of all the crew of the *Gacrux*. It was a power play. This particular gang was flexing their muscles, establishing their credentials. After all, if they could boast that they had the actual Navy in their pockets, well, that would be one hell of a coup. They'd have one over all the other gangs, even though operationally, it didn't make a whole lot of difference. But once word got back to the cartels that one of the Dominican *naciones* had the Navy where they wanted them, then that would be a big deal.

He'd almost told his XO several times about his conundrum. Ronny Sanz, a junior lieutenant – a corvette lieutenant, *Teniente de corbeta*, was Dex's best friend. While Ronny was a few years younger, the two men had serendipitously followed each other through the fleet, serving on the same ships. When Dex had been given the *Gacrux*, he'd requested explicitly that Ronny be his XO.

'So, what's going on, Dex?' Ronny said. When they were alone, they didn't bother with the formalities of rank. 'Haven't seen you like this since you got burnt over that Camila woman. Is that it? A *chica bonita* giving you sleepless nights?'

Here it is, Dex thought. What do I say? Is this the moment I lose everything? My best friend, my command, maybe even my life? He turned to Ronny. 'There's an added complication to this night's work.'

'Yeah? Like what?'

Dex ran his hands through his hair, grimacing. 'What you might call a predicament.'

Ronny stared at Dex blankly. Then, 'Holy Mary, mother of God.' He wagged his index finger, pointing at Dex. 'It's that shithead Saul. I'm right, aren't I?'

Dex nodded.

Ronny clasped his hands behind his head, expelling air through puffed cheeks. 'That *hijo de la gran puta*. What's he done now?'

Dex told him.

When Dex finished, Ronny was silent. Then, 'How do we fix this?' Ronny gestured toward three sailors on the fo'c'sle, one leaning into his 12.7mm machine gun pedestal mount while the other two had tripod mounts for the lighter 7.62mm. 'These guys are itching to play with their toys. They're already rehearsing the stories they're gonna tell their girlfriends.'

'You okay with this, Ronny?'

'We don't know what *this* is yet. But, yeah, all the way, boss.'

Dex picked up his binoculars. 'Trouble is, I don't know if Saul is with the narco boats. I'd be tempted to blow them out of the water if I knew he was not. Nobody'd be any the wiser.'

'Not if they got an SOS out,' said Ronny.

'Ideally, they wouldn't have time. Wouldn't know what hit 'em.'

In the distance, eastwards several miles away, Dex picked up a glint of metal, a momentary moonlit reflection.

'Company,' said Dex, thinking, *What do I do?*

CHAPTER 5

RV *Lemuria*,
Saturday, 2355 hours
North Pacific Ocean (31°47'51.4"N 140°37'34.8"W)

Jack enjoyed the evenings the most. Down in the scientists' mess hall. Relaxing with a few drinks. It was an excellent way to end the day. A good time to swap sea stories. Tonight, most of the scientists had turned in early. The only stragglers were Chief Scientist Margie O'Hanlon and a young Asian guy called Johnny Sato. O'Hanlon's bag was aquaculture, while Johnny's was tides and currents. Johnny liked to joke that his research area was eerily apposite given that he often felt like a piece of driftwood with nowhere to call home. Jack suspected that the 'joke' was more to elicit sympathy from Margie. Though at least twenty years older than Johnny, she was charismatic and good fun.

'I'm about all plum-tuckered,' said Margie, stretching and yawning ostentatiously. 'Think I'm going to turn in.'

'Aw, just one more story,' Johnny piped up, like a young kid desperate to stay up just a little longer.

Jack looked over to Margie, shrugging. 'Kid wants a story. Wouldn't want to get in the way of that.' He winked at Johnny.

Margie sighed. 'Okay, one last one. Set the drinks up, Johnny, and we'll begin.'

Johnny came back with the drinks, and Jack started. 'It's a quick one, really. And not much of a story, just something that, well, happened.'

Jack took a generous swig of his margarita. The kid did cook up a mean one. There was hope for him yet.

'Go for it, Jack,' Margie said.

'Yeah,' said Johnny, sitting down and stirring his margarita with the non-business end of a spoon. 'I've got to have my bedtime story, or else I can't sleep.'

Jack leaned back in his seat. 'Like I say, it's not much of a story. It's more just something you come across now and then. But it happened. I can vouch for the truth of it. And it gave me a serious dose of the willies.'

'Good intro, Jack,' said Margie, doing a small, soft handclap. 'Got me right on the hook.'

Jack smiled. 'That's the thing with true stories. They don't need much to get you invested. They kind of speak for themselves.' He let his hand curl around his glass, enjoying its coolness. 'Back in my Navy days,' Jack said, 'I got a temp draft on *Sylvia Earle*.'

'The survey ship? Nice work if you can get it.'

'Yeah, it was cool. It was mostly crewed by civilians, a detachment of Kiwi marine biologists. It was a little bit like *Lemuria*. You know, no Navy BS. For me, it was like a vacation. But they were short of a helo pilot, and I was in the area, and I was seconded.'

'You were in the area,' Margie said somewhat tartly. 'Of course, you were.'

'Hey,' Jack said, 'I was a popular guy in those days. People wanted what I had to offer.'

Though Jack was reasonably sure both Margie and Johnny knew about his SEAL bona fides, neither of them had ever expressed any interest in that part of his life, and Jack was grateful for that. Besides, when he occasionally thought about those long gone days, it was like he was remembering someone else's life, not his own, like a third-person memory.

Part of his psyche, the part that gravitated toward high-risk deviltry, wasn't always necessarily about violence. No, it was the simple, giddy impetuosity of spur-of-the-moment decision-making. It was what had gotten him into the deep stuff with Erin—why he'd jumped at the *Lemuria* voyage opportunity without thinking through the consequences.

'Hey, maybe people still want what you've got to offer,' said Johnny archly.

Jack laughed. 'I'll keep that in mind, but don't hold your breath.'

'The story, Jack,' Margie said, visibly flagging, checking her watch.

'I'm getting to that. Anyway, we were in the Tasman Sea about two hundred miles west of Auckland, monitoring a tagged great white. A twenty-footer, five thousand pounds, would you believe? She was swimming around on the surface, I don't know, just enjoying the day, as you do. When it happened. That old shark sort of dropped a couple of thousand feet in as many seconds, dragged down by something far bigger and meaner than her.'

'Shit,' Johnny said.

'Yeah, but get this. Her body temperature shot up by over twenty degrees. Twenty degrees, man.'

'I don't get it,' Margie said. 'Shouldn't the shark's body heat decrease at that depth?'

Johnny leaned forward, his elbows on the table, resting his head in the V of his hands. 'Yeah, it should. Unless –'

'Unless?' Jack said, enjoying their bafflement.

'Something …' Johnny said, extending the word. 'Something swallowed it. Like whole.'

'A whale?' asked Margie.

'Nah, not in those waters, that time of year.'

'Then what?'

Jack shrugged. 'Who knows? I've never seen a bunch of boffins so shook up, though. It's kind of funny—those fellas having a big hole punched into their reality.'

'Aw, man. That's a good story,' said Johnny, finishing his drink. 'Is it true, though?'

Jack smiled.

'And there's the rub,' said Margie. 'Is the man telling the truth?'

Jack folded his arms. 'The man is telling the truth. I shit you not.'

'It sounds like something we would have heard about,' Johnny said. 'Something like that, it's pretty out there.'

'You know how it works,' Jack said. 'Science is the only story in town. Anything that happens outside the science box is not allowed to exist. It didn't happen.'

'So, what? They sat on it?' Johnny cracked his fingers and stretched his back, useless against the epically unergonomic chairs.

Jack nodded. 'What happened to that big-ass shark - it made no sense. There's no beast big enough to munch wholesale on an adult great white and take her down that fast, that deep. Our oceans haven't been stocked with that kind of thing for over sixty million years.'

'Therefore,' Margie said, 'it didn't happen.'

'They attributed it to wonky equipment cranking out wonky data. Blame your tools, boys, why don't you? Though the gear on the *Sylvia* was all leading-edge, the best money could buy.'

'But the gear could've been wonky,' Johnny said.

'Yep,' said Jack. 'Could've. Wasn't. I know when a person's shook up. And those guys, they were shaking more than Elvis. They were scared, Johnny. Trust me, I've seen scared.'

Jack had other stories, ones, unfortunately, that he couldn't tell. One story in particular was thirdhand, word of mouth, SEAL tales, and, if true, classified. It was not for public domain consumption.

This particular one was about how, on a routine reconnaissance mission off the Solomon Islands back in 2004, a team of U.S. Navy SEALs encountered something very weird. The mission's objective was a standard reconnaissance of an uninhabited island believed to be a potential site for illegal activities. However, the SEALs were not prepared for what they were about to discover beneath the ocean's surface. As they approached the island, the SEALs deployed underwater drones to survey the seabed. The drones captured images of an underwater cave, showing unusual bioluminescent activity. Intrigued, the team decided to investigate further. Equipped with advanced diving gear, they descended into the depths. Inside the cave, the SEALs encountered creatures that could only be described as hybrids. These beings had the upper bodies of humans and the lower bodies of large, powerful fish. They were about seven feet long, with translucent skin that emitted a soft, blue-green glow. Their eyes were large and adapted to the low-light conditions of the deep sea. The humanoids appeared to be communicating through a series of melodic sounds and gestures. Initially, the SEALs kept their distance, observing the creatures – *mermaids?* - from behind natural rock formations. The creatures seemed peaceful, curious about the SEALs but not aggressive. One of the SEALs, a marine biologist by training, attempted to communicate using a series of hand signals and simple sound mimicking. To the team's astonishment, the creatures responded with similar gestures and sounds, indicating a basic understanding. The SEALs collected data, including high-definition footage and water samples, ensuring they did not disturb the mermaids or their habitat. After several hours of observation, the team surfaced, bringing with them unprecedented evidence of the encounter.

In fact, it was Skeeter who'd yarned the tale after downing several pitchers of good old Maryland Natty Boh. Skeeter claimed he'd heard the tale from a buddy of his. He'd refused to say who, tapping the side of his nose.

To this day, Jack didn't know if Skeeter had been spinning him one or was, in fact, relaying kosher gen. By nature, Skeeter wasn't inclined to indulge in outré speculation, so it made Jack wonder. In fact, so unsettled was Jack by Skeeter's unexpected apropos-of-nothing story that he'd gone online and checked out the Solomons for legends of humanoid sea marine life. To say that what he found was a major source of discombobulation would be an understatement – the Adaro. A unique figure in the mythology of the Solomon Islands, particularly within the culture of the Makira people. The Adaro was often described as a malevolent ocean spirit, distinct from the more benign spirits of the sea. It was said to have a humanoid form but with certain features that set it apart. For instance, it was sometimes depicted with fins and gills. The Adaro was also known for its harmful and dangerous nature. *Ah*, Jack had thought. *Gotcha.* The fish guys in Skeeter's account had been friendly sorts. Then he read: *These days, however, they are now amicable and benign, having evolved from their former fearsome selves.* Just as Skeeter had told it – peaceable.

Interrupting his musing, Margie said, 'What are you really here for, Jack?' The margaritas were taking hold, and Margie was beginning to feel comfortable asking personal questions.

'Oh, grist for the old curriculum vitae, research paper opportunities. Crustaceans, they're like the new way of divining the future. Their behavior tells us much about where we're headed as a planet. In Roman times, a guy called a haruspex used to mess about in sacrificed chickens' entrails, looking for omens. Even today, shamans in Cameroon practice *nggàm*, studying crabs' behavior. Yes, crabs. According to the shamans, how a crab moves can tell us much about what will befall us. Makes me part of a living tradition.'

Over the main Tannoy, the officer of the watch called the deck party helicopter crew to standby for embarkation. Jack looked at Margie quizzically. 'Seems late for a helo arrival,' he said, frowning. 'How far out from Hawaii are we?'

Margie shrugged. 'A day's sailing, five hundred miles or so.'

'Some kind of emergency?' said Jack. 'They couldn't wait another day?' He made a quick calculation. Given the average helo's limited range, this helo must have refueled in flight. The first frisson of anxiety crept around Jack's brain.

'Anyway,' said Johnny. 'You side-stepped Margie's question nicely, Jack, but I think our Chief Scientist here suspects you have ulterior motives.'

'You think I believe crustaceans are psychic?' Jack joked, trying to ignore the worrisome tug of the mystery helicopter. 'Okay, I admit it. You got me there.'

'It's just that,' Margie said, 'I've seen you down in the hold with your tanks, checking out the day's catch, how you handle the little fellas, how you're careful to put 'em right back in the sea at the end of the day. I've heard you talk to them, Jack. So sweet. Admit it, you're obsessed with the little buggers.'

Jack looked theatrically to his left and right as if making sure no one was listening in. 'You're right,' he said, mock sotto voce. 'I'm looking into Crustacean sentience.'

'Way to go, Jack,' said Johnny, offering an enthusiastic fist bump Jack only belatedly took up.

'I think,' said Jack, all seriousness now, 'no, I believe, that the only way forward is to accredit some kind of sentience to all living things. And maybe, when we really understand the ubiquity of it, that we as humankind, well, maybe we'll stop being so destructive, so fucking shitty to each other, to the planet, to everything.'

Jack realized that Johnny's margaritas were working their magic on him, too. But at this moment, he didn't care if these people thought his cheese had finally slipped off its cracker. It was what it was.

The swing doors opened into the dining hall, and a chunky squat guy came in wearing a baggy white T-shirt and Bermuda shorts. 'Mr Tarr,' he said. 'You got a conference which requires your attention.'

Jack recognized the stumpy guy as the ship's radio officer. 'Conference? You mean like a Zoom thing?'

Another quiver of anxiety fluttered through Jack's solar plexus. Erin? He stood up quickly, knocking his chair over. 'Who is it?'

'It's the Navy, sir. A three-star vice admiral named Clewton.' The RO hitched up his Bermudas. 'He doesn't seem like the patient type.'

Relief flooded through Jack. Erin's alright, she's all good. His relief was followed by a wave of righteous annoyance. *Clewton.* No-clue Clewton. Jack slowly sat down. 'I'd like you to tell Vice Admiral Clewton to go and slowly boil his balls.'

The RO grimaced, rubbing and smoothing his towheaded omnidirectional hair with one hand. 'It'd be better – for me, at least – if you told him. He's just arrived.'

'Alright,' said Jack, rising from his seat once again. 'I'll do that.'

CHAPTER 6

RV *Lemuria*
Sunday 0002 hours
North Pacific Ocean (31°47'51.4"N 140°37'34.8"W)

Jack took the deck route to the skipper's quarters, eying the helicopter parked precariously on the helopad. Although he didn't know its specific moniker, it was clearly a rejigged riff on the old CH-53E. A bird known for its long-range, multipurpose abilities. Midstep, he halted his purposeful midnight strides. *Deep breaths*, he self-instructed. Calm down. There was nothing No-clue Clewton could do to Jack. Jack was a fully signed-up civilian now, and the only ship he needed was citizenship. So why did he feel so on edge? He moved to the guardrail, slowly drawing air deep into his lungs. To be sure, he could make a pretty good guess why No-clue's unannounced visit was raising his hackles – the man's unwanted presence was like some species of home invasion. *Lemuria* – albeit temporarily – was his home, and No-clue had invaded it. It surprised Jack how much he did not want the Navy back in his life. Twelve years ago, Clewton had been a lowly commander that Jack had fallen out with big time.

Somewhat more in control of himself, Jack reluctantly pulled away from the guardrail and resumed his march across the deck. He reached the ladder and took it two steps at a time up to the starboard bridge lookout post and to the external door of the captain's cabin. Resisting the automatic urge to knock, he twisted the handle and walked straight in. Clewton stood with his back to Jack, his hands clasped behind his back, only turning around when Jack shut the door. He was dressed in civvies, obviously not wanting to appear too Navy-like. Just a regular guy, visiting his old pal Jack. Except Clewton was not a regular guy, and he certainly was no pal of Jack's. Not now, not ever. Not after what he did.

In a way, Clewton was one of the reasons Jack left the Navy. Just over a decade ago, Jack had been part of a team that had conducted a raid in the northeast of Yemen, a hundred miles from their ship in the Gulf of Aden. While they'd managed to rescue several Yemenis and take out fifteen militants, ten SEALs had become separated from the Yemeni counterterrorism operatives they'd been embedded with. Jack suspected they'd been captured by the terrorists. He wanted to return, locate, and helovac the lost SEALs. But Clewton had pulled rank. Said the guys were almost certainly dead and that there was no way he was risking more lives. Besides, the mission was completed, and it was a success.

Yep, Clewton. The ultimate buddy fucker. Somebody should have deep-sixed him years ago.

Clewton smiled, the one that never quite reached his eyes, offering his hand. Reflexively rather than by intention, Jack shook the admiral's proffered mitt and immediately felt vaguely soiled by the brief physical transaction. Clewton still exuded his bent shitcan of a personality.

'Long time,' Clewton said.

'Not long enough, Val,' Jack said. There was no way he was going to *sir* this guy. Besides, Clewton didn't deserve the honorific. Hell, Clewton didn't deserve to be in the Navy. But here he was.

Clewton was attired in an open cream shirt and green corduroy pants, clearly going for an off-duty look. Only his big fat gold Navy signet ring on his right-hand pinkie gave the game away. Jack became aware of a strange smell that seemed to waft off Clewton's person—a familiar smell—disagreeable, like rotting food. Accompanying it was the distinct odor of expensive bourbon.

Ignoring Jack's dig, Clewton sat down at the captain's desk. Without waiting to be asked, Jack sat down in the chair opposite. Again, if Clewton was annoyed by Jack's presumption, he showed no outward sign of it.

'Whatever it is,' Jack said, 'the answer's no.' Though, truthfully, Jack was a little curious about the reason behind Clewton's visit. How could you not be?

'I get it, Jack, I do,' Clewton said, the epitome of reasonableness. 'But I wouldn't be here ruining your evening if I, the Navy, didn't find ourselves in something of a … pickle.'

Jack rolled his eyes and slowly shook his head. 'The Navy's always in a goddam pickle, situation normal, etcetera, etcetera.'

'Except,' Clewton said, 'this isn't your regular Navy pickle. In fact, it is decidedly irregular, what you might call a *cornichon marine extrême*.' While Clewton did hail from the South, Jack hated his good-ole-boy act. In reality, Clewton was as waspish as they came.

'That supposed to get me on the hook? Get me all interested?' Jack leaned forward, elbows resting on his knees, his face getting into Clewton's psychologically owned space. 'Val, I'm a civilian now. You know this. There's nothing to discuss. We are both wasting each other's time. I got a life now.'

'Once Navy, always Navy. There's no me or you in this, only we. And we're still on the same side.'

'No, we're not,' Jack said emphatically. 'Leave no man behind. Remember?'

Clewton shook his head. 'That's right. And we didn't.'

'You can't know that,' Jack said, working hard to contain his anger. 'That was the point.'

'To this day, Jack, nothing has been heard of those guys. Not from the Yememis, not from the militants. If the Yemenis knew what happened, they'd tell us. If bad guys had 'em we sure as hell would've known about it.'

Clewton was plain wrong. You made damn sure you left no one behind. They hadn't made damn sure, and it was an unforgivable dereliction of duty. Clewton should have been keelhauled or some such, drummed out of the Navy, his insignia ripped from his uniform. He wasn't, though. Old families. Old money. A couple recent ancestors who'd already worn the Navy blue. It all helped. And here he was, a three-star ranking officer. Rewarded for failure, failing upward.

Jack leaned back in his chair, studying Clewton. 'It seems a bit odd sending you, of all people. I guess you told the powers that be about our history?' he said.

Clewton's fisheye smile once more crept across his features. 'To be honest, it's why I was given the honors. The reasoning was I'd get your attention. If they sent anybody else, they might not even get as far as an audience with you.'

Clewton's answer did sound like your typical Navy ass over teakettle, counterintuitive rationale. 'Okay, you've got my attention.' Jack couldn't help feeling that he'd been played, outmaneuvered somehow. But he had to admit he was curious about what could possibly need his input. 'Two minutes.'

'This is all on a need-to-know basis and is above secret. I'm sure I don't have to tell you what that means.'

'I'm already losing interest. Do you expect me to be impressed because of some upper-echelon classified bullcrap? I've been out over ten years, and I reckon I still know more black data than you've had hot dinners.' Jack checked his watch. 'Minute and half.' Jack was going to enjoy giving Clewton a big no.

Clewton scratched his head, hints of a glower moving about his face. Jack could tell he was struggling not to bite back at Jack's jibes. By God, they must want me something awful. And again, he would be lying if he wasn't intrigued as to what that something was.

'I'm working out of AUTEC now, Jack. You know what that is?'

'Where the Navy tests out their new toys. Mostly underwater stuff. Down in the Bahamas.'

'Andros Island, to be precise,' Clewton said. 'We got a lot of research and development going on, and not just in submersibles.'

'The guys used to joke it was the Navy's Area 51,' Jack said. 'That the AUTEC boys were knee-deep in all sorts of spooky crap. UFOs, invisibility cloaking. I presume the reality's a lot more mundane?'

'Mostly,' Clewton said. 'There's a small percentage that's ... not entirely mundane.'

'Admiral, may I suggest you have a long conversation with your ass and see if you can tell which is making more sense?'

'Come on, Jack, I'm being serious here.'

'So you *are* reverse engineering UFOs and making warships disappear.' Jack slapped his thigh. 'I knew it. Wait till I tell the folks back home.'

'No UFOs, Jack. Or invisible ships.' Clewton studied Jack as if wary about spilling what he had to say. 'But we do have a biotech facility, which is pretty out there when it comes to cutting edge.'

'I have no idea what you're talking about, and I'm still not interested.' Jack looked at his watch. 'One minute, then I'm out of here.'

'We've got an issue – with a new species of marine life. Something that dredged itself up off Andros. Never seen anything like it. Likely, one of our experimental vessels got its attention. Either way, we managed to capture it, study it. Let it swim around a sea pen. But it escaped. Thing is, this creature – this *crustacean* - is potentially dangerous. It needs to be recaptured. Put out of service. No place for such a thing in this world.' Clewton paused, biting his lower lip. 'Jack, we need someone with your specialist knowledge. You are literally one of the world's leading carcinologists.'

'There's others,' said Jack. In fact, he knew them all. The close-knit carcinology community was as small as the ocean was big. But what Jack wanted to ask, was desperate to ask, was: *What the hell have you found? And lost?*

Clewton continued. 'We want you to find it. You'd have your own team and access to any equipment you ask for. This creature, it's large and it's an unknown. If you capture it, I can guarantee you first dibs on research as well as discovery accreditation. Plus, a handsome Navy payment for services rendered. I'm talking about the high-end of six figures. Of course, we'd see to it that your university faculty received generous US Navy research grants on a regular basis. Enough to make your department a contender with the big boys.'

Jack leaned back in his chair. Clewton was offering him the world. But there would be a catch. Still, as a marine biologist, to sit on top of a discovery of a significant-sized unknown, well, it would make his career and then some. 'I say again—there are others out there who'd jump at the chance.'

'But none of them have your … expertise.'

Jack assumed Clewton was referring to his SEAL days. 'Jesus, Clewton, I don't have that expertise. It's been over a decade.'

Clewton ran a cursory eye over Jack. 'You've obviously kept in shape.'

'You know what I mean.'

'Still, you're the only PhD marine biologist with a certain type of training.'

As much as Jack wanted to grab hold of Clewton's hook, he had to think of Erin. He couldn't afford to complicate matters further. Besides, working with Clewton was a moral no-no. It was time to set No-clue straight and get him back on his goddamn helicopter. 'I'm going to have to give you a hard pass, Admiral. And your time's up.'

'I haven't quite apprised you of the whole situation, Jack.'

'Well, fuck you kindly, Admiral, but I say again, your time's up, and I'm out of here,' Jack said, making for the door. It felt good walking away from an actual admiral, especially No-clue, the man who'd trampled on the unofficial creed. It felt damn good.

'There's another reason it should be you, Jack,' Clewton said. Jack didn't like the glint of triumphalism in his eyes. 'Your buddy Skeeter. He was part of the, ah, project. He's MIA.'

Skeeter. Jack was kind of surprised that Skeeter – at least, up until recently - remained in the land of the living. He'd almost convinced himself Skeeter had lit out for the wide blue yonder years ago, *still on patrol*, as they called those who'd died in combat. It would explain why he never got in contact. Death will do that.

Clewton delivered the coup de grace. 'Leave no man behind, right Jack?'

CHAPTER 7

Narco Boat *Challenger*
Sunday, 0044 hours
Greater Antilles, Caribbean (22°02'25.2"N 74°59'57.9")

The forty-foot *Challenger* skimmed the glass-like ocean like a flat pebble thrown by a schoolboy. For Saul, it was both exhilarating and nerve-wracking. If all went well, he would be seen as a kind of cool guy within the organization. Something he so desperately craved. If it went ass-up, well, he'd probably be dead.

The boat sliced through the inky black water with a mighty roar, its engine's deep, throaty growl resonating through the hull. The wind whipped his face, cool and salty, tugging at his hair and clothes and carrying the spicy scent of the sea. Saul's grip on the boat's railing was tight, knuckles white, as he braced against the sharp turns and sudden shifts in momentum. The sound of the wind and the engine combined in such a din that it drowned out all other noises, heightening his focus, increasing his awareness. The blend of speed, night, and the looming unknown made for a heady mix of adrenaline and, yes, apprehension.

Above, the bloated moon gave them all the light they needed. Perfect conditions, Saul thought, as the go-fast boat topped out at over sixty knots, nearly seventy miles per hour. Nautical miles an hour. Saul chuckled to himself. What would Papi think about both his sons being seafarers? When Big Bro Dex became a bigshot officer in the Republic's Navy, Papi was overjoyed. And now little Saul was in the Navy too, the Narco Navy. The traffickers liked to joke that the Narco Navy was bigger than the actual Dominican Navy. Except it was no joke.

Gripping the *Challenger*'s sides, Saul breathed in deeply, seawater spraying his face with fresh salty droplets, trying to stay in the moment and enjoy the simple pleasure of being alive. No past, no future, only now, right now. The other boat, the *Alboràn*, was running parallel. It, too, carried three *narcotraficantes* sat on two tons of cocaine. The only niggle was the boat's name – *Challenger*. Who names a boat after a blown-up space shuttle? Bad luck, man. Bad luck.

On the *Challenger*, Skipper Antonio was at the wheel while Daniel, navigating, sat next to him. Clenched between his knees, Saul's assault rifle, an IMI Galil liberated from the Columbian National Police, felt warm to the touch. Soon, Saul would have his own narco boat, and he'd be sat in that fat shit Antonio's seat. Captain Saul. Up yours, Big Bro.

And he'd be getting paid upwards of thirty thousand dollars for his trouble, and to hell with the measly two grand for babysitting a couple hundred million dollars of prime Columbian white. Since the mid-sea arrangement with Dex, Bossman Aranda, the leader of Saul's gang set, had been Saul's best friend. Now, all he needed for that 'friendship' to continue was for Dex to be where he said he'd be.

To be honest, when Saul had told the bossman that he had Navy contacts, he thought he might have overreached. Saul didn't want to be a mere *bandelero* all his life, usually a short life. But he was so keen to get on and up the hierarchy that he couldn't help himself, and he'd boasted to Aranda that he could wrap his big brother around his little finger. Besides, Aranda also had ambitions. He wanted to go places, to become kingpin, a big shot. Currently, Aranda controlled the sets, and he controlled the gang. He wanted more, though, so Aranda reached out to the Latin Kings, informing them how useful he could be to them. And Saul thought Aranda was the type to pull off a stunt like that. Unlike most *bandelero*, Aranda came from a respectable upper-class Dominican family. And he had the confidence that came with that, the talk, the walk. Saul reckoned that if he could hang on those coattails, he, too, could walk the walk. Become a big shot. Show the world, show his brother.

To be honest, Saul was more than surprised when Dex had agreed to his proposal – he'd always thought that Dex was kind of up his ass when it came to honor and all that shit and that there was no way he would play fast and loose with his sanctimonious morals. But, hey. As they say, if the price is right, anybody – even righteous asswipes like Dex, could be paid off. Saul frowned. He wondered how much his brother was getting paid. He didn't like the idea of him getting a bigger payoff. That didn't sit right at all.

'Hey, Antonio,' he shouted above the *Challenger*'s four engines. 'Antonio!'

Antonio either couldn't hear Saul, or he chose to ignore him.

Saul edged his ass, scooting along the portside slatted bench closer to Antonio. 'Hey, Antonio.'

Daniel tapped Antonio on the shoulder, yelling in Antonio's ear, thumbing in Saul's direction.

'What?' Antonio shouted. Despite the roar of the engines, Saul detected the annoyance in the man's voice. He was such a miserable bastard. When Saul had his own boat, he'd make his trips something to be enjoyed. Hell, it wasn't like they were going to get caught. The narcos had most of the Caribbean in their pockets.

Saul ass-walked a couple inches closer to Antonio. 'Hey, man. How much you paying my brother? He getting more than me?'

Taking one hand off the helm, and without even turning round, Antonio flipped Saul a reverse bird. 'You talk too much,' he yelled. 'Shut the fuck up.'

Saul was about to answer back but thought better of it. Antonio was pissed off because Saul was in with Bossman Aranda. It was why Saul was on the boat in the first place. Antonio hated that his regular shotgun guy had been side-lined. He'd barely spoken to Saul all night.

The high-pitched scream of the boat's engines became more throaty. The boat was slowing down. Across the way, the *Alboràn* was doing the same. With one hand on his rifle and the other on the side of the boat, Saul stood up. Straight ahead, about a mile away, a patrol vessel bobbed in the moon's gleam.

'Is it the right one?' Antonio asked Daniel. 'The *Gacrux*?'

Daniel shrugged. 'I think so. Do you think they've seen us? Visually, I mean. We're too low in the water for radar. At this range. Maybe?'

'*Gacrux* needs to signal first. We need to be sure it's him more than he needs to be sure it's us.' The *Challenger* slowed some more, the *Alboràn* following, copying.

'It's all optics, man,' Daniel said, echoing Saul's exact thoughts. 'Theatre. Aranda wants the performance out here on the high seas to prove he's got the Navy dancing to his tune.'

Antonio nodded, killing the engines. 'I ain't getting any closer. My boat, my decision.' He turned round his bucket seat, addressing Saul, 'All your fault, *hijo de la gran puta*.' Antonio shook his head in disgust. 'There is no point to this.' He sighed and bent over in his seat, rummaging in a medium-sized black holdall, retrieving what Saul knew was a night vision camcorder.

'Make sure the moon's behind you. Otherwise, that thing's going to be next to useless.'

'What Aranda wants, Aranda gets,' muttered Antonio. 'He's got ambitions, gonna get us all killed is what.'

Daniel nudged Antonio. Daniel didn't want Saul to hear Antonio badmouth the boss. Daniel didn't trust Saul either. Yeah, and you're right not to.

Antonio, though, was on a roll. He held up the camera. 'Who does Aranda think I am? Tarantino?' He switched the camera on, flipping out the small screen, raising it above the elongated cigar-shaped bow, and waving it in the general direction of the *Gacrux*.

'Make sure I'm not in your goddam movie, Antonio,' Daniel grumbled. 'Don't need to be no movie star to do my damn job.'

C'mon, bro, Saul thought. *Don't mess this up for me. Flash the damn light.*

It was as if Dex had telepathically read Saul's thoughts; there were three short flashes and three long ones from the vessel.

'Alleluia, holy mother of God,' Antonio whispered. 'It is the *Gacrux*.' He restarted the engines and edged forward toward the patrol ship.

Saul looked over to the *Alboràn* to make sure she was taking her cue. He blinked. There was no *Alboràn*, nothing at all. Just the eerily calm Caribbean. No wind, tiny waves slopping against their hull. Saul stood up, cupping his hand over his eyes against the moon's glare and its reflection on the ocean. Still no boat, no *Alboràn*. The *Challenger's* sister narco boat had simply vanished.

Saul tapped Antonio on the back. Pissed, the skipper turned round. Saul pointed to the *Alboràn*'s last position. Antonio squinted into the moon's flaring silver light. 'The fuck?' he whispered. 'The actual *fuck?*'

By now, the *Gacrux* was a couple hundred yards away, and Antonio slowed down some more.

Saul lurched forward, falling over, knocking his head on the bench seat. Dazed, he lay on his back, staring up at the stars. Millions, billions. How beautiful. Away in the distance, he could hear someone shouting, no, two people shouting. No, screaming. The hell? Had they crashed into some rocks? Shit, were they sinking? He blinked several times, trying desperately to retrieve his brain. Saul sat up, rising on shaky legs, using his assault rifle as a crutch.

Antonio and Daniel were nowhere to be seen. They'd vanished. Like the *Alboràn*, he remembered. Where was everything going? Why was everything disappearing?

'Saul!' somebody shouted. It sounded like his brother, Dex. He turned around, stumbling over his own feet. It was Dex! Dex stood on the bow of his vessel, maybe thirty yards away.

'Saul!' Dex was screaming now. Was his brother one of the screamers from before? Why was everybody screaming tonight? And disappearing; they were doing that, too. Saul didn't understand any of it.

'SAUL!'

And then he felt a sharp scrape across his neck, and his head seemed to drop like a stone, smacking into the side of the boat before tipping into the sea. He blinked a few times and tried to get his arms and legs to work and swim. But he didn't seem to have a body. It was like his head was his body, like his head was all he had become. Bobbing in the sea. Before his eyes closed for the last time, Saul watched as Dex leaned over the guardrail, his face a mess of horror and love, as if, maybe, despite everything, he did actually give a shit about his brother, little Saul.

But, yeah. Calling a boat Challenger? *Man, that's asking for trouble.*

CHAPTER 8

Hercules Transport, 28,000 ft
Sunday, 1304 hours
Gulf of Mexico (19°27'43.5"N 95°17'54.4"W)

Strapped into his seat in the aging C130 Herky, Jack glowered at Clewton sitting opposite him. For his part, No-clue at least had the decency to look as sheepish as hell. Jack closed his eyes, feigning sleep. At one end of the aircraft, a small detachment of marines chatted quietly with each other, occasionally chuckling over some likely in-joke. A couple of seats up from Clewton sat two men dressed in black pants and jackets. Jack could see they were armed. Although he wasn't sure, he thought they might be with Clewton. Jack didn't like the way they kept staring at him. He knew the type. Some species of spook. They were in their early thirties and looked like they'd been around the block a few times. Their tanned, somewhat lined faces sat below identical crewcuts. Tweedle Dum and Tweedle goddamn Dee. One of them had an impressive scar cut into the skin below his eye.

Erin's Zoom face had been crystal clear on Jack's laptop. Jack's ride—the Navy's troop and cargo transport workhorse—was nothing if not Wi-Fi friendly. Their conversation—not an easy one—had taken place a couple of hours ago.

'There's been a change of plan,' Jack told her, raising his voice, even though his military-grade chat headset mitigated the aircraft's notorious internal noise level.

'I get that part,' Erin had said, yawning. The five-hour time gap meant that Jack's 2300 hours was Erin's four in the morning. 'It's the rest of it that makes no sense.'

Jack had told Erin some of it: how it was a marine life containment issue, how an invasive species had been accidentally introduced into an ecosystem, and that the species involved happened to be firmly in Jack's research ballpark. He said nothing about Skeeter.

'But why you?' Erin had insisted.

'It's my thing, honey. It's the Navy. They wanted to work with one of their own. They trust me to keep a lid on it, is all.'

'But the *Lemuria* thing was your big break, Jack,' she said. 'Your voyage of the *Beagle*.'

'And it still will be, hon,' Jack said. 'This isn't going to take more than a couple days. I'm in an advisory capacity. That's all. Then I'll be back on *Lemuria*.'

'Okay,' she said slowly, stretching the two syllables and running a hand through her already tousled hair. 'It worries me, though, Jack. How this might affect you. You've come a long way. We both have.'

Jack knew what Erin was referring to. When he left the Teams, he'd worked hard to move on and segue back into a life out of uniform. And he'd been able to do it. In part, it was because he'd walked away from it in his own good time. When it was the right time. But the most important part was that he'd met Erin.

Jack had been lucky. He'd left the military with a positive attitude and a clear idea of what he wanted to do. But deep down, he knew that most of the ease with which he'd transitioned into his new life was because of her.

As a psychologist, she understood that, in a way, Jack needed to play a role and that he needed to swap one uniform for another. To move from camo fatigues into bespoke professorial mode. *Like Indy Jones*, she'd said, only half joking, *between adventures and lecturing at some modest Midwest college*. And so Jack embraced the scholarly look. Tweed jacket, elbow patches, and corduroy pants. He grew his hair out and swapped his aviator-style frames for a pair of tortoiseshell horn rims. And it had worked. Every time Jack caught a reflection of himself, he saw the new guy, the teacher, not the other fella, the one trained to kill.

A lot of guys left the Teams because of some beef, real or imagined, with the Navy itself. They became embittered and cynical, carrying that bitterness and cynicism into civvy street, carrying all the things that meant they would fail. And while Jack loved the US Navy, he'd walked away because he didn't want his whole life to be shaped by one thing - the SEALs - and all it entailed. His main reason for leaving the past was philosophical. He'd wanted to grow as a person. As for the Navy, he simply suspected he'd outgrown it and that whatever itch he'd had, he'd scratched that bad boy. It was time to move on – besides, he'd seen the older guys, unable to return to civvy street, somehow embedded, concretized in all their past glories, unable to move on, unable to let it go – like the whole point of their existence was so that they could remember the past.

And the Navy he'd joined, that Navy, it didn't exist anymore. It was a Navy run by the likes of Clewton. It wasn't necessarily about incompetence when Clewton left Jack's guys in Yemen. It was something far worse. It was a decision made about resources over men – simply, it wasn't worth risking the expensive hardware over a few guys – who were almost certainly dead anyway. Jack saw it as the corporatization of the Navy. A soul-dead ethos that basically dishonored all those men and women who'd given their lives for their country. Guys like Clewton epitomized the new tranche of officers – it was always about the promotion, not the betterment of the Navy or the world.

Clewton. That SOB. Jack was aware that the admiral still wasn't telling him the whole story. The entire thing felt wonky, off – and from Jack's perspective – certainly career-wise, too good to be true. But Clewton knew exactly which buttons to press and so here Jack was.

Being back on military transport brought back a whole slew of memories, an uneasy collage of all the times he'd been in this situation — on a mission, flying at great inexorable speed to God knew what. Except this time, it wasn't a win-or-die situation. He wasn't going in armed; he didn't have to kill anyone. Nonetheless, while he was still wary about what he'd signed up for, he couldn't deny the pleasant adrenaline rush he was currently buzzing on.

But this was different from the old days. For a start, Jack was sat on his own – Clewton didn't count – surrounded only by the memories of his old unit, Skeeter and the rest, not the men themselves. Those men had his back, and he theirs. And back then, he might have been shit scared about what he was about to do, but they were all shit scared together.

A year ago, Skeeter's ex-wife, Abena, had died in a hit-and-run. The culprit had never been brought to justice. At the time, Jack had assumed that Skeeter himself would personally track down the motherfucker who'd killed his girl, make sure the bastard saw jail time. The Skeeter that Jack knew would have moved heaven and earth to make it right for Abena, even if she was his ex. But Skeeter failed to fetch up at the funeral, his inexplicable absence a massive hole in the proceedings. Maybe Skeeter had changed. Maybe these days, he didn't have your back. He certainly didn't have Abena's.

The marines shared another joke over their headphones at the other end of the aircraft. They seemed so young, and Jack felt ancient. This wasn't his world anymore. When they occasionally looked over at Jack and Clewton, all they saw were two middle-aged men, probably civilian contractors or something.

No. This wasn't Jack's life anymore. It belonged to the younger guys. There and then, he made up his mind to do whatever the Navy wanted him to do, then take the money and run. Don't look back. Never look back. He was an interloper.

Up to a point, Jack understood he'd been played. Clewton had presented the Skeeter card, and the only way Jack could play that particular hand was to do what Clewton wanted him to. But Clewton had also appealed to the marine biologist in Jack. It was a double whammy: On the one hand, he could rescue his old buddy, and on the other, he could get first grabs at a significant marine life discovery.

Clewton had been eyeballing Jack all night when he thought Jack wasn't looking or was asleep. Jack was an old hand at feigning sleep, observing while being observed. The skill had even saved his life once. Clewton's body language gave mixed signals, and Jack couldn't get a clear read. The admiral plainly had something he wanted to say to Jack. No, not merely say, confess. He was guilty about something. It was hardly detectable, but it was there. Alongside Clewton's ghostly guilt, there was also something else. This was harder to pin down, but in Clewton's furtive Jack-directed glances, there was something proprietorial in them, as if Jack were now an owned man, that he'd walked into some sort of trap. The third thing, though, was yelling at Jack, beating its chest, demanding attention. It was in the sweat on Clewton's brow, his dilated pupils sat in wide eyes, the shortness of his breathing, the way his hands trembled. And his face, it was the color of soured milk. Trampling over and subsuming the weak echoes of guilt and gloat, and coming through loud and strong, was fear. The actual top shelf, refined stuff. Vice Admiral Clewton was afraid. No, it was more than that. The admiral was terrified. And his terror was rising incrementally the closer the Hercules got to the Bahamas, Andros Island, and the Navy's Atlantic Undersea Test and Evaluation Centre.

CHAPTER 9

AUTEC - Atlantic Undersea Test & Eval Center
Sunday, 1433 hours
Andros Island, Bahamas (24°70'60.2"N 77°77'37.6")

The Hercules' wheels hit AUTEC's runway, jolting Jack from an agitated, unfeigned sleep. As the aircraft came to a standstill, he rubbed his eyes with the palms of his hands. He checked his watch.

'If you're wondering what time it is,' said Clewton, unbuckling his seat belt, 'it's two in the afternoon. You've lost a lot of hours.'

'Feels like more than a lot,' said Jack, walking past the admiral to the ramped exit at the tail end of the aircraft. Out of the corner of his eye, he clocked the Tweedles following the admiral. Damned if he was going to wait for No-clue.

As Jack stepped onto the loading ramp and out into a hot, cloudless day, the aircraft's kerosene exhalations filled the humid air. The combined odors of spent fuel and baked tarmac triggered more end-of-mission memories.

In the past, placing his two feet onto post-op terra firma usually meant a temporary yet intense bout of physical exhaustion, his mind and body relaxing as they simultaneously realized they weren't about to die. But he had the jitters right now, and it wasn't due to the time difference. Behind, someone shouted his name. Clewton. Jack waited for the admiral to catch up. The Tweedles tailed Clewton several yards behind. Jack was damned if he was going to give Clewton the satisfaction by asking why they were being followed around by a pair of spooks. They'd either been detailed as bodyguards or to make sure Jack didn't do a runner. Either option was worrying.

As Jack waited for Clewton to catch up, a grey Ford minibus with smoked glass windows pulled up behind him. A marine corporal jumped out of the driver's side and saluted Clewton before opening the sliding door.

'After you, Jack,' said Clewton, guiding Jack toward the bus. 'Guests first.'

It hadn't escaped Jack's attention that the corporal had worked hard not to make eye contact with the admiral. Almost as hard as Jack had worked to not punch Clewton in the face.

Guest. The patronizing yahoo. Jack absently took in the approach to the base proper – a heavily fortified entrance, manned by armed guards and a tech overdose of surveillance equipment. High, reinforced concrete walls topped with barbed wire and sensors surrounded the base, in theory ensuring maximum security. The gates were thick steel, automated, and presumably designed to withstand significant force. Upon entering, after Clewton had shown the marine guard his security pass, they moved slowly through a series of low, nondescript buildings. These ugly-fuck structures were built with sturdy, reinforced walls and minimal windows. The roads their vehicle followed were wide and well-maintained, lined with discreet signs and markings indicating restricted areas and access levels.

Further in, Jack noticed larger hangar-like buildings and warehouses. The hangars were massive, with high ceilings and large retractable doors. He wondered what freaky beyond top-secret military hardware they hid – decided he didn't want to know. As they moved closer to the heart of the base, the architecture became more sophisticated. The central command building was a fortress-like structure with multiple layers of security, including biometric scanners and guarded checkpoints.

'When do I get to see the, ah, asset details?' Jack asked.

Clewton nodded, 'Yes, I get it, Jack. You want to get this rolled out ASAP. But you, my friend, need to rest and freshen up. As do I. When we meet Dr Tammes – head of research – we must be as sharp as possible. He's got a lot to share, and you need to be at the top of your game.' It looked like Clewton was attempting a smile, but it came out as a wince as if he had a stomach ulcer playing up. Jack remembered the fear he'd seen on the man's face earlier.

'I know all the crustacean guys,' said Jack. 'Tammes isn't ringing any bells.'

Clewton stared out of the window at the Caribbean's blue sea in the distance. 'I'm not surprised he's not on your radar,' he said wistfully, almost as if speaking to himself. 'Lucas Tammes has been off the grid for many years working on various R and D projects.' He turned to Jack. 'At one time or another, Dr T has been familiar with all the non-existent departments in every Navy Echelon Two organization. Before AUTEC was lucky enough to snag him, he was at DARPA, the advanced research for defense –'

'I know what DARPA is,' said Jack, interrupting Clewton. 'What I don't understand is -'

'But,' Clewton jumped in, 'do you know what DARPA does?'

'Last I heard, they weren't interested in crustaceans,' Jack said. The SEALs, on occasion, had trialed some of DARPA's in-field inventions, often leading to unforeseen, dangerous outcomes – on the SEALs themselves rather than any presumptive enemy. When the DARPA guys got things right, they could come up with pretty cool stuff. Still, their military-use concoctions were often too out there to be feasible.

Clewton smiled his creepy smile. 'Hmm. That's funny.'

'I'm not even going to ask why,' Jack said.

'Maybe not funny,' Clewton mused. 'Perhaps … ironic. Of course, you're right, as such. The DARPA guys thus far have steered clear of the subphylum Crustacea. But, you know, transferable skills and all that.'

'Listen, Clewton, if you carry on being a cryptic dick, I'm going to transfer my skills right back to Honolulu.' In the seats behind, Jack felt rather than heard the Tweedles tense. He guessed it wasn't often they heard their boss called anything but sir.

Clewton appeared unruffled. 'Like I say, I know you want to get in and out, but what you need to hear is best heard from Dr Tammes himself. He's a scientist. You and he speak the same language. It'll be better coming from him.'

'I can't wait,' Jack said, leaning back into his seat and closing his eyes as the delayed fatigue caught up with him. The more he thought about it, the more he realized nothing about this situation made sense. He should have concentrated more on what Clewton was saying while still on *Lemuria*. But Jack had been three or more margaritas in the bag, and his bullcrap radar hadn't been fully operational. Idiot, Jack thought, wondering how he – one man – was supposed to locate a solo marine animal. The Caribbean Sea covered an area of over one million square miles.

Five hours later, Clewton had picked Jack up outside his temporary accommodation in the officers' quarters. Clewton was driving this time and had swapped the minibus for a tandem seater all-terrain vehicle. As Jack strapped himself into the navy-grey ATV, he realized that the Tweedles were no longer in attendance. *Looks like I've been accepted back into the fold*, he thought. Clewton was still out of uniform, and again, Jack wondered if this was to decrease the military vibe, some small psychological trick to make Jack feel like he was among civvy buddies and not the big bad military, keep him off his guard. Despite his earlier jitteriness and time-zone-befuddled head, Jack had surprised himself by falling instantly into a deep and dreamless sleep. He'd showered and shaved and was now feeling unexpectedly refreshed.

The ATV rapidly accelerated northward away from the officers' quarters toward the sea. Despite the open-air ride and the warm wind buffeting Jack's face, he could smell the booze on Clewton's breath. Dutch courage, thought Jack. In Clewton's estimation, whatever Jack was being taken to see required a whiskey top-up. And in Jack's view, Clewton clearly had not chugged enough – on top of the whiskey, Clewton still had the fear stink. The admiral had the ATV racked up to about sixty miles an hour, and Jack hoped Clewton was a high-functioning alcoholic and not just an occasional drunk.

They turned off the main base through-road onto a narrower tarmac trail, still heading north. The trail cut through an area of low swamp, and the smell of the ocean grew stronger. It was only a short time before the ATV was out of the AUTEC complex proper. As the darkening sky threw a twilight veil over everything, it was easy to imagine that they were racing through a true wilderness. As the road became more potholed, the ATV slowed down. A pack of wild potcake dogs burst into action, their lean bodies darting through the lush greenery as they chased the ATV speeding through the swamp. The evening sun filtered through the tree canopy, casting dappled light on their short, wiry coats, glistening with a mix of mud and sweat.

Jack had come across the potcakes before, on other Bahamian islands, and he remembered how he'd loved their independence, their mix of curiosity and playfulness. In fact, he realized, he'd first been introduced – if that was the right word – to the dogs' existence when on some well-earned R and R with Skeeter. There was something about the dogs that reminded Jack of Skeeter. Their zest for life, the way they looked out for one another. They didn't seem to have an alpha-male setup, more an ensemble, where they all mucked in together.

These dogs—some with floppy ears and others with erect ones—barked excitedly, their tails wagging in unison as their paws splashed through shallow puddles, sending sprays of water flying as they navigated the twists and turns of the marsh. The ATV roared ahead, kicking up clouds of mud and grass, eventually leaving the dogs behind, still bounding over fallen branches and weaving through the thick underbrush, their keen eyes and agile movements showcasing their adaptability to the wild terrain.

Occasionally, one of the dogs veered off to sniff at an intriguing scent only to leap back into the chase as Clewton's ATV rumbled on. For his part, Clewton seemed not to notice the dogs at all.

After about ten minutes, silhouetted against the westering sun, a tall chain-link fence came into view. Jack saw two barbed-wire chain links with a triple concertina wire fence in the middle as the ATV drew closer. The lab was its own compound within the greater AUTEC compound.

Jack had been wrong about the Tweedles – they hadn't been stood down. Instead, they'd doubled in number. There were now four black-clad men waiting at the entrance of the windowless squat building at the top of the steps leading down to the entrance. And while they still carried their holstered Glocks, they now were toting AR-15s. It looked like the 15s had been customized to each man's preference. *These boys know their way around firearms.* But he was still having trouble placing their provenance. They didn't have a special forces vibe about them. Many special forces guys presented as easygoing, laid back, belying their razor-sharp operational selves. These black-clad goons acted like they each had a firework wedged up their ass. So, yes, spooks. Probably. Some subspecies of CIA field operative? But not CIA Special Activities – those guys mainly were from Tier One units, like Jack's old crew. He thought about asking Clewton but doubted he'd get a straight answer.

If this was Tammes' lab, its structural aesthetic was full-on blast-shelter chic. Jack was familiar enough with military architecture to know that a steel-reinforced concrete edifice of this sort was usually an ammo dump. Tammes' lab exterior had all the signs of an officially designated Potential Explosion site. A further two men were standing by the entrance. And even though the sliding steel blast doors had been fitted into a thick composite frame, those self-same doors were lying mangled and twisted on the ground. On top of that, Jack noticed that whatever was responsible for the doors' ruination had come from within the lab. Someone or something had broken out.

What the hell had he got himself into? Whatever had blasted through those doors, it was no explosion. Something had sliced through the steel, something big.

CHAPTER 10

AUTEC
Sunday, 1902 hours

Dr Lucas Tammes waited for Val Clewton to arrive with Jack Tarr. In Tammes' view, it wasn't one hundred percent vital that this Jack Tarr fellow was on board with the project. Tarr was only here because Val had insisted. And Tammes owed Val big time. This whole black Research and Development gig right in the heart of AUTEC would have been impossible without the admiral's patronage, with him making all the obstacles disappear. Still, despite Val being a three-star senior officer, he must have had support from the higher-ups. Not for the first time, Tammes wondered who was pulling Val's strings. If it had not been for Val, all that unpleasantness at DARPA would have been the end of the trail, possibly the end of Tammes himself. Val's intervention not only let him off the hook but also gave his precious research a new lease of life. He sighed. In this life, you had to play the odds. It was a no-returns game if you didn't dare. Tammes was open to all corners and shortcuts in pursuing that persistence. For a man like Tammes, his need to succeed was a biological imperative.

Tammes was also a longstanding affiliate of the Zaldas Group, an under-the-radar corporation that, over the years, insinuated itself into the warp and weft of the US military-industrial complex until customer-supplier demarcation was all but meaningless. All this with nominal oversight. How they got away with this was another mystery. However, the corporation's claim to covert fame was its hundred percent success rate in reverse engineering other countries' stolen biochemical secrets. After the DARPA *situation*, Zaldas had loaned Tammes – with Val greasing the wheels - to AUTEC. Before Tammes' arrival, AUTEC had been sitting on some very interesting organic substances that had defied any attempt at replication. And while Tammes had been unable to duplicate the materials so far, he had been able to apply those materials in a way that profited his pet project.

There was an additional problem, however. Said organic substances had not been appropriated from another country this time but from another department of the Navy. *That* department – the one nobody ever talked about - was not impressed. Tammes and, by default, Clewton were in its sights. It was an unwritten rule that you didn't mess with these people, even if *people* were the right word. Tammes shivered. It took a lot to make him shiver: he was used to being the shiver itself, the presence that made other men blanche.

All that mattered was the project, he told himself.

Of course, Tammes could see the logic of having Tarr onboard. But, yes. The outsider's presence wasn't a necessity. It was a contingency. The man might be useful in certain circumstances. And for the moment, Tarr did not know the real reason for his being there. He just hoped that Val could keep his damn mouth shut. He'd always been a drinker, but it seemed like the admiral had been constantly in his cups since the incident. Val was not good with pressure. And while this situation could still blow up in their faces, there was a good chance that it wouldn't and all would be resolved. And besides, whatever happened, Tammes had all his research locked and sealed, accessible only to him. He could always quietly drop off the radar. Other navies and countries would pay handsomely for what he, Tammes, had to offer. Of course, it was never about the money. It was the research, always the research. Still, a nest egg would be nice.

Outside, through the destroyed outer doors, Val's ATV pulled up. There were two voices, one of them Val's. The voice he didn't recognize must be Tarr's. Several booted feet clattered down the steps into the lab anteroom. Tammes swallowed hard. He was not in the mood for sharing. This was his business, nobody else's. Not even Val's. Not even the shadowy types Val answered to. Sometimes, he wished that everybody would leave him alone.

*****

As they moved through the anteroom and into the lab proper, Jack and Clewton were followed by the Tweedles, the two original guys from the Hercules.

He now knew their names. The one with the scar was called Graaf, the other Dantz. Anyway, that's how Clewton had addressed them.

Instinctively, Jack registered the lab occupants: a tall, well-built man in a white lab coat, late forties, gray-streaked ponytail, and pinched mouth. And four more security personnel. Two more creepy spook sorts and two SEALs, young guys who would have joined up way after Jack had left the Navy.

Though Jack was aware of the five pairs of new eyes on him, he worked hard to ignore them. It was time to establish that he was no green-ass pushover, take back a little control, and let them dance to his rhythms. He'd just about had enough of being messed about.

'Professor Lucas Tammes,' Clewton said, gesturing toward the lab coat man.

'Doctor will suffice, Mr Tarr,' Tammes said. For a big man, his voice was thin and reedy, carrying an odd quality, almost as if it were AI-generated and not a human voice at all. His eyes were shark's eyes, dead, flat.

'Yeah,' Jack said, making a big show of studying the lab. 'Pleased, I'm sure.' He ignored Tammes' proffered hand. As far as he was concerned, this wasn't a handshaking gig. He was never going to be friends with these men.

He recognized most of the equipment in Tammes' laboratory. A lot of it was your standard lab setup: magnetic stirrers and vortex shakers, both designed to mix and shake it up; centrifuges for separating liquids; an array of powerful microscopes; several different types of cooling systems; analytical balances for the weighing of materials. There was also tomography gear, alongside CT & magnetic resonance scanners, as well as MRI imagers. Together, this kit could produce a three-dimensional image of the internal structure of the human body.

But this being AUTEC, much of it Jack didn't recognize. The stuff he did recognize—chain reaction machines, sequencers, spectrophotometers, UV light boxes—was all within the ambit of genetics, a subject that Jack knew very little about.

The lab also had that slight whiff of acetone that all labs had, due, in part, to the constant washing and cleaning of various types of test glassware. Present also were the sharp, bitter odors of the frequently used chemicals, sulphuric and nitric acid.

And then there was the waxy odor. Some kind of catastrophe had occurred recently, but trust the Navy to find the time to buff and polish the deck. He absently wondered who'd ordered the buff-up and who'd carried out the order. Not Tammes, for sure.

But underneath all this, the unmistakable stink of crustacean molt came through like a strong base note in some hideous perfume. The more Jack became aware of the odor's presence, the harder it was to ignore it. Usually, when a crustacean went through the process of shedding its exoskeleton to accommodate an increase in growth, it was accompanied by an unpleasant, albeit faint, rotting fish smell. This smell, though, lying beneath the usual lab smells, was something else. It was the whiffy baggage that Clewton had carried about him when Jack met him on *Lemuria*.

What was unusual about this lab was the panoramic underwater view from the wraparound convex windows, which covered over a hundred degrees of the lab's circular design.

'Fused quartz, three inches thick,' said Clewton, noticing Jack's interest.

The windows opened onto a sizeable underwater pen, easily visible through the prism of a crystalline Caribbean Sea. Jack wondered what had been swimming around inside the pen. The thick reinforced mesh that defined its limits was attached to the side of the lab. What made the setup feel off to Jack was that the same mesh arrangement acted as a cover for the pen—as if whatever had been in it had been capable of leaping out of it.

Jack's attention was drawn to a row of four upright, slightly angled incubators. Their laminated glass frontages allowed you to see what was happening inside. The incubators were huge. They must be, Jack estimated, eight feet tall and four feet wide. Now what in the hell would go in one of those damn things? One of the incubators' viewing windows was cracked wide open, leaving a space for something big to crawl through. Radial cracks stretched outwards from the hole's edges like zigzagged spokes. Whatever had been inside had simply exerted enough pressure on the glass to push through.

'Alright,' Jack said, turning to Tammes. 'Talk. This ... new discovery, this creature, what is it?'

Tammes glanced over at Clewton, and the admiral nodded. Tammes slumped into a swivel chair beside a large aluminum desk with banks of enormous, curved micro-monitors. He gestured to Jack to sit in the opposite chair. Tammes gazed around the lab. 'You've undoubtedly noticed the somewhat odiferous underswell permeating the place?' He raised his eyebrows questioningly. 'Perhaps a touch stronger than you're used to?'

'Some kind of crustacean molt,' said Jack, his eyes moving to the enormous incubators. 'And you're right. It's a hell of a lot more potent than is customary.' Jack rubbed his chin. 'Japanese spider crab might do it. Something big.'

'Something bigger,' said Tammes. 'And a little more solid.'

Jack breathed in, sniffing the air. 'You've got more than one of the specimens?' To explain the intensity of the smell, there must be several animals junking their shells at the same time.

Tammes raised his index finger, a faint smile playing across his blandly handsome features. 'One animal, Jack. Only one.'

Jack slowly shook his head, grappling with the implications. 'But that means one animal would be experiencing several molts in quick succession. Which is impossible.' Jack leaned forward. 'It is, right? Impossible?'

Again, Tammes glanced over at Clewton. Whatever was going on with these two was a double act that was getting on Jack's nerves. Surrounded by people like Tammes and Clewton, the Tweedles, Jack had the sensation he'd entered the uncanny valley, that he was in the company of facsimiles of humanity, not the real thing. The professor leaned over to the nearest wireless keyboard, tapping a key. One of the widescreen monitors came to life, revealing what looked like a 3D cutaway image of a crustacean Jack knew well. A mantis shrimp. Jack leaned into the monitor, squinting, realizing this was no generic stock image. It was a specific animal, a live animal, its interior organs revealed by medical imaging. And when he looked closer, he realized that something was wrong with the animal or something different. Several different things. With shock, he realized that the animal had been modified.

Genetically?

Jack sat back in his chair, his mouth dry and his heart thudding—his tell-tale pre-combat fight-or-flight body reactions. Now he knew why Clewton had crawled into a bottle, why the admiral was sweating fear. They'd done something to a mantis shrimp that wasn't technically a shrimp at all. In fact, a mantis was a stomatopod, a crab relative, and a lobster's next-of-kin.

'There never was a new species, was there?' Jack said, standing, his brain racing. *What have these idiots done?* Jack felt a fool. He'd believed he'd been on the way to working with the new coelacanth, the new giant squid. This mantis wasn't a discovery; it was a creation.

Once more, Jack looked over to the destroyed incubator. 'How big is this thing?' he asked.

Tammes sighed and tapped another key. Instantly, the original image was overlaid with striated lines aligned with the animal's external dimensions. Jack's heartbeat increased.

Three meters long, one and a half wide.

By the looks of it, a Peacock Mantis. But a peacock was a smasher, not a splitter. This thing's claws were designed for splitting.

Jack paced the room. 'A splitter?'

Tammes' eyes gleamed. 'We combined the peacock strength with the most useful underwater tool. Smashing stuff up is fine, but we wanted something more refined and accurate. Hence the mods.'

'You *what* now? A nine-foot splitter mantis?' Jack stepped forward, intending to do nothing more than get in Tammes' face and maybe ruffle his pristine lab coat a little. Graaf and Dantz lifted up their weapons, pointing them at Jack. Jack halted his advance, not because of the guns trained on him but because of his promise to himself and Erin. Violence was a thing of the past. And it needed to stay there. The flash of fear on Tammes' smarmy mug, though, was sweet.

'You can see why we need it back,' said Clewton. 'Why it needs to be back in its box. Why you are the man to do it.'

'Of all the dumbest of dumb things, why a mantis?' Jack refocused on the ruined incubator, marveling at the sheer power required to break out.

Tammes said, 'Come come, Mr Tarr. You know the answer to that. Can you imagine what a weaponized, supersized mantis would be capable of? How its ... particular abilities would enhance any Navy's armament?'

'Sink ships, take out subs? That sort of thing?'

Tammes grimaced. 'Maybe. It's possible. But there's no sign of that out there at the moment.' The professor seemed almost disappointed that his creature hadn't, in fact, sunk any ships.

'But why, Tammes? Why a peacock? You talk about its strength, but others have similar capabilities and better camouflage. They don't light up the whole ocean with their colors.'

Tammes smiled; if such, it could be called. It was more like something had stepped to the tune of the Death March across his face. 'Come, come, Jack. You're supposed to be the authority here. Aren't you forgetting something?'

And then Jack remembered. *Shit.* 'Polarised light.'

Tammes slow-hand clapped. 'Took your time getting there, *expert.*'

'A peacock,' Jack said, 'uses polarised light to blend into its surroundings. It's only seen when it wants to be. Almost like having a natural biotech capacity.'

Tammes yawned ostentatiously. 'Yes, that's the one, Mr Tarr. But, you know, when it comes down to it, I wanted to work with the peacock because, yes, at the end of the day, I'm just really, *really* drawn to all its pretty, *pretty* colors.' The thing disguised as a smile crawled across his face again.

This chode's legit apeshit crazy, Jack thought. 'I'm not doing this. Get someone else.'

Clewton stepped forward. 'Jack, we've already tried that.'

Ah. Jack had forgotten. Skeeter. Skeeter was already out there. Skeeter and his team. 'What happened to them?'

'We lost contact.'

'Where?'

'Somewhere off Anguilla Cays,' said Clewton. 'East of Great Bahama Bank. About thirty miles west of here.'

'How many guys was he with?'

'Six-man team.'

'And nothing from any of them?'

Tammes shook his head, eyes lowered.

Clewton said, 'Over forty-eight hours of radio silence.'

There was something off about both men's answers. Jack couldn't help but feel he had been sold another damn line. They were holding back yet again, not giving Jack the whole picture. Were they giving him the mushroom treatment because Skeeter and his guys were already shark shit?

But all Jack said was, 'What kind of boat?'

'Mark 5 special ops.'

From memory, Jack brought up a mental image of the vessel. Over eighty feet long with decent main and secondary armament. 'Okay, better than a RIB.'

'And they had helo support. It was the birds that first reported them missing.'

'And this was because of a confirmed sighting of the creature?'

'From the helos, yes.'

Mantises often swim near the surface. The massive mutated variety would be possible to spot in the clear waters of the Caribbean, especially given its bright blue-yellow colors. If the helo crew knew what they were looking for.

'What was the plan?'

'Kill it,' said Clewton simply. 'It didn't work out.'

CHAPTER 11

US CGC *Confidence*, Heritage Class
Offshore Patrol Cutter
Sunday 1913 hours
Cay Sal, Bahamas (23°41'28.8"N 80°23'15.2"W)

On the bridge of US CGC *Confidence,* Lieutenant Commander Liliana Gil closely watched the Officer of the Watch as he navigated the vessel's passage through the treacherous rocks toward Cay Sal, a tiny now-uninhabited island. She thought young Walker, a newly minted Junior Lieutenant, was doing alright, his seamanship skills up to the job. Still, she was ready to step in if the weather worsened or he slipped up. The mean wind speed was around nineteen knots, occasionally gusting up to twenty-one, taking the conditions up to three steps below a gale. *Confidence* wouldn't be making this parlous approach to the key unless it was a literal matter of life and death. And it was.

Liliana shuddered. Cay Sal. Just its name whispering in her head gave her the jimjams. At ten years old, twenty-five years ago, Liliana Gil had sat on this same key with her father, mother, and younger sister. The halfway point in the perilous journey between Cuba and Florida. Except Liliana's family hadn't been marooned, they'd stopped off to pick up food and fuel supplies provided by the underground network of migrant facilitators. Liliana wished they'd never stopped at the island, that they'd continued on their way. But her father had been unwilling to take the risk without refueling.

There was something wrong with the island. There was a reason why it had been abandoned. Several times. She knew that the last time it had been inhabited was in the 1970s when the Bahamian Police had used it as a base to look out for drug smugglers. They hadn't lasted long before they, too, fled the island. Or at least that's what happened if you believed the rumors. And Liliana did believe the rumors, or, at the very least, she gave the rumors some credit. She had the unfortunate memories of her own experience to thank for that.

And now an unknown number of Cuban illegals and their rickety boat had floundered in the heavy-ish weather off the key's northern shoreline. They'd been lucky to make it ashore. The Cubans were now sheltering in the ruins of the abandoned Cay Sal Lighthouse.

A budget handheld VHF marine radio had allowed the leader of the shipwrecked men, women, and children to send out a distress call. The radio tower on the nearby island of Water Cays bounced and boosted the signal out to *Confidence*, twelve miles away. It was just happenstance that *Confidence* was in situ returning to her homeport at Cape Canaveral.

Liliana was keeping an eye on the digital barometer. The atmospheric pressure was falling fast, and though there'd been no full-on storms forecast, Liliana always put the evidence of her eyes first. Already, the moderately-sized white-horsed waves had started to take on the tell-tale roll of larger seas. As soon as the pressure tipped into force six territory, she'd take over from Walker.

The peculiar AUTEC communication bothered her, too. They never communicated with the Coast Guard. Ever. Nearly twenty years at sea, and she couldn't remember one single AUTEC message.

And now:

RELAY ANOMOLOUS UNIDENTIFIED PHENOMENA – SURFACE, UNDERWATER. VISUAL, SONAR, RADAR, ACOUSTIC.

No other explanation. No details. Just ... what? Look out for weird stuff?

She raised her binoculars. They were now three or four miles from where they needed to be. She envisioned a quick in-and-out. Around the rock shelf the Keys sat on, the sea was shallow enough to drop anchor. Then send out a RIB to the island and back, pick up the survivors, and get the hell away from the island. Because of the navigational hazard posed by these waters, she told herself.

Not because of the other thing. After all, she reminded herself, I am a thirty-five-year-old woman with my own command. I don't believe in ghost stories. Even when they're mine.

The lighthouse tower, still standing high, had weathered nearly two hundred years of storms. Built, she knew, by the British to last. And their lighthouse had lasted far longer than their presence on the island. They, too, had eventually left, suddenly and mysteriously, no longer interested in their strategically useful lump of rock.

She picked up her VHF two-way. 'Cal Sal Key, this is Patrol Vessel *Confidence*, over.'

Nothing but static.

She repeated her message. Again, only the eerie crackle of white noise.

'Do you think they're okay?' Walker asked, not turning to her, keeping his eyes on the waters beyond the bow.

'Battery fail, I should think,' Liliana said. 'Those little handhelds, they don't pack much juice. They're lucky we picked up.' *Unlucky for us.* Liliana tried unsuccessfully to push the unprofessional thought out of her head.

'What are the chances?' Walker said, marveling at the unlikely odds that the *Confidence* had picked up the distress. 'Ma'am,' he said, lowering his voice as if embarrassed. 'Do you believe in God?'

'If there's help on offer,' she said, 'I'll take it.' Truth be told, she didn't know what she felt about God, about the possible existence of some supreme being. What she did know was that there were more things slinking around the world in the dark than you'd like to think. More *things* that science at present was reluctant to accept. At least officially. And some of those things slunk around that damn Cay Sal Lighthouse. Her mother, an *Iyalawo*, a Santería high priestess, had told ten-year-old Liliana that the spirits haunting Cal Sal were tutelary spirits. Guardians

And that they had nothing to fear from them; the spirits were there to protect them. Liliana had so wanted to believe her mother. If her mother were right, why then had those very same spirits scared the living crap out of her? Years later, her mother confessed to teenage Liliana that she'd lied. Telling her that she'd raised something to protect them from whatever was on the island. Because what hid on the island and lurked in its waters, *it* was not a good thing.

She closed her eyes, willing her rational self to return. Almost certainly, her memories of Cay Sal were false, a child's misremembering through a filter of fear and superstition. On the other hand, the memories seemed so *real*. She sighed. It was a frequent and familiar debate with herself.

The port lookout's designated bridge speaker crackled into life, his voice competing with the buffeting wind. 'Unknown contact, bearing zero-four-five, maintaining range three-eight-zero yards, keeping parallel course with *Confidence*. Unknown has surface mass of approximately seven square feet, one point five feet out of the water. Indeterminate color. Possible whale, over.'

For a brief moment, a wave of nausea passed through Liliana. It happened so quickly, it was like she'd imagined it. Maybe she had. She shook her head. This damned island.

Liliana acknowledged the watchman's report. Anomalies. Gotta be a whale, a humpback, a baby humpback, or a pygmy whale. But she knew that humpies stayed mainly in the east Caribbean; at least, that's where all the tourists went to hopefully catch sight of them. From experience, Liliana knew that the humpies didn't tend to stray too far west.

Again, she thought, should I report it? And again, she held back, unable to unite her two minds.

Goddamn anomalies.

The ship tilted noticeably to starboard. It was almost time to take over from Walker. The seaman helmsman had surreptitiously looked over at Liliana, a clear sign that *he* thought it was time for the skipper to start giving the wheel orders. Just a few more minutes, she thought. Walker's good for a while yet. Besides, she was damned if she was going to act on an able seaman's hint, no matter how good or experienced a helmsman he was. It would be undermining to Walker, and she, as a Latin female in the Coast Guard, of all people, knew what that was like.

The VHF hissed into life. '*Ayuda.*' *Help.*

'Cay Sal, this is Patrol Vessel *Confidence*, over,' Liliana said.

'*Ayuda*,' the voice wheezed through the electrical hiss.

'Cal Sal, this is *Confidence*. Estimated time of arrival three zero minutes, over.' Liliana was aware that, with the exception of Walker and the helmsman, all of the bridge crew was watching her.

'Cal Sal, do you read me, over?'

There were a few staticky clicks and what sounded like heavy breathing, then: '*Por el amor dios ... ayuda.*'

For the love of God, help.

From what seemed like a million miles away, Walker said, 'Fifteen degrees starboard.'

The helmsman repeated the order.

'Keep her so,' said Walker, checking the rudder angle indicator before moving onto the binnacle, checking the ship's heading.

'Cay Sal, this is *Confidence*, over,' Liliana said, her voice sounding ineffectual even to herself. The hiss suddenly strengthened, sweeping the bridge in a shrill wave. Then nothing. Utter silence.

Liliana checked her watch. They were in danger of losing the light before they could evacuate. She estimated there was probably an hour's worth left, so they had just about enough time to do it.

Damn it, she whispered. Why did everything have to be so *challenging*? For once, couldn't the variables be on *her* side? Calm seas, excellent visibility? They weren't at SNAFU-FUBAR quite yet, but they were getting close.

Oh Sovereign and Mysterious spirit Shango, who directs the destiny of our lives, watch over me and my ship.

The prayer slipped into Liliana's head before she realized it was there.

It was the prayer – or some version of it – her mother had used on the island, a prayer that asked for the protection of the God Shango. Mighty

Shango. It was Shango, her mother had said later, that had helped them locate the food, the fuel. Without Shango's help, they would have perished. Furthermore, her mother had insisted it was under Shango's care that allowed them to finally reach Florida safely. And it was Shango who'd protected them from whatever haunted Cay Sal.

But that first night on the island, as they huddled in the ruined lighthouse outbuildings, having no clue where the immigrant facilitators had hidden the food and fuel – her father having lost the map at sea – her mother's spirits seemed anything *but* friendly.

By lamplight, her mother muttered in the corner of the roofless stone building, her voice lost to the howling wind, the roaring sea. Father cradled little Maria, rocking slightly, lost in a miasma of his own misery. The voyage, the sea had unmanned him. He felt, she knew, useless. That this was all his fault. But then the wind had suddenly dropped, and the sea ceased its ferocious roar. From her prayers, Mother had looked up at the now clear sky, at the stars, letting out a blood-chilling wail. And then Mother slumped into herself, breathing heavily as if in a trance. Liliana remembered staring out into the heavy, velvety dark.

Liliana had heard it first. Footsteps on the shingle, something big, heavy, getting closer, making its way toward the ruins, toward them.

Then silence. No footsteps, nothing coming closer, nothing at all. Whatever had been coming toward the lighthouse had stopped and was present no longer. Young Liliana had thought|: *Shango has saved us!*

And in her mother's dreams, Mother whispered, *Shango.* The very sound of the word, a susurration of waves on a pebble beach.

Shango, Shango.

The port lookout's voice once more cut through her thoughts. 'Unknown contact, bearing zero-four-five, maintaining range two-eight-zero yards, maintaining parallel course with *Confidence*, over.'

'Thank you,' Liliana acknowledged. Whatever was out there, it had gotten closer.

CHAPTER 12

AUTEC
Sunday, 1932 hours

'Kill it? What the hell with?' Jack reminded himself he didn't want to stand next to Clewton for too long in case the admiral's stupid rubbed off. He was the kind of man who mistook platitudes for wisdom.

'416s,' said Clewton.

Jack doubted that 416s, a heavy-caliber assault rifle, would have much impact against an outsized mantis' armor.

'We figured we'd hit on him close to the surface. Do it dry. No need to get wet.'

'These modifications,' Jack said. 'Do they extend to its shell?'

Tammes nodded.

'You sent guys out on Mark Fives with pop guns against a bulked-up mantis with an enhanced shell?'

Clewton had the decency to look defensive. 'It was about getting them out there ASAP. We aimed to get at it before it became accustomed to its new habitat. Besides, Skeeter wasn't interested in our new toys.'

That did sound like Skeeter. He was always a beans, bullets, and black oil type of guy. He'd resist deploying ordnance he wasn't used to. Jack sat down. 'Jesus. Tell me it's tagged.'

'It is,' Tammes said, 'but contact's intermittent. Unforeseen signal degradation or something. I probably should have opted for analog, not digital. A design fault. It will be rectified.'

'Last we got a reading,' Clewton added, 'it was headed northward, into the Antilles.'

'Any other sightings?'

'*Bloomington* out of Port Canaveral reported unusual activity. Off Black Point.'

'Elaborate.'

'Something made physical contact with *Bloomington's* hull. Scraping sound, unknown source. And it seems the animal has started moving northeast. Its presence was noted by a Dominican patrol vessel drugs picket. Something killed the crew of a narco boat they were about to board.'

'A normal-sized mantis can swim thirty times its body length per second,' Jack said, working out the math. 'A nine-foot version should be able to move around 270 feet a second, 0.05 miles. So in a minute ... what's 60 times 0.05?'

'Three miles a minute,' said Tammes.

'One hundred and eighty miles in an hour.'

Jack turned to Tammes, 'But of course you knew that.'

'What's your point, Jack?' asked Clewton.

'If it's been out there for days, it could be thousands of miles away. But it isn't. Why?'

'It's acclimatizing to its new environment?' suggested Clewton.

'Maybe,' said Jack. 'Or maybe it's staying here for another reason.'

Again, that knowing look between Clewton and Tammes.

'It's a crustacean, Jack. It ain't reasoning,' said Clewton, turning on his southern diphthongs. Something he did, Jack realized, when he was nervous.

'Yet,' Jack said, 'two incidents have both included military vessels.' Jack scratched his head. 'Why would it be attracted to military vessels? There's plenty of merchant shipping out there, leisure craft.' Jack shook his head. 'Could the accelerated growth affect its ... cognitive abilities? Increase them?'

And there it was yet again. The creepy we-know-more than-you look between Clewton and Tammes.

'Yes,' said Tammes. 'It's possible.'

'So, what ...' said Jack, 'it's messing with US Navy vessels because it's pissed off with Uncle Sam?'

'As you say, there've been no civilian-based incidents,' said Tammes.

'Not that you know of,' said Jack.

'Fingers crossed,' said Clewton, ostentatiously crossing both sets of fingers.

Jack looked at Clewton with disgust. 'You do know that Skeeter and his team are likely dead?'

Clewton nodded. 'Nevertheless, his status remains MIA. There's still a chance.'

'What, then?' said Jack. 'While searching for the mantis I might serendipitously come across Skeeter and his team?' Jack ran both his hands through his hair. 'I don't get it. What's the priority here? The mantis or Skeeter?'

'The mantis,' Tammes said. 'We need to have it back. It can't be out there ... unsupervised.'

'Unsupervised!' Jack exploded. 'It's a nine-foot killing machine. Not some two-year-old kid gone walkies.' Jack paced the lab. Stopped. 'Okay, so let's say that Skeeter's still out there, whatever the reason. I guess it's possible. It's a combination of engine failure and comms going wonky. It happens.' He resumed his pacing. Halted again. 'No, it doesn't work. It's a busy shipping lane. Someone would have seen them, picked them up, or called it in.'

'It's December, Jack,' Clewton said. 'Not so busy.'

'December is only relevant to tourism,' Jack said. 'It makes no difference to commercial shipping.'

'Ignoring the ins and outs of current freight traffic,' said Tammes, 'what's the plan, Mr Tarr?'

'Who said I'm even on board with this?' Jack said. 'I'm only here because I'm a world-class idiot. I believed the admiral's bullshit about a discovery, a new species. Not some Frankenstein experiment gone wrong.'

'We need you, Jack,' Clewton said simply.

Jack studied the admiral's face, looking for the lie – failed to find it. 'So you keep saying.' Damned if he's not telling the truth, Jack thought. But why me? What am I bringing to the party? It's not my ops talent. I'm way rusty in that department. And the Skeeter connection? No relevance at all. Plus, there's no way they need a hotshot crustacean guy to second-guess what the damned thing's likely to do. The only guy who could get close to doing that is Tammes – the chump who created the creature.

Jack sat down, baffled.

'And in recompense for the modest false pretenses in getting -'

'The lying,' Jack cut in.

'To reiterate, there'll be a significant financial settlement—enough, for example, to fund a research project for years.'

'You already said that' Jack sighed. 'I need to think this through.'

'Sure,' Clewton said, shrugging as if he didn't care. 'Just don't take all night about it. We'll be in the anteroom.'

Clewton nodded to the two spooks and Tammes, and they trailed out of the lab after him, the professor giving Jack a furtive glance before he exited. Jack relaxed back into his chair, glad to have time to himself. He'd already made his decision. He just wanted a break from breathing the same oxygen as Clewton and his groupies. Their mere presence somehow defiled the lab's already shitty air. Without an iota of doubt, he knew he wasn't being given the whole picture, but he could work with that. When he was in the Teams, they often had no idea why they were doing what they were doing. Sometimes, the operational context was simply above his pay grade. He didn't need to know. And as long as any built-in knowledge deficit didn't get him and his guys dead, he was content. Clewton had Jack in the bag while still on *Lemuria*. As soon as Clewton dropped Skeeter's name, there was no way Jack could walk away, even though Clewton's smarmy act had triggered all of Jack's fight-or-flee buttons.

Nemo resideo, as the Roman legionnaires called it. Leave no one behind. All those years ago, Clewton had stomped all over the code. Clewton had left guys behind, and Jack had despised him for it. There was no snowball in hell's chance that Jack would end up squatting in the same box of despicables alongside the likes of No-clue. He wouldn't be able to live with himself. Besides, he owed Skeeter. He'd lost count of the number of times Skeeter had saved his sorry ass. Hell, everybody who ever served regularly alongside Skeeter was in for a sorry ass-saving or two. Skeeter never left anybody behind. Never.

Still, Jack was a realist, under no illusions. It was, indeed, likely that Skeeter and his guys had perished. No matter what Clewton said, the Antilles was a busy shipping lane, even in winter. Someone would have seen something. Was the mantis responsible for Skeeter's disappearance? Would it be capable?

Of course, it would. The creature was a splitter—a mantis that size would be able to open a small boat's hull like an old-school can opener.

Jack shouted out to Clewton and the rest.

Moments later, Clewton, Tammes, and the spooks trooped in. Jack couldn't deny that ordering a vice admiral around felt sweet. What a penny-ante fellow I am, he thought, smiling. Still, simple pleasures.

'Well?' Clewton said.

'I'm in,' Jack said. 'But I got a couple of provisos that need greenlighting.'

'Okay ...' said Clewton, drawing out the two syllables.

'First, I'm not killing anything. I'm done with all that. Any means of creature capture will be non-lethal unless, of course, there's no choice. This means we can access deadly alternatives, but they'll all be last-option solutions.' Hyperintuitive, Erin would smell the killing on him and know by the look in his eyes. He might be able to live with it, but she wouldn't.

'Second, there'll be a limited timescale to my direct involvement in creature capture.'

'How long?' said Tammes.

'Seven days. I'm out if we have yet to capture or contain the creature within one hundred and sixty-eight hours. However, I reserve the right to stay in-field searching for Skeeter and his team – if we haven't found them by then. And with appropriate Navy backup.'

'How long?' Clewton asked.

'As long as it takes, Val,' Jack said. 'You know that. As long as it takes.'

Clewton nodded. 'Anything else?'

'Last,' Jack said, 'I still get my research donation regardless of mission outcome.'

'Yes to two and three, Jack. But as for non-lethal capture, I can't sanction that.'

'Then I'm out,' said Jack, hedging his bets.

'What about Skeeter, Jack? Are you comfortable leaving him and his guys hanging in the wind?'

Something twisted in Jack's gut, demanding release. Whatever it was, it must have reached Jack's eyes because Clewton looked suddenly wary, taking a step backward. 'I've got my orders, too, Jack. You've no idea how low on the food chain I am with this thing.'

'Not my problem.' *But it is,* Jack thought. *What about Skeeter?* 'There's a whole damn book on operational discretion. In-theatre contingencies. Means justifying the ends. Just war theory. If you really want me, I'm sure you can twist at least one of those to get me onboard.'

'You mean, a fudge?'

'It's what the Navy does best, *Val.*'

Clewton glanced over at Tammes, who shrugged.

'Alright, Jack. Let's reverse things. I want you to kill it. Therefore, you will be issued with ordnance capable of that preferred outcome. However, if a situation arises where you think you can bring the asset in alive, if you sense an opportunity, you do that.'

'Agreed.'

'But you only get one chance.'

'I can accept that, too.'

'Very good. Consider it done. And there's an NDA to sign.'

'Not until I see the paperwork.'

'Trust issues, Jack?'

Ignoring Clewton, Jack said, 'I need to meet my team. Discuss mantis restraint strategies and non-lethal weapons.'

'And lethal,' Clewton chipped in.

'Yeah,' Jack said sadly. 'Those too.'

As Clewton strode out of the lab, Jack couldn't help feeling he'd been played yet again; that Clewton's meeting Jack halfway had been performative, that Clewton, ultimately, would have agreed to anything to have Jack onboard.

CHAPTER 13

US CGC *Confidence*
Sunday, 1955 hours

As *Confidence* approached Cay Sal, Liliana noticed the familiar curving finger of volcanic rock jutting into the sea, running parallel with the island, creating a natural harbor. She couldn't help thinking the crooked digit-shaped 'wall' looked like a witchy invite: *Come hither, child.*

Waves crashed against the ship's hull, sending sprays of salty water into the air, causing the cutter to pitch and roll, each movement requiring skillful adjustments to keep on course. The island was, as Liliana remembered, an unsettling sight, rising abruptly from the churning sea. Barren and treeless, with rocky, jagged cliffs, it loomed menacingly against the darkening sky. The shoreline was a mix of must-avoid sharp rocks and narrow strips of gravelly beach, barely distinguishable in the dimming light.

They were now less than one nautical mile from the narrow entrance of the harbor. According to the chart, the inlet was deep enough for the patrol ship's draft, and once they were in, they'd drop anchor. Get the RIB crews ashore, evac the people, and get out.

The natural harbor was the only viable entry point to the island. According to the chart, the narrow, precarious inlet was flanked by treacherous rocks and hidden shoals, which inevitably meant powerful currents and swirling eddies. Navigation would be a formidable challenge. The rocks around the entrance were slick and black, barely visible, their jagged edges promising disaster in the event of screwup stations. With the light fading fast, the visibility was poor, adding to the complexity of the approach. It didn't help how the horizon blurred as the last vestiges of daylight slipped away, leaving a muted, gray twilight.

The cutter inched forward, its powerful searchlights piercing the gathering darkness. Beams of light swept across the water, illuminating the chaotic waves and the scarily hazardous course ahead.

After all this time, Cay Sal still gave her the creeps. That strange communication from AUTEC didn't help either. Anomalies. Be on the lookout for. What the hell did that even mean? She picked up her bridge mic. 'Port lookout, contact update, over.'

'Contact maintaining parallel course, distance unchanged, ma'am' Was it Liliana's imagination, or did the young man's voice seem a tad shaky? And what had happened to the people on the island? There'd been no contact with them for over thirty minutes. All the VHF was giving her was hiss and sizzle.

Goddamn anomalies.

She hated any type of Bermuda Triangle-type bullshit. Hated any kind of superstition, period. This was why she was so annoyed with herself, with the undeniable fact that Cay Sal was still pitching her some major-league jitters. And it wasn't anything to do with the weather. Physical danger, she could handle. Being in physical danger often was her job. It was what she was paid for. What she wasn't paid for was to be spooked like a goddammed child. She was the skipper of a forty-million-dollar ship, responsible for the lives of over a hundred hairy-rumped matelots. She was no greenback and had every right to wear her big-girl boots. *I am a United States Coastie sailor, dammit.*

'Unknown contact maintaining bearing zero-four-five has closed to range two-two-zero yards, still keeping parallel course, over.'

Frowning, Liliana acknowledged her port lookout. *Damn.*

Report the damned creature, she thought. You have no clue what the hell it is. Ergo, it's an anomaly. But no, she couldn't. Not just yet. Give it a few more minutes; whatever it is, it'll get bored and move out to the open sea where it belonged.

'Sonar,' she said, addressing the duty watch ping jockey, 'are we getting anything on side-scan?'

'Very faint, ma'am.'

'Enough for a species ID search?' The larger CG cutter-sonar now carried a species identification chip. In the context of climate change, more of the CG's operational time was spent reporting unusual marine-life behavior.

'On it, ma'am,' the sonar operator replied.

It'll be a baby humpback, Liliana thought. Confused, lost.

'Bridge?' It was the pinger. Behind her back, Liliana crossed her fingers.

'Yes, sonar,' she replied, trying to keep the hope out of her voice.

'No luck, ma'am. Contact's too faint for ID.'

Damn.

Report or not to report.

If news got out—and it would—that newly minted skipper Liliana had been mistaking humpies for sea monsters, the powers that be would never let it rest. It would define her and what was left of her career. She might as well to hell with it and report that they were being stalked by the Loch Ness monster. It was at times like this that she needed her dad. Pàpa would know what to do, dependable, solid Pàpa.

A sugarcane cutter from Guantanamo, her father had traveled with his family cross-country to the big city, bright lights. He got his family a one-room wooden shack in Los Mangos, a ramshackle settlement sprawling over a hilly area in the Havana borough of San Miguel del Padron. Their shack, made from wood recovered from the garbage dump, squatted behind the baseball stadium. As a little girl, Liliana used to watch Pàpa, listening to the roar of the baseball crowd as if it were a sound from another world, a world he could only dream of. Her dad had worked every job he could to pay for their passage to Florida. A receipt ripper at a store entrance, a nail polish bottle recycler, even a disposable lighter repairman. Now, in Miami, Dad owned his own taxi company.

Yes, Pàpa would know what to do.

Report or not to report? That was the goddamn question.

Even if this thing out there was AUTEC's anomaly – was it dangerous? Damn them for being so vague.

Okay, she said to herself. She was calling it in if the unknown got closer than two hundred yards. If she called it wrong, she'd handle the ridicule. She'd tough it out. She'd weathered far worse.

She couldn't un-forget what happened here all those years ago. And no matter how many times she told herself that she'd been just a kid and that kids misremember stuff and make shit up, she couldn't forget the fear she'd felt.

Yes, there was no point in denying it. She'd been good and scared. So, too, had Dad, holding Liliana's little sister to his chest, visibly trembling. Her brave, lovely father was never scared; he always stared life right down its barrel, unflinching. Not that night.

And Màma hadn't helped with all her Santeria mumbo jumbo, calling on the spirits to protect them and summoning ancient gods to watch out for them.

Shango.

That's who Màma had cried out for. To keep them from harm from whatever lurked on the island.

She shook her head. Get a damn grip, girl.

Focus.

The light was still just about serviceable, but she knew they were on the edge of darkness and how quickly darkness fell in these parts. The weather, too, visibility-wise, needed to be better. The wind had already tipped over into Force Six territory, making her nervous. While the thin promontory of rock would offer some protection, it was too low in the water to risk waiting the storm out.

'Starboard ten,' she said.

The helmsman repeated the order. Then, 'Ten of starboard wheel on, ma'am.'

'Very good,' Liliana said. 'Steady as you go.'

'Steady as she goes,' the helmsman confirmed.

She'd stood Walker down and taken over from him herself. Her junior lieutenant had done well, and she'd told him. The approaches to the Cay Sal were deceptive. Navigating an unfamiliar stretch of water with a mix of half-submerged rocks and choppy seas took steady nerves. Especially when people's lives were at risk. The compliment had made the kid blush, which was sweet. Liliana knew how important encouragement was. She'd known the rough end of a particular type of loaded criticism far too often when negotiating her way through the pitfalls of a still-largely male environment. Hell, it still happened.

She ordered the engine room to cut revolutions to Half Ahead. It made the ship trickier to handle against the shove and pull of the waves, but she needed to be cautious. The rocky approaches were treacherous, and she'd only have one chance to get it right. *Confidence* was her first command—it wasn't going to be her last.

'Unknown contact maintaining bearing zero-four-five, now range two-zero-zero yards, still keeping parallel course with *Confidence*.'

As the channel narrowed, the animal altered its course accordingly yet kept its distance. Liliana couldn't shake the feeling that she, *Confidence*, was being pursued. Whatever its ultimate intent, it seemed set on following them into the inlet.

'Slow ahead,' she said. The engine room repeated her order. As the ship's speed reduced, the sea's growing power became more pronounced, and Liliana had to grip the edge of the chart table to stop herself from stumbling across the bridge. It would not be a good look for a commanding officer.

'Both watches of seaman muster midships,' Liliana barked into the primary Tannoy mic. 'Make RIBs ready. RIB crews stand by. Foc'sle standby to drop anchor.' Despite the wind's increasing ferocity, the on-deck clatter of heavy-duty steaming boots penetrated the bridge's sealed doors.

They were now at the entrance to the inlet, *Confidence* at dead slow ahead.

'Unknown contact lost, assumed submerged, bearing zero-four-zero, range one-eight-zero yards.'

Less than six hundred feet away.

In Liliana's mind, her father's voice said, *'Mija, pequeño,* you need to tell someone.'

Not yet, Dad.

As *Confidence* drew nearer to the harbor, her movements became more deliberate, almost cautious, threading through the narrow, rock-strewn passage. The tension on the bridge was palpable, each wave threatening to push the cutter off course. The bridge personnel were laser-focused, their hands - Liliana noticed - gripping whatever they could hold on to, their eyes darting between the navigational instruments and the treacherous waters ahead. Finally, the cutter breached the harbor's entrance, the waters calming slightly as the protective arms of the inlet embraced them. Liliana let out a breath she didn't realize she was holding. The island's desolate landscape was now clearer, stark, and haunting.

Liliana took *Confidence* into the dead center of the harbor and dropped anchor. 'RIB crews ready,' she broadcast, scanning the coastline with her binoculars. But the shoreline was empty, devoid of people.

'RIBs away,' she said.

Then, she felt the first subtle vibration resonating through the ship's hull.

Liliana swallowed hard, turning to her radioman. 'Sparks, I need to send a message. Now.'

Beyond the inlet's walls, the storm tipped over into a Seven.

CHAPTER 14

AUTEC
Sunday, 2047 hours

Clewton introduced Jack to his new team. Of the four SEALs who faced Jack in the lab's small briefing-cum-downtime suite, two were stony-faced, studiously neutral. These guys were relatively young, mid-twenties. The admiral gestured to the nearest of the two SEALs, a wiry, bearded blond guy called Cal. The other sailor, similarly stringy, though Black, went by the moniker of Detroit, or Det for short. Both were Petty Officers on the lower end of the scale.

'Chief,' they said almost in unison, inclining their heads toward Jack.

'Chief?' Jack said, addressing Clewton.

Clewton smiled. 'You've been temporarily returned to your former rank for our little op. *Senior* Chief.' He turned to the third operator. 'You might even remember Mac,' Clewton said, turning to a familiar-looking smirky guy with a boxer's face. 'McCloud. Chief McCloud.'

McCloud's smirk was not enough to be classed as silent contempt, but it hovered on the edges. Jack wondered if this smirky man was going to be a problem. Even in a tiny four-man fire team, you still got your Navy standard-issue asshole.

If McCloud was a Chief, he was probably a platoon leader. One below Jack's old rank. Jack's higher rank reinstatement explained why McCloud might have a whizbang stuck up his fundament.

Jack remembered McCloud now. Ten years ago, when Jack was about to muster out of the Navy, the smirker had been the newest member in his platoon, straight out of training. To the regulars, he was a tadpole yet to prove himself. Jack hadn't known him long enough to get a handle on him. But one thing he did remember: during downtime, McCloud could be often found sharpening his non-regulation T-bar punch knife.

But before Jack could say anything, McCloud held out his hand. 'I'm Mac,' he said good-naturedly. 'I can tell by your expression you think I'm the mandatory asshole, right?'

'I'm catching a lot of smirk,' Jack said.

'It's my face,' said Mac. 'I can't help my face—people want to punch it.' Jack studied the large, broken nose and the chipped teeth.

'Are you going to be a problem?' Jack said.

Mac pointed to his own face, 'Like I say, default expression.'

'You're smirking now.'

Mac raised his eyebrows. 'At the danger of repeating myself, factory fucking settings, man.'

'That's all it better be,' Jack said, shaking Mac's hand firmly, still thinking about that vicious piece of weaponry *Mac* loved.

'And finally,' Clewton said, turning to the remaining SEAL.

Jack turned to the final member of the team. Oh, shit, he thought, as *this* SEAL gave Jack a big fat seductive smile accompanied by an ostentatiously lascivious wink. *Zadia goddamn Breaux. This just gets better and better.*

'I believe you knew Chief Tarr, Ms Breaux, back in the day?'

'Aye, sir,' she said, waggling her eyebrows. '*J'ai de la chance.*'

Jack cleared his throat. 'Zads,' he said, acknowledging her. The female SEAL raised her eyebrows, clearly getting a massive kick out of Jack's discomposure.

Zadia Breaux. Jack had often wondered what had happened to her. And here she was in the flesh, that vital energy that defined her still burning fiercely in her eyes. According to her work dress insignia, Zadia was now a Petty Officer First Class. Zadia Breaux, the Navy's best-kept secret – a female SEAL.

'Assume,' Clewton said, turning to Jack, 'that your team, hereafter designated as Foxtrot-Tango-One, knows as much as you. Over to you, Chief.'

'Sit yourselves down, FT1,' Jack said, pointing to the table and chairs in the center of the room. His brain was feverishly trying to get into ops mode, his mouth suddenly dry, wondering what he was going to say. It'd been a while since he'd last done this, and Foxtrot-Tango-One knew it. Jack glanced quickly at each of his team's expressions. While Cal and Det remained masterfully inscrutable, Mac's allegedly accidental smirk face smirked away. Only Zads seemed to be unequivocally glad of his presence. He just prayed she wasn't too glad. Jack had history with Zads, and it was a history that could not be repeated at any cost.

'I know you're all hacked off,' Jack started, looking each of his team in the eye, 'to find yourselves under the command of a civvy-street Navy-retiree. But all I have to say to you is tough shit. And that re your predicament: my heart pumps purple piss. Is that clear? You all know the United States Navy is an organization you absolutely should have no contact with if you can't take a joke. Well, this situation is *that* joke. The joke to end all jokes. I didn't ask for this any more than you did. The upside? This situation is temporary. Seven days, to be exact. You have one hundred and sixty-eight hours only to detest my presence. Make the most of it.' Jack paused for effect, taking in his team once more. 'Also, I -'

Zadia slowly raised her hand.

Give me a break. What now? 'Yes, PO?' Jack said, failing to keep the annoyance out of his voice.

'For the record, I just want to say that it's a pleasure to be working once more alongside Senior Chief Tarr.' She fluttered her eyelashes.

'For Christ's sake, Breaux,' Clewton said, slamming his fist on the table. 'Not the time or the place.'

Zadia leaned back in her chair, suitably chastised, clearly unused to the un-admiral-like outburst.

Clewton nodded to Jack to continue.

'As you know,' said Jack, 'the operation is in two parts. One, to -'

There was a quick, perfunctory knock on the door. The door opened, and one of the spooks walked in and gave Clewton a word tablet. Clewton scanned the tablet, his lips moving as he read.

'We've got a report,' he said. 'A sighting. Two hundred klicks west.'

'Skeeter?' asked Jack.

Clewton slowly shook his head.

US CGC *Confidence*
Sunday, 2058 hours

There was another slow, almost languid scrape along *Confidence's* hull. It was like something was testing their defenses or, worse, toying with them.

'Away RIB Alpha,' Liliana said into the Tannoy mic. Once more, the clatter of booted feet was audible outside the bridge. She'd decided to send one RIB only. No point in putting all three in danger. *But danger from what?* She wondered if she should move from defense watches to full battle stations. In her report to AUTEC, she'd asked what level of risk they were potentially under – if, indeed, what was stalking *Confidence* was their anomaly. She needed to know what the risk was. She needed information. All she'd received from AUTEC so far was acknowledgment. Which was just about as useful as a store receipt. She told the radio room to get off another message to AUTEC, requesting a risk assessment.

She watched, praying, as RIB Alpha sped toward the shoreline. So far, whatever was baiting *Confidence* didn't appear to be interested in the smaller craft.

Without warning, the scraping intensified – reaching an ear-splitting screechy crescendo reverberating through the ship like some unearthly harbinger. Something was making its presence known. This time, the creature applied more pressure to its scraping movement, and Liliana could hear *Confidence's* hull creaking.

'Ma'am?' Walker said.

'Have the men ready the remaining RIBs,' she said, clenching the navigation table.

'What is that thing, ma'am?' Walker said, his eyes wide. She noticed that the rest of the bridge, too, had their eyes surreptitiously on her.

'When I know, I'll let you know,' she said lightly as if it were another regular working day. Under no circumstances could she reveal to her crew the gut-wrenching fear she was feeling. That wouldn't do at all.

She waited for the creature's next scrape, nerves taut as piano wire. But for the time being, it remained silent. Worse, in a way. To keep occupied, she moved out onto the port bridge wing, raising her binoculars at the solo RIB speeding toward the shoreline. It was then that she saw people on the beach. They were waving frantically at the approaching RIB. Liliana estimated that there were at least twenty or so, primarily women and children. Unsurprising. It was common for the men to make the journey first, and then when they'd established a foothold in their new home, the women and children would follow. Liliana wondered where their boat was. She could see no sign of wreckage in the sea or on the beach. Had they all managed to reach Cay Sal safely? Or were they even more traumatized because they'd lost family members?

RIB A made land as the would-be migrants ran toward her sailors. 'All RIBs away,' she said. Moments later, three more RIBs plowed through the choppy waters. It was as they approached the shoreline that something inexplicable happened. And it happened so quickly and with such ferocity that, for a time, her brain could not compute or translate the images her eyes were sending.

RIB Delta, to starboard of the others, was cutting through the water, skimming. Doing what RIBs do. Ahead of the RIB, by about twenty yards, the sea suddenly frothed and seethed, bubbling like hell. Like a boiling pot of water. But the spumy bubbles had nothing to do with the storm, the tide. It was something else. It was an emerging, living thing, an animal. And worse, it had a glistening claw-like appendage, dripping with seawater. Then, moving so fast that it was virtually invisible, the claw struck the RIB. The reality of its action was only confirmed by the carnage in its wake. Her sailors, her boys, her girls. Cut in half, their legs collapsing, kicking into the RIB, blood geysering in long, violent spurts, their torsos momentarily airborne, arms yet flailing, their brains unaware they were already dead.

Then.

The RIB, too, impossibly, somehow became airborne, as if punched out of the sea itself. Thirty, fifty feet into the air, aided and lifted by the strong winds. The empty RIB then started to fall to earth, surrendering to gravity and the wind's whim, dancing in the air.

On the beach, men, women, and children scattered.

CHAPTER 15

Sikorsky Seahawk, 1500 ft
Sunday, 2256 hours
Straits of Florida (23°46'17.8"N 79°49'12.6"W)

Strapped into the Sikorsky with its vibrations jangling his molecules, Jack couldn't help slipping into his old pre-op mindset. It was like putting on a comfortable pair of shoes. Or, rather, these days, a well-worn, past their sell-by date, uncomfortable pair of shoes. In the past, Jack had thought of the odd state of mind as almost like a Zen thing. The paradox of being so focused that you lose all sense of self. A strange paradoxical calm where there was no past, no future. There was only a present and a very narrow, limited one, like stepping outside your material body and monitoring yourself from the contradictory viewpoint of intense disinterest. Put another way, all the sound and fury of everyday life, all the shit, simply disappeared.

Jack had told the pilot to fly at the lower end of the Sikorsky's flight capability so that they could keep a lookout for Skeeter and his team. It was a gesture, Jack knew, more than a realistic chance of finding his old friend, but sometimes the odds, however weighted against you, came up with the goods. Occasionally, some mysterious quirk of the universe very similar to what you might call 'fate' gave you a break. The same principle when nothing more than a hunch saved your life. Still, it was a long shot, and everybody knew it. It was possible that the Sikorsky's transponder would pick up a distress signal from Skeeter. Just very unlikely.

Jack couldn't help but notice that Zads, McCloud, Det, and Cal were all going through their own habitual pre-ruckus processes. All of them were leaning forward slightly, eyes closed, slow breathing in, slow breathing out. By different means, the four SEALs would end up in the same mind-place. Some men found their way by counting beads on a rosary, others by conjuring up images of their loved ones. A lifetime ago, one old hand had confessed to Jack that he achieved his composure by thinking about his dog, a lurcher. Though truth be told, Jack suspected the breed didn't matter.

'ETA Cay Sal,' the pilot said over the intercom, 'will be 2312 hours.'

Moving out of his calm place, Jack checked his watch. Fifteen minutes.

As soon as the team was up to speed about the fatal brouhaha on Cay Sal, they took their readiness up a notch and stepped into a higher gear. As folks say, Jack thought, shit just got real. Not that there'd been any fooling around or light banter in this team, but the feeling their trip was more banyan than battle was gone.

The storm buffeted the helicopter like a kid's toy, and the pilot seemed to be riding the gusts like a bird with a broken wing trying to skim thermals. It took no more than sitting in the back of a chopper for a few minutes for Jack to figure out if the pilot was on top of his game. This guy was not.

The fact that Clewton had declined passage to Cay Sal came as no surprise to Jack. Clewton was your classic La-Z-Boy warrior. He was a man at peace with his conscience as he sent others into harm's way, seeing no contradiction in how he prioritized his personal safety above all else. A career man through and through. Jack knew that as far as Clewton justified his actions to himself, it didn't get much further than you can't have much of a career if you're dead.

Tammes, on the other hand, Jack thought he might have come along. Slimy creep that he was, Tammes, at least, seemed to be invested emotionally in his hideous creation. Even if that investment was for the sole purpose of personal gratification. Besides, Tammes might have been operationally useful. After all, he, more than anyone, knew what the damned thing was capable of.

Which brought Jack back to the ongoing niggle: What am I doing here? Why me? What am I not being told?

At first, Jack found it hard to accept what Tammes had done and what Clewton had facilitated. The whole project didn't seem possible. Yet here they were. And now the USCG was one RIB crew down. What the hell were they going to tell the families as they gazed, broken and confused, at their loved ones' closed caskets?

But now, what surprised Jack most was how quickly he'd assimilated the idea of a mutated animal rampaging around the Caribbean into his personal worldview. He briefly wondered if his rapid acceptance was connected to his SEAL training – situationally, from one evolving moment to the next, the unofficial mantra had constantly been adapt or die. Because whatever the set of circumstances, once you've woken up and smelled those particular – for Jack, Ethiopian Yirgacheffe - beans, it is what it is.

He eyed the three big metal toy boxes strapped to the helo's deck. A combo of lethal and non-lethal playthings. The bigger exclusion nets and electric cables had been left at AUTEC, too unwieldy for a small team of SEALs. However, they had the smaller iteration of the nets through net launchers, several types of repellent devices, and some pretty impressive state-of-the-art camouflage diving suits. Harpoon guns with ultra-quick sedation reaction times via tranquilization darts and energy beams; magnetic field manipulation devices to guide the mantis into nets; holographic barriers to influence the creature's perception; and acoustic and light devices. Some of this equipment was present due to Jack's specific requests, but AUTEC magicked up the rest. Face it, Jack mused, sourcing somewhat esoteric tech was a cakewalk compared to creating crustaceans of Brobdingnagian proportions. They'd have stepped up if he asked for a cloak of invisibility.

Once more, an angry gust grabbed the helicopter and yanked it out of its favored flight path like a leaf or a feather. The others' faces remained impassive, seemingly impervious to the death-defying maneuvering. Jack hoped his face held the same neutrality. Zads caught Jack's eye and winked. He had to work hard not to wink back.

Zadia Breaux. She was, indeed, a character. Jack was surprised she was still in harness. He'd always assumed she'd rotate back to general service as soon as she proved her point. He wondered if she was a female SEAL one-off. Zads, after all, was a one-off kind of gal. And that was the understatement of all time.

'ETA Cay Sal five minutes,' the pilot said.

Zads' roots stretched deep into Louisiana mud. To be precise, St Mary's Parish in Acadiana. St Mary's was fifty percent water, and when Zads was doing her training, she liked to joke that she was already half-frog. Ms Breaux was not exaggerating. Moreover, Zads had enough 'blood quantum' to legally call herself Chitimacha, a federally recognized tribe. It was this, she claimed, that allowed her to read water like a book. Except it was more than that; she communicated with it. Water talked to her, and she to it. To her, water was a living thing.

Zads was a striking figure whose presence instantly commanded respect. Jack suspected she had what most folks would have called charisma. Zads' modest height and lithe and wiry build belied her formidable strength. Her muscles, while not bulky, were finely tuned, giving her an athletic and agile appearance. She moved with a fluid grace, reminiscent – Jack always imagined - of the creatures in the swamp she grew up with. Her sun-kissed skin was a testament to the countless hours spent outdoors, and her eyes were sharp and observant, always alert and assessing her surroundings with the keen awareness of a predator.

Despite her slender frame, she could perform feats of power and endurance, leaving others in awe. She was renowned for her exceptional swimming abilities, gliding through the water with the speed and agility of an alligator. Her movements in the water were uncanny, a skill honed from years of navigating the bayous and swamps of her home. Her fellow SEALs knew damn well that they could rely on her in the most critical situations, trusting in her unyielding spirit. She was, Jack believed, a genuine inspiration, her blend of swamp chic and Navy SEAL prowess sealing the deal.

As the pilot angled his approach, there was a bright, external flash as he switched on his landing light. The pilot aimed for the red flares burning on the beach area as miniature human-shaped figures backed away from the makeshift helopad.

As the helo approached the landing zone, the pilot was distracted by a gusting change in wind direction, driving them close to the sand berm that followed the beach line, acting as a barrier to the island's interior. It was clear to Jack the pilot had misjudged the altitude and proximity of the sand ridge. Jack instinctively braced himself as the pilot pulled up sharply, trying to avoid imminent collision.

The helo skidded across the top of the berm, causing a mini sand storm, losing all visibility. Fighting to regain control, the pilot attempted to level out, but the chopper's tail rotor, instead, sliced into the berm, causing the aircraft to spin uncontrollably.

Jack closed his eyes, clenching his teeth, waiting for impact. Waiting to kiss his ass goodbye. *Nice knowing you, ass. Wish we could have had more good times together. Sorry, Erin.*

Descending rapidly, its skids hit the beach with a hard thud, bouncing before settling unevenly. The engine sputtered and died, leaving an eerie silence except for the creak of stressed metal.

'Are we there yet?' Jack asked the pilot.

'Sorry, guys,' the pilot replied. 'You okay?'

As Foxtrot-Tango-One mumbled their individual affirmations, Jack tried to ignore the shakes in his legs, his horribly dry mouth. *Goddamn it*, he thought. *Not used to this game of sailors.* He unbuckled and swung open the sliding door as the others jockeyed the heavy containers into the disembark position.

A cold cocktail of wind and rain hit Jack in the face as he jumped out onto the sand, the chopper's blades slowing their rotation. He jogged to the Coast Guard seaman hovering outside the flares' circle. Meanwhile, Zads and Mac lugged one container into the night while Det and Cal heaved the other.

Jack shook hands with the sailor, a tall, Black twenty-something with a Texas accent. Several more Coasties hung back behind him. Tex was having difficulty forming words and was understandably in shock. His men didn't look like they were doing any better.

'Show me what you got, Tex,' Jack said after introducing himself. The young man gazed uncomprehendingly at Jack briefly, wondering what Jack was talking about.

'Oh, right,' Tex said, getting it, scampering off into the dark, Jack following.

Tex stopped up-beach about fifty yards away from the helicopter landing site. Slipping out his flashlight, Jack switched it on, its beam illuminating a sad-looking heap of tarpaulin. As Jack moved forward, a sinking sensation in his solar plexus gained gravitational pull with every step. He leaned over and pulled up one corner of the canvases. Despite the fresh wind, ignoring the sweet, coppery blood smell underneath the tarp was hard. It was a while since Jack had been close-up and chummy with this particular bouquet, and he hadn't missed it one damn bit.

What the hell am I doing here? I should be home in bed with Erin. This is nuts. And the weather. The wind wasn't quite up to shrieking stations, but it was getting close.

He gently pulled off the tarp with one hand, like a parent preparing to scoop a small child from its bed. The wind threatened to take the tarp, and Jack gripped it tighter. He steadily held the flashlight with his other hand, pointing at what lay beneath.

The bodies.

'What's up, Chief?' Zads asked, joining Jack, while Mac, Det, and Cal remained in the flares' circle of light checking the equipment.

And then she saw the bodies.

'Mon Dieu,' she whispered. *'Maudit.'*

CHAPTER 16

Team *Tango Foxtrot One*
Sunday, 2344 hours
Cay Sal

'Yeah,' Jack said, extending the one syllable until it drifted into the night. '*Damn* is right.'

'We've both seen worse than this,' Zads said. Then, 'But … *effrayante*.'

'Say again.'

'Creepy.'

'You're not talking about the bodies, are you?'

Zads looked around into the blustery dark. 'This place. What's *wrong* with it?'

'I feel it, too. Thought it was my imagination. Put it down to my new civvy-faced sensibilities.'

'It's one of *those* places, Jack.'

He knew what she meant. Cay Sal was a place that wasn't *right*.

He refocused on the three bodies. Three mix-and-match cadavers. The sailors from *Confidence* hadn't paid too much attention to their dead comrades' body-part allocation. They'd been in a hurry to get the corpses covered up and out of view. And who could blame them? One big guy's torso was coupled with a more diminutive girl's lower half, and his massive football player legs now conflicted big time with the slightly-built female sailor's upper body. The third man's upper and lower parts had been matched correctly but had been placed side by side, so he now stared vacantly at his own groin.

Jack turned round to Tex. 'How'd you recover the bodies?'

Tex swallowed, biting his lower lip, slowly shaking his head. He pointed further up-beach to where the migrants milled around a small fire. 'Three of the … halves, the top halves, they washed ashore coupla hundred yards up yonder.' He lowered his arm. 'Everything else kinda fell from … above.' Tex looked upwards warily, unconvinced the sky was done with dropping human remains.

'The torsos were – what? - thrown on the beach?' Jack said. Trying to extrapolate the meaning from the bizarre sequence of events.

'No, man,' Tex said, close to tears. 'Just dropped. Out of the sky.'

Jack hunkered down, giving his flashlight to Zads, getting closer to the dead sailors. Each Coastie had been cleanly severed in half just below the ribcage, their intestines trailing into the sand. Two had lost a boot, and one still wore his PC cap. Each stared sightlessly into the night sky, their faces expressionless except for, perhaps, a faint look of surprise. Whatever happened to them had happened fast. Which would be, he knew, the exact MO of a mantis, outsized or otherwise.

'Did you see what attacked them, Tex?' Jack said, his eyes remaining on the dead sailors. 'When you saw them approaching?'

'Nothing, man,' the Coastie said, his voice catching. 'None of us, we weren't really watching the other RIBs, we were attending to the Cubans. You know, first aid. Making sure they were hydrated. Then ...' Tex looked up again. Likely, he'd never trust the night sky ever again.

'It's gotta be *it*, Chief, don't you think?' Zads said, keeping her voice low.

Jack nodded, forming a picture of what happened in his head, like a crime scene detective. So. *The RIB skimmed toward Cay Sal; the mantis, mostly submerged, matched the RIB's speed. Then one or maybe both claws emerged at such velocity that it was invisible, cutting the three in half, their torsos falling into the sea to be washed up later. The lower half of their bodies, their legs, then collapsed into the RIB. The mantis dived under the RIB and punched it out of the water, and the RIB and lower extremity body parts launched into the air with unholy acceleration.*

Jack stood up, his knees cracking. He was getting too old for this—a cliché, but true. He was already nostalgic for his sedentary life. All this action-man stuff didn't fit right anymore.

Confidence's searchlights scanned the natural harbor's dark waters about three hundred yards offshore. 'Zads, can you get a sitrep from *Confidence* and see if they've had any confirmed visuals or more hull contact?'

Zads nodded, extracting her multiband Team radio from her utility belt. She moved inland a few yards, away from the sea's clamor. As Zads moved into the relative shelter of the rocks leading to the island's interior, Det was suddenly by his side.

'What's the plan, Chief?' he said, frowning as his eyes strayed to the bodies. 'Mac wants to know what gear we will be using.' He seemed to sense something, tensed. 'Hey, weather's less pissy all of a sudden. That's good, right?'

Det was right, the storm seemed to have dropped.

Without hesitation, Jack said, 'We need to get a clear run at the mantis. We don't want to be doing this with a bunch of bystanders getting in the way, rubbernecking. Besides, Clewton wants this under wraps. That means getting the civilians and the Coast Guard off and away from Cay Sal.'

'Looks like a helovac's out the window, Chief. Pilot says the helo's too bent out of shape to take off.'

As Jack covered up the dead Coasties with the tarp, Zads emerged from the shadows. 'Has *Confidence* had any visual or audio contact with the animal since the RIB was attacked?'

Zads checked her watch. 'The skipper, Lieutenant Liliana Gil, tells me over three hours ago.' She shoved her radio into her belt. 'Well, Mr. Crustacean Man, is it possible the mantis has got bored and skedaddled?'

Jack ran his hand through his wet hair, running generic mantis behaviors through his brain. 'Yes. They don't tend to stay in the same place for long. Unless they're returning to their breeding grounds. Then they'll hang around. But this isn't the breeding season. So, yeah, he could be gone.'

Zads smiled. 'Only one way to find out, right?'

Oh, yes. The team would have to go out in one of the remaining RIBs and test the waters, so to speak. Besides, the harbor wasn't that big – if the creature was still present, there was a good chance *Confidence* would have picked it up with her spotlights. Probably. What's more, Jack reasoned that there was no motive for the animal remaining. It wasn't here to breed. It wasn't here for sustenance – there was far more prey out in the open sea than in a size-restricted inlet. But then, what the hell did he, Jack, know? They weren't dealing with your regular mantis here. Instinctively, Jack knew that the animal's size wasn't the only variable in play. The data Tammes had given Jack and his team was selective. There was something else going on with the animal. A mantis fed on fellow crustaceans – crabs and mollusks, that type of thing. Was it possible it was mistaking ships' hulls for aquatic prey? It didn't seem likely. And attacking the RIBs, killing the sailors? That didn't fit with its predatorial profile. A mantis would only use its mighty claws in the pursuit of food or to defend itself. It was a damn scary animal, but it wasn't a psycho. The only psycho in this mix was Tammes. No, there was something wonky about the mantis' behavior.

'Jack?' Zads said. 'You okay? You zoned out there, buddy.'

'I'm taking one of the remaining RIBs out. To *Confidence*. Then back here. Trial run. If it's safe, we get everybody off the island.'

'If it's safe,' said Det, 'then there's no need for us to be here. The animal's moved on.'

'Agreed,' said Jack. 'Tell the pilot to contact AUTEC. Get another chopper. And I need to speak to Clewton when I get back.'

If I get back, he thought. 'Oh, and tell Mac and Cal to ready the beam harpoons and magnetic nets.'

As Del trotted back to the helo, Zads said, 'If it's safe, Jack?' She shook her head. 'It's a big if.'

'Who's the expert here, Zads?' Jack smiled. 'It's what I'm here for, right? Be the guy who knows shit?'

'I'm coming with you,' she said. 'If you have to, you can't navigate and repel at the same time.'

'Sure,' said Jack, knowing there was no point arguing with Zadia Breaux when she got a bee up her butt. 'Let's both die together.' Besides, she was right – there needed to be at least two in the RIB. If Zadia was surprised at how promptly Jack accepted her proposal, she kept it to herself. 'Alright, let's go,' he said, jogging toward the migrants' fire. 'You, too, Tex. Nothing you can do for these guys. We'll evac them later.'

Most Cubans who sat around the fire warming themselves were women and children. They were exhausted and resigned, barely acknowledging the newcomers' presence. Zads beelined to the group, introducing herself and checking to see if any medical attention was required. A small group of Coasties, who Tex joined, were stood huddled on the edge of the fire's reach. The few migrant men present stood behind the women and children, arms folded, silent, staring into the flames. One of them, a sinewy old fellow with close-cropped gray hair, moved toward him, his tired face an open smile, tears in his eyes. He grasped Jack's hands in both hands, thanking Jack, tumbling over his words in English and Spanish. The old man surprised Jack by grabbing his shoulders and pulling him into a tight hug. The guy was strong. Embarrassed, Jack extricated himself from the man's embrace.

The man pointed to himself. 'Bembe.'

Jack matched Bembe's generous smile. 'Pleasure's all mine, Bembe. I'm Jack.' They shook hands. A form of greeting Jack was more comfortable with. Bembe's grip was firm, his palm calloused. Jack asked Bembe if they'd lost anyone at sea, and Bembe knelt on his right knee in the sand, earnestly praising God again in another spill of English and Spanish.

All safe, *toda Seguro*. All safe. *Gracias a Dios*.

Jack helped Bembe to his feet. 'Did you see anything when you were out at sea?'

'No, Jack. Only … we feel.' Bembe shook his head, his hands.

'I don't understand.'

'There was a … a tremble in the water, a rumble. It makes us sick. But not for long. But we see nothing, Jack.'

'The sea trembled?'

Bembe shook his head. 'No, no. We tremble. A *sonido*, a sound, it comes from the sea.' He did his shaking thing again.

'Okay, Bembe, I hear you. A sound that makes you feel ... unwell?'

Bembe nodded. 'Yes, yes, *indispuesto*.' He gazed solemnly into Jack's eyes.

An idea started to form in Jack's mind, one he reluctantly shelved for the time being. It was frustrating because the idea had legs, but he needed to focus on getting these people off the island. He told Bembe his plan, and all the while, Bembe nodded gravely.

'Yes, Jack. This island, it is ... *malvada.*'

Evil.

Jack made to move over to the Coasties, but Bembe grabbed Jack's elbow, his eyes beseeching. '*No, no el mal, más allá del mal.*'

Beyond evil.

Bembe then got a hold of Jack's hands once more, pumping them enthusiastically before finally letting go. Jack tried to dismiss the old man's words. *Beyond evil.* He desperately didn't want to let the idea inside his head. To take root. It was a concept he was familiar with. In the past, he'd seen people do inexplicable things. Things that seemed to have no place in the universe. Unless, of course, the universe was, at its heart, rotten to the core, something that Jack refused to accept.

But this place.

He stared purposefully into the old man's eyes, eyes lit by the flickering flames. 'I'm here for you, Bembe. You aren't alone.' For his part, Bembe smiled sadly, then drifted back to his people, standing on the rim of the fire's limit, a ghost on the edge of night.

Collecting his thoughts, unnerved by Bembe's blind trust in him, Jack walked over to Zads and the Coasties. Tex introduced Jack to his five remaining shipmates. Their responses were muted, perfunctory, clearly looped into their own thoughts, keeping whatever it was that twisted through their minds to themselves. Jack wondered how much of it was due to losing their shipmates or the island's peculiar hostile vibes. Bit of both, more than likely. Cay Sal, vacation destination it was not.

'Petty Officer Breaux and me,' Jack said, 'are going to RIB it out to *Confidence* and back. Then, all things being well, we're going to ferry you guys, including your clients' - Jack nodded to the Cubans - 'off this damn island. Simple.'

As Jack finished his preamble, Mac, Det, and Cal materialized out of the dark, weapon-laden.

'Good timing, fellas,' Jack said, accepting the weapons. 'They good to go?'

Mac gave a thumbs up before sloping off into the darkness, Det and Cal following. Jack assumed they were going back for the electromagnetic hubs for the hologram net or whatever the hell. When one of the Tweedles, Dantz, had given him the introductory spiel on the newly minted defense system, much of it had whooshed over his head, and he was rather hoping one of the others was taking it all in.

Jack became aware of Tex, eyeing the hardware. 'You got any more of those?'

'You sure?' Jack said, offering the man a beam harpoon.

The guy nodded.

'Me too,' said another CG man, stepping forward. Zads gave him the remaining spare beam gun. More the merrier.

According to Clewton, Skeeter had been offered the same state-of-the-art weaponry. Skeeter, being Skeeter, had refused, preferring to stick with what he knew. Besides, Skeeter had wanted to get out there while the trail was yet fresh. Only conventional weapons had been readily available. Clewton's description rang true. Jack could easily imagine Skeeter having no truck with beam harps and magnetic fields. *Just give me a gun*, Jack's mind's-eye Skeeter demanded.

Jack showed the two men where the safety was, the trigger. 'Then point,' he said. 'There'll be an infinitesimally short delay while it charges.' He grinned evilly. 'It'll feel a lot longer.'

The wind now was almost a distant memory, and the natural harbor's waters had stopped producing white horses, oddly calm. The speed of the changing conditions struck Jack as some kind of omen. Though good or bad, he had no idea.

Probably a climate change thing.

CHAPTER 17

Team *Tango Foxtrot One*
Monday, 0025 hours
Cay Sal

Like Tex, the other Coastie volunteer—a guy named Jedson—was somewhere in his mid-twenties. They wanted payback for their slain pals. Also, Jack guessed, their lust for revenge was clouding their judgment. 'You know you could die out there.'

They nodded in unison, their eyes never leaving his.

They knew.

Well, alright.

Never did a RIB look so vulnerable, Jack thought. Fragile. It was nothing to what was possibly out there in the enclosed waters of the natural harbor, waiting. Or not. Jack was rooting for the *not* option.

Mac and Co emerged again from the dark, hauling the remaining box of goodies over the sand, panting from the exertion. Cal immediately volunteered to crew the RIB. Mac didn't, Jack noted. Not that Jack blamed him. Whether they reached the *Confidence* and back was a coin flip, fifty-fifty.

Fiddy-Fiddy, as Skeeter would have said. His Bronx accent always came to the fore when potentially lethal risk was imminent. Ditto Erin. When she lost it with Jack. *Erin.*

'It's a fair offer, Cal,' Jack said, addressing the young SEAL, 'but I need you, Mac, and Det shoreside to take up the slack. You know, in case we don't … well, you know.' He looked where *Confidence's* searchlights still strobed the dark waters. He turned back to Mac. 'You okay to step up?'

Mac nodded.

'And stop with the smirking.'

Cradling his beam harpoon, Jack turned to the two CGs. 'As I said, this weapon is about pointing in the appropriate direction and squeezing on the trigger. If we're taken by surprise, this is what you do – aim, pull the trigger. Quick as you can. Once latched on to a target, the weapon's AI will automatically analyze its size and movement. If it's a match, and you pull the trigger, it'll do its thing. If not, the weapon will remain in neutral, and you will be unable to fire. Currently, the weapon is set to stun, not kill.' *Just like on Star Trek.*

Jedson muttered something to Tex.

'I know, guys,' Jack said, 'I know how you feel about this particular animal. But there's a bigger picture here, bigger than you or me.'

Jack kept referring to the mantis as an animal to keep the situation within the realms of relatable reality for the CGs and the Cubans, some of whom had wandered over to listen into the conversation.

Tex raised his hand. 'Hey, Chief,' he said. 'If you've got the data to recognize that thing, does that mean you know what it is?'

Shit. The young Texan was a quick study.

'You don't need to know what it is, just how to stop it.'

'Kill it, yeah?'

'Neutralize,' Jack reiterated. 'Whatever it is, it needs to be studied. There might be more of them.' He was surprised at how easily the lies came.

Tex held up his gun. 'And this baby'll do the trick?' Tex was working hard to inject some gung-ho into his voice, kind of failing.

Jack nodded. 'Several things will happen in quick succession once you've squeezed the trigger. The plasma beam will stun the animal. A microsecond after that, the harpoon will impact exactly where the beam did. The harpoon has a specialized tip for penetration, with barbs and hooks attached. The harpoon is calibrated to pierce the animal's carapace and no further. This will allow the tranq to be delivered sans target death. There will be significant recoil. Get that butt snug into your shoulder. When you acquire the target, you'll even get haptic feedback via the harpoon stock. Each harpoon gun carries three spears.'

'Chief?' Tex said.

'The butt'll vibrate into your shoulder,' Zads said. 'Just like your phone.'

'You feel that buzz,' Jack said, 'even without visual, you pull that trigger. Trust the tech.'

'Trust the tech,' Tex whispered to himself.

Jack turned to the other Jedson. 'You okay to cox the RIB?'

The kid nodded. 'I brought us over here. I'll get us back.' He looked at his weapon. 'What the hell's this, Chief?'

'A net launcher. Unlike the beamer weapons, you have to judge yourself when you're good to go. You only get one go, choose good.'

'Yeah, but what does it do?' Jedson persisted.

'It launches a titanium steel net. The heat at the time of launch allows the net to expand; when it hits the water and, hopefully, the target, the cold causes the net to retract, enclosing the target. The optimal deployment window is when the target has already been incapacitated, but it can be used as a weapon of the first instance.'

'Cool,' said Jedson. 'What do you mean the first instance?'

'*Mon loup*,' Zads purred, 'you can use it anytime you want.'

'Cool.'

'Hooyah,' Zads whispered.

Yeah, Jack thought, the kid had the right stuff. Walking a little from the others, he quickly radioed *Confidence*, informing her that the RIB would approach her stern perpendicularly. That way, he reasoned, the cutter's searchlights could light up the sea ahead, astern, and starboard without blinding them. The blind spot, of course, was everything to port.

And everything underwater.

Jack turned to Mac and Cal. 'Can we get some of those hologram doodads on the hull? Three ought to do it.' He turned to the two CGs. 'Can you tip her up?'

While the two CGs put their shoulders into the RIB, lifting her off the ground, Cal and Mac took the holo projector hubs – gray cubes, small enough to fit into a big man's hands – and crawled into the space between the sand and the hull.

'One forward, two aft,' Jack said.

When Jack left the Navy, holo tech was in its infancy. In fact, apparently, it still was. But these holographic projector hubs were an effective piece of kit—at least, he hoped they were. The hubs were designed to be attached to the hull of small craft potentially vulnerable to large marine animal incursions—read, sharks. The stuff used to attach the hubs was—Clewton had told him—a substance that bio-mimicked the unique properties of gecko toepads. Stickier than sticky.

The linked hubs projected incandescently bright images of a steel net hanging vertically – regardless of speed - from the vessel's hull. Jack was doubtful whether the illusion would deter the mantis. Frankly, he hoped the creature was long gone, and they wouldn't have to try out any of their new toys. And he couldn't help thinking, *What would Skeeter do?*

With the holo-hubs secured, Mac and Cal crawled from under the RIB. The remaining CGs helped push the RIB across the sand while Jack's throat constricted with fear and his asshole puckered with the same stuff. They were good to go. With the RIB in the shallows and everyone aboard, he said, 'I'll take forward lookout, Tex starboard, and Zads the dark side. I need your swamp-eyes for that.'

Zads gave him the OK sign.

'Heads on swivels, everybody.'

Crouching in the apex of the RIB, harpoon tucked tight, Jack let the tide do its work. The RIB, accordingly, drifted into the harbor. There was no need to start the engine until they had to. As the RIB moved further from safety, the fire on the beach diminishing in size, the wind had now dropped to a full-on eerie silence. *Confidence* was no more than half a mile away, but it might as well have been a thousand. The mantis could finish them all in seconds if it chose to. If it was nearby. Though the tide was taking them out toward the patrol vessel, it wouldn't take them directly to her. At some point, they'd have to start up the engines. There was no getting around the fact. That was when they'd be at their most vulnerable.

Mantis shrimp 'heard' sounds with their whole bodies. The mantis' body was covered in sensory hairs that picked up low-frequency rumbles. They used the hairs to detect other mantis communicating with them. The noise of a RIB engine propellor would, he knew, rest right in the middle of the low-frequency range.

Had the mantis attacked the RIB because it mistook the boat's aquatic bass rumble for a fellow disproportionately-sized mantis? Maybe it had attacked in confusion or frustration when it realized that the RIB wasn't a fellow traveler. Which sort of brought Jack back to his earlier thought, an almost lightbulb moment. Something Bembe had said. About a *tremble* from the sea, a rumbling sound.

Jack became weirdly aware of the way his heart pounded in his chest, and he couldn't help wondering whether the full-bore thudding was regular for him – his old normal. It was so long since he'd been scared-shitless that he didn't know if this was how he'd always reacted. And if *he* was feeling like this, he hated to think what the two CGs were going through. But then, this kind of thing was a young guy's game, and young guys always had a skewed slant on their chances of survival. Belief *it* was unlikely to be *them* was how they did what they did.

The four strained their eyes, scanning the waters as the inky dark sea took them further out. The ocean had calmed to such an extent that it was now like an expanse of liquid obsidian, a blackness that seemed to hold its breath. The only sound was the gentle wash of wavelets against the RIB's sides. Each splash, each lap, like the precursor to something far bigger brushing up along the hull's sides. The slightest ripple could spell doom, the beginning of the end. His finger squeezed the fancy harpoon's trigger. He realized he had no damn idea how much pull it would take for the weapon to fire. He stopped squeezing, letting out a long, slow exhalation of breath.

Need to calm down, he thought. He glanced back at the others. Zads and Tex had their weapons tucked into their shoulders at the ready, scanning the water, moving with their whole body. Jedson stared straight at Jack, his face a white oval in the darkness; as instructed, his weapon was beside him on the RIB deck. Jack needed him to be one hundred percent Cox. If required, Jedson needed to be on it yesterday.

'It's out there,' Jedson whispered. 'I can feel it.'

'No, you can't, son,' Jack whispered back. 'Don't let your imagination make the running.' And then Jack – *I'll be damned* – wondered if he, too, didn't 'feel' it. A subtle vibration in the pit of his stomach, threatening to move a notch up from subtlety and into naked, unbridled body-juddering horror. *Imagination, Jack, remember. You're not feeling anything.* Sweat popped on his scalp, like worms writhing, before rolling down his face, between his shoulder blades. He suddenly felt exhausted, really plum-fuckered. The mother of all sugar losses. Hell's the matter with me?

Tex said, 'I feel it, too.'

Jack noted how Tex kept his eyes on the starboard, remaining vigilant.

'Tex, you feel that butt vibrate, then you can feel it.'

Zads sniggered.

'Petty Officer Breaux, how old are you?'

It was Tex's turn to snigger.

Jedson took a deep breath. 'It's gone now.'

'Yeah,' Tex said.

Jack breathed in, feeling better and cooler. His inexplicable mega hypoglycaemic moment gone. The hell?

The moment of tension – whatever its source - passed. Okay. The two CGs would be all right now. Still shitass scared, but not letting it get in the way. Never volunteer, guys.

The thing was, were Tex and Jedson right? Jack tried to get a reading on his own instinct, what it was telling him. He failed. Rusty. 'How 'bout you Zads?' he said.

She didn't reply immediately, then, 'Not sure, Chief. Got nothing to work with.'

Jack knew what she meant. The danger they were in now was a first, unique. There was no similar set of circumstances with which she could compare notes.

'Take it easy, guys,' Jack whispered. Then, 'But not so's you fall asleep.'

Another chuckle from Tex. Jedson remained silent.

The minutes stretched into agonizing eternity as the sea retained its uncanny silence as if the water itself was the predator. In a way, Jack mused, the sea was a predator. You took your eyes off it for one moment, and it could be the end of you. Yes, men and women loved the sea. But the oceans were never going to love you back. She was never your partner, your girlfriend. It wasn't that it was all one-way traffic. The sea, she gave up her treasures often enough. Food for sustenance, watery roads for trade and commerce, and even recreation. What's more, if you were an island nation, she was your best line of defense. It's just that it was never an equal partnership. The sea, she was more the femme fatale type. Yep. Lower your guard, let her in, and she'll get you killed. Or kill you.

CHAPTER 18

USCG *Confidence*
Monday, 0020 hours

Liliana squinted into her binoculars as the RIB, crewed by two of her sailors and two SEALs, shoved off the beach and out into the inlet proper. Trying to ignore the tremors surging through her hands like light electric shocks, the binos suddenly seemed extravagantly heavy, as if she were raising a dumbbell to her eyes. But she had to do something; her nerves demanded it. Ever since the evac RIB had exploded out of the water, it was like she'd stepped into an alternate universe where the standard rules of engagement no longer existed. A scenario for which the playbook was not yet written. In her mind, Liliana was already writing letters of condolence to her dead sailors' families, wondering what the hell to say.

On the radio, the SEAL guy's voice was calm and reassuring when he told her the plan and that two of her crew members were involved.

That she was conflicted was an understatement. She was both proud and horrified that two of her boys had the cojones to get back on the water. Proud her two boys were honoring the US Coast Guard's core value of devotion to duty, horrified at a selflessness that would odds-on mean more letter writing.

Walker was doing a good job directing the searchlight operators and keeping the lights out of the RIB crew's eyes. Apart from a thin sheen of sweat on his upper lip and brow, he seemed to be holding up. Liliana hoped she was projecting a similar air of unflappability as her XO. As long as the crew could see their skipper unfazed, oozing confidence and composure, then they'd be all right. Even if the worst thing happened, the boss would get them through it.

Whatever had punched RIB A high into the air was lying low. No eerie hull-scraping, no sonar or radar blips, no anomalous visuals. It had been several hours since the incident.

Foxtrot Tango One, RIB
Monday, 0037 Hours

Jack was calculating the exact moment he'd signal to Jedson to start the RIB's engines. They were almost at the point where they'd drift away from *Confidence* and not toward her. Peering through the beam harpoon's telescopic sights, he could see *Confidence's* closed-up battle-stations deck crew keeping a close eye on the RIB's progress. The one thing Jack did not expect to feel when he sailed into the water was relief. Yet he could not deny it. The further they drifted from the shoreline, the weird sensation of being watched eased, and the unseen threat lessened. The malevolent pull of the island was losing its power. Jack knew when to trust his instinct, like all special ops folk. The uncanny atmosphere of Cay Sal would be unconsciously stored and analyzed in Jack's brain, becoming data, something to factor in, to consider. That is, whatever it was, was it going to be a problem?

It was what you did. After a while, you didn't even realize the doing of it. A collateral effect of being operational, whether at sea or on land. To survive and increase your chances of returning home, you had to be more than embedded; you had to be immersed. Become as one with the terrain, watery or otherwise. And in those desolate spots, those ofttimes mountainous, desert, jungled, inhospitable places, you had to commune with the sand, listen to the rock, the way the wind seemed to speak. And the vast majority of locations, the all-too-human threat notwithstanding, were good, open, and honest. But sometimes you fetched up where you weren't wanted, a place that didn't want you.

Places that just felt damned. Places inimical to the doings of humankind. Again, in so far as you were aware of your thought processes - it was never a metaphysical thing. What was hinky with a place was never articulated in terms of the paranormal or some such. No. Whatever it was, whatever was going on, it was always just a factor to be aware of. The more aware you became that, in some sense, everything around you was alive, the more likely you were to stay that way yourself. Clocking up a high mission tally meant you were able to adapt to the perspective of a kind of willed atavism, an embracing of skillsets that so-called civilized society had long buried – conjuring a mindset familiar to our ancestors hunting on the African savanna. Go full paleo hunter, and you'd usually get to see your loved ones again.

Cay Sal was one of those places where a paleo mindset could come in handy. Planet Earth and her environs had mostly become user-friendly, the obvious dangers—geographical and human-related—clearly flagged. This shitty little nub of land in the middle of nowhere was a salutary reminder to sleepwalking humans that the universe still had surprises up its cosmic sleeve.

But yeah, Cay Sal. A wrong place. For Jack, the combination of haunted locale and mutant creature hinted too readily at the presence of a world, a universe that didn't play by the rules. Here on this lonesome rock of an island, there was no existential safety net and it got to him. This place didn't want humans. And regarding the creature's apparent absence, it didn't want monsters either.

And then hell – pretty much all of it - broke loose.

A thin, electrical-sounding whine increasing in volume penetrated Jack's eardrums. Similar to the high-pitched buzz a camera flash makes when it's pumping the voltage for the next shot. It was coming from behind him. Before he could turn around, a flash of tracer-like orange arrowed across the water, followed by a deafening crack. Fifty yards away, on the port side facing the beach, a huge splash of water erupted into the night, sending shockwaves rippling through the boat.

Then another whine, another flash, ripping like thunder across the bay, the sea again, exploding upwards, drenching them with water. It was much closer this time, a hundred feet or so.

Zads. Zads was firing her weapon, one harpoon after the other, the gun recharging consecutively. Tex moved into position beside her, and he, too, fired into the sea. The boat rocked more, and more water cascaded onto them.

Jack had his weapon aimed to port a moment after the first explosion but couldn't see anything.

'What is it?' he yelled.

Zads was pressing buttons wildly on the gun's LED console. 'I can't turn the damn thing off!' she screamed. The weapon whined up a notch, preparing to fire, then cut out, the LED lights all turning red.

'Three harpoons, Zads,' Jack said. 'It's all you got. Calm down.'

Zads sat back down in the RIB. 'Shit,' she said. 'Shit.'

'TEX!' Jack shouted. 'Stand down!'

But Tex wasn't listening, and he fired his gun, aiming at where Zads' last harpoon had hit. Jack waited to be drenched again. Finally, Tex's weapon's LEDs blinked into the red.

Jack scanned the water, waiting for the worst to happen. After the cacophony of detonations, the relative silence rolled in like an invisible fog.

'Zads?' Jack said.

'Shit,' she said again, quieter, embarrassed.

'The hell?' Jedson said, pale face paler, looking anxiously around. 'Where is it?' He looked at Tex.

Tex pointed at Zads. 'I was following her.'

'Zads?' Jack repeated.

She stared at the weapon in her hands, slowly shaking her head. 'I dunno what – I must have ...' She shrugged. 'Shit.'

'Did it lock onto something?' Jack asked, still scanning the water, convinced they were about to be attacked at any moment. If the animal hadn't known they were on the water – it knew now.

'Stupid computers,' Zads muttered. 'Sorry, boss.'

Jack knew that Zads was dying inside. A rookie mistake. In front of the baby CGs, too. Way to go, girl.

'Forget it, Zads. These weapons - you heard Clewton - they're still in development. Crap happens.'

'I thought,' said Tex, staring at the weapon in his hands, 'that it'd only fire if the gun recognized the creature's stats?'

'Haven't you heard, Tex? The SEALs, we're only here to iron out the bugs.' He turned to Jedson. 'Turn on the engine, cox'n. Get us to *Confidence* as fast as you can. There's no point in tip-toeing now.'

USCG *Confidence*
Monday, 0055 hours

After the brief, unexpected firework display out in the harbor, Liliana slowly lowered her binos, surveying the scene without the aid of Swiss optics, the RIB approaching at a heady rate of knots. She didn't want to hex the RIB's final hundred yards, but it looked like the creature had indeed moved on. The tension on the bridge in the last few moments had palpably decreased. Liliana realized the crew's hitherto tightly contained fear was draining away. She felt it in her own body, the awful thrill of probable imminent death dissipating, fading, as if through the soles of her feet into the gridded deck. Her legs felt shaky and wobbly, and she hoped with all her heart that it was more than adrenaline keeping her upright. That when the adrenaline receded, she had the wherewithal to remain upright.

Walker picked up the Tannoy and ordered the port watch of seamen to stand by to receive the RIB. Liliana noted with satisfaction that Walker's voice was calm and quietly authoritative. Business as usual. She turned away from him, from the rest of the crew, leaning over the charts as tears welled. Damn, she was proud of these people. The only thing now is, is this ... creature toying with us, or has it *really* moved on?

CHAPTER 19

USCG *Confidence*
Monday, 0112 hours

'What about the bodies?' was the first thing the CO of *Confidence* asked.

'We're taking care of that,' Jack said. 'They'll be taken to AUTEC for autopsy, then flown back to Florida where the remains will be released to the families. I've been assured that repatriation is being expedited.' Jack hoped he was telling the truth. He didn't like the idea of shithead Tammes lingering over the deceased, getting a kick out of what damage his monster was capable of inflicting.

'So, what's your thinking?' Lieutenant Commander Liliana Gil addressed Jack and Zads, but mostly Jack. Even women of power, Jack thought, often unconsciously adopted the so-called male gaze. Neither Jack nor Zads sported rank insignia. As Jack had learned, it was a particular bugbear of Erin's.

They were all squeezed into Gil's private quarters. Jack sat opposite Zads at a small writing table built into the cabin's white-painted bulkhead. The CO paced the cramped space, clearly not at peace with herself. Jack recognized the look. He'd seen it on enough men's faces after their first action. Sure, some of it was shock, but most of it was a kind of incredulousness that such lethal violence could take place and that, somehow, they'd lived to tell the tale.

'Are you asking me if I think it's safe, ma'am?' Jack said, fielding the CO's question with one of his own. Jack saw no reason to appraise the CO of his civilian status. It would muddy the waters. He studied the Latin woman. She reminded him of Erin. Not in looks but in how both women's slender frames belied the reality of immense inner strength. He wondered if Liliana Gil bought into the kind of stuff that Erin was interested in. Though a professional psychologist, Erin's worldview accommodated some pretty out-there ideas. She was, for example, partial to mystical ways of thinking. For example, she owned up to the conviction that she was somehow destined to meet Jack and that there were unknown unknowns in our lives pulling strings, tweaking, and so forth. She had other notions, too, notions that were probably not a good fit for twenty-first-century psychology. Not all of which Jack automatically characterized as hokum, just most of it. Not that he'd tell her that; these days, he was all for live and let live. And ultimately, what the hell did he know?

Yep, Liliana Gil would have had to work hard to get to where she was.

She nodded.

Jack looked at Zads. She shrugged, and he turned back to Liliana. 'Ma'am, I can't give you a black or a white. Best guess is *yes*.'

'With provisos,' added Zads.

'Okay,' Gil said, frustration flashing in her eyes, 'but what's the balance between the *yes* and the *provisos*?'

'I'm erring on the side of the *yes* camp,' Jack said. 'If you want me to, I'll personally go straight back into that RIB and start evacuating.'

'You're asking for my permission?'

'It's your call, ma'am. Your mission, your men, your survivors.'

'Options?'

'You could wait for a helo-evac. No saying how long that would take. Plus, this weather front's circling, coming back, bigger and badder.' In fact, Jack had no idea what the weather was doing. He just wanted Gil to make a quick decision. 'It's a moveable feast out there. In more ways than one. As for us, we've got places to be.'

Gil stopped pacing. 'You're talking about the ... the creature, aren't you?' Jack raised his eyebrows, cocking his head to one side, smiling slightly. He hoped Gil got the hint that she was straying into need-to-know territory.

If she did, she ignored his gentle warning. 'That thing killed three of my sailors.' Despite her low voice, he could sense the white-hot anger bubbling beneath. 'I need to be able to tell their families *something*. I need to tell my crew *something*.'

She was right. Her sailors would want to know what happened to their shipmates. But his hands were tied. He couldn't tell her anything. 'I'm sorry, ma'am. This has gone right up to CG HQ.'

'Washington?'

Jack nodded. 'When you get shoreside, you, your officers, and crew will be debriefed. It'll be ... handled, everything. It's out of my hands, out of yours. That's what you tell your crew. Be honest; be angry about it. Tell them the truth.'

'Tell them nothing, you mean.' A statement, not a question.

Zads said, 'Ma'am, you tell them as much as you can. Jack's right. And when you've done that, tell them they know as much as you. They'll believe you.'

'You both know what it is, right?' This time, the CO eyeballed Jack and Zads with equally intense stares.

'We know what we've been told,' Jack said. 'I doubt we've been given the full picture.' He sensed Zads turn to face him, surprised, he guessed, that Jack, too, felt he was being kept in the dark; surprised that he'd been that upfront with *Confidence's* skipper.

'Alright. I can do that. Tell it how it is.'

Jack gave her time to marinate her thoughts and get her head in order. Then, 'Ma'am, I don't wish to rush you, but we're on the clock. Do you want to resume the evacuation?'

Gil walked slowly over to the door, 'Give me a couple of minutes,' she said, exiting, leaving Jack and Zads with their thoughts.

Earlier, when Jedson let the RIB's speed rip, they'd made it to the *Confidence* without further mishap. Jack knew that Zads felt terrible about what had happened with her harpoon. He also knew that to tell her it was okay wasn't what she wanted to hear. What she'd done, it wasn't okay. If that thing had been around, it would have cut them to pieces in seconds. It was mostly because of this, that Jack thought the odds for the creature's absence were good. But it was true what he told the CO. He couldn't be a hundred percent sure.

When they'd boarded *Confidence*, Jack had told Gil about her two stand-up guys, Tex and Jedson. About how they'd risen to the occasion. And they had. It may even be worth a mention in dispatches.

Jack had also requested a secure line to AUTEC. Sitting in the radio shack on his own, once he got through, he filled in Clewton with what had happened, what he needed, and what he was going to do. The admiral had been silent for a few seconds, before greenlighting all of Jack's requests. For now, at least, No-clue was fulfilling his part of the bargain. Creating monsters aside, maybe Clewton had cleaned up his act. Maybe finally, he understood the importance of doing the right thing by his in-theatre personnel.

When Gil returned, she looked at Jack and nodded. 'Get them off that island.'

Jack and Zads returned to the island without incident, Jack steering, Zads tucked up in the RIB's bow with Jack's beam harpoon. It was Jack's way of telling her that all was forgiven. Tex even volunteered to do the return trip. His boss soon put the kibosh on that idea, telling him he'd done enough. And he had. For his part, Jedson decided, as far as he was concerned, that discretion was, indeed, the better part of valor. By the look on his face when he and Jack shook hands, it was clear that Jedson was all volunteered-out. Back on Cay Sal, Mac, Det, and Cal had organized the remaining CGs and migrants. They'd all seen Jack and Zads make the journey twice now. After Jack had explained the fireworks display, most of them were convinced that the crossing was safe. He'd told them that it was *his* weapon that had malfunctioned. That harpoon was a typical piece of shit Navy-issue. It was an explanation that everyone seemed eager to accept. They didn't want to believe that they'd actually engaged the monster and that it was still out there. Besides, it was almost the truth.

When Jack's boots hit the beach, he again felt the island's wrongness. Given the earlier excitement, he'd pushed it out of his mind. But here it was again, pressing into his temples. And again, there was that thought, circulating with other thoughts, not yet connecting.

The sea trembled, Bembe had said.

Yet part of Jack's reasoning that the evacuation was probably safe was that the creature, the mantis, had not liked the island either. That it, too, felt compelled to go elsewhere. But that reasoning was ridiculous. Animals didn't sense ... *spiritual* danger.

Or did they? he wondered, thinking about dogs barking at nothing, cats hissing at blank walls. And snakes doing crazy shit before earthquakes.

But they did sense when a threat was present, far quicker in most scenarios than a human could. Some animals did pick up on changes in atmospheric pressure and electromagnetic fields. Still, if the animal had felt the island's dark influence ... what did it mean?

That it was thinking? After all, a mantis boasted a centralized collection of nerve cells, which by any other definition was a brain. Not a very big one, but a brain nonetheless. So, yes, it could think. Would artificial enlargement make a difference? It shouldn't. Though bigger, its brain would, presumably, still be the same set of limited nerve cells. But something was wrong. Wrong, like this island.

What Gil told them about the creature's behavior. It had followed *Confidence*, stalked it, and toyed with it before attacking the RIB. That sort of behavior was more than a collection of nerve cells. It was a *plan*.

What was it that they weren't being told?

'What's the deal, Chief?' Zads asked.

Jack looked at his watch. If Clewton followed through with his promises, there'd be two helos landing in an hour's time. One helo would ferry Jack and his crew off the island, the other would take the bodies back to AUTEC. To the ghoul Tammes.

'Chief?'

'Petty Officer Breaux,' Jack said, 'how do you feel about doing some picket duty?'

CHAPTER 20

USCG *Confidence*
Monday, 0202 hours

As soon as Jack and the scary lady SEAL left the cutter, *Confidence* weighed anchor. Liliana had intended to stay in the inlet only for as long as she had to. Now, she didn't have to. Her sole aim was to get underway. ASAP. If she succumbed to the tsunami of unanswered questions circling like winged predators about why this day's work had turned into such a shitshow, she would not be able to do her job. Those thoughts, she knew, would eventually peck a way in. And she would deal with them one at a goddamn time.

But for now, *Confidence* was heading north to Port Canaveral. Her traumatized guests would disembark, and then they would be the authorities' responsibility. Responsibility was the right word. But to her eternal shame, earlier, she'd been characterizing her guests in terms of *the problem. These people, they're my problem.* Until she'd briefly met the shivering, in-shock Cubans before they were taken below decks for a medical examination, yep, she'd viewed them as a problem. The head guy, Bembe, much older than the rest, had thanked her profusely, eyes wide, ingenuous, staring into hers. And it was then she saw her father's eyes, her mother's, baby sister's. He caught it, too. Her recognition. He knew she was looking into a mirror. That magically, this *mujer jefa* – female boss – was a fellow traveler, and she had stood in his shoes at some moment in the past. So comforted by this revelation, the man didn't even ask what would happen to him or his people. He nodded. It was an almost imperceptible movement. *These people, they are my people. I am answerable to them, and they are most emphatically not a damn* problem.

The reassuring sound of the anchor being raised and rattling into its chain locker cut into her retro-embarrassed musings, and when the fo'c'sle part-of-ship officer confirmed the action completed, Liliana ordered the engines slow ahead. Through her binos, she could see the five silhouetted SEALs standing by the fire, awaiting their transport. She guessed they would be glad to be leaving Cay Sal. Everyone was glad to be leaving Cay Sal. It was curious how the big SEAL, Jack, articulated his feelings about the island. She hadn't expected that. Not from a SEAL. And she was surprised too that she'd offered her own personal experience from all those years ago.

What's more, she knew that he was spooked by the idea that whatever it was that had killed her sailors had somehow picked up on the island's lousy vibe. It had influenced his thinking to the extent that he had risked his life on the hunch. The creature, too, wanted to avoid hanging around the island. But as Jack insisted, that made no sense. Cay Sal was a sanctuary for all manner of wildlife, birds in particular, but seals also. Cay Sal didn't bother them. So, what manner of creature *was* affected by the island? That is, apart from the human kind?

Forget it, she told herself. *Way above your pay grade.*

As they reached the open sea, she handed the bridge to Walker, realizing the circling predators had, indeed, pecked through her defenses.

It was then that she received another message from Port Canaveral, relayed by CGHQ, Washington.

And AUTEC.

Sikorsky helo, 1000ft
Foxtrot Tango One
Monday, 0307 hours
Caribbean (24°06'53.6"N 80°58'37.2"W)

Jack once more settled back into the resulting shake, rattle, and roll of the helo's turbine-powered engines. The atom-jangling vibrations, however, were an improvement on the old piston-driven jobs.

They'd left when their original pilot and the bodies were picked up and taken back to AUTEC. Nobody had said anything, but by unsaid mutual consent, it was deemed unfair to let the pilot wait for his lift on the island on his lonesome. Even if he was a bit of a flake. To Jack, it would be on the continuum of leaving a man behind in enemy territory, even if the enemy, in this instance, was a figment of their collective imagination. They didn't need to wait long anyway, the second helo arriving ten minutes after theirs. It gave them time to stow their gear, their new toys.

Zads, Det, and Cal had slumped into an apparent deep sleep as soon as they'd strapped themselves into the chopper. Clearly exhausted, it was good that they got to recharge. Mac remained awake, sharpening his punch knife on a tiny, pin-like piece of tungsten carbide. Jack wished he, too, could plug into some upright rack time. But his head wouldn't let him. It was *Confidence's* CO's fault. Liliana Gil. What she'd told him. About the wildlife on the island. What she'd said, all that about the local fauna not giving a hoot about Cay Sal's malevolent atmosphere, struck a chord, bringing into focus the elusive thought spinning around Jack's head ever since he'd been mapping the creature's behavior. And why he'd taken the RIB risk. The hunch the creature, too, might not be comfortable with the shitty energy any more than humans would. But that was before Liliana Gil appraised him about the de facto animal sanctuary stuff. That the local fauna appeared not to give two shits about whatever bad mojo permeated the place.

Which meant …

Which meant the creature was something other than an animal. But it's already that, you idiot. It's a nine-foot mantis.

Which meant …

Earlier, when Jack and Zads had returned from *Confidence*, he'd allowed the possibility that the creature, with its rudimentary brain, was thinking and making decisions. Yet if Jack's theory about the creature's sensitivity to the island's wonky atmosphere were true, it would mean that the creature was making more than just decisions. It was …

Which meant …

Jack's head slumped forward, ambushed by sleep, sliding into a deep, abysmal blackness, a place without dreams.

USS *Frank E Sublett – Stealth-Class Destroyer*
Monday, 0440 hours
Picket Line, Florida Straits (24°38'34.6"N 80°78'14.8"W)

Jack didn't wake up until they landed. In fact, he must have been unbuckling when he'd still technically been asleep. Fully conscious now, he was already rising from his seat. Ingrained habits, and so forth. Jack was mildly pleased he'd slipped back into his old-time state of readiness but also a shipload dismayed. Now that he was with Erin, he liked to think he was more civvy than SEAL.

It wasn't until his boots touched the warship's flight deck that he remembered his plan. It wasn't much of a plan, to be honest. It was broadly – get in the way of the creature and its possible destination. Possible. Not probable. And nowhere near likely. Again, a hunch.

Zads and the others offloaded the gear, their legs and torsos moving with the yaw of the ship, a destroyer by the looks of her. A new one. Jack had deliberately not kept up with the Navy's changing, hopefully improving, seagoing stock. It was an itch he desperately wished to scratch, but he'd manfully resisted. He didn't need to know that stuff anymore. Given his current circumstances, the clunking irony didn't escape him.

He was greeted by a junior deck officer, who, without much ado, whisked him away to the bridge and the CO, a tanned, youngish man. They shook hands. The CO introduced himself as Captain Cleeves.

'What's our situation, sir?' Jack asked.

'We're still sailing into position. It could take another thirty minutes or so. We're the lead ship, so we'll sit somewhere in the middle of the rest, coordinating.'

'What have you been told?' Jack asked.

'Not much,' the skipper admitted. 'We were headed for Puerto, told to change course, that we were to form a picket. Get in the way of the Keys, go into the Strait some. Advised that this was not an exercise.' He paused, looking around the bridge at his men and women. 'Got a mix of Navy and Coast Guard in the line. Best we can do at short notice. As soon as we all get in position, we'll be pinging like there's no tomorrow. We've even got a new sonar code from AUTEC that will apparently help with the incoming's detection.' Cleeves paused. 'And then once it's detected, it's over to you, Chief.'

'How many helos have we got?' Jack asked. The helos would use their sonar in front, staggered between the line of ships, like an early warning system.

'Aiming to have at least one from every ship in the line, so at least twelve.' Cleeves turned to Jack, lowering his voice. 'I don't suppose you can tell me what we're expecting. How much trouble might we be in?'

Fair questions from the CO, ones that Jack had been expecting. 'It's an experimental submersible bioweapon.'

'Is that AUTEC-speak for dolphin with a bomb strapped to its nose?'

'Something like that,' Jack said. 'It needs to be stopped. Taken back.'

'To AUTEC?'

Jack nodded.

The CO muttered something unintelligible under his breath.

'As to the threat level,' Jack continued, 'if it comes to it, nobody should be in the water except me and my team. The … weapon is ship-curious, particularly warships and CG cutters. Anything really that gives off a military vibe.'

'And when we get into position?'

'We wait,' said Jack, looking out of the bridge into the dark night.

CHAPTER 21

USS *Frank E Sublett*
Monday, 0501 hours

Zads and Co had been allocated a cabin—a private space—to check their gear. Jack remained on the bridge, sipping strong coffee, lost in thought. Suddenly, everyone on the bridge came to attention.

'Stand easy,' said Clewton airily with a wave of his hand, strolling onto the bridge. And then, as an afterthought, 'At ease,' signaling to the bridge guys to return to their duties. He was followed by Tammes, Dantz and Graaf.

'Jack!' Clewton said, all hail fellow well met, clapping him heartily on the shoulder, causing Jack to slop his coffee onto the deck. Jack's look of surprise must have shown. 'Got some news. Thought I'd deliver it personally. Good news, in fact.'

Jack nodded, unhappy to be once more in Clewton's company. And Tammes. The admiral's goons lurked in the gloom by the SATNAV, its green glow giving their faces an eerie cast. 'Something wrong with the plan, Val?'

If Clewton thought there was, he kept it to himself. 'The plan's all fine and dandy, Chief. Simple but effective, I'd say.'

A sudden streak of white-hot hope shot into Jack's chest, his heart suddenly thudding against his ribs. 'Skeeter? There's news on Skeeter?'

It happened so fast that Jack thought maybe he'd imagined the look of confusion pass over Clewton's features. As if the admiral had no idea at all about who Jack was talking about. Whatever it was, he recovered quickly. 'Sorry, Jack. Not Skeeter. Something ...' Clewton trailed off.

'Better?' Jack said, voice harsh.

'I was going to say *helpful*.'

Liar.

'Go on.'

'Not here. Come with me.'

Taking a deep breath, Jack followed Clewton's rapidly disappearing form off the bridge, aware of Tammes and the Tweedles keeping up behind him.

The brightly lit officers' dining hall was hard on the eyes after the soft dark of the bridge, and it took Jack a few seconds to acclimatize. They had the hall to themselves. Prearranged by the admiral. As the ship's senior officer, he could technically do pretty much whatever the hell he wanted. Not that commandeering the cake eaters' mess was such a big deal.

Dantz and Graaf had stayed outside. Jack imagined them hovering malignantly in the passageway, the heat from their stary eyes boring into him through the steel bulkhead.

'Take a seat, Jack,' Clewton said, indicating a plastic-molded, garishly yellow chair tucked under one of the Formica-topped mess tables.

'Just get on with it,' Jack said, remaining standing.

'As you wish,' Clewton said, his body language suggesting one big shrug, as if he couldn't give a shit whether Jack stood or sat. Mocking Jack's modest rebellion, Tammes noisily flopped into one of the chairs, folding his arms, pointedly staring at the overhead.

Jack had gotten his wish with Tammes' presence. Operationally, it made total sense. But straightaway, on the bridge, he'd been aware of the stink of Tammes' wrongness. The professor was, Jack realized, a flesh and blood version of Cay Sal and could hardly bring himself to look at the guy, let alone engage with him.

'So,' Clewton said, looking at Jack, 'I ran your request up the line.'

'Request?'

'Non-lethal force and so forth.' Clewton smiled. The smile where he left his eyes out of the process. 'You've got the green light to bring the creature in alive. That is now the preferred option.'

'Okay,' said Jack, drawing out the second syllable. 'Why the change of heart?'

'I think you can take it as a measure of how much the brass want you onboard.'

Jack noticed that Clewton seemed to be telling the truth. The powers that be wanted him, but *why* they wanted him was still a mystery. Again, Jack felt the weighty presence of a bigger picture, a picture he was unable to grasp.

'One thing,' said Jack.

'Anything you want to say, Jack,' Clewton said, the epitome of reasonableness. 'This is your show.'

'The creature's behavior at Cay Sal. It didn't sit right.' From the corner of his eye, Jack saw Tammes' scrutiny of the overhead now directed at him. 'Its, ah, some of its behaviors, to my mind, weren't what you'd expect from such an animal, regardless of its size.'

'Care to elaborate, Chief Tarr?' Tammes asked, his trebly voice belying his bulk.

'Not really,' Jack said. The last thing he wanted to do was get into a debate about the existence of metaphysical evil with Tammes, especially as Tammes – to Jack's mind – was quite possibly the human embodiment of it. 'Call it a hunch – I haven't fully thought it through. Just that something's off.'

Once more, that brief swap of eye contact between Tammes and Clewton.

'I'm right, aren't I?' Jack insisted. 'Something is going on with it.'

Clewton stepped in. 'Take the win, Chief. You've got what you wanted. No killing.'

Tammes, hands behind his head, his gaze again directed at some invisible spot on the overhead, giggled. If Jack hadn't known the giggle's source, he would have sworn a schoolgirl had somehow stowed away on the ship.

'Hell is wrong with you, Tammes?'

Tammes continued to stare at the overhead. 'The admiral is right, Jack. It would be best if you took the win. Non-lethal strategies – just as well, considering -'

'LUCAS!'

Indifferent to Clewton's intervention, Tammes continued. 'I was going to say, maybe it's just as well we're now - as it were - on a shoot-to-stun policy, given -'

Red-faced, the admiral stepped toward Dr Lucas Tammes. 'Lucas, for the love of -'

'God?' Tammes said, his voice rich with mockery. 'Val, what has some non-existent Sky Daddy got to do with any of this?' Tammes stood up and stretched his arms above his head, joints popping. He moved a few steps toward Jack. 'We don't need God. This is all on us. Well, *me.*'

Now, just a few feet from where Jack was rooted to the spot, Tammes' aura of chemical wrongness was almost overpowering. His pores seemed to secrete some kind of anti-pheromone—a form of concentrated, oleaginous corruption.

'What's he talking about, Clewton?' Jack demanded, unsure he wanted to know the answer.

Clewton ran both hands through his thinning hair. 'Jack, when you say the asset is acting beyond the parameters of crustacean behavior, what do you mean exactly?'

Jack breathed out. 'It's making decisions.'

Clewton sat down. 'A lot of animals make decisions.'

Jack bit the bullet. 'Humanlike decisions.'

Tammes turned to Clewton. 'I told you he'd get there. You might as well tell him the rest. If he's going to bring it in, he needs to know.'

'Excuse me,' Jack said, suddenly furious. 'I'm stood right here.'

'Sorry, Jack,' Clewton said tiredly. 'Lucas is right.'

'About *what*?'

'The mantis. It's possible that it is, in fact, executing humanlike choices.'

'And why's that?' Jack said as a slow, creeping sense of dread reached out from the pit of his gut.

'Because,' said Clewton, 'there's a human component in the creature's genetic makeup.'

The saliva in Jack's mouth dried as a wave of horror swept through his chest as if he'd started a fatal fall from a great height.

Tammes folded his arms. 'I have managed to isolate what you might call the intelligence gene. This gene – or set of genes – is responsible for advanced cognitive functions in humans. I call it the ICG, the Intelligent Gene Complex. As the mantis grew, it became possible to integrate the ICG into the mantis genome. The consequence of this is a process called neurogenesis – the enhanced production of neurons, leading to a larger, more complex brain. We are at the boundaries of genetic engineering here, gentlemen.'

It was Jack's turn to sit down. He squeezed the bridge of his nose, shaking his head slightly, trying to take in the implications of Tammes' story. 'Just how human is this thing?'

Tammes smiled; if such, it could be called. 'Mr Tarr, none whatsoever. The animal, while more cognitively advanced than its natural brethren, still negotiates its environment through the filter of its mantis perspective. It's just that it's a perspective that's more enhanced.'

'It's cleverer?'

'That it is,' said Tammes. 'But you have to remember, it's still going to act, broadly speaking, like you – a carcinology expert – would expect it to.'

'You should have told me this earlier,' Jack said.

Clewton nodded, spreading his hands out, palms up in an apparent gesture of capitulation, as if to say, *Got me there, Jack.*

'Is there anything else you're not telling me?' Jack looked into Clewton's eyes, his BS radar on high alert.

'No, there is not,' Clewton said with finality.

Jack nodded slowly as if accepting Clewton's word, knowing that, for whatever reason, the admiral was a lying son of a bitch. Both Clewton and Tammes were still playing hard to get with the full picture.

*   *   *

Jack managed to find his way to the Petty Officer's mess, where his SEALs were temporarily billeted. The mess was located midships, designed to minimize noise and motion from the ship's general operations. The bulkheads and overheads had a sleek, modern look with muted, non-reflective surfaces. The lighting was soft but sufficient, avoiding harsh glare and creating a comfortable environment. *All modern conveniences,* Jack thought. *Not how I remember ship accommodation.*

The only one of his guys awake was Zads. She was checking and rechecking her personal gear. Apart from being a damn fine operator, her pre-op meticulousness was one of the reasons why she still walked Planet Earth.

Not having his own well-used personal kit was another reason why he was still feeling like a fish out of water, to mix his metaphors. Your personal gear – weapons, diving kit, whatever - became a second skin or appendage. You didn't own this gear; it was an extension of you. When you used your own stuff, there was no bodily middleman – a foot, arm, trigger finger – between the brain and said gear. Though the time difference between threat and response could be measured in less than a second, that tiny advantage often made all the difference.

Itemizing your kit was an excellent way of dealing with the imminence of putting yourself in danger's way. Lose yourself in the details, the planning. Let the mechanics of the thing take over, sidestepping your fears.

Despite Clewton's yielding to Jack's non-lethal sensibilities, yet again, it still felt like he'd been hoodwinked. Still, at face value, it was a victory. He could return to Erin with an ethical bounce in his stride. Jack could now wholly apply himself to the task at hand now that he didn't have to kill the damn thing. In his head, it clarified things significantly.

Right from the get-go, he could feel his hard-won civilian sensibilities being eroded by the mere fact of his presence in a Navy context. It was so much easier to have principles when those principles were abstractions, beliefs that would never have to be tested. In a military environment, the weight of those principles suddenly became real. He was well aware they were the sort of principles that could get you and your buddies killed. Survival was about contingency, expediency. In particular, adaptation. The things that kept you alive. Jack would put himself and his team into a situation where the priority was to take the target alive, potentially making the operation much riskier.

'What's new, Chief?' she said as he entered the cramped space.

Jack relayed Clewton's revelation about the human component in the creature's genetic makeup. She nodded slowly, not overly freaked, unlike Jack. When he finished, he looked above and around, 'Just wondering what the hell is this thing?'

She laughed. 'The *Frankie*?'

'The what?'

'The *Frank E Sublett*—aka the *Frankie*—is a whole new breed of destroyer. Stealth-class, with all the bells and whistles. Black sails ops are her natural habitat.'

'Like *this* op kind of black sails?'

Zads smiled, that odd combo of sad and sexy that had driven Jack nuts back in the day. 'This op isn't black sails, Jack, this is damage limitation. Half the ships in the damn 4th Fleet are in the line or will be. At least those available. Coast Guard, too. Difficult to slip this under the radar.'

Jack, also, was surprised at the amount of tonnage assembled thus far. He'd expected something more modest when he suggested the picket line idea to Clewton. And while he was reassured he was being taken seriously by the higher-ups, he couldn't help feeling nerved-out about this sudden-seeming escalation.

Jack nodded to the tactical net launcher she'd been checking. 'You used those before?'

'Oui. Though not in anger. Yet.'

'They do what they're supposed to?'

'I'd say so. I mean, yes. The net is launched, spreads, finds the target, and wraps itself around it in a big hug. Smart metal is all the rage now. Metal memory. The net is *deformed'* - she air quoted – 'when compacted inside the launcher, cold as hell frozen over. When it is launched, the sudden heat causes it to expand. But then, the ocean's cold reminds it of its original shape. So, it becomes compacted again, trapping the unfortunate target in its remembered form. It is an awe-inspiring thing.'

'OK,' said Jack. 'Give me the *but*.'

'Oh, *Boo*, you and your sweet talking.'

Jack sighed, briefly looking at the overhead. 'Come on, Zads.'

'The *but* is what the *but* always is—*will* it stop whatever's trying to put you out of the game?'

'So it's anybody's guess whether the net will hold?'

'Always the quick study, Jack.'

'I liked it better when it was just guns and bullets.'

'You have the beam harpoon. Isn't that gun enough?'

'It'll do,' Jack said, thinking, *no wonder Skeeter got himself MIA*. He was carrying guns and bullets. Skeeter had gotten old and refused to adapt when the changes came in. Jack, on the other hand, had seen the wall, the one with the massive font-size writing on it; he'd carefully read that damn wall, heeding its message. And he got out. As they say, he swallowed the anchor.

The trouble with Skeeter was that he was such a VIP in the Teams that no one dared challenge him. How do you pin down and take issue with a legend? Consequently, Skeeter had more than likely got himself split in half by an overgrown crustacean simply because he ignored one of his own cardinals – adapt, baby, *adapt. Oh, Skeeter, you damn chump.*

Yes, at his age, Skeeter should've hit the bricks, sitting on his porch chugging on bottles of Natty Boh, listening to his beloved Delta blues. Not gallivanting around the Caribbean, getting himself lost to fuck. Silly old goddamn fool.

A remembrance of Skeeter singing softly while majorly in his cups.
Oh, lord, have mercy on me,
I don't know if I'm going to see tomorrow.
'Boo, you got S on your mind?' Like a wistful Cajun ballad, Zads' voice was soft, low, and lyrical. She could always read him like a book. Mind you, Erin could, too. Jack liked to imagine that when his face was at rest, its default setting was poker-faced implacability. His lady friends, however, past and Erin-present, made him feel like he must be presenting as wide-eyed and guileless.

He sat down on one of the lower bunks. 'You ever second with him? Skeeter? I mean, recently?'

Zads shook her head slowly. 'He didn't want me, Jack. After all the things we went through, he left me out. It was cold, the way he was.' She sighed a big one. 'Now that I am older, I understand why he was like that.'

Jack said, 'You know he and I, when I got out of the Teams, we never spoke. Not once. I tried at first. Called a few times, texted, that kind of thing. Kinda half-assed, I know. Got nothing back. Thought, To hell with you, S. To hell with you and your holier-than-thou grandstanding bullshit. Always taking the moral high ground, like he had the leasehold on it. And ...'

Zads smiled. 'Life took hold, no? Your new life.'

'I guess. But I should have tracked him down, got in his face. But I was stubborn, and I did nothing.'

'Ah, yes, stubborn. But you learned from Skeeter, the master.'

'Hmm.' Jack stretched, knowing he'd have to wake up the others soon and apprise them of the upcoming fun and games when he remembered something. 'What did you mean, Zads, about Skeeter, about understanding him?'

'Skeeter, he was playing mother hen to his little chicks. He kept me out of his clique, his inner circle. He was protecting me.'

'And who did he want in this inner circle?'

'Guys like himself, guys who'd been in the game too long. The ones who knew there was no way back. If you'd stayed in, guys like you.'

'Are you saying that's why he ghosted me all these years?'

Zads offered a big Gallic shrug.

'But what was he protecting me from? I'd already got out.'

'You know how it is, Jack. You get outside and can no longer access the other land. The land you left. You lose the language.'

'I'm speaking to you, Zads. It seems easy.'

'You know what I mean. All you need to know is that Skeeter loved you like a brother.'

'Funny way of showing it.'

'But that's exactly his way of showing it – keeping you away from all the crap, all the bullshit. Giving you a clean start. If Skeet became a regular fixture in your civvy-faced lifestyle, you'd never really leave the Navy. You'd be in a limbo land – neither civvy nor SEAL. Skeet understood that even if you don't.'

'Yet here I am.'

'You see, Jack, even in the SEALs, delicious irony is still a thing.'

Jack chuckled at that.

Over the main Tannoy, a female urgently voice-piped Jack and his team to the bridge. *Time to get in the water.*

CHAPTER 22

Sikorsky Delta Bird, Team FT1
Monday 0633 hours

When they took off from *Frankie's* flight deck, dawn was a glowy Caribbean hint. Jack was facing forward, talking to the pilot over the Sikorsky's comms; Zads and the rest were strapped in behind, all tightly clad in a permutation of a specialist type of foamed neoprene wetsuit, their flippers – as was the tradition - draped over their right arms. One of the helos from the hastily improvised rag-tag of destroyers, frigates, Littoral Combats, and Patrols had got a bite from their specs-recoded sonar matching the unknown incoming's kinetic profile alongside its allometric specs. Or something like that.

As they climbed to a decent altitude and headed south, Jack studied the two end-of-line ships. The penultimate vessel in the P-Line was USCG *Confidence*, Liliana Gil's ship. He wondered how she was feeling about her new orders. Pissed, no doubt. Beyond the horizon's curve, the last ship of the southerly P-Line hove into view. At first, Jack couldn't get a handle on it. As a type, the warship looked vaguely familiar. She had a destroyer's dimensions, but there was something odd about her lines. The destroyer struck Jack as a blend of conventional military design but with some disturbingly eclectic elements thrown in for good measure. Yep, she was an unsettling sight. While she retained the sleek, angular silhouette typical of US Navy destroyers, and her gray hull cut sharply through the water with military precision, she'd clearly undergone subtle, oddly disturbing modifications, apparent even from a thousand feet worth of height. The hull of the ship, while primarily standard Navy gray, also appeared mottled with patches of darker, almost black, discoloration. No US Navy vessel would be allowed to go to sea looking like that. You'd only get that kind of paintwork if you'd been at sea for years. Nonstop.

And then he realized why she was familiar. She was—or what was left of her—an old Forrest Sherman class from the 1950s. He knew it was a Forrest Sherman because when they left service in the late 1980s, at least one of them became a museum ship, one that Jack had taken a guided tour of as a kid—one of the only days out he could remember with his parents.

But why was this one back at sea?

She was still too far away for Jack to get a proper visual on her, and then, anyway, the Sikorsky veered east, away from the ship, and he lost sight of her.

He made a mental note to ask Clewton about the old girl. There was something about her strange presence that niggled him.

They were now fast approaching the datum point, the furthest southerly edge of the P-Line's sensory reach, twenty klicks from the *Frankie*. The co-pilot fed Jack a steady flow of information as the creature approached. It had slowed down to a steady fifteen knots, which was odd in itself. The creature's apparent caution worried Jack. It was like the beast was considering its options. Jack was still cautious in accrediting the animal with that much cognitive insight. Allowing the creature that much brainfuck would open the floodgate to all of Jack's concerns about what it was that Clewton and Tammes were keeping from him. And they *were* keeping something from him. He'd bet the farm *and* the Native American burial site it was built on that he was being mushroomed. If Jack's understanding of crustacean sentience was in the ballpark, it would need more than genome enhancement to reach that level of cognitive wariness.

'Ten klicks to drop off,' the copilot said.

Jack knew that if it so chose, the mantis could zip through the P-Line in mere seconds. Its slowing down to a constant lower speed contrasted big time with the species' usual method of forward propulsion. The mantis was a metachronal swimmer – it swam to a rhythm, pushing itself forward in regular bursts of speed, somewhat like the human breaststroke. Again, it felt to Jack that the creature was searching for something – and whatever it was looking for, it was connected to the military and the Navy in particular. Was this behavior simply because its genesis was at AUTEC, a Navy military base? Could it be that straightforward? But then why wouldn't it just return there?

Because that was where it was mutated, genetically stretched into something monstrous, alien, a stranger to itself. Whatever had happened in Tammes' lab must have been a never-ending sequence of unimaginable torture for the animal.

Maybe death for the animal was the better outcome, Jack thought. But no, he'd sworn off any more killing. It wasn't his place to act as judge, jury and executioner. He'd done it too many times, whatever the rights and wrongs, and it had been poisoning his soul. He was becoming separated from himself, his feelings, his emotions. He knew that if he didn't leave the Navy, the umbilical-like cord that kept him connected to his humanity would be forever severed.

It was like being slowly encased, entombed inside an armor-like carapace, an invisible exoskeleton that made him feel invulnerable, more or less than human. Was that what it was like for the creature? A feeling of being trapped inside its own mutated body? Jack shuddered.

'Five klicks, standby.'

Something like it had happened to Skeeter. Skeeter had left it too late to get out. His cord had been cut, like a spacewalker's safety tether, jettisoning him into the dark outer reaches of his mind. No way back. Jack should have intervened, done something, and helped his friend wake up and smell the coffee. But he hadn't. He'd been preoccupied with his post-Navy rehabilitation. He thought back to what Zads had told him about Skeeter ghosting her, dropping her from his inner circle, from being one of his regulars. Skeeter had cut his tether, surrounding himself with other untethered guys, men who considered themselves invincible. Men who knew in their secret hearts that they were only leaving the party through their own slow-boot shuffle off the mortal coil. No civvy street for them.

Jack shook his head, trying to clear his mind, as the helo rapidly descended to hovering thirty feet or so above the sea, maintaining the same position. Mac slid the helo door open, and Jack crossed his arms to his chest. It was a long time since he'd done a helocast jump, and it suddenly occurred to him that the doing of it did not appeal to him one iota. Before he could further consider the absurdity of leaping out of a perfectly serviceable aircraft into the deep blue sea, he jumped out of said perfectly serviceable aircraft into the deep blue sea. Reaching the limit of his plunge, he was aware of the others doing likewise, on his nine and three, rapidly descending in a streaming rush of bubbles. An individually calibrated weight belt-buoyancy compensator combo allowed the SEALs to remain at a constant depth of thirty feet.

The moment Jack shot beneath the sea's surface, the water held his body like an embrace. The world transformed as the ocean enveloped him, creating a gentle pressure. His focus narrowed on his immediate surroundings as he reflexively adjusted his buoyancy, feeling simultaneously weightless yet somehow anchored to the ocean floor.

Once they were all in the water the helo moved off northwards, hovering in proximity, standing by for extraction. Jack checked comms with Delta Bird, the helo's call sign.

Over Jack's earbuds, Delta Bird reported, 'Three klicks, closing. Maintaining course and speed. Closest point of approach eight minutes.' Delta Bird's voice was as clear as the proverbial bell. Subsea diver, satellite-boosted comms systems had been vastly improved since Jack's day. Presumably encrypted, too.

Jack acknowledged the sonar update as the team consolidated their positions, forming a curve some forty yards long, each SEAL eight yards distant from their neighbor. All were facing northwest. Jack was in the center. On his three, Det and Cal. Nine-ward, Liliana, then Mac. As agreed, the two flankers, Det and Mac, toted the net launchers while Cal and Zads were on harpoon duty. Jack had pointedly put her hands on the harpoon again, despite her Cay Sal goof up. *I trust you, Zads.*

'Lights when you're ready.'

'Roger that,' Delta Bird said. Two light buoys dropped into the water a couple of yards in front of Jack's team. The light hubs dangled twenty feet under the sea's surface.

'Initiate,' Jack said.

'You got it,' Delta Bird replied, activating the two hubs. Instantly, the light show began, with UV and polarised light shooting away from the team, dopplering blurrily beneath the waves toward the target's predicted arc of approach. A mantis boasts exceptional UV vision and can also detect – as well as use - polarised light. Jack was guessing that the illuminations using those wavelengths would catch the creature's attention and draw it in. Though it appeared to be swinging their way anyway, Jack wanted to ensure it stayed on course.

'Six minutes, guys.'

'Standby, team,' Jack said.

'Standing by,' they answered in unison.

'Harpoons only if nets fail,' Jack said, submerging to ten feet below the surface, the others following his lead. 'Harpoons on stun.'

'It'll be with you in four,' Delta Bird reported, the tension tuning the copilot's vocal cords to a higher pitch. 'Course, holding, speed down to ten.'

'It's noticed the lights,' said Zads.

'Yeah,' said Jack.

Delta Bird said, 'Amended ETA *twelve* minutes. That's one-two.'

'Have we scared it off?' Mac asked.

'Hope not,' Jack said, wondering if he'd overplayed his hand with the underwater discotheque.

'Coming your way again, guys,' Delta Bird advised. 'Ten knots constant.'

Jack peered out into the murk. While the visibility was getting better by the minute as the sun edged out of the eastern horizon, it was still suboptimal. This was the wrong time of day to be doing this. It had been a cloudless, starlit night, and when the sun rose proper, they'd have a sight range of at least eighteen yards, maybe up to thirty. While NV goggles did work underwater, Jack was banking on the hubs' regular light flashes alongside the UV and polarised illumination to light up what was coming their way.

As if reading his mind, Zads said, 'Glad we're not doing this at night.'

'Have you got your infrared switched on?' Jack asked.

'Yes, *Maman*.'

Someone chuckled. It sounded like Det. Or Cal. They were peas in a pod, those two.

'This is unpleasant,' Mac said, kind of to himself.

Yeah, Jack thought. The waiting, not the thing itself, often unmanned a fellow. 'Whites of its eyes, guys, whites of its eyes.'

'How many eyes it got?' Cal asked.

'It's a little tough to pin down,' Jack said. 'They've got compound eyes—eyes within eyes. Trust me, they can see better than you or me.'

'CPA two minutes,' the pilot said.

'Team, if you're not already standing by,' Jack said, 'stand by.'

He got a few murmured yes bosses-chiefs back. His team was feeling it, like him. But for them, this type of thing was their bread and butter, their everyday. For Jack, this type of thing most certainly was not his goddamn everyday. So what the hell was he doing dicking in the Caribbean, his mouth, despite being surrounded by millions of liters of water, as dry as a Dan Aykroyd joke? Why wasn't he on *Lemuria* waiting for regular-sized crustaceans to pop up? Better still, why wasn't he lying beside Erin in his own bed?

Even to himself, his order to Foxtrot Tango One had sounded like a variation on the old joke about US Navy prevarication – *stand by to stand by*. He felt a delinquent chuckle wend its way up his throat. *Piss off, chuckle*. It wouldn't do if he lost it to a bout of hysteria. Not good at all.

'Six-zero seconds,' the pilot said, his voice almost a whisper as if he thought the creature might hear him.

The hubs' regular lights were fixed, and Jack stared into the distance using their powerful beams. Of course, it was possible the creature was swimming below the beams, coming at them from underneath. But knowing mantis behavior, Jack trusted it to go right to the light source, as was its natural, nature-given predilection.

But this ain't no ordinary shrimp, Jacky-boy.

Now he'd had the thought, it was impossible to unthink it: the mantis coming at them stealthily from below, catching them off-guard. He dismissed the notion of alerting the others. If his nerves were anything to go by, they'd be spooked good and proper enough.

'Target's with you,' the pilot said, now full-on sotto voce. 'Northwest of your position.'

And then there it was. An explosion of iridescence, a coruscating blast of color that somehow remained in a constant state of detonation. *It's letting us see it. It's letting* me *see it.*

'We got company,' Mac whispered unnecessarily.

Hanging motionless in one of the hub's regular lights, facing the team, facing Jack. As if considering the pros and cons of its next course of action. As if weighing up the threat the team posed to its well-being. The creature raised its flattened, paddle-like abdominal appendages – s*wimmerets* – and propelled itself gently forward by, maybe, six or seven yards, maintaining its depth, staying inside the beam, coming to rest once more, still watching.

Watching me, Jack thought. Letting me watch it. Not camouflaging itself.

Why?

CHAPTER 23

Team FT1
Monday, 0645 hours
Southwest Datum Point

The net launchers' max effective range was forty-five feet. Anything even slightly above that would be hit-and-miss—literally. The other problem with the nets was that they also had a minimum range of thirty feet. Anything less than that, and the nets didn't have enough time to open. The sweet spot left them fifteen feet to play with. And with the net launchers, one shot was all you got. If Det and Mac missed, there would be no second chances.

'Nets?' Jack whispered. 'Focus on the swimmerets, slightest movement, fire.'

But the creature just hung in the light, unmoving just out of the nets' range, as if it knew the extent of their weapons' reach. Jack wondered if Tammes had used the net launchers on the creature before and that it had some memory of what it faced.

It's a crustacean, Jack. It doesn't have memory. At least, not in the way humans do.

Above, the sun was rising into a new day, the increasing visibility incrementally revealing the mantis in all its glory. And it was glorious, this thing, this aberration.

'My God,' Liliana whispered. '*C'est beau.*'

'Roger that,' said Mac, his voice full of awe.

'A Peacock Mantis,' Jack said to no one in particular as the nascent sun filtered through the water, striking the creature's motionless body and revealing a kaleidoscopic formation of colors glimmering like precious gemstones. Bejeweled with vibrant blue, green, and gold tints, its many eyes seemed to stare at Jack with an otherworldly fire. On its approach, it had slipped through the sea with the grace of a dancer.

'It's only got eyes for you, Boo,' Zads whispered.

'Steady,' Jack said, more to himself than the others. And then, almost instantly, the creature was no longer in the regular light's beam. It was so quick; it was as if it had dematerialized, vanished into thin air—or, rather, water.

'Shit, where'd it go?' Det asked.

'Has it gone?' Zads asked.

'Assume it's still with us,' Jack said. 'Delta Bird, activate Buoy Two.' Behind them, the second light hub started pushing out light in a broadly south-easterly direction. 'Cal, Liliana, about turn, cover our six.' Jack requested an update on the creature's position as the two SEALs turned on their bodies' axis.

'North of you, Jack. Two hundred yards. South-easterly course, ten knots. I don't want to alarm you, but it looks like it's circling.'

'Consider me alarmed,' Jack said, twisting round in the water, a full one-eighty, telling Det and Mac to do likewise. 'Det, for the moment, it's on your starboard ninety. Eyes peeled.'

'Chief,' Det acknowledged.

Buoy Two's constant beam streamed before them, fanning at a generous one-fifty degrees. One-eighty would be better, thought Jack. The thirty-D blind spot on Det's side was worrying. He willed the creature to swim into the beam. At least then, they'd know where the damned thing was.

'Delta Bird?' Jack said.

'Target maintaining south-easterly trajectory, ten knots constant.' The animal was moving away from them, toward P-Line Orange.

'Delta Bird, inform *Frankie* they've got incoming,' Jack said.

'Huh,' Det grunted. 'We live to fight another day.' The relief in his voice was palpable.

'Everyone keep your focus,' Jack said. Instinct told him that the fat lady was still singing somewhere out there. 'Maintain readiness.'

'This is Delta Bird. *Frankie* informed. Target course constant, ten knots steady.' Jack could hear the pilot's breathing over the comms. 'You guys had enough fun in the paddling pool?'

'Damn right,' Mac said.

'What's its distance from our position?' Jack asked.

'This is Delta Bird, half a klick, increasing, I – '

'Delta Bird?'

'Wait. It's slowing. Seven knots, four. Shit. Chief, it's … it's stopped.'

'Guys,' Jack said urgently. 'It's going to take a run at us. Remember what I said? How fast can it go? Delta Bird, as soon as it disappears from your sonar – and it will, just like before – you give us a big Fox, loud and clear.'

'You got it, Jack.'

Fox. *Fire.*

'Listen, guys, as soon as Delta B gives us the Fox, net launchers launch. Straight ahead. Pull the trigger; don't wait for visuals; assume it's upon us. Det? Mac?'

Both Det and Mac gave Jack a thumb and finger OK.

'This is Delta Bird. Target incoming on your position, ten knots, still constant.'

'Harpoons, on my word.'

Liliana and Cal acknowledged.

'Incoming, altered three degrees, your port, ten knots.'

'Cal,' Jack barked. 'Move out to Det's ninety, cover him.'

Det swam out from the line. Jack was painfully aware that, technically, Cal was now taking point. He hoped he hadn't unnecessarily exposed him, wondering if he should have taken the de facto point himself. The creature's three-degree course alteration had thrown Jack. *Damn, I'm out of practice.*

'This is Delta Bird, course unchanged, speed fifteen knots, increasing.'

'Any second now,' Jack said.

'This is Delta Bird, twenty knots.'

Jack's harsh breathing joined his team's chorus of harsh breathing, everyone trying to manage their body's response for when the time came, more than likely hoping their breathing wasn't the loudest, that by implication, they were the least in control.

For the thousandth time, Jack quickly scanned his team's whereabouts, ensuring they maintained positional integrity—that nobody had drifted into the line of fire. It was easy to do this in the sea—easy to drift out of your designation, easy to lose your orientation, especially if you were focused on something that was out to kill you.

Something's wrong.

Jack eyeballed his team's positions again, his vision slightly impaired by the now strong sunlight slanting across and downward from the east.

What is it? What's wrong?

Cal! Where's Cal?

'FOX! FOX! FOX!' Delta screamed out.

The nets were already shooting forward, fanning out before Delta Bird's second screamed *Fox!* A silvery detonation exploded from the net launchers, the sun's watery rays reflecting off the almost liquid metal.

'I got it!' Det yelled. 'I got it! I got the shithead!'

'Det!' Jack shouted, 'Hold position. Everybody, hold position. Let the net do its work.'

As the churning water cleared on Jack's forty-five, he could see something struggling inside Det's net. *Something's not right. Where's the jewels, the precious stones?*

'*Oh, shit, oh, God, God!*' Det cried out, his voice full of horror.

And then Jack saw what Det saw: *Cal.* Cal was struggling inside the net, entangled, panicking as it slowly contracted, incrementally reducing his small swim space. The net's tensile strength was set to the mantis, a mantis with an inch-thick suit of armor. Without the mantis carapace, the net would cut straight through Cal.

'*Fuck,*' Zads said.

'This is Delta Bird, sitrep, over?'

Ignoring Delta Bird, Jack started swimming toward Cal. 'Zads, cover me. Mac, standby with launcher. Det, hold.' As Jack retrieved the cutters from his utility belt, he said, 'Delta B, target update?'

'This is Delta Bird, target three hundred yards, stationary. Sitrep?'

'We've got one WIA,' said Jack, almost on top of Cal. The net had now closed to a couple of feet around the snared SEAL.

'Medivac?' Delta Bird said. 'I'm in position. SPIE rope deployed for wet extraction. Just give me the word, Jack.'

Jack acknowledged Delta Bird, lifting his cutters to the net. Cal's breathing was loud through the dive audio, his eyes wide with panic. 'Deep breaths, Cal,' Jack said, trying to keep the panic out of his voice. 'Take it easy.'

'Get ... me ... out ... Chief,' Cal stuttered.

'Boss?' Zads said. 'He OK?'

'Oh, Christ. Oh, sweet Jesus,' Det said.

Jack brought the cutters to the mesh, gripping them tightly. Nothing. He tried again. The cutters were useless.

The net, in places, was now touching Cal's body.

'We're gonna have to evac you, Cal. The cutters aren't doing it.'

Cal nodded.

'Delta Bird,' Jack said, 'surfacing for extraction.' He grabbed the ultralight net and started tugging it, adjusting his own buoyancy with his free hand. Slowly, he and Cal floated upward, ascending into the new day, breaking the surface.

'*Get it off me, get it off me,*' Cal's terror-struck voice blubbered over the radio.

'This is Delta Bird, target, ten knots, incoming, northeast.'

Shit.

'Let's get vamoosing down there,' Delta Bird added unnecessarily.

Zads, Det, and Mac bobbed, hooks at the ready, as the helo came in slowly, trailing the SPIE rope in the water. 'Cal first,' Jack shouted. As the rope approached, Jack caught it, hooked it with Cal's dive suit carabiner, and tugged. 'Det, you next, then Mac and Zads.' As his team okayed him, Det hooked on and was hoisted up a couple of feet by the winch guy.

Get it off, get it off.

Delta Bird said, 'Ten knots, two hundred yards, course steady.'

Mac was hauled out of the water. Somebody was screaming. Cal or Det. It sounded like Det.

Zads hooked on next and was winched up, ready for Jack.

'One hundred yards, incoming,' Delta Bird said.

Jack hooked onto the rope, and as the Sikorsky banked upward and away, Jack aimed his harpoon at the sea to the right of the now blazing sun. Where he'd been treading water seconds before, the rainbow-colored mutant rolled out of the sea briefly before submerging again, the sun glinting off its radiant carapace.

CHAPTER 24

Delta Bird, 800ft, *Team FT1*
Monday, 0811 hours

Jack unbuckled, shrugging off his tanks, peeling his hood over his head. Cal was lying on the helo's deck, Zads, and Mac, their backs to Jack, crouched over him. Cal's breath rasped as his chest strained against the mesh. Sat to one side, Det's arms were wrapped around his knees tight against his chest, unable to witness what was happening to his buddy. His face blanched, bloodless. Mac was attempting to cut through the net with the helo's heavy-duty emergency bolt cutters, grunting with the effort. Frustrated, he threw the cutters to one side, shouting something unintelligible. Jack pushed past Mac and knelt. The net was now cutting into Cal's face and into his body, its shape mirroring Cal's. Cal could no longer shout or scream – the air was being forced out of him, denying him any lung expansion.

Compressive asphyxia.

'The net,' Jack said, thinking out loud, 'expands with heat and contracts in the cold. How do we heat the net?' Jack stared into Cal's terrified eyes. 'Oxy torch?'

'Won't find one on a helo,' said Mac, confirming what Jack already knew.

'Propane torch?' Jack asked, on the off chance that safety advances had been made.

'Nah,' said Zads.

Jack pressed his mic, speaking to the pilot. 'Get *Frankie*, standby with oxy torches. Ask Clewton what cuts through titanium.'

He felt helpless, trying to squeeze his fingers under the net, but there was no gap. The net was so snug against Cal's body that he could no longer move. Only his eyeballs flicked from left to right, up and down, bulging as his face took on a blue tinge.

'Thermo blankets!' Mac shouted, releasing the thin silver-colored covers from their holder. 'Wrap them around him,' he said. 'Might buy him some time.'

Jack and Zads lifted Cal up while Mac mummified him inside the foil.

'ETA *Frankie*?' Jack shouted out.

'Couple minutes. Can he hold out?'

Jack shook his head. 'Don't know, maybe.'

'Clewton here.' The admiral's voice was loud and clear.

'The net, what can cut through it?'

'Laser, plasma cutters.'

'Anything like that onboard *Frankie*?'

'Standby.'

'CLEWTON!' Jack yelled. But the admiral was already gone.

Standby? What the hell does that mean?

Stand by to stand by.

Blood started to seep in between the foil blankets' folds, running down the sides of the entrapped Cal.

'The thermo Bs, I don't …' Zads paused, bringing her hand to her mouth. 'They're not working.'

Mac nodded toward Cal. 'The body, Chief. His *body*, man.'

Mac was right. The blankets seemed … loose, *looser*. Jack placed his hand on top of Cal. Wished he hadn't. There was too much give, like touching a parcel with no actual damn contents. Without thinking, Jack tore the blankets off Cal's head. *Shit! Sweet Jesus.*

The net had sliced into Cal's head, shrank into it by at least an inch, cutting into his cheeks, chin, his skull. His eyes, though, they'd been spared, perfectly framed by two wire squares, orbs staring sightlessly at Jack.

The *Frankie's* aft-flight deck hove into view as the ship moved into position to retrieve its bird. Delta B bounced on the deck a few times before she was secured. The sliding door was flung open from the outside, and Jack and Mac slid Cal's body onto the waiting gurney, blood now pouring through the blankets' folds, dripping onto the flight deck to the wheeled stretcher. One corpsman pushed the gurney while the other cut through the foil. Suddenly, he stopped. He turned away, swiveled on the balls of his feet, bending over, dry retching. The other corpsman stepped away from the gurney, turning his head toward Jack and his team, who had now exited the helo and were jogging toward him.

Way, way, too late, Clewton emerged from the after-hangar with two sailors in coveralls, both carrying torches. Jack carried on past the gurney, past the medics, and reached Clewton.

Dantz and Graaf quickly inserted themselves between Jack and the admiral. For his part, Jack slipped into a loose stance, ready for them. Zads and Mac stepped up beside him. Det, however, screaming with rage, charged full-on into the Tweedles, taking Graaf down with his momentum. Clewton shouted, 'Enough! Stand down!' Det ignored him, continuing to pummel the downed man, blood spurting from Graaf's exploding nose. His pal hung back, unsure what to do, clearly wanting to override his boss' order.

Jack and Mac dragged Det off the fallen Tweedle. Once Det was separated from his target, he crumpled into Jack's arms, falling to the deck on his knees, a couple of feet down from the admiral. In the entrance to the hangar, Tammes stood silently, face impassive.

Ashen-faced, Clewton stared at Jack with undisguised contempt. Jack waited for the admiral to outline the nature of his team's punishment – thrown in the brig, dropped from the mission, maybe *both* - but it never arrived. Instead, Clewton said, 'Can we all calm down? I get it. You think I'm to blame. You think I sit on my ass all day long while you guys do the hard yards. But it's not like that. And I do understand. One of your guys got killed. But Jack, Cal was one of *my* guys, too. Your loss is *my* loss.'

Not trusting himself to open his mouth, Jack nodded curtly. Clewton was so full of bullcrap. He'd convinced himself that he actually did give a shit about Cal.

A young sailor, a seaman, a bridge runner saluted the admiral and gave him a piece of paper. Clewton scanned it, his lips moving.

'No rest for the wicked,' he said eventually.

USCG *Confidence*
Monday, 1023 hours
Picket Line

Liliana stood on the port bridge wing, watching her MH-65 helo return with the SEAL from USS *Frankie* – the team from Cay Sal. As she observed them exiting the helo, she was surprised to count five. Thirty minutes ago, news had come down the wire that they'd lost a guy. Or gal. They must have had a replacement. She wondered if the poor guy knew what he was letting himself in for.

As for *Confidence*, the only ship's exterior lookouts she'd posted were on the bridge wings. When the SEALs were in the air returning from their op, the creature had somehow reached the P-Line and started snatching sailors off several ships' lower decks, two CGCs, and one Navy ship. CGC *Astounding*, CGC *Flamboyant*, and USS *Shadow*.

Damn, but this thing was fast.

All of the vessels that had been hit were to the north of *Confidence* in the line, and it seemed likely that if the creature maintained its southward trend, then she was due a visit. Accordingly, Liliana had ordered her aft and midships lookouts to stand down. She was determined not to suffer any more casualties. Three was more than enough.

The sailors who'd died or gone missing on the other ships were all lookouts on the lower parts of the ship. Liliana wasn't sure whether the bridge wing platforms were out of the creature's reach, and like the two port and starboard lookouts, she kept a wary eye on the water immediately below.

Now that the sonar had been recalibrated to the creature's specs, Liliana was a little easier in her mind that *Confidence* wouldn't get caught out. The call to redeploy to the picket line had made her heart sink, not that she could show her disappointment. As usual, she was painfully aware of how closely the bridge watchkeepers scrutinized her. So she relayed the news as if it was just an everyday annoying bug and not a duty that was potentially placing them inside the equivalent of a combat zone.

XO Walker mirrored his boss' reaction, and the bridge crew seemed to exhale a sigh of relief. Liliana knew that she and her officers had again passed the unsaid test. If either she, Walker, or the other bridge junior officer had shown the least smidgeon of alarm, it would be all over the ship before you could say heave-ho. It was the nature of ships – especially the smaller ones – that anything the skipper did would be analyzed and chewed over by all the lower messdeck yap jockeys.

Returning to the bridge's warmth, she couldn't help gripping her rosary underneath her uniform blouse despite her ambiguous relationship with God.

Still, at least she didn't have the Cubans onboard. They'd been ferried off to the bigger ships and thence to the mainland. She prayed they were okay and that they'd *be* okay. The bridge interior doors swung open and in strode the SEAL team leader, the one called Jack.

'Morning, ma'am,' he said. 'We're ready to assume position.'

'Chief,' she said, returning his tired smile. 'What's the odds it will come sniffing this way?'

Jack shrugged. 'The odds are good. You're next in line. It attacked three ships in a row. One after the other – fast as hell. For some reason, it seems to have held back from attacking *Confidence*.'

'Any particular reason?'

'Not a clue, Captain,' the SEAL answered.

Because, she thought, *it's waiting for* you *to get into the water, Chief.* The crazy thought came from nowhere, unbidden.

'Your comms synced with ours?' Jack asked, looking at her curiously as if he'd somehow, telepathically, clued into her insane thought.

'Good to go,' said Liliana.

'Any spooky pings, visuals, ma'am, let us know.'

'You got it, Chief,' she said, glad she wasn't the one getting into the water, close up and physical. Not her thing at all. She loved her ship's hull and how its standard, inch-thick, carbonized, manganese steel kept her insignificant self and the deep, dark ocean apart. 'Anything else?'

'There is one thing,' the chief said. 'What's your take on that old Forrest Sherman out there?'

It was Liliana's turn to shrug. 'Taken out of mothballs for some reason?'

The chief nodded slowly, 'Could be, could be.'

She watched Chief Tarr leave the bridge. *It's waiting for you, Jack.*

CHAPTER 25

USCG *Confidence, FT1*
Monday, 1103 hours

Jack kept to a steady depth of thirty feet beneath *Confidence's* starboard stern, once more squinting into the crystal clear Caribbean Sea. He estimated a sight range of up to or slightly over thirty yards. To his far three, under the bow, Zads maintained a similar position, as did the new guy, Harper, suspended, as it were, midships. Harper was toting a beam harpoon. Harper the Harpoon. Way to go, nominative determinism, thought Jack. Another concept Erin had brought into Jack's hitherto emptily conceptual life. Good old Erin, educating her sailor. Harper quickly became Harps, stepping into Cal's vacated space with grace and sensitivity. It's not easy replacing a dead man.

Det was a worry. He'd calmed down somewhat, but it was clear to Jack that he hadn't stepped on the road to self-forgiveness, let alone started to travel it. That process would come. But not today, not next week. A year or two down the line, maybe never. He hadn't realized Cal and Det had been – as Zads discreetly apprised him – an *item*. Zads had been good with Det, confessing her similar – albeit non-fatal - faux pas with the beam harpoon back on Cay Sal. And Jack, briefly gripping Det's shoulder in what he hoped was a reassuringly avuncular fashion, told him, *Experimental weapons, Det. You know the drill, there's no telling how they'll perform in-field. It's the first time these things have been used in anger. We're a case study. Useful idiots. After this op, they'll be withdrawn from service because of what happened. Modifications will be made. They'll be reintroduced. Lives will be saved. And that'll be on us – the guinea pigs.*

Det had nodded, his face full of sorrow and pain. There'd be an inquiry into Cal's death, but Jack would make it his business that Det be fully exonerated. Clewton could take that to the bank.

Jack had paired Det with Mac facing northward on the cutter's portside. Mac, the older man and more experienced SEAL, would keep an eye on Det.

As the creature had been moving northward, it had attacked the ships' portside. Jack didn't see why it shouldn't do the same with *Confidence.* That is, if it showed. He could see no reason it would break its attack pattern and avoid the CG instead. Still, you never knew. Jack had also made it a point to keep Det on the net launcher, figuring he was unlikely to make the same mistake twice.

Confidence's engines were shut down, removing any prop danger. Back in the day, Jack had been taught all about the Bernoulli Effect and how not to get sucked into ships' propellers. You'd be reasonably safe on the surface, but it wouldn't be pretty if the props started suddenly turning at this depth. It was not a way he wanted to leave this vale of tears.

For its part, the sea was calm with hardly any wind; therefore, the drift speed was minimal, probably half a knot or so. They would not be too far adrift from the picket line when and if the creature came their way.

'Chief, *Confidence*, over.' Liliana Gil's voice came over loud and clear.

'Chief, over,' Jack said.

'Sonar target, identical species calibration, five-hundred yards, one-four-five degrees, course three-zero-zero, speed five knots.'

Jack acknowledged *Confidence*. 'Zads, Harps, at the risk of stating the obvious, the target will attack or won't. If it gets personal and goes for *you* – you won't know anything about it. It's that fast. If it attacks any other of the team, you either net it or shoot it. Don't worry about your buddy getting in the crossfire – he'll already be dead.' Jack emphasized this last for Det. Det needed to understand that even before he netted Cal, Cal was a dead man swimming.

If, that is, the creature had been attacking Cal. It was another mystery. One that Jack hadn't the time to give the thought it deserved. Given the creature's speed, somehow Det had ensnared Cal before the creature got to him, which was impossible when he thought about it. If the creature had wanted Cal, it would surely have gotten him. And if it were true—that for some reason, the creature did not want Cal—then his order to ignore any potential blue-on-blue issues would get people killed. On the other hand ...

Harps said, 'So if it stays on its present course, and it comes at us, one of us is going to luck out.'

'Something like that,' Jack said.

'Great odds, Chief,' Zads said.

'As the song says, two out of three ain't bad, yada yada.'

'Hey, boss,' Mac said, 'what if it comes under us?'

'It didn't before. It hit us head-on – no reason to assume otherwise.'

'Unless it's learning,' said Det, his voice low, flat. 'You know, trying out new strategies.'

Zads said, 'I don't want to think about *that*.'

Me neither, thought Jack. Det's thoughts mirrored his own. If the creature was learning, they'd have their work cut out. *Am I endangering their lives?* Only if the harpoon's stun facility was a piece of shit – which Tammes assured him it wasn't. When in captivity, the beam was used daily in its 'training' – the stick alongside the carrots.

I am so the wrong person to be leading this team, to be here. And again, the niggle, the worm in the apple. Why *am I here?* Clewton didn't need an expert in the water – hell, Jack could offer advice via Zoom. And as for the Skeeter connection, that was irrelevant, water under the bridge. No, something was bent out of line. He just couldn't figure out the angle.

'This is *Confidence*, contact bearing one-four-zero, four-zero-zero yards, course zero-four-five, speed five knots.'

Any second now. Scrub that. Any millisecond now.

Visibility was good—exceptional, in fact—far better than this morning. Jack estimated twenty-five yards or so. If it wasn't for the mantis' uncanny speed, he'd be confident about not being caught unawares. As it was, the seventy-five-foot cushion was no cushion at all.

'This is *Confidence*. Contact bearing one-three-eight, three-four-eight yards, stationary.'

'Standby,' Jack whispered into the dive mic.

Several standing bys whispered back.

A cloud moved over the sun, and the water darkened, dramatically decreasing visibility. Though the water temperature remained constant, Jack shivered. The creature was out there, biding its time, just like before, considering its options.

Several things happened at lightning-speed velocities. From roughly east to west, something zipped across his vision on a bullet-like trajectory before disappearing out of view. A tracer of rainbow color, a glint, and a glimpse, and it was gone.

'*Jesus*,' someone whispered into their mic. Zads?

Excited shouting from *Confidence*. 'Say again,' Jack yelled back, willing Liliana to calm down.

'Contact bearing zero-nine-zero, two-one-two yards, stationary.'

'On your two-seventy, Harps,' Jack said, looking at the new guy.

'Shit!' Zads said.

'Zads?' Jack asked.

Confidence said, 'Bearing zero-zero-seven, one-three-two yards, stationary.'

'On my ninety,' Zads said quietly.

'What's going on?' Mac asked.

'Stay calm,' Jack said, trying to stay calm. 'Hold positions, vigilance, froggies.'

'Boss?' Mac again.

'It's checking us out.' *Wondering if we're worth the hassle.*

Jack felt it before he saw it. A tremor, a shiver, in the water, a subtle precursor heralding its arrival, its immediate presence. And then a sense of something rushing toward him, a bright blur of red and green and orange and blue and –

He was face-to-face with it, in its 'face.' Its many, many-eyed face. It hung there with him in the silent, still sea, watching him, seeing him in the way only a mantis can see. Jack listened to the yells and shouts from *Confidence.* From Zads, Mac, and Harps. Even Det. He listened, yet heard nothing.

With exquisite slowness, the creature unfurled its appendages, its claws.

CHAPTER 26

USCG *Confidence, FT1*
Monday, 1137 hours

'Hello, fuckface,' Jack said. He might as well land an insult before he died.

Dimly, Jack was aware of a distant babel of voices, a confusion of competing input, and those voices slowing, running down, like an old-time analog record player cut off from its power source.

The creature's two compound eyes seemed to bore into Jack. But that was impossible. The two eyes weren't eyes at all; they were *compound* eyes. Eyes within eyes. *So why does it feel like it's staring directly into my soul?*

Because, Jack, the marine biologist thought, it's not seeing you in the same way you're seeing it—a visual image—it's 'seeing' you, experiencing you *neurally*. The reality of your presence is created by what passes for its brain, the cumulative effect of its two prominent eyes containing thousands of small eyes, independent photoreceptors, and it is experiencing you directly, uncut, as it were. *The thing itself.*

Eyes within eyes.

And why am I having these thoughts? How am I having these thoughts? I should be dead.

Am I dead? Mechanically, he looked down to see if his legs were in situ. They were. Splitter hasn't split me. Still intact.

And something about the creature ...

And then, to his left, in his peripheral vision, Harps was turning toward him on his axis, raising his net launcher, preparing to fire.

Something about the creature was ... off.

Newbie Harps was following Jack's order. If you see the creature on a buddy, don't hesitate; don't worry about blue on blue. Because by the time you fire, your buddy's a goner. But I'm not. I'm still here, alive and kicking.

Something. Not just its exaggerated size, something else ....

And then, to his left, more movement—this time, Zads. She was pointing her beam harpoon directly at the creature, at the yet motionless animal still floating effortlessly in front of Jack.

In my personal space, dammit!

Then the voices in his ears, the formerly faraway voices, grew closer, increasing in volume. Jack yelled into his mic, except he didn't. Instead, a slow-motion metallic croak issued forth between his lips. And in the world outside his mask, his suit was changing, speeding up, revving up to its normal tempo. And the sense of being ... experienced, probed, by the creature faded, melted away.

There was more movement. Harps raised his launcher, no longer in slo-mo but back in real-time, upheaving his weapon like a netter about to net his fish.

Somehow, Jack had time for several thoughts: I'm about to be netted. Along with the creature. Crushed into the animal's carapace as the net contracted.

But there was no net and then no creature. All was absence. Because newbie Harps was also absent. Gone, man. Simply not there anymore. Except some of him was. The man had been replaced by a blooming, now billowing red cloud.

The hell?

'HARPS!' someone shouted, someone desperate, panicking. It took a second for Jack to realize he was the Someone, the despairing and panicked. It was him. Get a grip, man, he self-instructed.

And then, underneath *Confidence's* chatter and his team's tsunami of questions, came a noise that would haunt Jack until the end of his days.

'QUIET!' he shouted out, ears straining.

There it was again, a faint ululating scream. No, not a scream, a plea - forlorn, wretched. Wordless, a wail, and implicit in its eerie cry was an entreaty for help.

'He's alive,' Mac said. 'Harps is still alive. Shit.'

'Where is he?' Det asked.

'Quiet!' Jack demanded again. Then, 'Harps, Jack here. Can you hear me?'

Again, that wordless wail, now growing fainter each second.

'Harps?'

Nothing. Static. White noise.

'*Merde*,' Zads said.

'*Confidence*, target position?'

'This is *Confidence*, target bearing three-one-five, course three-one-five, three-point-seven kiloyards, speed erratic. Heading away from the line, toward the Keys.'

Head still spinning, Jack said, 'Roll call.'

When Zads, Det, and Mac signed in, Jack requested that *Confidence* get them out of the water.

*   *   *

Later. The surviving team members sat out of their dive suits in Liliana's cabin, drinking from big mugs of hot, strong coffee. Though they'd known Harps only briefly, his absence still sat heavy. And like Cal, the manner of Harps' going didn't sit easy with the team. No one aired the thought, but it was a good guess that they were all wondering if Harps was still alive. And, if so, what the hell was the creature playing at?

There was a knock on the cabin door, and Liliana entered her domain. 'Your ride's here, guys,' she said.

'Ma'am,' Jack said. He'd already debriefed Clewton via the VHF. He'd given the admiral a somewhat truncated version, leaving out the weirdness that had ensued when he'd had his close encounter of the in-my-goddamn-face kind – the high strangeness time-slow thing, the sense of … of what? Of being examined? No, it was more than that. It had been like an interrogation, a wordless third-degree. Like it was asking, What are you? Maybe even, Who are you? And why are you in my way?

Ridiculous, of course. Which was why he'd scrimped on the truth. As far as Jack was concerned, all Clewton needed to know was where the creature had been and where it was likely headed. The admiral had Jack on a need-to-know leash, so he was merely returning the favor. Let us all not have a damn clue what the other knows or is up to. It was, after all, the Navy. Being in the dark, not knowing what the other hand's doing, Standard Operating Procedure.

The Keys? the admiral had said.

Uh-uh.

Why?

To move into the Gulf? Jack had suggested.

But why*?*

No idea. It was true. Jack, like the admiral, was clueless.

Then, a voice in the background. Tammes.

So what's the takeaway? From … this latest … encounter?

The launchers, the beam harpoons. The thing's too fast. We're not getting a chance to use them.

Again, Tammes' voice, metaphorically speaking over Clewton's shoulder.

'What's he say?' Jack demanded.

'Jack!' Tammes said, taking over from Clewton and greeting a long-lost buddy.

'Sounds like you've got something you want to say, Tammes.'

'I'd like to hear what you've got to offer first. You're the expert, Jack.'

Obsequious asswipe. 'We need to get an advantage,' Jack said. 'So far, it's been playing on its home turf.'

'What sort of advantage?'

'I think you already know, Tammes. Its next destination is not the Gulf but the Keys, or, rather, one particular Key.'

'Go on.'

'Mantis shrimps can survive out of water for several minutes, especially if the weather is humid or wet. They've been found on roads near beaches. Possibly dropped by birds, but also perhaps an indication of terra firma capabilities. And unlike all other marine species, our guy has abdominal gills. This could allow him to survive out of the water a tad longer than his fellow marine brethren. And also, Tammes, I have – oh, let's call it a hunch – that our guy's gills have been tinkered with – and that you know damn well it can operate on land.'

'Hmm. Got me there, Jack. You're right. My mantis is amphibious, though I didn't have time to test the extent of this before it escaped.'

'Nevertheless.'

'Okay, yes, nevertheless. Fair enough. Yes, it should be able to live out of water for … extended periods.'

'And there,' pronounced Jack, 'is our advantage.'

'Catch it out of water?'

'It's our best chance. Before my team and I return to the water, we need to reassess and consider new strategies.'

'I agree.'

'But first,' said Clewton, coming back online, 'We need to decide what to do *now*.'

'Yeah, well, we've lost it again.'

'That is not strictly true, Jack. We just got a couple of beeps from its tracker by Western Sambo Reef before it went dead again, and it was heading for Key West—well, Boca Chica Key, to be precise.'

'The Naval Air Station.'

'It could be, Jack.'

'What does Tammes think?'

'Giving me the thumbs up as I speak.'

'Listen, Clewton. This thing. It's targeting Navy assets. It's like it's searching for something. Care to enlighten me? What's it been trained to do?'

'Search and destroy. That's its whole raison d'etre. It ain't got no deep feelings about anything, Jack. It's just a glorified goddamned crustacean. You know that, right?'

Clewton was lying. Why was he lying? What was he lying about? He asked, 'Have you alerted the base?'

'Yep, they're on red, awaiting you.'

Jack yawned ostentatiously. 'We're a little frazzled. We haven't had any shuteye for getting on forty-eight.'

'Appreciate that, Jack. Once you're at Boca Chica, and everybody's up to speed defense-wise, and everything's quiet, you can rack out.'

'What have you told them?'

'Oh, that there's a terrorist threat. Guys hiding out in the swamp. That kind of thing.'

'If it does decide to visit, you'll have to upgrade, tell them the truth.'

'We'll get to that if and when. No need to complicate matters. Be ready in thirty. Clewton out.'

Clewton, the mook.

CHAPTER 27

Naval Air Station (NAS) *Key West*
Monday, 1212 hours
Boca Chica Key, Monroe County, FL (24°57'34.1"N 81°69'40.0"W)

Midmorning, Jack and his team arrived at Naval Air Station Key West. Despite its KW designation, the station was situated on Boca Chica Key, the second-to-last key of the Florida Keys.

It was a beautiful day, with clear skies and a gentle breeze. It was not too hot, but that would come.

Boca Chica, Spanish for 'small mouth' or, as some insisted, 'girl's mouth,' was likely named for the entrance to Saddlebunch Harbor, which, with a ton-load of artistic license, resembled two pouty lips. If the creature approached from this direction, it was possible that it would hit the northeast side of the station. Jack, on the other hand, believed it was more plausible that it would advance from the south. The southern approaches to the station consisted mainly of swamps, granting the creature unimpeded access right into the heart of the base.

'That's what you'd assume,' Clewton had said.

'What, you're now saying it's capable of second-guessing?' Jack had countered.

Clewton looked like a naughty schoolboy who'd been caught out. Tammes, meanwhile, just looked like his default shifty dickwad self. 'Ain't like that, Jack,' Clewton said. Once more, the admiral slipped into his faux cracker good ole boy accent as if he thought that countering one falsehood with another would somehow wipe the slate clean of all his confabulating.

'What is it like?' Jack said.

'The animal has limited operational functionality,' Tammes said airily. 'In several basic scenarios, it can decide to take the road less traveled, as it were, and surprise the enemy. It's not like it's making its own decisions; it's more a matter of programming. It has access to a few responses to potential in-field eventualities.'

'Sounds like thinking to me,' Jack said. 'You've just described any operator in the field.'

'All we're saying,' Clewton said, 'is don't expect the ... expected.'

Jack was about to respond when they were interrupted by the duty security officer, a thirty-something marine, who introduced himself as Captain Lance Fugat. A sweaty, befreckled individual, Fugat's expression was all what's-the-fuss-about, clearly psyching himself for a tirade against the incomers messing up his day. Jack understood why Fugat might misapprehend his place in the hierarchy of men he'd just joined: Clewton unshaved, sporting a garish gold-red Hawaiian shirt; slug-underbelly pale Tammes practically screamed civilian contractor, while Jack, unruly hair, stubbled, stained, sweat-soaked T, looked like he'd just stepped off a Gulf oil rig.

'Captain,' Clewton said, holding out his hand.

Fugat, ignoring Clewton's offered paw, looked like he was gearing up for a major asshole-tearing fest when he clocked the Tweedles standing behind Clewton. Graaf, with his ruined nose, clearly itching to ruin someone else's nose. Dantz, scarred and mean, looking for all the world like some nineteenth-century Prussian duelist hoping to run someone through with the slightest provocation. Even an idiot could tell the spook Munsters would not be allocated to anyone less than a commodore. And then his eyes flitted over to Zads and co, slouching in the cool shadow of the helo. And being a good marine, he knew Tier Ones when he saw them. The captain looked a little closer at Clewton, seemed to recognize him, came to attention, saluted. 'Admiral, sir!' he said smartly. All this had happened in a second or two. Still, long enough for everybody to notice, and if anybody were going to be asshole-rearranging, it would be the admiral. But again, Clewton surprised Jack by letting Fugat's rookie mistake go. And again, Jack suspected this was not down to any good guy-ness on the admiral's part but merely a prioritization of what needed to be done. If only Clewton gave this much of a shit for the actual men under his command, Jack thought bitterly. With Clewton, everything was contingency and expediency. And he wouldn't put it past Clewton to give Fugat a shitty write-up when all was done, bar the shouting.

'Captain,' said Clewton sardonically. 'Here's what I need. First off -'

'All due respect, Admiral,' Jack jumped in. 'Here's what's going to happen.'

Clewton remained silent for what seemed like an age, glaring at Jack, his already heat-red face getting redder. Then he smiled and held up his hands, palms outward. *No problem, you carry on.* 'Captain Fugat,' Clewton said, 'Chief Tarr. Allow me to defer to the, ah, Chief's experience.'

'Thank you, Admiral,' Jack said, all business.

'First, my people need to be billeted immediately – they've had no proper shuteye for two days.'

Fugat nodded to one of the men behind him. The man jogged over to Jack's team and led them away. Jack would join them later. As soon as, he thought, stifling a yawn. He was running on empty. He needed to get racked ASAP. His team, even Zads, had been strangely subdued around him. In fact, come to think of it, not one of them had really said anything to him since the incident underneath *Confidence.* He wished he understood people better.

Turning to Fugat, he said, 'What's the setup here, Captain?'

'Well, Chief, here at Boca Chica, we're not considered high value enough to require a Marine Corps Security detachment. Though Lord knows, I've requested the presence of the aforementioned enough times.'

Shame, Jack thought. The guys from the MCS regiment were about as good as it got in terms of defense and protection.

'And,' Fugat continued, 'we—the Corp on NAS—don't have a formal hierarchy of platoons and squads, even though we've got a company-size number of marines on security detail.'

'I understand,' said Jack. And he did. What the captain was alluding to – albeit politely, in probable deference to the admiral – was that when sailors and marines co-existed alongside on shore bases, operational waters, to some extent, were muddied. It seemed that this station was no different – a muddle-through matelot-Jarhead combo. What could possibly go wrong? 'What's potentially coming our way will likely not appear until after dark, giving us over six hours to prep. As of now, all security detail shore leave is suspended until further notice. At thirteen hundred hours, all watchkeepers will muster, and they will be briefed, brought up to speed, and issued with appropriate ordnance panoply. At sixteen hundred hours, Admiral Clewton and Dr. Tammes will brief you and your men about the nature of the threat. Can I see a layout of the base?'

One of Fugat's guys stepped forward, unfolding a large-scale map and passing it to Jack. The base cut an inverted V-shape into the southern approaches, where Clewton had guessed the creature would come. He would deploy more heavily on those two V prongs.

Before Jack could continue, Clewton jumped in. 'You will deploy a quarter of your people on each side of the south-facing V, with the rest split evenly between the north, east, and west perimeters.'

Clewton paused to check if Fugat was taking it all in. He seemed to be.

It was Jack's turn to step in. 'Let's not get ahead of ourselves, Admiral. I need to check out the map.'

Clewton nodded as Jack scrutinized the base layout. Damned if Clewton wasn't right. That southerly V would be about the best place to lay in wait. Jack nodded to the admiral, agreeing to his personnel deployment strategy. He said to Fugat, 'You mentioned you had about a company's worth of marines? How big a company would that be?'

'Around two hundred.'

'Sailors?'

'Hundred or so.'

'Okay, so seventy-five defenders on each side of the V.' Jack paused. 'How long's each prong?'

'One klick.'

'Spread thinly then, Captain,' Jack said. 'Your guys will have to be on their game.'

'They will be, Chief,' Fugat said, though his doubt was clear.

'Any questions?'

The captain shook his head slowly while obviously having a stack of questions. 'Ah, no, Chief, I don't believe I do.'

'I'll leave you in the capable hands of Admiral Clewton. I'll see you at sixteen hundred hours.'

Fugat detailed another of his men to escort Jack to his quarters. Jack reckoned on getting four or five hours. He needed it. He was dead on his feet, a dead man walking.

*   *   *

Jack's room was in the same corridor as the rest of his team. Stentorian snoring was coming through the doors of several of the rooms. In an ungentlemanly way, he wondered if one of the snorers was Zads. She didn't used to snore. The marine corporal opened the door, and Jack entered. It was the usual monastic setup: single bed, desk, chair, closet. He quickly stripped off and showered, patting himself dry, the heat doing the rest. He slumped naked onto the bed, too hot already, even for sheets. He thought he'd drop off straight away, but sleep remained elusive. Too damned much zapping around in his head. The last few days had been a rollercoaster of sensory overload. The oleaginous Tammes, multi-faced Clewton; the stone-faced Tweedles; the mutilated CG bodies; Liliana Gil's tired, haunted face; Cal's horrible death; Harps – what happened to poor Harps? Was he maybe, against all the odds, still alive? And Zads. He'd never forgive himself if he got her killed.

And Erin. God, he needed to be with her, to hold her.

Yet, it wasn't the horror of the creature that kept zinging into his exhausted mind. His brain seemed to be protecting him from the close-up reality of the deadly animal, denying its presence traction in his head. For which he was immensely grateful. Instead, it was Skeeter. His old buddy-mentor. Jack knew that the last few days had quickly moved away from a provisional rescue operation for Skeeter and his team and had segued into a full-on monster hunt. He couldn't help but feel that though his old friend was almost certainly dead, he was somehow letting him down. Again, Jack cursed himself for not getting in contact with Skeeter. He should have ignored Skeeter's clean break theory, that the two shouldn't see each other. Christ, how much Jack missed him, how much he just wanted nothing else but to shoot the breeze over a few – or many – cold ones.

Sure, being with Erin, Jack felt like he'd inherited the Earth, the proverbial luckiest man alive. But, oh my, the cliché about combat vets was true. You could only talk the talk with the people who'd been there and back. For the first time in a long while, he allowed himself to miss Skeeter's easy camaraderie. He allowed himself to simply miss his friend.

And then even Skeeter fell away, alongside the fierce midday heat, as Jack slipped into the calm dark waters of dreamless sleep.

CHAPTER 28

NAS *Key West*
Monday, 1600 hours

Jack and his team joined Clewton, Tammes, and Fugat on the podium at the beginning of the 1600-hour briefing. Jack felt the excitement in the room, in his bones. Three hundred-odd personnel were crammed into the Briefing Suite, a grandiose designation for a spacious rectangular hall. There was only standing room at the back, while most sat on rows of minimally padded standard-issue plastic chairs. A combo of air conditioners and fans hummed and oscillated varyingly, their actual chill provision desperately wanting.

Earlier, Jack had managed to contact Erin. Again, she looked pale and seemed subdued. 'When're you coming home, Jack?'

'Coupla days, week tops.'

'Where are you?'

'Florida. Too hot. Missing damp, rainy Rhode Island. Missing you.' And he was. He suddenly wanted out. Out of the Navy's clutch. Out of the whole shitty mess of monsters and mutants and MIA buddies. It wasn't his world anymore, his home.

Something of Jack's inner turmoil must have played out across his face. Erin said, 'It's okay, babe. Once this is done, whatever this is, you don't do it again. I'm not going to let you.'

Jack had nodded at that, smiling. *I've been forgiven!* Jack punched the air, feeling like a tremendous weight had been lifted. And then he'd lost the connection.

In Clewton's attempt to downplay the significance of the facts of the case, he stuck to the party line that they were looking for a marine animal that had escaped from The Navy's Marine Mammal Program. The same program that had previously trained sea lions and dolphins to guard against underwater threats. Except this program was a program within a program, and we're not talking about mammals – we're talking amphibious.

Naturally, there'd been a shitload of questions re the nature of the mysterious probable incoming. Clewton told them the target was a hitherto undiscovered marine species. He added, leaning forward over his lectern, 'All entre nous, I don't need to tell you the importance of keeping a lid on this Ultra Secret project. Ladies, gentlemen, this is a matter of national security—it doesn't get any higher than this.'

Clewton's shtick was a well-used technique, making everybody feel special, that they were somehow part of the chosen few entrusted with great responsibility, that the future of Western civilization as we know it rests on your shoulders, yada yada, and so on. The snake oil merchant he was, Clewton's routine went down well. The admiral loved holding forth listening to the sound of his own sweet voice.

He even told his rapt audience about the possible effects of the creature's subsonic signature tune and that its aural calling card could cause some personnel discomfort. The admiral went on to list the varieties of affliction, ranging from mild nausea to instances of immediate syncope—*that's* fainting *for you crackers out there*, Clewton added, earning him a few uneasy titters.

Even when Clewton projected a photo of the creature on the large white screen behind him, his audience lapped it up despite a few nervous chuckles. Jack noticed that the image had been somewhat airbrushed. Its colors had been toned down, its appendages stunted, and its overall shape rendered more anthropomorphic. The whole crustacean thing had been Disneyfied. It looked more mammal-like, less monster, a beast you wanted to befriend, not kill. Jack thought, Why not to hell with it and stick up a picture of Bambi?

The admiral had even hinted that the creature was more comrade than enemy, trained to be a sailor's teammate, just like the aforementioned dolphins and sea lions.

Later, Fugat split the company into sixty small teams of five personnel, each mirroring Jack's fire team. Each team sported two launchers and two harpoons set to non-lethal. The fifth guy was armed with a fifty-caliber anti-armor sniper rifle, a conventional weapon of last resort. Fugat's men and women had been told the target must be captured alive, that a lethal outcome was not the favored option.

Under the pretext of a bio-terrorist threat exercise, the base had been shut down for thirty-six hours. No one in, no one out. All on-base activities had also been shut down, too. Civilian residents advised to remain in the accommodation, while off-duty military personnel were confined to barracks.

As Clewton's presentation ended, the various security teams filed into the blazing sun to familiarize themselves with the weapons at the firing range.

When Jack asked Clewton how the weapons training for the sailors and marines went, the admiral shrugged as if to say, *When it comes down to it, it's all aim and fire. Oh, and make sure the safety's off.* That was pretty much what he'd told Jack when he'd had his crash course in high-tech weaponry. Yeah, and look how that turned out, he thought, as dead Cal's terrified, dying expression jumped into his head.

Jack watched the company fan out to their respective positions, some on foot, others in a range of light utility vehicles. The more or less default expressions on the young men and women's faces—Jack noticed with dismay—were one of barely suppressed excitement. They thought this was the real deal, what they'd signed up for. Finally, some action, anything to break up the monotony, the boredom of shore-based life.

Clewton's having immediate access to so much unconventional ordnance bugged Jack. There was no way your run-of-the-mill naval air station would stockpile beam harpoons and net launchers. The weapons must have been shipped over from AUTEC. And therein lay the bug. It was like Clewton knew his mantis was likely to hit the NAS. But he'd let Jack think it was his idea that the creature might do so. *Why is Clewton manipulating me? What's the purpose, the play?* Whatever might be going on, no doubt searching for Skeeter had been completely thrown out the window. It seemed that Clewton had Jack exactly where he'd always wanted – chasing after his damned monster.

But it always came down to: *Why me?*

Jack tried to return his thoughts to operational matters, insisting he and his team were right on the tip of the southernmost V sticking out into the swamp. His gut hunch was telling him that for once Clewton was correct, that the creature wouldn't pussyfoot around and that, seeing as it was coming from the south, it would hit the base at the point most southwards and closest to the sea. Of course, it was all guesswork, all best guess. But then, that was all this kind of thing was ever about. Naturally, the best guessers stayed alive; the best guessers were those who returned. Skeeter had been the best guesser *ever*. Even when Skeeter got it wrong, he was never *so* wrong that it got him or his team killed. Even Skeeter's occasional bad calls were better than most operators' good ones.

Because Foxtrot Tango One would be at that southernmost base tip and had easy access to the marsh channels, Jack had requested a couple of Keppler kayaks. While Clewton had allowed the Kepplers, he had made it clear that he did not want Jack and his team out in the swamp without his – Clewton's - express say so. While Jack agreed to Clewton's proviso, he knew damn well that if the need arose, he would most certainly ignore it.

One odd thing had happened, though. Another damn thing that seemed to confirm Jack's epic suspicions that something ultra wonky on a colossal scale was going on. And that Jack didn't know the half – perhaps even the quarter – of it. Jack remembered asking Clewton about the ancient Forrest Sherman he'd spotted on the southern edge of the picket line. Clewton had instantly paled, frozen as if he were a drama student in some tiresome still-image tableau of one. The admiral had proceeded to stare into the far distance, his only movement the flex of his jawline muscles. For a moment, Jack wondered if he'd had a seizure. 'Admiral?'

Slowly, animation returned to the admiral's body, and he stiffly turned to Jack. 'That ship. It doesn't exist.' The admiral's voice wavered as if speaking was taking up all of his willpower. 'That's all you need to know.'

And before Jack could ask his follow-up question, Clewton had stalked off.

Another goddamn mystery.

At 1715 hours, Jack found himself alongside Zads and the two Kepplers, sitting in a clump of young paradise trees on the edge of the tidal mangrove swamp, facing south. Jack had also been able to procure NVG protective helmets for FT1, which boasted infrared mode as well as night vision. Mac and Det were several yards away, positioned in a similar thicket, surrounded by thickish brush. Jack had been pleased to note that Det had looked near-as-dammit sane after his rest. Gone was the deranged, barely concealed rage, now replaced with a quiet purposefulness. Det was still out for revenge but wouldn't be an idiot about it. Jack was about ninety percent sure Det had come through the danger zone. The zone that gets you dead.

Zads shifted uncomfortably on the soggy ground. 'Well, this sucks big fat monkey balls.'

'The trouble with paradise trees,' Jack said, ignoring Zads' comment, 'is that they smell like rotting cashews.' Overhead, a couple of gulls wheeled, cawing.

'Nah,' said Zads. 'It's *merde*, smells like *merde*.'

Jack sniffed again. 'Hmm.'

'Yeah?'

'I don't know, yeah, maybe.'

'No maybe about it, Chief.'

Jack felt the sweat beading between his shoulder blades. Mosquitoes flitted in the gloom, and he slapped one in his neck. 'I do believe I'm wilting.'

'SEALs don't wilt.'

'I'm a civilian. And civilians are allowed to wilt.'

The radio crackled into life, and Zads told Fugat that team Yankee-Tip was all good.

'I should check with Det and Mac, Zads, you know, to see if they're still alive.'

'Yo, Mac! Det!' Zads shout-whispered. 'You girls still with us?'

'Hanging on,' Mac said.

'See? Everything's fine.'

'Yep, epically copacetic, just like always.' Still, at least his guys were talking to him again. Maybe he'd imagined their distancing themselves from him. Whatever he'd done, they'd forgiven him. Like Erin. Maybe his luck with this monster mess was changing. He was, he reckoned, due a break.

Zads fell silent, letting the buzz of mosquitoes and sandflies take center stage. Occasionally, there was a loud pop where a mussel or clam had burrowed into the mud. Jack wondered if they should be worried about crocodiles. It would not be wise to disturb one of those babies.

As if reading his mind, Zads piped up, 'So how big do these Keys crocs get?'

'Oh, not too big, maybe, oh, let's say twenty feet, give or take.'

'No shit!' Zads shook her head slowly.

'Yes shit.' Jack didn't tell her that it was very rare that one got to be that big. It would keep her on her toes, he reckoned, more focused. That and the look on her face had been priceless.

'Makes me nostalgic for good ole Louisiana gators.'

The paradise trees' shadows grew longer as the sun descended westward into the Gulf. The insects' noise increased as the shadows lengthened as if they were syncing their cacophonous buzz with the shadows' advance.

Jack sniffed the air. 'Rain.'

'Not a cloud in the sky, Jack,' Zads said, looking out across the swamp toward the darkening horizon.

'Rain.'

Zads muttered something under her breath.

'Say again,' Jack said.

'Really? Twenty feet?'

'Fraid so.'

This far south, night didn't fall. It pounced like a big black tomcat, scooping you up in its claws and swallowing you, making you wonder who put the goddamn lights out.

'Night vision time,' Jack said, the wind picking up. 'Rain. Soon.'

Zads remained silent. Jack knew her well enough that there was a question coming. A big one. A question that he'd been expecting all day. It was a question he'd avoided asking himself, even though it was a question that needed to be asked.

So when Zads whispered, 'Boss? How come you're still with us?' he knew what she meant.

'You got me, Zads.' With some satisfaction, Jack noticed the lowering skies, the clouds rolling in from the east. 'I was … *this* close to it.' He gestured pointlessly in the dark.

'Looked like you were dancing with it, Chief.' Zads clicked her tongue, thinking. 'And then it took poor Harps. Not you. Why?'

'I think … Harps was … he was going to shoot it. He was a threat. I wasn't. I froze. I -'

'No, you didn't freeze, Jack, it was more like you were …'

'What, Zads?'

'Jack, it was more like you were saying *hello*.'

CHAPTER 29

NAS
Monday, 1844 hours
Southern Perimeter

'It was, like, half a second, Zads. I turned round. It was there. It was gone. That's all.' Her *hello* observation had riled him. It was too close to the mark, raising all the questions he'd been busy ghosting. He remembered, all right. *Hello, fuckface,* he'd thought, utterly convinced those four silly syllables were to be – as it were - his last words. The creature was in his face for a second, two tops. All that stuff zinging in his brain about the creature seeing into his soul, his very Kantian-thing-itself goddamn essence, *that* was all post-experience. Crap he'd tagged on to the encounter to make sense of it – retrospective additions. It's what the human brain did – it filled in the gaps because, boy, did the old gray matter hate lacunae. Another Erin-ism, he realized with a pang of loneliness that stabbed him right in his heart. He missed her quirky insights into the vagaries of the human condition. Missed her providing him brain food, things he'd never even considered before.

'Boss?'

'Sorry, Zads. Klicks away.'

In the distance, something cried out. An eerie high-pitched sound, almost like a … scream? *The hell?* Whatever it was, it gave Jack the creeps. As predicted, a flotilla of black clouds drifted landward, blowing in from the sea. The air buzzed with electricity.

'Bird,' Zads whispered. 'Male Limpkin. They can kinda sound like a person in distress.' Though Jacked detected her doubt.

Another eerie wail. This time further away. Jack's skin crawled.

'Hell's that?' Mac, all sotto voce.

'Bird,' Jack hissed back. 'Apparently.'

'Yeah, well,' Mac said, 'I've just managed to unclench my buttocks from the last encounter. I've no desire to re-clench. Makes me walk funny.'

Despite the dark, Jack was close enough to see Zads studying him, concern writ large on her delicate features. He knew that when she got a bug up her ass, the only way of dislodging it was – to mix metaphors – leap into the breach. 'What you said before, about me and the … kinda odd thing to say, Zads.'

'What? About you making out with a giant shrimp?'

'Just a second or two.'

'Nah. More'n a damn second or two, Chief.'

'What're you not telling me?'

'Chief, you and that … thing, you were, um, head to head for … *shit*, you and *it* were vis a vis for over a … *minute.*'

'No!' Jack said, emphasizing the word in a harsh whisper. 'No damn way.'

'Wasn't just me saw it. Det and Mac. Harps -'

'It was *seconds*, Zads.' Jack shook his head, unable to understand what Zads was alleging. 'Couldn't have been a minute. I told you – if one of us gets company, open damn fire because … it won't matter. It'd already be too late.'

'And that almost happened, Jack. When the creature appeared, I was good to go … but something stopped me and the others too. I, we, instantly knew this wasn't like the other times with … *it.*'

'What do you mean?'

'You were alive, Jack. *Alive.*' Zads breathed in sharply, trying to control her emotions. 'I stood everybody down – *let it play out.*'

In the dark, Jack shook his head slowly.

'Longest minute ever,' Zads said to herself into the night.

'But -'

'Damnedest thing.'

'But Harps, he -'

'Yeah, he counted the full minute, too. Stood down with the rest of us. But he still had his weapon at high port. I don't know. He was trying to get comfortable with the position or something. And the creature, all it saw was a sudden movement, a threat, and -'

'Alright, Zads. I know the rest.' He felt like he was deflating into himself, physically imploding under the enormous weight of his mistakes. *You got Harps killed. Probably Cal, too. Too out of touch with this shit. You've no idea what you're doing.* Explained why Zads and the others had been off with him, unable to look him in the eye. 'Ah. You all think I should have died. Not Harps.'

'*Non,*' Zads said forcefully. 'Not that at all. It's just that there seemed to be some kind of interaction between you and the creature.' Zads sighed. 'Was there, Jack? Anything?'

'No!' he said, equally forcefully. But unlike Zads, Jack didn't know if he was being truthful.

The radio hissed into life, making them both jump. 'Yankee-Tip, this is Mike-Base, over.' Fugat said.

'Yankee Tip,' Zads said.

'You guys okay?'

'All quiet on the Southern Front.'

'Ditto all teams,' Fugat said. 'Gonna be a long night.'

'Yes, sir.'

'Fugat out.'

From across the marshlands, another otherworldly wail, closer, longer. Like a *plea*. 'Are you sure,' Jack said softly, 'that's a ... whatchamacallit?'

Zads was silent for a few moments. Then, 'A Limpkin. And no, I'm not. Not a hundred percent. Actually, this time, it sounded like a person.'

'So, what? Did somebody get themselves lost in the swamp? A tourist?'

Zads shrugged. 'Some guy fishing? Got cut off? Tide's incoming.'

'Or it could still be one of your Limpkins.'

'Yeah, that, too.'

'NVGs aren't picking up anything.' Jack squinted in the monochrome-green rendered world. Despite green being easy on the eye, the goggles were still a pain if you had to wear them over an extended period.

'Me neither,' Zads confirmed.

Another hair-raising keen. Yet closer. Maybe two hundred yards, Jack thought. 'I'm going out there,' he said. 'Have a look.' A strange idea had snuck into his brain, one that, once it was there, it was impossible to kick out. It sounded like a man. A wounded man. But there was more to it than that. The wail seemed to carry with it all the pain of the world, an ululation that had too much burden, a soul seared by an unendurable horror. And for this soul, there was no way back to this world, to sanity.

'Is that ...'

'No,' said Jack. 'Our boy, he has no lungs or vocal cords.'

'Are you sure?'

'Absolutely not.' Zads was right. Jack had no idea what Tammes had done, how creative he'd been. For all he knew, the mantis did have a larynx or voice box, an esophagus, and perhaps, even a goddamn supporting role in *La Traviata*.

'But we know what sound it makes.'

'Sometimes makes, not always.'

'Whatever. That low rumble, like a base buzz. I'm not feeling it. You?'

'Nope.'

'I'm going out there,' Jack said.

'I'm coming, too,' Zads said, her voice almost lost in the rising wind, the increasingly heavy rain.

Jack nodded. 'Tell Mac and Det. Tell them that if we're not back in thirty minutes, assume the worst and that Fugat might want to concentrate more guys on the V tip.'

As Zads trotted off to the others, Jack cut two stout saplings from the lower part of the paradise tree with his knife, skimming off any unwanted foliage. The impromptu walking sticks would assist in testing the waters, assessing the risk as they moved forward.

When Zads returned, Jack presented Zads with her cane, which she received without comment. 'Just thinking about those crocs, Jack.' She let out a low whistle, automatically twisting her NVG monocular into position, Jack doing the same. 'Twenty feet. Oh, boy.'

The wind carried another lost wail as they moved through the gate and onto the jetty. Mooring rings & dock posts stood sentinel alongside the rotting wooden pier, suggesting that the silted channels had been dredged at one point to allow seagoing craft to come alongside. The sagging structure may even have preceded the existence of the base.

The rusty, unhinged perimeter gate they'd stepped through wound around the edge of the marshes. It always struck Jack how lackadaisically half-assed the security of some military bases could be. In the marshes, among the rotting wood-slatted jetties and their decaying pilings, it felt like this unused section of the base hadn't seen a security patrol since World War Two. Unforgivable, really - an ocean-adjacent naval base open to hostile incursion on its seaward side. Jack knew how something like this could happen. Assumptions. For half a century or more, a procession of base commanders had assumed there was a fence line out there in the swamp. That his or her predecessor had kept it maintained.

Jack and Zads looked at each other, pointing in the same direction, nodded, then carried forward. The end of the jetty was littered with driftwood and dried seaweed, humidity hanging in the air. Jack was careful to step onto the bank that followed the narrow inlet. The mangrove swamp was on their left, with the open-terrain estuary mud banks to the right. The voice seemed to be coming from the estuary side. At least they didn't have to go into the mangroves.

While the bank's tufted grass had a worrying, spongy feeling, it was solid ground. In a wildly meandering fashion, the bank broadly let them move southward in the direction of the voice. The further they moved outward, the narrower the bank and wider the channels. They were getting closer to where the marshlands met the sea, a dangerous hinterland unfavorable to human safety – hungry, sucking mud; rapidly rising tide; generic features, so easy to get disorientated – to name a few.

Behind him, Zads' heavily breathing presence was a source of comfort. The last twenty-four hours or so had dented Jack's confidence. The sudden, no warning appearance of the creature, alongside Zads' revelation about just how long that encounter had gone on for, had unnerved him more than he cared to accept.

And then another sound. A low rumble, short, like thunder, truncated. And then again. It was very similar to the sound the creature made underwater. The sound of it rattling its damn carapace above water. If Zads had heard it, she didn't say anything. Maybe he'd imagined it. Perhaps it *was* just thunder.

But then Zads stopped.

Jack stopped, too. 'What is it?'

'Are you thinking, *mon ami*, what I'm thinking?'

'That this is a trap? Oh, yeah.'

Zads smiled. 'Okay, you have the thought, but do you think it *is*?'

Before Jack could open his mouth, Zads was answered by the mysterious, plaintive call. This time, it was to their left as if they were level with it. No more than thirty yards.

'Hello!' Jack called out.

Silence.

'C'mon,' he said urgently. 'This way.'

Several yards later, the bank narrowed to the extent that Jack and Zads had to get on their haunches and crawl the last couple of yards. 'Hello?' said Jack.

Silence. Then, a low moan ended in anguished sobs. As the last of the banks gave way to mud, Jack could see a lighter green shape on the darker green of the mud, mere feet below him.

'You okay, Jack?' Zads said, whispering.

Wary of the bank giving way, Jack slid forward onto his stomach. 'Zads, grab hold of my belt.'

As Jack edged forward, the shape stretched across the mud rolled over, looking up at Jack, eyes wild.

'Oh, God,' the man said, his voice less than a croak. '*Godohgodohgod.*'

It was a familiar voice.

'Bembe?' Jack said.

CHAPTER 30

NAS
Monday, 1947 hours
Southern Perimeter

The marsh was now soaked in deep-dyed shadow. As the tide rose, the mud on which the man lay was becoming more porous, less substantial, his prone body sinking inchmeal into the foul-smelling morass. 'You got me, Zads?' he asked.

'I'm losing traction, boss,' she said. 'You go any further, we're both going in.'

'Hey, Bembe, are you hurt?' *Dumb question*. The man's only response was a low moan. Jack's NVGs were next to useless in picking up on wounds, but all his limbs seemed present and accounted for.

There was another low, suddenly truncated rumble, and Jack stiffened. 'What is it, Jack?'

'I'm not sure, but we might have an uninvited guest.'

'The target?'

'That rumbling.'

'Just thunder, Jack. It's circling. It's what it does. You've done Met 101. You should know this.'

'I'm wondering if it's the sort of noise it would make if it were out of the water, a touch more trebly, more rattle than buzz.' Jack sighed. 'Yeah, probably nothing.'

'Any nausea? Sweats?'

'I don't think so. Maybe a little. I don't know - when your mind gets a hold of the idea, it kind of makes it so.'

Bembe moaned again.

'How the hell did he get here?' Zads said. 'He's supposed to be putting his dogs up Canaveral way. I don't get it.'

As Zads asked her question – perhaps, even *before* she asked it – the whisper of a grisly thought – not yet fully formed – did the rounds inside Jack's head. A thought suggesting the only way that Bembe could be present in this dreary place is if he'd been inserted. Why, though? And who would do such a thing? And again, even as he asked the question, he suspected he knew the answer. But it was too horrific, too … even for …

Once more, the bass rumble growled across the marshes.

'Boss!' Zads said. 'You with me?'

Zads' voice snapped Jack out of his uneasy ruminations, and he immediately deployed his improvised cane, holding it out as far as he could stretch, prodding Bembe. But Bembe remained inert, his body slipping further into the mud as the upcoming tide undercut it. They only had minutes to get him out. 'Dude! For Chrissakes, grab the pole.' Again, Bembe's only response was that low, uncanny caterwaul.

Shit, he heard Zads say. Yeah, shit, indeed, it didn't seem possible that a noise like that could issue forth from a human throat.

Jack suddenly jerked forward, sliding closer to the man. 'Shit, Jack,' Zads yelled. 'I can't hold you, the bank's caving. I'm gonna pull you up.'

'NO!' Jack called back. 'I'm almost on him.'

But Zads wasn't listening; she was heaving him back to the bank's precarious incline. Bembe started moaning louder, his cries soundtracked by a low rumble of thunder. In the distance, lightning forked into the Caribbean Sea. The wind gusting through the nearby radio towers' wires created an eerie whistle. And then again, that low-bass rumble. From the south. Closer, Jack noted. Not thunder. Probably not thunder.

As Zads tugged Jack onto the bank, he rolled over, picking up the launcher. 'Is there any way we can use this damn thing?'

'You got a plan?'

Jack shook his head. 'I don't know. I was thinking along the lines of a scrambling net.'

'I don't understand,' Zads said.

Holding up the net launcher, Jack said, 'Could we launch this into the mud? I mean, underneath him? I could climb down, haul him up. Maybe use the net's contraction to haul him up?'

'Perhaps,' Zads said. 'Risky. Easy to get tangled caught in it when it starts to shrink.'

'I think I'd be alright. If it's not shrink-wrapped me in the first place, it's not going to take me with it when it compresses. What do you think?'

Another non-thunder rumble. Yet closer. Less than a quarter-klick, Jack estimated.

Followed by another uncanny, inhuman wail from Bembe, as if the two were somehow connected. He was almost covered by the viscous, sucking mud. 'Let's do it!' Zads said.

'Go for the bank base, about two feet above his head.'

Zads took up the launcher and knelt on the bank's edge, pointing it downward. Bembe's body was only several feet away, and it was impossible to get the shot wrong. Still. *BOHICA*, Jack thought. Yet again, I'm about to do something impressively stupid.

More thunder, closer. *Like two concurrent rumbles, one shorter than the other. The legit thunder was hiding, covering the creature's rumble. To hell with it, let's call it.*

'Hold for a minute, Zads. Radio it in first. We got a survivor, request medical assist, and –'

'Boss?' Zads said, lowering the launcher.

'Alert Fugat. Target likely approaching southern V.'

Finger hovering over her push-to-talk button, Zads said, 'Likely?'

Bembe moaned.

'It's the creature.' He could feel it in his bones. Actually, kind of literally. 'Do it, Zads.'

As Zads touched base with Fugat, Jack once more lay down on the bank's edge, his brain running all the variables regarding the target's possible presence. *What if I'm wrong?*

A small, dull detonation instantly dragged Jack back to the task. The net launched, hitting the mud in precisely the right place. Due to the heat from its launch, the net was spreading and widening, giving Jack enough handholds to scrabble down. When he made contact with it, the net seemed to shiver and move like a living thing. And beneath his gloves, he could feel its heat, smell the rubbery odor as it charred his clothes. Within seconds, he was down with Bembe, grabbing the collar of his shirt and pulling him upward, the mud's surface viscosity helping him move closer to safety. Jack felt like a fly scrambling on a spider's web. The net reached its limit and was now starting to retract as the water cooled its initial heat burn. Jack didn't like how the gaps in the net seemed to be getting smaller. If he got a hand or foot caught ... He tugged Bembe up beside him so most of his body was above him, pushing him up with his shoulder, at any moment expecting to feel a vice-like grip claw around his ankle. Inch by inch, he shoved him toward the bank's top.

Above, Zads shouted out, 'Another foot or so, Jack. Keep him coming.'

The man was a total deadweight. The net's gaps were decreasing, and its shrinkage rate rapidly increased, reaching the danger zone. They'd be trapped if Jack and his rescue didn't get off ASAP. But it was no good. Jack couldn't push up quickly enough. He was inching his way up, and inching wouldn't cut it. And then the net quivered again, its metal-flesh rungs vibrating ominously. Shit! Time's up!

Someone screamed. Zads. Jack wanted to scream, but he was out of breath, out of strength, out of everything. And then there was movement, a sense of rapid ascension, of skimming upward. Jack was up on the bank, Bembe still in front, Zads rolling him off the net, screaming at Jack.

GET OFF THE FREAKING NET!

Jack got off the freaking net just as it seemed to slide into itself, rolling up into a nice, neat package. Ready for use once more. Jack lay on his back, breathing deeply, desperate to get air back into his lungs, luxuriating in the fat globs of tropical rain spattering on his face. He was only dimly aware of Zads attending to Bembe.

When Jack was fairly sure he wasn't having a heart attack as that vital organ galloped apace inside his chest, he rolled onto his stomach and heaved himself onto his knees. 'How is he?'

Zads said, 'Alive. Got all his limbs. Can't see any wounds. Can't get any sense out of him.'

'In shock,' Jack said.

'It's more than that,' she said as Jack hooked his arms under the man's elbows, dragged him to his feet, squatted down, and rolled him onto his shoulders.

'Yeah,' Jack said, his legs wobbly under Bembe's weight.

'There's something wrong with Bembe,' Zads said.

'No shit, Watson.'

Zads moved to the now prone Bembe, stretched across Jack's back. She was quiet for a few moments. She seemed to be patting Bembe down. 'What're you doing, Zads?'

'There's something not right here. I'm just -'

'What? You're just what?'

Silence.

'Zads?'

'His legs are fractured.' Her voice was flat. 'Each leg, in exactly the same place. Someone deliberately broke his legs. *Merde.*'

Oh, Christ, Jack thought, feeling like this night's obsidian grasp would never let him go. It was like Cay Sal's malevolent mojo had followed him here and that something was trying to poke through the fabric of reality or, at least, testing its limits. The grisly suspicion Jack had been striving to keep at a safe distance pounced back into his head. They broke Bembe's legs. They left him there. Closing his mind to the implications, exhaustion hammering behind his eyes, Jack focused on staggering forward, back toward relative safety. Muscles burning, he had no choice but to take it slowly – with Bembe onboard, even the bank sucked at his boots. *If I can't have the Cuban,* the swamp said, *I'll take you, Jack—Fair's fair.*

The sound of his boots clumping on the wooden jetty was music to Jack's ears. There was more clumping as Mac rushed toward him, sliding

Bembe onto his shoulders and jogging away to the arriving corpsmen, their vehicle's lights silhouetting the paradise trees. As Zads edged by him on the narrow walkway, he bent over, clutching his knees with both hands, severely winded. Somewhere behind, back in the marshlands, that low rumble and its abrupt cessation again. Closer. Not thunder. Ground level.

Standing upright, he followed Zads, Mac, and the arriving reinforcements. Jack reached the circle of bright lights, searching for Fugat. From the corner of his eye, he saw Clewton and Tammes approaching. Jack did a quick side step, avoiding their approach, and found himself next to Mac and Zads. They stood by a gurney, watching a corpsman wash away the mud from Bembe's face as another corpsman strapped him in. Jack remembered Bembe's face on the *Confidence*—full of hope and joy at being alive. But this version of Bembe, this version, was destroyed, defeated, his eyes wild, sightless.

'Bembe,' Jack said softly, taking his hand.

Suddenly, Bembe yowled out loud.

'Careful,' the corpsman said to Jack, shaking his head. 'What the bejesus happened out there?'

CHAPTER 31

NAS
Monday, 2040 hours
Southern Perimeter

Bembe. Why's he not on the mainland? Twisty roots of possibility—like the above-water mangrove roots—continued to probe his brain. Explanations, possibilities. *Something to do with why Clewton didn't want us using the Kepplers, going out into the swamp.* As soon as the admiral had arrived at NAS, he'd been shiftier than usual. More furtive.

But before Jack could ponder Bembe's inexplicable presence further, the creature's deep-base buzz rumbled ever closer, the disarming overture heralding its approach. And this time, it was unquestionably the creature, not thunder. Jack observed several men and women halting mid-task, bending over, hands on knees, clearly struck by differing degrees of queasiness. Some were gagging, others were retching, and one or two were vomiting.

He turned away from the ambulance, looking out again toward the swamp. Zads, Mac, and Det materialized out of the tumult of sailors and marines, suddenly by his side. From the swamp's edge, further south, shouts, and screams, regular firearms. And on the wind, Jack thought he heard a net launcher's faint, strangely dull pop. Then silence. Beyond the fence, away from the chain link perimeter, Fugat shouted orders, his sailors and marines fanning outwards into the swamp proper, crashing through the dense fauna, their flashlights slicing through the night.

Apparently, the swamp was now officially open to visitors. Clewton must have greenlighted the incursion, though he hadn't contacted FT1.

Jack told his team, 'Let's grab the Kepplers,' knowing full well that Keppler use remained unauthorized. 'The tide's filled the channels, and we can cover a bigger grid.' They heaved the kayaks, squeezing them through the gate and sliding them into the water off the jetty, unthinkingly twisting their monocular NVGs into sight position.

Jack and Zads pushed off first, then Mac and Det in the other Keppler. Slicing through the water effortlessly, they made decent time, moving out of the marshes and into the mangrove swamp proper. The modest turbulence their paddles caused sent whorls of water-cooled air into the stifling Florida night. The searchers crashed through the undergrowth on both sides of FT1's channel. The pathfinders were swearing, cursing, making heavy weather of it. Sailors would have no idea how to navigate a mangrove swamp, and the marines would be fairing no better – the closest they got to this sort of terrain was on a jungle combat course. Unless, of course, they were engaged in an actual mission in the actual jungle. Under the weight of night, the trees seemed bowed in obeisance, though what they were obeisant to was anybody's guess. It certainly wasn't to the puny humans haphazardly roaming through the trees' domain.

Jack had a good idea of what they were experiencing. Enter a mangrove swamp on foot, and there's a transition zone where the vegetation gets denser, and the ground becomes waterlogged and saturated. And then the heat hits you, the lung-crushing humidity, like an insidious slow-motion waterboard.

You'd get entangled in the intricate root systems of the mangrove trees, your boots sodden in the shallow, brackish waters. The exposed roots would be slippery as hell – algae was partial to a bit of mangrove root. In the dark, to up the crapshow ante, you'd be walking into low-hanging branches, the younger, thinner ones whiplashing into your face, maybe taking out an eye, as the guy in front pushed through. Within minutes, you'd be covered in insect bites, all scratched to hell.

No wonder the poor mothers were cursing the day they were born. 'What kind of stupid sends people out into this?' Mac whispered.

'The Clewton kind,' Zads whispered back. 'Why won't he let them use the Kayaks?'

'He doesn't want them – us - to go too deep into the swamp,' Jack said, slowing down his kayak, raising his hand, stopping.

Mac bumped gently into him from behind. 'What is it?'

'Can you hear that?'

'What?'

'Those guys, they've gone silent.'

Jack looked over to where the platoon on the left had been thrashing around. One solitary flashlight beam gave up its position. The platoon had ceased all movement. Thirty seconds ago, several beams were waving about, a lot of noise.

'It's the target,' Det whispered. 'It's close. I'm getting the jangly molecules thing.'

'Ditto,' said Zads. 'Christ it's … it's …'

'Yeah,' Jack said softly, 'it is.'

Jack had thought he'd somehow become relatively immune to the subsonic sounds. But here it was, yet again. He realized that the sound only came through the creature's choosing to rattle its carapace, not just the simple fact of its presence. He knew, though, that if he was suffering

Guy One. He screamed in horror and backed away from his buddy's failing legs. Then he, too, was scooped up by the creature.

On the air, the smell of cordite and copper, the stench of violent death. The cordite always won, but it was the blood you remembered.

'LAUNCHER, GO!' someone shouted.

Guy One's screams turned to howls of pain as the net wrapped around both mutant animal and man.

Who the hell had ordered the fire?

And why was Guy One still alive? Why hadn't the creature killed him, too? When the creature had held Guy One up in front of its eyes for the briefest of moments, it was as if the creature had been studying the man.

Like it did with me, Jack thought.

'Standby with harpoons,' Jack said, wondering if they'd need them. If the net would be enough. Guy One's howling once more became screams as he realized what was happening, that he was trapped with the monster inside the shrinking net.

'Andy!' shouted one of the men from Guy One's platoon, moving forward, only to be yanked back by Zads.

Andy's screams grew louder, more anguished as the net tightened across him, pulling him into the creature's carapace.

'Oh, Christ,' muttered Det. Jack guessed he was remembering Cal.

'Andy!' someone else called out.

A wave of nausea spread through Jack, causing him to bend over and retch emptily into the night air. Beside him and beyond, others, too, were vomiting or collapsing to the watery ground. The creature continued rattling its carapace. Jack glanced up at the creature as the tree it had cut finally fell into the clearing, no longer being kept upright by the dense undergrowth. As it fell, the tree, still held by several vines, seemed to swing sideways, knocking the animal across the glade and into the edge of the trees. As the subsonic sound moved into the hearable spectrum, the nausea and headaches vanished, and Jack stood up. Another sound started to cut through the creature's growing bass hum, a high-pitched ... singing – the sound railway tracks make when a train is coming your way.

The tree fell into the middle of the clearing, crushing at least one man, his scream rushing through the night. *The sound a ship's hawser – a thick wire rope – makes when it's about to snap.*

The steel net was singing!

Beyond the tree edge into the woods proper, a sudden sound of something breaking, snapping, rent the night.

The creature was free. It had broken through the net.

Silence. Silence, too, in the direction of the creature. The creature must have found a water channel and was now escaping.

And then something started to emerge from the edge of the tree line—a man or, at least, man-shaped. Jack tore off his NVGs and squinted into the dark.

Harps?

CHAPTER 32

NAS
Monday, 2259 hours
Southern Perimeter

As Det helped Zads get Harps into the rear seat of the kayak, Jack told Mac to remain with the platoon survivors, instructing him to get them back to base. Zads had given Harps a quick medical once over, reporting that nothing appeared to be physically wrong with him, despite Harps' dive suit being torn to strips, with ugly tears on his arms and legs. But it was his eyes that haunted Jack. It was as if they'd beheld something ineffably wrong – a kind of metaphysical wrongness – and wrongness that had somehow obscured Harps' essence, his soul. If Harps was somewhere in there, he was hidden behind those eyes. Clearly, he was in deep, deep shock – in fact, catatonic.

They made good time returning to the perimeter fence and soon clumped down the wooden jetty, Harps between Det and Jack.

Harps.

How the hell had he gotten here? He was taken over a hundred klicks away. It must have been the creature. But why? And why hadn't it killed him? What the hell was going on?

Several corpsmen rushed forward and took Harps to a waiting ambulance. The gurney with Bembe on it was gone. As Harps was loaded into an ambulance, Jack allowed his mind to return to the Bembe conundrum, to the terrible suspicion rising from the depths of his mind, tightening his chest with its implications.

How was Bembe here? He should be in Florida.

Clewton. *No*. Not possible. Not even Clewton would stoop so low.

Clewton was so sure that the creature would come from the south.

Bembe lying in the mud, both legs broken.

Bait.

Don't take the kayaks out, Jack. Don't want you finding the bait.

Jack looked into the crowd and found Clewton, caught his eyes. The admiral immediately looked away and said something to Dantz and Graaf, who started moving toward Jack. Clewton must have seen something in Jack's face to send his goons over like that. And despite aching, screaming muscles, Jack strode purposefully to the approaching Tweedles.

Save them a journey, he thought grimly, fired on by the growing certainty that Clewton and his men had crossed the line. They had done something so beyond redemption that, for them, truly, there was no going back.

As the gap between Jack and the Tweedles rapidly closed, his brain triaged the situation, prioritizing incoming threats alongside immediate objectives: take out the Tweedles, get to Clewton, and demand answers.

And then the Tweedles were upon him, one on either side, still closing. Jack immediately stepped backward, keeping them in front of him so he could see them both. Jack went for Graaf, who seemed to have authority over Dantz. Or, at least, he was the one who spoke. If attacked by more than one, take out the leader. Jack gave him a hefty kick in the groin, and Graaf went down, squealing, actually squealing.

Spinning to his left, he dodged a throat punch. Now pivoting sideways, Jack grabbed Dantz' arm with both hands, using the other man's momentum to sharply twist his wrist at an unnatural angle, breaking it and propelling him into the group of gawp-faced personnel watching the fight play out. Before Graaf shakily rose to his feet, Jack swung round and kicked him in the temples with the tip of his boot. He went down. Stayed down. Jack raised his boot above the man's neck to issue the coup de grace.

Stopped. *No.*

Instead, he swiveled around. Dantz was a couple of feet away, his right arm dangling uselessly by his side, a knife in his good hand. From within the crowd, Clewton shouted something, then Zads. And then Dantz dropped the knife, crumpled to the ground, eyes wide with surprise. Det stood behind him and nodded to Jack.

The encounter had been less than a minute. But it had felt like an age.

'What's this about, boss?' Zads asked.

'Bembe,' Jack said, gasping for air.

'What about him?' Mac asked.

'Bait.' Jack bent over, hands on his knees, trying to get air into his lungs. 'Clewton went fishing, thought he'd snag a monster.'

'Jesus Christ,' Det said.

'No way,' Zads said, her voice a whisper.

'That's what I intend to find out,' said Jack, standing upright, not liking the deadness in his voice. It sounded like someone else, someone he knew a long time ago, someone he'd hoped he'd never meet again. His brain no longer seemed capable of forming words. In a kill-or-be-killed world of immense and unrelenting cruelty, words were a luxury, an irrelevance. But this burning, twisting inner turmoil - this rage – felt good. And it was righteous. That familiar existential fury at life's never-ending shitshow of injustice. It seared his soul – and how he resented being brought back to this place in his mind, a place he thought he'd left forever. There was only one man responsible for his being here.

Jack turned round, scanning the crowd, trying to find Clewton. *Clewton.* 'Clewton.' The two syllables felt strange in his mouth as if he had never spoken, as if language was new to him, an alien concept. '*Clewton.*'

There was more buzz-rumbling from beyond the chain-link fence. Some part of Jack's brain registered that it was close to the wooden jetty. Fugat abruptly appeared before him, saying something that Jack couldn't catch. Fugat's eyes were imploring, apparently desperate for Jack's attention. But Jack pushed by him, stepping around the captain.

'Boss?' Zads said.

'Jack?' Mac said.

Someone grabbed hold of his arm, but he shrugged out of it.

Far away, Fugat's *urgent* voice barked out orders. Zads', too. And somewhere in the mix, Det and Mac joined in. The big group of sailors and marines spread out purposefully, moving to defense positions. The ambulance with Harps sped off, its lights flashing. But all this was mere background noise to Jack. And now Jack marked Clewton. And then Tammes. They were standing next to some class of light armored vehicle, one new to Jack. They were with a third guy, a commander, a large man with a stern face and a rigid stare. Most likely, he was the base head honcho, Fugat's boss. Jack briefly wondered why he hadn't been at Clewton's briefing. Maybe he'd been struck with a bad case of extreme peevishness. You know, *his* base being taken over and all. The admiral looked over to Jack, speaking urgently to the commander. The commander replied with the same urgency as Clewton nodded toward Jack. Jack did not heed the commander, hardly noticing him; his eyes were for Clewton only. For his part, Clewton looked like he wanted to get back in the LAV. Tammes, meanwhile, had sidled behind the admiral.

As Jack walked steadily toward the group, expression neutral, he felt his brain click into gear, some part of his rational persona returning. 'Yo, Admiral,' he said, keeping his voice even, trying not to sound like the maniac bubbling just below his surface equanimity. 'A word, please.'

'Jack?' the admiral said, hesitant. 'Shouldn't you be with your team?'

Out in the marshes, the unique detonative pop of a net launcher cut through the wind, the rain. Both Clewton and Tammes glanced southward briefly, jumpy.

Ignoring the indirect order, Jack said, 'If we take a walk around the other side of the LAV, out of this wind, we can talk in private.' Clewton and Tammes, then the commander, walked around to the sheltered spot behind the chunky vehicle.

'Ah, that's better,' Jack said, joining them and rubbing his hands. Behind him, he was aware of his team's presence. He could even sense how primed they were. 'It's just that I was wondering why you were so sure that our boy was, in all probability, going to hit us from the south? And this marshland in particular. Awful good guess, *Admiral.*'

'I don't care for your tone, *mister,*' the commander said.

'And I,' said Jack, addressing the commander – clocking his B Williams name tag - 'don't care for the company you keep.'

'Stand down!' Williams shouted.

'No,' said Jack quietly, showing him his crazy eyes and raising his net launcher. 'You stand down.'

Clewton stared in horror at the net gun. 'Bob, do as he says.'

'Yeah, *Bob,*' Jack said, giving him some more crazy, waving the launcher around.

'But -'

'Williams!' Clewton was close to losing it. He knew what it would be like to die caught in the net.

Commander Bob stepped back.

'There's no coming back from this, Jack,' Clewton said.

'That's funny, *Val.* I was thinking the same about you.' More launcher pops out beyond the perimeter. 'I'd like you, *Val,* to tell Bob here how you knew the target would be hitting this part of the perimeter.'

'Mr. Tarr,' Tammes said in his whiny, nasally supercilious voice, 'it's called working with the data – also known as an educated guess.'

'Commander Williams,' Jack said. 'Tell me, how long is the perimeter fence all told?'

'Four miles or so, give or take. Why?'

'Four miles, Admiral. Yet you insisted we concentrate here, in this specific spot. Funny that.'

Shouts, screams, more net pops, and the rat-a-tat-tat of regular ordnance. Williams glanced out at the darkness beyond. Clewton swallowed. 'It's probably time for us to get back to HQ; leave you professionals to it.'

Jack sighed. 'Take a step toward me, Admiral. This won't take long.'

'You're way out of line, son,' Williams said.

'Piss off, Bob,' Jack said amiably. 'Now, Admiral, if you will. My finger's getting kinda tired resting on the guard here. Reckon it's only a matter of time before it slips.'

Clewton stepped smartly forward. And just as smartly, Jack clubbed him to the ground with the launcher's butt before smartly training the weapon on Tammes, and Williams.

Clewton groaned.

'Tell Bob, Admiral. What you did.'

Clewton struggled to sit up.

'You can get up, Admiral. It was only a tap.'

'A means to an end,' Clewton spat out.

'Can't hear you,' Jack said.

'A means to an end. The tough decisions we have to make.'

'Yeah? What tough decisions were those, you piece of shit?'

Clewton wiped the blood from his chin, hands trembling. 'Collateral damage, Tarr. You know the drill. Grow the fuck up.'

'There's nothing collateral about what happened to that man. You broke his legs, and you rolled him out of your helo. Left him in the mud. For *bait*.'

'*Them*, Tarr. Fucking plural –'

'Val, for -' Tammes said.

'*All* of them in the mud,' insisted Clewton.

A mind's-eye image of the Cay Sal survivors flashed into Jack's head. Old and young, men and women. Children.

'I don't believe you,' Jack said.

Clewton spat blood from his mouth. 'Excuse me if I don't care two shits, Chief.'

The commander stared down at Clewton, disgust wavering around the edges of his face. 'Admiral?' For a big man, his voice was now notably small.

'Bait,' Jack said. 'It's why you were so sure this is where it'd approach.'

Clewton struggled to get to his feet, using the side of the LAV to haul himself up. Jack kicked his legs from under him. 'Stay down!'

Clewton's eyes, his irises, became black with hatred. He laughed. 'You're not walking away from this, Tarr. You're walking, but you're dead.'

Jack placed one boot hard on the admiral's chest, the end of the launcher barrel in his face. 'I'm not going to repeat myself. Tell Commander Bob what you did, Val.'

'I defended my country.'

Jack dug his boot further into Clewton's chest.

Clewton groaned, a noise dissimilar to Bembe's out on the marsh. 'I used the resources at hand.'

'You used *people* as bait.'

'I did.'

Jack turned away from Clewton. 'You hear that, Commander? You hear what this man did in my, *your,* name?'

Ashen-faced, Williams nodded.

Jack returned his focus to the admiral. 'Now tell me what's going on with that animal. What have you done?'

Clewton laughed again as much as his restricted lungs allowed, clearly moving into some category of hysteria. Jack had seen enough grown men go that way. Sometimes fear, the knowledge that the gig's up will do that. 'National Security, Jack. You know how that goes. We have to keep ahead of the curve. Can't get left behind.'

'But why me? Why am I here?' *But you know, Jack. You* know. *If only you'd let the thought in.*

'Because you're the best, Jack,' Clewton said, spitting flecks of blood onto his shirt collar. 'The Navy's not been the same since you left. I don't know how we've managed. We've *struggled.*'

'Last chance, Val.' Jack made a show of shoving the launcher's stock into his shoulder as if readying to fire. 'There are any number of guys you could have called on, guys on top of their game. Why me?'

'Jack, dear boy, haven't you heard? You're the world's leading authority on all things crustacean. How could we possibly not want you, *nay,* need you.'

'The only thing I can think of is …' The thought on the edge of Jack's mind circled yet again, yet remaining beyond his comprehension, but getting closer.

'Yes?' the admiral said. 'You're almost there.'

Jack pressed his boot further into Clewton's chest, leaning on the launcher's butt, sinking its nozzle deeper into his face. 'I'm not doing this all night, Admiral. I'm giving you one last chance … or we'll *wrap* this up.'

Clewton nodded. Jack removed his boot, taking the launcher out of Clewton's skin. Tammes helped him to his feet. Williams stayed where he was, still chewing over what the admiral had done to innocent civilians.

'You know, Jack, you've been woefully slow for an intelligent man. My God, did you ever think we'd called you up because you're so indispensable?' he chuckled. 'You did, didn't you? You actually thought—yeah, need a job done well, call up old Jack Tarr. He's the only living, breathing operator to get stuff done.'

'It's Skeeter, isn't it?' Jack said. The hitherto circling thought had finally been snagged—the unthinkable hunch that Jack had been grappling with all along.

Clewton offered a slow handclap. 'The only thing that makes sense, huh, Jack?'

'You wanted me because ...'

'Yeah, it's your buddy Skeeter out there, more or less. Less, I reckon.'

Jack raised the launcher once more.

Alarmed, Clewton put his hands in the air. 'And before you get all righteous, there's something you should know.'

'You think?' Jack sneered, finger tightening on the trigger.

'Your buddy Skeeter, he signed up for the project. With full knowledge of the possible consequences, he signed a waiver. He *volunteered*.'

Yes. As much as Jack hated the thought, that sounded right. Over the years, it wasn't that Skeeter had been cumulatively scarred by his experiences in the SEALs; it was something far worse – he had been transformed, changed into a man suited for one environment only, a figurative version of what he'd become. Becoming a literal monster wouldn't have fazed Skeeter if that was what he believed he already was.

'Sir,' Williams said to Clewton. 'Is this true?' The commander had paled yet further until his pallor matched virgin-white paper. 'What he says, it can't be right. Sir?'

'Oh, fuck off, Bob,' Clewton snarled. 'May I remind you, this all happened on your watch. And if this gets out, you're where the buck stops. Tammes and my good self, we're invisible.'

Williams' mouth opened in a perfect O.

'Oh, don't worry, Commander,' Clewton said, 'what happened here, it goes no further.'

Jack said flatly, 'The creature's gone. Those guys out there, they're spooked, shooting at shadows. Commander, you tell Fugat to change the operation into a search and rescue—find every single one of those people this cunt used as chum.'

CHAPTER 33

NAS
Monday, 2344 hours

Fifteen minutes later, Jack, Clewton, and Tammes sat around a scarred wooden table in a cramped, nondescript cube. The building was also featureless on the outside - a cinderblock construction with a bland external veneer. Inside, the room smelled of wet cement, as if they'd just finished constructing it for this specific meeting. The only illumination was two lights with a long metal shade hung above their heads. Clewton and Tammes sat opposite Jack, their downlit, chiaroscuro faces eerie in the shadowed room. Outside, thunder rumbled, and hard Florida rain drummed on the sole window.

Jack seethed, *raged*, inwardly. His head was slumped forward, his forearms resting limply on his thighs. He didn't trust himself to speak, to move. He couldn't bring himself to look at Clewton, at Tammes. All he wanted to do was leap across the shitty little table and knock their heads together until they were an unrecognizable, pulpy mess. Fuck. *Fuck.* What these two men had done. It felt *beyond* evil. Bembe and his people. Skeeter. It was a kind of hell just being in the same room as these two. Malevolence emanated from them, and the very air they exhaled felt like it was coated with an oily residue. It was as if Clewton and Tammes, all along, had only been imitating being human. These two were walking-talking living violations.

With all his willpower, Jack forced himself to look at them.

'Apologies for the melodrama,' Clewton said, looking around the compact space, up at the dim bulbs. 'Nearest available room, short notice and all that.' Clewton was all back to business, the recent unpleasantness forgotten, much ado about fucking nothing. Again, Jack marveled at how quickly Clewton seemed to move on from being found out and exposed as someone beyond contempt. That the admiral was in denial didn't come close. Clewton's epic cognitive dissonance must be the only reason he could live with himself.

The admiral rubbed the side of his head where Jack had knocked him. Though Clewton's eyes were shadowed, Jack imagined they blazed with hate. Clewton was right – he, Jack, had crossed a line. If he were still in the Navy, he'd be in the brig, in chains, not metaphorically. But the line Clewton had crossed was of a whole different order. For a while, though, Jack was safe. The admiral still needed him to lure in Skeeter. Clewton was right about one thing: whatever Skeeter had become, he was still his buddy. Right now, both Clewton and Jack needed each other. Without the admiral, Jack wouldn't be able to get to Skeeter.

Jack made an ostentatious glance around. 'Hush-hush chic,' he said, working hard to match Clewton's all-pals-together conversational pitch. There was no sense in confirming what was going on inside his head – about how there would be a reckoning. 'Highly appropriate, considering what you two clowns have been up to.'

Clewton leaned forward. 'I meant what I said, Jack. Perhaps I shouldn't have put it the way I did. Still, I genuinely believe that your actions are explained by you having been contaminated by immersion in civilian street. You know how the military works. You know it's all about the greater good, for Uncle Sam. Defending this great country – my profound privilege – has always been about expediency, contingency, and getting the upper hand. And it never was and never will be about morals. Morals are for the guys that lose. I've always, *always* put the needs of the Navy first.'

Clewton was right up to a point. And, yes, Jack felt a touch of cognitive dissonance between his civilian self and his Navy alter-ego. But in his heart, he had always believed that there was some unwritten line that should not be crossed. When he had been in-field, an operator, he held to the belief that, if it came to it, he would refuse an order if he deemed it unconscionable. He didn't know exactly what that line was, but he was sure to know it when he saw it. And now he'd seen it. With what Clewton had done to the Cay Sal survivors. With what he and Tammes had done to Skeeter. Skeeter had known that line, too. In all the times when Jack had worked with Skeeter, he had never seen his former mentor take the easy way out and put non-combatants at risk. 'Tell that to the Nazis, Saddam, Ceausescu, all of those pricks who believed that morals, humanity, didn't apply to them.' Jack paused to breathe. 'It applied alright, and then some.'

Jack wondered how men like Clewton got away with what they did. But he already knew. The Navy was a granular organization with wilful, deep-rooted interdepartmental blindness. This way of organizing the military and the Navy, in particular—created the perfect conditions for a certain type of skulduggery, where one hand never knew what the other was doing, where nefarious schemes could exist with seeming impunity, sans accountability, oversight. A natural habitat for men like Clewton and Tammes. Men who gravitated toward the gray areas, where morals without imperatives thrived, truths minus absolutes. Shadowy areas where self-issued licenses granted them the freedom to do what the hell-ever they wanted. Tammes would have been given a set-in-stone mandate as long as so-called needs were met and the Navy got first dibs. A lot of it was just one big boondoggle – pissing money up the wall on fraudulent projects. It made Jack want to weep at the amount of public funds shoveled into so-called black projects. But there was always an administrative fiat greenlighting projects whose relationship with the law was tenuous.

Ordinary enlisted men and women assumed they were in the cheap seats and were not getting the bigger picture. The thing with the Navy, though, was that nobody was getting the bigger picture because there was no actual bigger picture. It was just a bunch of disparate people doing disparate things. Everybody was in the cheap seats, even goddamn POTUS. It was all so utterly ass-about bonkers and wearisome as hell.

Clewton said, 'Tell me, Jack ... when you were in the Teams, in theatre – in particular, ocean-based ops – did you ever hear rumors of other, uh, let's say, operators with advanced skillsets, even more so than the SEALs?'

Jack had. Several times on sea-going missions, he'd been aware of other SEAL-like protagonists in the mix, taking care of business on the other side, so to speak, of an objective. The compartmentalization of involved assets wasn't a new thing in the military. If you didn't need to know what the other fellow was doing, then you didn't need to know. When you got high in the Tiers, you realized there were all sorts of hinky outfits out there, some of which were presumably even beyond Tier One clearance. And, of course, the SEALs talked among themselves. Rumors, speculation. *Kaffeeklatsch*, as the Germans would say, coffee gossip. In Tarr-speak, bullshit. Still, you never knew. All he said was, 'Yeah, the usual messdeck scuttlebutt. So what?'

'For some years now—when you, in fact, were still in the game—we, the Navy, have been using enhanced bio-skills tech. Not on the Skeeter scale, but physical enhancements that increase endurance, dive depths, subsea maneuverability, and so on. As you can imagine, this allows a great and significant advantage over the enemy. What's happened to Skeeter is the natural evolution of these bio-enhancement programs. There was a certain inevitability.'

Tammes jumped in, 'The point is, Mr Tarr, that we can't fall behind in the bio-arms race. And that's what this is: an arms race. Like the atom bomb, getting into space. We *know* the Chinese, the Russians, *et al.*, right now have programs in place working – right *now* – on enhanced-human bio-weaponry. Transhumanism is all the rage. Or, at least, it will be.'

Jack imagined Tammes' feverish eyes and the ubiquitous sweat on his forehead as if he were perpetually too hot or anxious about being found out. 'You lied to me. All of it lies. Like you said, 'I'm here because I'm bait, the lure. And yes, I was stupid not to see that.' *Maybe not* that *stupid*, he thought. *From the get-go, I* knew *Clewton was keeping something up his ass.* But, *stupid enough.*

'Jack,' Clewton said, opening his arms across the desk, palms up, all Mr Reasonable, 'I admit I stretched the truth. But try to see it as a measure of how desperate we were to have you -'

'Yeah, yeah, ends justify the means, national security, blah blah. I get it.'

'Not all lies, Mr Tarr,' Tammes said. 'A hefty fee for your efforts will facilitate future research projects.'

'But not on bio-weaponry.'

'Yes, not that.'

'So you're just paying me off.'

Clewton grunted. 'I know it may seem like that, Jack, but your input into this ... operation is invaluable, incalculable.'

'For all the wrong reasons.'

'What do you mean?'

'Skeeter. First off, you wanted him dead. It seemed like he was a dud, an experimental impasse. You couldn't control or get him to do what you wanted. Cognitively, he appeared limited, dumber than dumb, an uncontrollable monster, your very own Frankenstein's creature. And then he escaped. The Caribbean is a big place. How are you gonna find him, kill him? Oh, yes, yeah, bait. This is where I came in, but you changed your mind. You started to like the things Skeeter was doing. Tracking vessels, avoiding detection, having a purpose, even though you didn't, and still don't – know what that purpose is -'

'And you do, Jack?'

Yes, I think I do. But ignoring Clewton, Jack continued. 'You started to realize that cognitively Skeeter-mantis, while not firing on all cylinders, still had the mental faculty to plan, to strategize, *learn.* And then the icing on the goddamn cake.' Jack fell silent and leaned back in the creaky chair, folding his arms. *I, too, can be melodramatic.*

Sighing with annoyance, Clewton said, 'He started killing.'

'He started killing,' Jack echoed. 'Moreover, he outwitted a highly trained SEAL team several times. And then he attacked the ships on the picket line.'

'That was ... unexpected,' Tammes said.

'And that's when you decided you didn't want Skeeter dead. Instantly, he ceased being a target, a bogie, and, once more, became an asset.' Jack chuckled. 'And here's me thinking I'd convinced you, charmed you with my eloquence, my big civvy-street words, to take him alive, that I'd somehow appealed to your better natures.' He laughed again. 'Another big chunk of stupid on my part.'

'No, Jack,' Clewton said. 'We were, in fact, in two minds about reinstating Skeeter's asset status. Your request for non-lethal strategies tipped the balance.'

'Oh, even now, knowing all you've done, with all your shitty excuses, how I'd like to believe that, Admiral. That somewhere in your black, shriveled heart, a tiny piece of it is redeemable.'

Clewton cleared his throat. 'About the immigrants -'

'They've got names,' Jack said, voice harsh. 'For example, the guy we rescued, his name is Bembe; the others ...' For a moment, Jack couldn't get the words out; his throat and chest were not his to control. He was in danger of breaking down, sobbing uncontrollably. It was then that he knew he was going to kill Clewton. Kill Tammes. And their departing would not be easy for them. But not now, not yet.

'This, uh,' Clewton continued, 'goes much higher than me. I've got powerful interests pulling my strings. And, um, Bembe and his people got caught in the ... put it this way, I was heavily leaned on to take the action I did.'

Powerful interests. That was more than likely true, Jack thought. But in his heart, Jack knew that what happened to Bembe was all on Clewton. The admiral had form when it came to playing fast and loose with other people's lives. Jack remembered Yemen. 'Tell me the truth, Admiral. Are your men out there right now, picking up Bembe's people?'

'I swear, Jack. As we speak.'

'You will let me know the outcome.'

The admiral nodded. 'Of course, of course.'

'Before we get onto capturing ... Skeeter -'

'You're still in?' Clewton's relief was palpable.

Jack nodded. There was one more thing Jack needed to hear. 'What I want to know, *Doctor*, is ... is this ... process reversible? Can you bring Skeeter back?'

Clewton laughed. 'Jack, once the genie's out of the bottle, you -'

'Excuse me, Val,' Tammes interrupted. He made a show of rubbing his half-rimmed reading glasses with a cloth. Jack realized that everything about the doctor was performative. A mask, subterfuge, distraction. Jack felt like ripping Tammes' face off to see what was behind it all – but he already knew – *nothing.* 'Yes, Chief, it is possible. Your friend can be brought back. A complex procedure, but not unachievable. That's why I opted for 100% organic – it saves all the tedious biomechanical interfacing, outer skeletons, and so forth – much better opt for biotic structures. And that's what we've got with Skeeter.

Every process at every part of the way was biocompatible - something that does not hurt the human body. And, probably needless to say, it's amazing what's biocompatible with the human body.'

Genetics. Jack knew shit from Shinola about genetics.

While Jack was willing to believe the professor, he was almost sure that Tammes was playing him, good cop to Clewton's bad. Give Tarr something to hold on to and keep him with the program. 'Go on.'

'It's something I've been thinking about,' Tammes said to Clewton, almost apologetically, Jack thought. Tammes continued, 'Getting enough servicemen and women to volunteer en masse for a program like this is problematic. Body enhancement to this extreme would be a challenging sell - unless it were... reversible.'

'Evidently, you sold it to Skeeter,' Jack said.

Tammes thought about this. 'Yes, of course. But your friend was, I would say ... atypical. You must understand that –'

'Yes, I get it,' Jack said. And he did, knowing Skeeter. An aging Skeeter, getting perilously close to being retired, taken out of active service. The Navy, the Teams, they were all Skeeter knew. There was no way he'd hack life outside the Navy. He'd crawl into a bottle and stay there. Yes, Jack could believe that Skeeter would volunteer for something like this. His desire to remain a contender. To hold on to being relevant. Jack could see Skeeter going for it. Be the big man again. It was his old buddy's weakness – he liked to be in the thick of it. 'So there's a chance?'

'Oh yes, but it goes without saying that we need to bring him in— unharmed. We have, of course, mapped his genome. Skeeter's blueprint is the journey's end, a destination to which we can return, to reintroduce Skeeter to himself.'

'In that case, I know where he's headed.'

CHAPTER 34

NAS
Tuesday, 0209 hours
Base Hospital

Jack sat in the chair next to Bembe's hospital bed. Minutes earlier, he'd left Harps' room next door. Harps had been sat on his cot clad in a white medical gown, frozen into a creepy, uncomfortable-looking position. His knees up to his chest while his arms dangled by his side, his hands contorted into angular shapes. It looked like he was being carried by an invisible ... something. His face was locked in a rictus grin, his eyes depthless, sightless pools of horror. Harps, seemingly trapped inside his uncanny posture, still as death, stared at Jack, behind him, then beyond, as if he gazed into some dark, cosmic abyss.

Why was Harps still alive? Jack, too? Why had Skeeter attacked and killed the RIB Coasties? Had Skeeter been under the malign influence of whatever lurked on that benighted island? It was a mystery. Another goddamn mystery.

'I'm so sorry, Harps,' Jack said, searching for life in the young SEAL's unseeing eyes, finding none. Jack felt for Erin's tags underneath his shirt. He tried to imagine what it would be like to be somehow transported, conveyed all that way to the marshes, clasped in the claw of a creature that could split you as quickly as a nut in a cracker. Instantly. Jack sighed, running his hand through his hair. Harps seemed like a decent kid, and Jack hoped he'd make it back from wherever he'd gone. Judging by the sense of permanence in the kid's vacant gaze, if he did return, it'd be a long journey.

Jack was aware that he, too, was on a journey of sorts. In this poky room, Jack was getting Cay Sal vibes - that the world was not what you thought it was. Part of Cay Sal's inimical screwy off-kilter charm was that it made it seem like you could feel the universe expanding, things getting further apart from each other, spinning into ever-increasing states of aloneness – the feeling got in your face, it made you aware of your tininess status, the utter irrelevance of your existence. It was all the more imperative that Jack saved Skeeter and that he got back to Erin and started rebuilding his world, a recognizable world that behaved – by and large – as expected. *When I get home, I will stick my head in the sand and enjoy what I've got. I don't need to know* shit.

Like Harps, Bembe had been given a private room. No surprises there, Jack thought. Clewton and Tammes would want to keep them apart from other patients. All the better to deny Bembe the chance to tell tales out of school. And it didn't look like Harps would be yarning anytime soon. For Harps, maybe it was the best outcome, his condition granting him immunity from Clewton's desire to close anyone down who knew too much.

The armed guard in the hallway bore testament to the admiral's intention to keep this whole sorry episode under wraps.

Well, we'll see about that. I'm going to take you down, Admiral. Grab you from the rock you crawled under and throw you into the light of day. Let the good folk of this great nation know what you're doing in their name.

Zads, Mac, and Det were out in the hallway, too, catching Zs. They were sprawled over uncomfortable benches not designed for ready-to-drop Navy SEALs who needed to spread their bones. They'd been mostly quiet since the Skeeter revelation, each with their thoughts. It was a lot to take in. Especially for Zads and Mac, they'd known Skeeter for a long time. And both of them owed a debt to Skeeter. He'd ensured they stayed on the right side of the ground, breathing God's clean air. Jack was still processing what had been done to his friend. But the saddest thing was not the transformation itself, Jack realized with a jolt, but that Skeeter had been desperate enough to throw his hat into the ring in the first place.

Zads had said to Jack, waking up before the others, 'Boo, this is like Cay Sal.'

As per, Zads was uncannily tuned to his wavelength. He asked her what she meant so she could air her thoughts.

'*Skeeter*. And what he's become. The island is wrong, and Skeeter is wrong. The world is not what she seems.'

Jack had offered her the merest of nods. *I hear you.*

But Zads wasn't finished with her train of thought. 'It's like we're on the border. Of a different world. One we don't know. Where we don't know the rules. Like all along, we didn't know anything. Not really.'

Jack looked into her brown, questioning eyes and saw the confusion there. While he knew she needed more from him, he placed his hand on her shoulder, briefly squeezing. It was all he had.

Immediately after telling Clewton and Tammes what they needed to know, Jack demanded to see Bembe. He had a little time to spare. Skeeter's transmitter, according to Tammes, was transmitting intermittently. Now, Skeeter was fifty klicks west of the Keys, about to enter the Gulf proper. The signal had been static for several hours, suggesting Skeeter was injured. Double-edged sword news, Jack thought. It was good that Skeeter was possibly incapacitated and, therefore, easier to contain. Bad. Worst-case scenario, Skeeter was dead or dying. He must have been wounded in the swamp.

Bembe was breathing steadily. His prematurely lined face looked at peace. Both legs were in plaster. Here was a fellow human being crammed full of hope for the future and love for his family. And now that future had been taken away, his family destroyed.

So.

How to avoid being killed by Clewton. How could he ensure his team remains in the land of the living? And how could he protect Bembe?

Williams. Commander Bob had seemed an okay type – once he'd lost his big hat attitude, once he understood what good ole boy Admiral Val had done.

Jack allowed himself a big internal sigh. For days now, he'd been living and breathing violence and brutal death. Red in tooth and claw. The last few days had exhausted him mentally as well as physically. The physical side he could handle. In the past, extreme endurance had been a way of life, an everyday fact of existence. What was going on in his head, though, was different. An unquantifiable mess of contradiction and confusion. Part of him was seduced by the high-voltage delirium dream of deadly ultra-violence. In contrast, the other part retreated in horror, appalled.

And the horror was stacking up. Cal. Harps. Bembe. The decimated platoon. And Skeeter – or what the bastards had turned him into. How much Skeeter was left? How much of that thing was his old buddy?

Erin. Think of Erin – the normalcy, sanity, the everyday glorious minutiae of regular life. He felt Erin's tags through the fabric of his work shirt. Immediately, the solid shapes, their tactile reality, started to work their magic. His head began to clear. As the fuzz dissipated and clear thinking once more became an option, Jack considered his situation. No doubt about it, he was in a pickle of monumental proportions. And it wasn't just about Skeeter's safe, non-lethal retrieval; it was about what happened afterward. More than likely, immediately afterward. It went without saying that Jack did not trust Clewton; if he could sacrifice innocent civilians to achieve his objectives, he could ensure that when Jack returned to Erin, it would be in a casket. Full Naval honours. Probably Zads, too. And Mac and Det. Bembe, also. Yes. Clewton was ruthless enough to make these things happen without breaking a sweat. As for Tammes, who could tell? That needledick was always sweating.

He looked once more at Bembe. The man's eyelids fluttered. He was coming round. *How the hell am I going to tell him about his family?* But Jack needed to do this. To Bembe, he was the only familiar face, a friend of sorts.

Bembe moaned and opened his eyes, a look of confusion and panic spreading across his face. He turned around, saw Jack, and calmed down.

'Chief Jack,' Bembe whispered.

'Bembe,' Jack whispered back, squeezing Bembe's hand.

He looked down at his legs, and his face changed from bewilderment to horror. 'What happened?'

'You're safe now,' Jack said. 'Stateside. You made it.'

Bembe's brow furrowed. 'And ... Maria. Carlos?' Wife, son.

Jack remained silent as he tried to control the anger, the rage bubbling within. Whatever Bembe saw on Jack's face, it was enough. Jack didn't need words. Bembe knew. He *knew*. Tears rolled down the side of his face onto his pillow, fat globs of liquid despair.

'I'm sorry,' Jack said, squeezing Bembe's hand tighter. Bembe stared up at Jack, eyes brimming. He tried to say something but couldn't. Instead, he just shook his head. What had happened to him was beyond words, beyond comprehension. Jack could imagine what he was thinking: *This is America. How could* America *do this?*

'Bembe,' Jack said softly. 'I will make this right.'

A half smile wandered over Bembe's features, a fragile, vulnerable thing.

'Bembe,' Jack said more forcefully. 'Listen to me. I swear I will make this right. Trust me, I will make it so. I need you to believe me. Do you?'

Bembe searched Jack's eyes, and whatever he found there seemed enough. He smiled. This time, Bembe's smile was strong, shot through with a fierce longing, a desire for things to be put right.

Call it vengeance, call it justice, I don't give a shit, Jack thought.

As Jack left Bembe, quietly closing the hospital room's door, Zads and the team came awake. SEALs. They could sleep anywhere and lightly do it. Jack nodded at them as they yawned, stretched, and scratched body parts that required attention. Jack turned to the guard, a marine Private First Class. Nodded to him. 'The guy in there is called Bembe. If you get the opportunity to speak to him, use his name. And you smile at him. You treat him with dignity and respect. Got that?'

'Yes, sir,' he said, not knowing Jack's rank, erring on caution.

'One other thing. You only let somebody in there if it's a direct order from the base commander himself. Got that?'

'Sir!' the marine said.

Jack stared into the young guard's eyes, ensuring he fully understood the importance of Jack's instruction.

'What now, boss?' Zads asked.

'House call. Commander Bob's. Appraise him of the situation.'

'And what is the situation?' Mac asked.

'I don't want Bembe going into the night, gently or otherwise.'

'Chief?' Det said. 'What're we talking about here?'

'Who, not what. Clewton.'

'And are we at risk of, uh, likewise of going into the night?' Zads asked. Always the quick study.

'Oh, yes,' Jack said smartly. 'Which is why we need to be on our guard as soon as we get Skeeter in the bag. As long as Skeeter's with us, we're safe.'

They followed the road from the hospital to the center of the camp proper. They remained silent for the few minutes it took to reach the officers' accommodation. Jack got the duty corporal to wake up Fugat. Said it was a matter of urgency. Fugat met them at the quarters' entrance five minutes later, rubbing his eyes. Jack told him he needed access to Williams and that he, Fugat, was his best bet. 'Sure,' Fugat said, leading them to his personal transport, a Mutt jeep.

'Haven't seen one of these for a while,' Jack said, taking shotgun.

'This is mine, my baby,' Fugat said. 'The Navy stopped using them in the 90s. This is a restoration project, and I love her dearly.'

The Mutt roared as it tore through the sleeping base, the cool night air whipping past Jack as the ancient jeep's tires crunched over the gravel roads, sending up small dust clouds. He gripped its dash as it bounced over the sometimes potholed, uneven ground. The base was sparsely lit, with street lamps casting pools of yellowish light at intervals. Shadows loomed large, and the buildings were outlined in sharp relief against the dark sky: utilitarian structures, low-slung barracks, and high-tech operational buildings passed by in an architectural blur. In what looked like the mess hall, a few lights were still on – in contrast with the training grounds, which were now silent and empty, like the hangars, their large doors closed and secured for the night. Palm trees lined some of the way, their fronds rustling in the breeze. The salty scent of the sea mingled with the earthy smell of their foliage.

Finally, Fugat veered onto a narrower path leading to the base commander's quarters, screeching to a halt outside. The house was slightly more secluded, set apart from the main operational areas. A modest but well-kept structure, with a small porch light illuminating the entrance. The lights in the downstairs room were still on. Someone twitched the curtains.

Bob can't sleep, thought Jack. *Wonder why.*

The front door opened as Fugat leaped out of the Mutt. Jack told his team to look out for Clewton's guys and trotted after Fugat. The commander swung the door open fully to let his marine captain and Jack inside, looking up and down the street as he did so. With Jack and Fugat comfortably sitting in the living room, Jack filled in Williams about the situation and his fears – what Clewton was capable of.

'Indeed,' Williams said. 'Haven't been able to sleep. This whole SNAFU is not to my liking at all.'

'There's no other way of putting it, Commander,' Jack said. 'But we're all in danger—you and Captain Fugat, too. Clewton's out of control.'

'Suggestions?'

'Make it clear to the admiral that you've created certain contingencies that will be executed immediately if anything untoward happens to yourself, the captain, and my team, including Mr Bembe Carlos and any other Cay Sal survivors.'

Williams nodded. 'Insurance policies all round, Chief?'

'That's the one,' said Jack.

'Understood,' the commander said. 'Anything else?'

'Take care, sir. You, too, Captain.'

There was a loud knock on the front door. Jack and Fugat followed the commander. On the doorstep was a naval lieutenant who had clearly just woken up.

'The target's on the move, sir,' he blurted. 'Moving north.' Then, turning to Jack, 'Just like you said.'

As he left the commander's house, Jack said, 'Oh, and Bob - you might want to get in a man to fix your fence.'

CHAPTER 35

Sikorsky Hawk, 2000ft, *Team FT1*
Tuesday, 0555 hours
Gulf of Mexico (26°11'14.0"N 84°70'20"W)

'What did Williams say, Chief?' Zads asked through her helmet mic, ensuring the comms circuit consisted only of Jack, Mac, and Det. Jack told her and the rest of the team about their insurance policy, which would likely expire when the Navy regained complete control of Skeeter. Unless, of course, the base commander put in place a failsafe that made Clewton think twice about taking extreme action. The commander's protection was an effective short-term safety net. However, outcomes would become extremely unpredictable once Skeeter was in captivity. Trying to solve the personal survival conundrum while focusing on the mission to recapture Skeeter was hurting Jack's head. It didn't help that he was exhausted.

They were high above the Gulf in another workhorse Sikorsky. The plan was to drop off at the Tanaquil oil rig, a floating platform, to await Skeeter's approach. Clewton and Tammes were in another bird flying parallel a quarter of a klick away on their starboard side.

'Where're we headed?' Mac asked. 'After we leave Tanaquil?'

'The Dead Zone,' Jack said grimly.

'Sounds fun,' Mac said.

'Six thousand square miles of hypoxic water,' Jack said, unconsciously slipping into college prof mode. 'Starting in the Mississippi River delta and stretching westward as far as Texas.'

'That's water without oxygen, right?' asked Det.

'Yes,' Jack said. 'All the shit – nutrients from fertilizers, mostly. Nitrogen, phosphorous, but also animal waste, sewage. Gets dumped in Old Man River's watersheds all the way from Montana, Minnesota, through Arkansas, down into Louisiana. No marine life – except jellyfish – can live there.'

'And that includes … what Skeeter's become?' asked Zads.

'That's what Tammes is telling Clewton.'

'Do you believe him?' Det asked.

'In this, yes. They want Skeeter – there's no gain from lying.'

'So this Dead Zone, we're safe, right?' Det asked.

'Use your brain, Det,' Zads said affectionately. 'We're in suits. We've got our oxygen.'

Det nodded sheepishly.

'I don't get it,' Mac asked. 'How do we know that Skeeter is coming this way? Why would he even try to go through the DZ?'

Jack told them. About his hunch, a gut feeling that was more sure bet than mere fancy. He told them about Skeeter and his wife, a second-generation Ghanaian force of nature named Abena Akuffo. How Ms Akuffo – a child prodigy, science-wise – had landed employment at the Naval Biodynamics Lab in New Orleans, where she met and fell in love with Skeeter. Skeeter was there on a loan draft secondment – a volunteer – to measure physiological responses to impact acceleration, particularly on the head and neck. 'Something like astronaut training, I guess.'

'I was just thinking, boss,' Mac said. 'Even then, Skeeter was the volunteering kind.'

'He was that,' Jack agreed. 'And what the biodynamics lab was looking into was something the Special Ops brass were very much interested in. You know the kind of thing, like how much shit can the human body stand? Anyway, they wanted one of their guys in the program. And Skeeter always wanted to prove a point. Even if it was to himself.'

Ah, Skeeter, Jack thought. *You never could rest easy with what you had—you always had to be trying for more.* Skeeter's favorite poet, some Brit, had written *Something hidden. Go and find it. Something lost behind the Ranges. Lost and waiting for you. Go*! Skeeter loved to quote the lines, often in theater. It was how he lived, always wanting to see what was over the next mountain. The Brit scribe must have written his poem with men like Skeeter in mind. Always needing to go the extra mile.

As part of her research remit, Jack told them that Abena also went to sea, shipping out on Coast Guard cutters in the Gulf and the Caribbean, studying their integration into combat roles. She sailed with the Navy and on bigger ships. She'd once told Jack that she felt closer to him when she was at sea, wherever Skeeter was in the world.

'Sweet,' Zads said.

'But -'

'Ah, always the *but*.' Zads again.

'You know how it is,' Jack said. 'Two people, no matter how much they love each other, if they're only meeting briefly now and again, over the years, it takes its toll. Abena wanted a family. Skeeter already had a family – the SEALS. There was no way he was going to give that up. So they drifted apart until, finally, they called it a day. Saddest thing ever.'

'So ...' Mac said, 'let's get this straight – you're saying that Skeeter's been drawn to the cutters, ships, and shore bases because of their connection to his ex-wife's work? He's checking out where he knew she'd been stationed?'

Jack nodded. 'That's my thought.'

'Wow,' whispered Zads. 'And Abena, is she still at this Biodynamics place in New Orleans? That's where he's aiming for?'

'No, and yes,' said Jack. 'Abena's no longer with us. About a year ago. She was killed in a hit-and-run. They never caught the culprit. Skeeter wasn't at the funeral. Now I know why.' Frankly, Jack had attended Abena's funeral not just to pay his respects but also to see Skeeter, to kind of ambush his ass.

'Too busy becoming a crustacean,' said Mac. Then, 'Sorry, shitty thing to say.'

'Don't sweat it, Mac.' *Gallows humor.* Mac's way of dealing with the situation as it presented itself. But Mac's callous remark revealed an uncomfortable truth. When they next fetched up alongside the creature, they would be all dauntingly aware of its provenance - Skeeter.

'He's trying to find the one person who ... anchored him,' Det said, more to himself. Jack suspected he was thinking of Cal.

Jack continued. 'They'd separated before Abena died.' Another reason Skeeter might have volunteered was to win back Abena. Skeeter might have calculated that after the enhancements, he would inevitably be seconded to the Naval Bio Research Station, maybe even as part of one of Abena's bodily stress and kinetics programs.

'He doesn't know she's dead,' Det said, his voice cut with sadness.

'You figure,' Zads said, 'he's aiming for *La Nouvelle Orleans* to be with his ex ... then, what?'

Jack shrugged. 'Maybe, in his mind, he's convinced she can help him. She is – *was* - a medical doctor. Perhaps he's conflated her expertise with that of Tammes'.'

Something caught Jack's eye out of the starboard observation hatch. A warship. They were less than a thousand feet, and Jack had a good view. There was the Forrest Sherman destroyer, presumably the one on the southerly ass-end of the picket line. She was steaming along at a fair old lick. Over thirty knots, Jack reckoned.

And what was it that had been done to her lines? There'd been something weird about her appearance when he briefly saw her on the picket line, but now he had a better view. For any ship that stayed in service long enough, she'd undergo mods and conversions to accommodate new tech, weaponry, and such. However, the changes in this Forrest Sherman were more profound and organic. It was like the whole ship had been altered. With its bridge, radar, and communication equipment, the superstructure looked normal at first glance. However, upon closer inspection, there appeared to be stringy lumps clinging to the metal.

Like … *growths*, Jack thought. Organic growths. The growths looked like actual vine-like tendrils. Tendrils that blended seamlessly with the ship's structure and … pulsing faintly, almost imperceptibly.

The hell?

Yet, she remained recognizable as a Forrest Sherman. Was the ship somehow connected to Skeeter or Clewton? Jack remembered how Clewton had paled when Jack had mentioned the old warship, looking like he was, for all intents, about to pass out. In the Teams, there'd always been rumors of a black sail DESRON, an extra, unaccounted-for destroyer squadron nobody was supposed to know about. Jack had figured it all for a Herculean bunch of messdeck bullshit – after all, he'd been top Tier; unquestionably, he would have come into contact with such a clandestine outfit because when you got right down to it, he'd *been* Mr Clandestine. DESRON 13, he remembered, was what they called it. *Thirteen.* Of course, it would be.

Clewton's voice intruded into Jack's thoughts as he came over the comms. 'Just to say, people, ETA Tanaquil platform in fifteen minutes.'

By way of an answer, Jack said, 'Val, I just saw our friend, that old lady Forrest Sherman. The hell's going on?'

There was a long, staticky pause. Then, 'Don't you mind her, Jack,' Clewton said. 'She stays on her side of the line, we ours.'

'Val, I guess I have no idea what you just said.'

'Well, Jack. *I* guess I'm not party to every damn thing that goes on in this man's Navy.' Clewton offered a half-choked chuckle. 'I got my territory, they got theirs.'

Jack broke comms. It was a conversation that was going nowhere. Besides, Tanaquil had just hoved into view.

Jack noted how the scene below was both breathtaking and industrially imposing. As a marine biologist, he hated what these rigs did to the ocean and what their produce did to the world. So it was with some irony that he appreciated how the horizon was painted with the soft, pastel hues of early morning—pinks, oranges, and purples blending seamlessly into the ocean's deep blue. And how the first rays of sunlight glinted off the calm waters, creating a shimmering, golden path leading to the rig.

From this altitude, the oil rig stood out starkly against the vast expanse of the sea. Its massive steel structure rose from the water like a mechanical behemoth, with towering derricks and cranes silhouetted against the dawn sky. The platform was a hive of activity dotted with machinery, pipelines, and helipads. Bright lights from the rig pierced through the early morning haze, reflecting off the water and adding to the surreal, almost otherworldly atmosphere. The rig's network of walkways and platforms was visible, crisscrossing the structure like the threads of a giant web. The sea's gentle waves lapped against the rig's pontoons and support columns, which plunged deep into the ocean. Small boats and support vessels were moored nearby, their lights twinkling in the dim light. As the helo descended, the sound of its rotors mixed with the distant hum of machinery from the rig, creating a symphony of industrial noise. The sheer scale of the oil rig became apparent, a testament to human engineering and white-hot naked greed.

Jack prepared for helo disembarkation.

Tanaquil Oil Rig, Floating Platform
Gulf of Mexico

Once the helo was safely clipped and tethered on the rig, Jack and his team jumped onto the helipad, leaving their equipment inside the bird. Their stay on the Tanaquil would be brief. They'd brought a couple of extra cases that Jack had insisted on. When he'd presented his new wish list to Clewton, the admiral had thought Jack was pulling his leg. *Just make it happen*, Jack had said. Jack got the same WT Actual F response from Zads, Mac, and Det. Jack didn't listen to them either.

As they made their way to the rig's control center, a dimly lit room filled with flickering screens and humming machinery, Jack detected the fumes of percolating roasted coffee beans. Just what the doctor ordered, he thought. Clewton was already in the CC, talking to a man about Clewton's age. The man looked fit and tanned, with short gray hair and blue eyes. He was dressed casually, wearing jeans and a plaid shirt. Despite the simple attire, there was something about it that shouted money.

At the other side of the CC, a group of men lounged around a coffee machine next to the sonar and radar consoles. They were all wearing thick, startlingly pale blue neoprene dive suits. There were eight of them, hard-faced and cut with muscle. They exuded an air of contempt and suspicion.

Some of them sported Zapata mustaches of varying degrees of structural integrity. They all had close-shaven heads and carried a merc vibe, likely originating from the same box of psychotic bastards out of Military Contractors Central. Jack knew the type, and he despised them.

One diver with a particularly thick mustache leaned against a console, his arms crossed and a sneer on his lips as he eyed the room with cold, calculating eyes. When he met Jack's eyes, he smiled—a cold and heartless thing. Jack mouthed a kiss back, and the man looked away. Another sat in a chair, his feet propped up on a control panel, casually spinning a diving knife between his fingers. His expression was bored and arrogant, but his eyes never stopped scanning his surroundings. A pair of divers stood by the door FT1 had just walked through, their stance rigid and alert, as if ready to pounce at any moment.

They exchanged low, muttered comments, their voices filled with disdain, clearly aimed at Jack's team. Their eyes darted suspiciously in FT1's direction, then around the CC, never settling on one spot for too long. Nearby, another diver with a large scar across his forehead checked his gear, his movements precise and methodical. He, too, cast a dark look toward Jack, his face a mask of hostility. The atmosphere in the control center was thick with tension and menace.

Jack figured them to be two four-person fire teams—the men that Clewton had promised Jack. Except that Jack had requested only one team. Four were manageable; eight, and they'd start getting in each others' way.

Something about these guys didn't sit right: Jack couldn't place their provenance. He didn't think they were SEALs, ex or otherwise. These geniuses exuded a freaky level of hypermasculinity - or some toxic iteration of it. Perhaps surprisingly, hypermasculinity wasn't that prevalent in the SEALS. By the nature of the training and the work, SEALs were comfortable in their masculinity. They had nothing to prove. Besides, the SEALs were all about cooperation, not competition – teamwork.

But these blue suits, mere toxicity didn't cover it.

Why would Clewton want to subcontract the wet work? Because it would be best to keep it all in-house; more manageable to keep it under wraps.

Jack waved to the men. Some of them turned his way, but not one returned the gesture. 'Do you know any of these guys?' Jack asked his team.

No, they did not.

Clewton noticed Jack and waved, strolling over, hand outstretched. Two long-term pals meeting in a park or a bar. As before, Jack ignored Clewton's proffered hand. And again, Clewton acted like he didn't give a shit.

'No Tweedles?' Jack asked.

Clewton frowned, confused. 'I'm sorry?'

'No matter,' said Jack airily. Maybe they'd been more hurt in the recent fracas than he'd thought. Couldn't have happened to a nicer couple of guys.

'Jack,' Clewton said, recovering, trying to lose the frown. 'I'd like you to meet an old friend of mine. Very old. We went to the same school, in fact.'

This time, Jack accepted the man's hand. It was cold and clammy. And while the man smiled, it didn't reach his eyes. None of Clewton's friends – it seemed - had mastered smiling. 'Robert Belknap,' he said.

'Rig manager?' Jack asked.

Belknap's face morphed into another species of smile—a smile Jack didn't like—this one supercilious and calculating. Clewton had given Belknap the lowdown on Jack's character.

'No, Jack,' Clewton said. 'Robert here is the *CEO* of the Petro conglomerate Almodovar-Belknap Energy.'

'Right,' said Jack, singularly unimpressed.

'No need to look so worried, Jack,' Belknap said. 'I'm on your side.'

'What he means is,' Clewton said obsequiously, 'Robert here is on the DoD payroll via the Pentagon, providing most of the black tea that keeps the Navy moving.'

'How about that?' Jack said, wondering about the relevance of all this. He couldn't help feeling that Belknap was somehow part of Clewton's post-capture Skeeter plan. He didn't like it at all. He nodded over to the blue-clad divers. 'Are these guys up to speed?'

'They've been fully briefed and know they are backup, not principals.'

'These extra guys,' Jack said. 'Who are they?'

'Robert's rig divers.'

'You sure it's not overkill?'

'It's not worth taking chances,' said Clewton. 'This time, we recover the, ah, asset. No mistakes.'

'Alright,' said Jack. 'As long as they follow my lead.'

Before Clewton had time to answer, one of the blue suits studying the sonar screen shouted, 'We need to get into the water, Admiral. Target's on its way.'

CHAPTER 36

Team FT1
Tuesday, 0832 hours
Mississippi Dead Zone
Gulf of Mexico

Jack was glad to be off the floating rig and once more in the air, even though it would be a brief flight to the edge of the Mississippi Dead Zone. The overly cozy, pally rapport between Clewton and Belknap had made Jack want to puke. The presence of the blue suits hadn't improved Jack's mood either. The other guys had been standoffish, uninterested in even the most basic social interaction. Partly, the new guys' chilly response to Jack and his team was, in all probability, down to the age gap. Except for Det, Jack's team consisted of old-timers, long in the tooth and ready to be shipped out to civilian life. Hell, Jack was over twice the age of most of Clewton's fresh recruits. He must've seemed ancient to them. But there was something else behind the particular brand of condescension the young hold for the old. Jack could feel it in his bones, something that went beyond mere contempt for one's elders. He hoped he was wrong, but Jack instinctively felt that whatever play sheet the new guys had been given, it was different from his. He wished he'd checked out what ordnance Clewton's boys had been carrying – he still had a suspicion that Clewton didn't care one way or the other whether Skeeter was taken alive or dead and that all the admiral cared about was that Skeeter was taken out of the picture.

'Hey, boss,' Zads said. 'There's your Forrest Sherman again.'

Jack squinted through the thick observation glass. Zads was right. Below, the aged destroyer gamely chugged through the Gulf's muddy waters. 'The hell she up to?'

'Something to do with us?' asked Mac.

'I don't think so,' said Jack, wondering if this was how it ended for them, how Clewton took them out of the game, snatched by a ship that wasn't supposed to exist. A ship that could appear out of nowhere and could just as quickly disappear. Taking them with her. Once again, the variables were stacking up. And Jack didn't like it one bit. It was exhausting watching your own back. 'Be careful down there,' Jack said unnecessarily. 'Remember, we trust each other, no one else. And after we've got Skeeter in the bag, we stick together. Vis isn't going to be too hot down there. Don't get separated.'

The helo pilot informed them that they'd arrived at the target location. They were now stationary, hovering at about fifty feet. As Mac heaved open the sliding door, Jack, Zads, and Det started sliding the cases with their buoys out into the water. The sea was mostly calm, with a gentle swell. The Gulf tended only to get rough when creating hurricanes. The rest of the time, it was mostly placid. As far as Jack knew, there were none in the making.

Clewton's voice came over loud and clear. Tammes had lost Skeeter. The signal had failed twenty klicks to the south of their current position. Skeeter's course, while somewhat erratic, was broadly headed in their direction.

From several hundred feet above sea level, Jack could easily see the Dead Zone's outline, where the ocean changed from gray to blue. The clear demarcation between marine life and marine extinction was as impressive as horrifying. And as the helo descended, an unpleasant chemical-type smell filtered into the cabin. How Skeeter thought he would make it through the DZ and into New Orleans was beyond Jack. Perhaps 'Skeeter' wasn't doing too much thinking. And if Skeeter was 'thinking,' maybe it was all about the destination, not the getting there. Skeeter had always been single-minded. It was as good as cinched once he'd set his mind on a particular outcome.

As soon as Jack jumped into the water, he felt the familiar absence of weight, feeling light and able to move in any direction with minimal effort. Even after the thousands of times he'd jumped into the water, he still felt that sense of keen anticipation and excitement – it was, after all, moving from one world into another. It all came naturally, and he equalized his ears without even thinking, even as he adjusted his buoyancy so that he remained at the correct depth. But it was the sense of freedom that he savored the most. Even now, with all the potentially life-ending variables swirling in his head, the initial sensation of submersion, of weightlessness, still did it for him. Jack welcomed the water's cold embrace.

Once again, Det heaved the buoyed lights out of the helo, their orange buoys denoting their position. Next, they shoved out the two similarly buoyed sound systems – Jack's new toys, which he hoped would ensure Skeeter came swinging their way. Once in the water, the SEALs' drift should match the buoys', so they shouldn't end up too far apart. About a hundred feet away, the blue suits' helo mirrored the stationary hover of its sister. Jack watched as its passengers slipped feet first, arms folded against chests, into the water. The helo then drew upward, moving to Jack's other side to facilitate the remaining team's entry into the sea. The three four-man teams would form a curve, its concave side facing outwards, southward. Jack's team was in the middle. This fact should have given some cause for comfort. It didn't. Instead, it made him feel hemmed in. Zads jumped in first, followed by Mac and Det. Jack was last.

The visual range was better than Jack had thought; not as good as the Florida Straits, but serviceable. Jack estimated that he could see up to thirty and forty-five feet, which meant he could just about catch the shadowy shapes of the other teams on both sides.

Jack activated the lights, pressing a red maintained push button on the jerry-rigged remote control attached to his suit's right forearm, creating an instantaneous underwater lightshow. The lights' beams slashed through the DZ murk. As before, the light humans couldn't see would attract Skeeter – infrared, ultraviolet, x-rays, and gamma. Next, time to turn on the music. Get down, low and dirty—no point in having a light show without the ear candy. Jack pressed the only other button on his remote, a yellow push. At once, the mournful rhythm of Deelie Thomas' Last Chance Blues pushed through the water. Jack was surprised at how good it sounded. For once, Navy-issue equipment was doing what it promised to do on the goddamned packaging. Okay, it was a little muffled, but it wasn't aimed at human consumption.

Sound traveled much faster through water, so if Skeeter were nearby, it would get to him damn quick. According to Tammes, Skeeter could 'hear' the music, but not in the same way as humans. Instead, Skeeter would experience the music through his body, through the vibrations. Tammes said that humans also experience music through vibrations, so, yes, it was possible that Skeeter would 'recognize' his favorite music. Jack also thought that if Skeeter recognized the music, it would appeal to his human side and maybe even signal Jack's presence and that he was available for an underwater tete-a-tete.

Whole lotta ifs, as Deelie said.

Take me to the last dance
Only have the one chance
Whole lotta ifs comin' my way

According to Clewton, each team was – more or less - equipped the same, which meant each team would have two net launchers and two harpooners. The team on Jack's right was Alpha T, Jack's was Bravo T, and the guys on the left were Charlie T. To avoid confusion, team leaders would only coordinate with their opposite numbers. Jack successfully established contact with Teams A and C, their respective leaders offering curt responses. The chilly reception and Jack's sense of something off surged again. He didn't need a love-in from these blue suits, but their sullen presence was grating big time.

He listened to his breathing in his earphones. Slow and measured, just as it should be. As they all hovered in the silence, the familiar feel of light pressure against the skin of his suit was, as always, reassuring. It was like the sea was holding him. In the past, he'd assumed that his enjoyment of the sensation was some manifestation of a primal desire to return to the safety of the womb. It was a thought he'd never pursued to any great extent. After all, he was a sailor, not a new-age guru.

Gradually, he became aware of the tiredness in his hands and realized he was gripping his harpoon too tightly. He was more wound up than he cared to admit. And the blue suits' overly manned presence was not helping. At the very least, they'd get in the goddamn way. Damn Clewton and his interfering. Jack suspected that the blue suits' presence was more about putting Jack in his place than operational efficiency. The tension between his team and theirs was chewable - it was like it was crawling inside his dive suit, trapped with nowhere to go.

For the moment, all was quiet. Yet every shadow, every peripheral visual shadow, and every ripple held the promise of instant death. The only sound was the swish of water against his suit. Time started to stretch. They'd only been in the water for minutes, but it felt like hours. The waiting, the vigil, this part was always the hardest. It was the anticipation, the expectation, that unmanned, coiling, hanging heavy in the water like an old-timey sea serpent. The battle, the confrontation itself, that was the easy part. But the strain of high tensile preparedness took it out of you, especially when you were exhausted, running on fumes you'd already burnt up.

Something swept in and out of view from below. It was so quick that Jack wondered if he'd imagined it. *Nerves. Trick of the light.* Not Skeeter. Even if what he thought he'd seen was a marine animal, it had no color. As Jack had suggested to Tammes, Skeeter's psychedelic carapace would have to be toned down if there were further iterations of what Skeeter had become.

'Jack,' Zads said. 'Did you see that?'

So he had seen something then. 'Trick of the light?' He squinted in the toxic murk. 'Det? Mac?'

'No, nothing,' Mac said.

'Negative, boss,' Det said.

'Teams A and C, catch anything beneath us?'

'Team A, negative, out.'

'Team C, negative, out.'

Jack said, 'What did you catch, Zads?'

'I don't want to sound like a fruit loop, and it happened so fast, but it … looked… like a person.'

'A person?'

'Yeah … swimming. Arms and legs. But it was so quick …'

'Tanaquil, this is Team B, over.'

'Tanaquil, over.' Clewton's voice was a little staticky but audible.

'Got any assets in the water I don't know about?'

Clewton paused. A long pause. Then, 'No. Confirm no assets … What's the problem?'

'Probably nothing,' Jack said. 'Team B, out.'

That was weird, Jack thought. *What's with the pause?* He didn't like that pause at all. And Clewton sounded off, too, more off than usual. One thing Jack was sure of, the admiral was not lying. Clewton gave off vocal tells when he was lying, and Jack hadn't detected any. No, it was as if the admiral had received bad news, and whatever that news was, it had put the willies up him.

'This is Team C, over.' The Team C leader's voice was low, almost a whisper.

'Go ahead, C,' Jack said.

'Looked like several contacts, forty feet, off my three o'clock. Hellish fast.'

'Looked like?' Jack said.

'Fast, ah, human swimmers. Just a glimpse, but …'

'Spit it out, C,' Jack said.

'Human-like, not … human.'

'Are you sure?'

'Negative,' C said. 'Like the lady said, too quick for visual certainty.'

Jack sighed. 'You seem cozy with Clewton. What's he not telling us?'

'It ain't this,' C said.

'Then what is it? What do you mean?'

'The admiral,' C said, 'he's telling the truth about these … potential unknowns.'

It ain't this, C had said. *Then what is it? What* is *Clewton lying about?* What was C not telling him?

Was this something to do with the seemingly omnipresent Forrest Sherman?

And then, a brief blast of low rumbling pulsated through the water, wrapping itself around his body, sneaking through his pores, messing with his vital organs. Skeeter's signature tune, his heavy-handed *hello*. The sudden nausea vanished.

A chill crept up Jack's belly and into his chest, and all thoughts fell out of his head. An icy cold – where there was no cold - pushed into his skin. In more ways than one, Skeeter was all around him.

There were no lights, no Last Dance Blues, no Zads, or other teams. No Clewton, no sullen blue suits, no mysterious unknowns. In Jack's world, all that existed was Skeeter, what Skeeter had become. Because there Skeeter was, hovering in the water, fifteen feet or so in front of him.

'Boss?' Mac asked.

Jack forced himself back into the here and now. 'Don't tell me,' he said, anticipating Mac's next utterance, 'We've got company.' Adding, 'Nobody does anything.' His voice was a distant echo as if someone else had spoken. 'Everyone, be still. No sudden movements.'

Skeeter drifted closer to Jack, his bright colors reflected and refracted by the combination of water and light show. It was clear that Skeeter wasn't doing too good. One of his claws was bent at an unnatural angle, and blood was leaking from a serrated hole in his carapace. Being in the DZ wasn't doing Skeeter any favors, either. Jack sensed that the creature was finding breathing difficult. As Skeeter drew closer, Jack willed himself to remain in place. He was ninety-nine percent sure that whatever constituted the vestigial parts of Skeeter's human side, Skeeter knew who he was – that here was his old buddy. The remaining five percent gave him heart palpitations.

A white noise-overloaded susurration briefly swamped Jack's stricken mind, and the world around him receded yet further. He gradually became aware that he wasn't alone in his thoughts, that there was another presence. One that didn't communicate with words and language but through emotions, feelings, and images—images of Skeeter.

Of Abena.

Of Jack.

A door, a portal, call it whatever, something had opened into Jack, and the part that endured as Skeeter was now within Jack, accessing his innermost thoughts and desires. But this process, this state, regardless, wasn't one-way; it was a sharing, and he, Jack, was in Skeeter's mind, Skeeter's consciousness. And then there was a jolt, a sharp stab of searing pain. Not physical pain, mind pain. Broken-heart pain. And Jack understood that Skeeter had read him too well – that he'd deciphered his ex-wife Abena's fate in the language of Jack's essence. That Abena was dead. Right down to the exact, precise second, Jack felt the fight go out of Skeeter. Skeeter's indomitable spirit that had seen him win so many battles over the years, the fire inside his old friend – mutant crustacean or human – died. And a million miles away, from within the still heart of the Dead Zone, came Mississippi Harry Jones' watery warble, his soulful rendition of See You Tomorrow.

Oh, lord have mercy on me

I don't know if I'm going to see tomorrow

Jack's right arm seemed to be moving of its own accord. It took a moment for him to understand that his arm, his hand, was being lifted gently by Skeeter's good claw. It was the hand that held the harpoon. With gut-wrenching insight, Jack knew what Skeeter was doing. Skeeter was asking Jack to kill him.

Jack shook his head, trying to bring images of Skeeter being transformed back into a man, a human being. But Skeeter pushed back and pushed into Jack, riding on a quiet, rolling wave of infinite blackness, profound dark. Peace. Skeeter was pleading for oblivion. And he wanted Jack to be the one who delivered it. Jack's arm ceased moving. The harpoon was now pointing into the ragged wound in Skeeter's carapace—a wound where Skeeter would be vulnerable.

As Jack's finger squeezed the harpoon's trigger, somebody grabbed both his shoulders from behind, jerking him around.

CHAPTER 37

Team FT1
Tuesday, 0922 hours
Mississippi Dead Zone

At first, Jack had assumed someone – probably Zads – had pulled him back because they thought they were protecting him from Skeeter. It wasn't until Jack saw a red cloud spiraling out of his forearm that he realized he was under attack, and the red cloud was, in fact, his blood. He'd been knife-slashed, his weapon arm. Somebody had yanked him backward, incapacitating his weapon hand at the same time. As the flash of steel arced toward his heart he parried the attacker's knife arm out of its lethal trajectory. A smooth, lightning-quick move he was almost unaware of executing. As the blue suit leaned into Jack, following the momentum of his attack, Jack jabbed him in the throat with the knuckles of his right hand. The slash across his arm hadn't cut any major arteries. The blue suit's hands moved automatically to his ruptured throat as if their presence would somehow help. The man's eyes looked out of his mask with hatred and terror as he tried to get air into his lungs.

Take me to the last dance
Only have the one chance
Whole lotta ifs comin' my way

Jack recovered his harpoon, which had been dangling on its lanyard since the unexpected attack, and brought it up neatly so that it was aimed at the man's torso, ready to deliver the coup de grace. His throat jab had not been powerful enough to cause fatal damage. The spear meant for Skeeter was now going to find another home. Jack froze. He caught himself about to kill another man, a fellow human being. The freeze lasted for less than a second, but it packed in a shit-ton of compressed thoughts. *Erin. She'll clock the death smell on me. She'll know. She'll just know.*

Better that than not returning at all.

Unfreeze.

As the oxygen-deprived blue suit continued to writhe before him, Jack caught a flash of brilliant color on his nine, about twenty-five feet away. And then it was gone. Skeeter. Still alive, then. On his three, black-suited divers battled hand-to-hand with the blue suits. Jack's team was outnumbered, and it was only a matter of time before they succumbed. He had to do something.

Two more blue suits were swimming toward the melee. These guys were aiming their weapons at Jack's guys. One of the weapons was an APS assault rifle that fired flechettes, better than regular ammo under water. The other guy's weapon, Jack didn't recognize. But it fired regular bullets, not darts. He knew because in the fractured second of his unfreeze, one of those bullets took Det in the shoulder, the force of it knocking him ass over tit. Deliberately or accidentally, as he backward somersaulted, a net shot out from Det's launcher, wrapping around one of the blue suits.

Det floated upside down, blood flowing from his wound. Not good. Immersion in seawater didn't allow for any healing process, including clotting. Jack glanced down at his arm wound. The blood flow had stilled to a trickle. Superficial, then. Not deep.

The two incoming blue suits were now preparing to fire again. Jack had to do something. He raised his harpoon at the nearest blue suit, the one with the APS, and prepared to fire. The guy with the other weapon— which looked like an underwater version of an AK—spotted Jack and turned toward him, aiming his rifle at him. Jack gave in to simple self-preservation and let his body do the talking, his harpoon swinging quickly toward the APS blue suit.

Because now it wasn't just about saving his skin. If he was dead, how would he give Skeeter peace? If he was dead, how would he protect Zads and Mac? If he was dead, how would he get back to Erin so she could roast his ass?

Then, before he could fire, from behind Jack, swimming above him, a blur of streaking -gray-green. He lost sight of it almost instantly. It was there, and then it wasn't. And when he refocused on the guy with the AK, the AK pointing at Jack, the man had vanished.

The hell?

Jack recalled the odd shapes he'd seen flitting around before. Zads had seen them, too. What was going on here?

Sensing movement out to his left, Jack spun around. The throat guy had recovered and was now coming for Jack, arms outstretched. Jack didn't wait to find out what the man thought he was going to accomplish with such a clumsy move and veered to his attacker's left, sweeping with his knife as he passed. The man's throat spurted arterial blood into the deoxygenated water. Jack moved away from the dying man and propelled himself toward Zads and Mac. It was four blue suits against two, and both Zads and Mac were wounded. They remained alive because close-quarter combat didn't allow the blue suits to use their underwater assault weaponry.

A blue suit was hanging back out of the scrum, aiming at Zads. Now beyond thinking mode, Jack just took the shot, and the man tumbled away into the murk, leaving a trail of swirling scarlet. At the same time, Zads managed to slash one of the blue suits across the chest, and he retreated, followed by his two buddies.

Jack swam over to Zads and Mac.

'How bad is it?' he said, taking in the thigh of her slashed neoprene suit.

'Looks worse than it is,' said Zads, giving herself a quick once over. 'Hurts like hell, but just skin deep.'

'Ditto,' said Mac, briefly studying his wound – a gash across the palm of his hand.

'Stay here,' said Jack, glancing over to Det. 'Back to back. There are four more of these blue suits out there. Use the net and harpoon if you have to. These guys, whoever they are, don't want us to get out of the water. And switch to Foxtrot Team One comms only. We don't want them knowing what we're doing.' He swam over to where Det was hanging in the water, blood flowing freely from his shoulder. 'Det?'

'Still here, boss,' Det said weakly.

Jack looked at the man's eyes behind the mask. His eyes were becoming glazed, and he seemed to be staring over Jack's shoulder at something behind Jack. Jack had seen that glaze, that look, before. Det was dying - a shoulder shot very often caused arterial blood to spill into the lungs.

'Still here,' Det said again, coughing, as he stared even more intensely at something beyond Jack, something approaching. Jack looked behind him. There was nothing there. Or was there? Fleetingly, Jack thought he might have caught another blue-green shimmer so quickly that it was like the idea of movement rather than the move itself.

Jack returned to his dying comrade. Det's eyes were closed. He was gone. Jack gently held onto Det's lifeless arm and squeezed it. 'Fair winds, buddy,' he said.

When he returned to Zads and Mac, Zads said, 'Is Det ...?'

'Yeah.'

As Zads absorbed the news, Mac said, 'Hell's going on, Jack?'

'The blue suits. Clewton ordered them to keep his asset alive. They saw me about to kill it. Skeeter. They know we're not on the same page anymore. Makes us expendable.'

'Aw, it's no fun being disposable,' Mac said.

'You were gonna kill it ... Skeeter, I mean?' Zads asked.

'Yeah,' Jack said. 'I think so.' *Was I?*

'Why?' Zads said. 'I thought you wanted Skeeter alive. Clewton and Tammes said there was a way back for him.'

'I don't know if I believe that,' Jack said. 'Besides, Skeeter ...'

'Skeeter what?' Zads asked.

'I think he ... he was in my head or I was ... he wants to die.'

'He was in your *head*?' Zads said.

'Yeah ... like, ah, telepathy, I guess. It was weird.'

'So, what? You he think read your mind? Knows his wife is dead?'

'It's nuts, but yes. Exactly that.'

'Hate to say it, folks,' Mac said, 'but with Skeeter out of the picture, there goes our way out of this mess.'

Jack said, 'He's not out of the picture. He's out there somewhere, and those blue suit bastards are looking for him.'

'I'll say again,' Mac said. 'You're still intending to rip up our get-out-of-jail voucher?'

Kill Skeeter. No. Set him free. Stop his pain. I'd want him to do the same for me.

'Mac's right, Jack. With Skeeter ... gone, we serve no purpose. We're loose ends. They'll be coming for us.'

'So we convince Clewton that we're not a threat – it's our only chance.'

'How do we do that?'

'Clewton's taken comms down so that no one on the surface can hear the admiral's blue suits offing Navy SEALs. Comms down, it works both ways. Those up there don't need to know what's gone on down here.'

'What happens underwater, stays underwater?' Mac said.

'That means -'

'It means,' said Jack, 'we take out the remaining blue suits. The only truth that resurfaces is our truth. And our truth is that Skeeter took out the blue suits. That's all Clewton needs to know. And that while the blue suits defended themselves against Skeeter, *they* offed Skeeter in the process.'

'Do we go after them?' Zads asked.

'No need. When the blue suits can't find Skeeter – and they won't – they'll come to us. Tidy things up.'

'What, we just wait until they come back?'

'Yeah, but not here. We need to get further behind the lights, behind the Delta blues. We need the advantage. The sun in their eyes, so to speak. The blue suits went off in a southerly direction, so they'll likely return that way. They won't have the time or the energy to outflank us. How are we doing for oxygen?'

Jack's SEALs had decided to ditch supplementary tanks for ease of movement, which meant there was no backup for their primary rebreathers. When they were out, they were out. And though they weren't that deep, they'd been pretty active. Active enough to dent air supplies.

'I got twenty,' Zads said.

'Thirty,' said Mac.

'Twenty-five,' said Jack. 'Okay, let's get in situ.'

As they swam to a deeper position behind the light and audio buoys, Zads said, 'What about the elephant in the room, guys? Is no one gonna bring that up?'

'Which elephant's that?' Mac asked. 'I've counted at least five.'

'She means we're not alone,' Jack said. 'We've got unknowns on the chess board.'

'Shit,' said Mac. 'You saw those, too? I thought I was seeing things. Like sleep deprivation hallucinations or something.'

'I'm not a hundred percent,' Jack said, 'but I swear I saw one of those things take out a blue suit.'

'Not Clewton's, then?' Zads said.

'Doesn't seem like it,' Jack said. 'Who are they? And why are they rooting for us?'

'We got company,' Mac said tiredly, as if wearying of his running joke.

The remaining blue suits emerged from the gloom, weirdly in sync with the four-four beat of Skeeter's favorite Delta blues, as if the whole thing were choreographed by some unseen hand.

CHAPTER 38

Team FT1
Tuesday, 1011 hours
Mississippi Dead Zone

Out of the gloom, three blue suits emerged, swimming in a tight arrow formation. If Mac could get the right angle, he could take all three out with his net launcher. By Jack's calculations, the blue suits should have numbered four. Maybe Skeeter had taken out the missing guy. Or maybe whatever else was out there had.

Echoing his thoughts, Zads said, 'Shouldn't there be four?'

'Zads, keep a watch across the full one-eight-o,' said Jack. 'I don't want any surprises.'

'Boss,' Zads said, immediately commencing checks on the three cardinal points not covered by Jack and Mac.

'I'm going to draw them in. Mac, if you can get them lined up, take them all out with the net.'

As Jack made a beeline for the blue suits, Mac broke away from him, moving to the blue suits' nine.

'Seems to be clear,' Zads reported.

'Okay, Zads. You cover Mac, not me. He's taking the shot.'

'Chief,' Zads whispered as if she thought the blue suits could hear her.

A glimmering effect caught Jack's eye. Flechettes, catching the light above, reflecting it, giving Jack less than a second to roll out of their way. The flechettes zinged by Jack, their water-distorted, elongated bodies missing him by mere inches. No noise accompanied the lethally swift, streamlined object. As he yawed to his front, he caught a brief glimpse of Mac, steadying his launcher, taking aim.

Jack fired a harpoon into the middle of the blue suit formation, taking out the lead diver. The man smashed into the two guys behind him, scattering them like nine pins. They recovered quickly, one aiming at Jack, the other at Mac. More shimmering arcs of deadly light shot toward Jack. This time, he wasn't quick enough to get out of the way, and he felt two thudding impacts on his upper thigh, causing him to accidentally misfire a spear that sailed harmlessly by the remaining blue suits. As Jack struggled to raise his gun, the diver who'd shot him moved in for the kill. And then, like magic, a harpoon appeared in the man's chest – Zads! - instantly leaking blood out of his suit. The man looked down stupidly as if he refused to believe the fact of his skewering.

The tell-tale dull pop of the net launcher on Jack's three caused him to swing around just in time to see the remaining blue suit entrapped in its deadly clutches. He made to regroup with Zads and Mac, but he remained stationary. His right leg refused to move, and his slashed arm now felt numb and sluggish.

Shit.

Instead, Mac and Zads joined him.

'I know I'm stating the obvious, boss, but we've got to get you out of the water.'

'But Skeeter,' Jack said, 'we need -'

As Mac came alongside Zads, he glanced up, glaring at something behind Jack. 'Oh, sweet Jesus,' he whispered.

Zads looked away from Jack, following Mac's line of sight. 'Sacre goddamn bleu,' she said.

What now? Jack thought, painfully twisting around.

Materializing out of the Dead Zone gloom, five, six, *shit,* eight blue suit divers. 'I've got two spears left,' Jack said quickly. 'Zads?'

'Three. I think.'

'And three short,' Mac said grimly. 'I got nothing.'

'Zads, Mac. Get out of here. I'll hold them off. I'll only slow you down.'

'*Non*, Boo,' Zads said. 'We stay where we are. Make every harpoon count.'

'Never know,' Mac added. 'Might get lucky.'

Doubt it, thought Jack, relieved he wouldn't die alone. Too tired, too weak to argue. When Zads got a bee in her ass, it was pointless anyway.

And then an array of shimmering darts came at them. One caught Jack in the calf of his other leg, and a fresh spiral of cloudy red bloomed from his suit. A stray flechette struck the edge of one of Zads' flippers. 'Damn,' she said.

Jack didn't have the energy to cry out. He was fading, he knew, and fast, an image of Erin forming in his mind's eye. *At least I won't be alone when I check out,* he thought. And then, *Have I already thought that?*

He was dimly aware of Mac lifting Jack's harpoon gun, its lanyard stretched to the limit. Mac was firing, Zads, too. More deadly glimmers of light flashed by. And way, way out in the distance, someone sang the blues. Sang the blues about how so goddamn blue they were—just like the sea, like the Caribbean.

As Mac tugged again on the lanyard to get a better line of fire, Jack spun around, now facing the attackers—another spear from Zads. Then, *I'm out.*

'One left,' said Mac, aiming for the last time.

'Sorry, guys,' Jack whispered, watching the blue suits advance, then stop, expertly hovering, raising their weapons for the final kill.

Jack closed his eyes, waiting for the inevitable perforation of his dive suit, his body. Found he wasn't afraid to die. Sad, though. So, so sad he would never get to be with Erin ever again. And, yes, a little pissed off. There were so many things he still wanted to do. And … *Why am I still alive?*

He'd had the singular thought the second time in as many days.

He opened his eyes. The blue suits' line was in disarray. *The hell?* And then he saw why. Those weird gray-green flashes were back. Slick, serpentine movement. Darting in and out of the blue suits, slicing them, cutting, with a curved, extended … what? Sword? The blue suits who still lived slowly disappeared in a fog of their blood, glancing frantically around, Jack and his team forgotten. Now, an attack from below, those sword things slashing upward, some between the blue suits' legs, cleaving them, one body half falling away from the other, slowly, strangely balletic in the water's lesser density.

Jack could hear Zads and Mac in his ears, but he had no idea what they were saying. It was like they were speaking a different language. He struggled to concentrate, afraid of missing something important. Before realizing his worry, his concern was that of a living man, not a dying one. *I don't need to give a shit about anything ever again.*

But I do. I do need to give a shit. Why?

And then, out of the billowing clouds of red, a rainbow formed. Long seconds passed before Jack comprehended what he was seeing.

More unintelligible words from Zads and Mac. What were *they* on about? And why had they stopped speaking English?

The rainbow—it was Skeeter's technicolored carapace. *Ah, that's why I have to have a care. I've got to do the honors. For Skeeter. See him alright.*

I'm dying, that's what. I'm shutting down, ceasing all operations, and clocking off, but not before I've done right by my buddy.

From somewhere and nowhere, Jackson Dupree was singing about how lonesome he was. Poor Jackson, poor Skeeter. All of us, fucking poor all of us.

As Skeeter approached slowly, with an eerie dignity, Jack felt a tug on his lanyard. Mac was raising Jack's harpoon gun. Jack turned to Mac and shook his head. Mac resisted for a few seconds before letting the weapon go. Using his dodgy hand, Jack nudged it into his good hand, lifting it until it pointed directly at Skeeter. Skeeter stopped, hovering for a moment, before positioning himself onto the barrel of the harpoon, its tip now snug inside his carapace. Just as he'd done earlier before they'd been so rudely interrupted. The weapon was wedged inside Skeeter, and all Jack had to do was squeeze the trigger until there was no squeeze left. Jack stared into Skeeter's compound eyes, the light in the many eyes, one by one fading, blinking out. And then Skeeter was in his head. Like before, but also not. There were no pictures, no messages, only a presence, a presence without requests or demands, only a presence that needed to be acknowledged.

I feel you, buddy, Jack thought as he reached the last of the trigger's squeeze, and his one remaining spear dug deep into Skeeter's body. For a moment, nothing. Then Zads and Mac shouted in that curious language, the one he'd never learned. There was a tug on his lanyard, and Jack was wrenched forward into Skeeter's carapace. Skeeter was sinking, taking Jack with him. The gun was stuck good and proper, and the lanyard was still shackled to Jack's suit.

As Jack descended, Zads and Mac's voices became even louder and more incoherent. He knew one thing: the voices were desperate and panicked. Their hands scrabbled at his arms, his waist, but he was sinking too fast. Why, anyway, would they want to stop him from sinking, from going with his buddy?

Then, the many-colored hue of Skeeter's rainbow shell turned gray and black. Then nothing.

CHAPTER 39

Team FT1
Tuesday, 1032 hours
Mississippi Dead Zone

As Skeeter sank into the depths, taking Jack with him, Zads grabbed hold of the lanyard with one hand and slid her knife out of its sheath with the other. Skeeter seemed to shift position as he descended, causing Jack to roll over. Jack's eyes were open, and he appeared fully conscious yet unblinking. A smile played around his mouth, and he shook his head. '*No, Zads,*' he said, with great difficulty, his voice the barest of whispers. Ignoring him, she brought the knife to bear on the rope, keeping Jack attached to Skeeter. But as she moved to bring down the cutting stroke, Skeeter lurched again, dragging Jack away from her once more, violently jerking the knife out of her hand.

Zads once more dove for Jack, but the rate of his descent was speeding up, probably as Skeeter's carapace flooded. Skeeter was, she realized, like a ship that the sea had breached. She reckoned she was at around eighty feet, fast reaching the point where the nitrogen build-up would impair her judgment. If she followed Skeeter any deeper, she wouldn't even be aware she was running out of air, asphyxiating. In the deeper gloom of the depths, she was losing sight of Skeeter and Jack, and all she could catch was a glimpse of a rainbow, a rainbow being consumed by the abyss.

Suddenly, something grabbed her right calf and gave it a fierce tug. She spun around, half-expecting to see another bunch of blue suits arriving for round three. But it was a black suit. Mac.

She felt herself relax, allowing herself to be wrenched out of her downward trajectory. She let Mac drag her up, up toward the surface, the light. She was aware of Mac shouting in her ears, but she couldn't understand a word he was saying, only that whatever it was, it sounded like he was angry. She wondered who it was he was furious with. It was very rarely that Mac lost his temper. Even in the heat of battle, he was always eerily composed. Always there for you. Got Your Back Mac was his brand, his trademark. So why was he practically screaming in her headset?

As they ascended, a wave of nausea passed through her, and she thought she was going to puke into her mask. Mac must have sensed something was wrong because he stopped shouting and looked at her, catching her eyes and making sure she was still conscious, she guessed. And by the time they'd swapped eye contact, the feeling of imminent vomiting stations passed, and Mac resumed his rescue.

By the time they hit the surface, Zads felt much better, more or less back in her senses. Less woozy.

'You okay?' Mac said.

Still getting breath back, Zads gave him the OK sign.

'We need a plan,' Mac said, looking around.

Zads did a quick three-sixty, observing two items of interest. On relative bearings at three o'clock, around ten miles distant, was the creepy warship that had been in attendance since the picket line—the one that had vexed Jack so.

Jack!

Jack was gone—it didn't seem possible. Even when he wasn't present, he was always present—not that she'd ever tell him that.

The other item of more immediate relevance, a high-speed craft of about a hundred tons, was aiming in their direction at about thirty knots.

Zads waited for Mac to say it. He didn't let her down. 'We got company.'

'The Clewton kind of company?'

'These days, what other kind is there?'

As the vessel drew closer, Zads got a better look at it. 'It's got the Tanaquil logo. She's a CTV, a crew transfer vessel. Probably a crew of three, maybe four.'

'That's good news,' Mac said.

Zads understood what he meant. 'Civilians.'

'Yeah,' said Mac. 'I don't think they're gonna off us with an audience.'

'They don't have to. As Louis A said, they've got all the time in the world.'

'Apart from not getting killed, Zads, what's the plan?'

'You need to be the mangenue to my ingenue,' Zads said.

'Yeah, that's not helping any,' Mac said wearily.

'We play it innocent, play it straight like how Jack said. Skeeter killed the blue suits. And Det. Jack. That's it.'

'Do you think Clewton'll buy it?'

'I don't know, but we can always muddy the waters by mentioning the unknowns, the green-gray things, put a little extra in the pot, a pinch of misdirection.'

As the CTV approached Zads and Mac, she slowed down. On deck, Clewton and Tammes, Graaf and Dantz were leaning over the port guardrails. Even from this distance, Zads could feel the animosity seeping out of Clewton's pores.

You're a dead man, Admiral. You just don't know it yet.

Her whole life she'd built, her career, her standing in the world was about to burn. Jack would be avenged. Skeeter, too. Cal. Det. And Harps. She turned to Mac. 'I've got to tell you something. In addition to the plan.'

Mac turned to her with raised eyebrows. 'Oh, yeah?'

Zads told him.

When she'd finished saying what she needed to say, the CTV was now close enough for Zads to read its name, the *Ponce de Leon,* out of New Orleans. Two crew members collapsed a section of guardrail, unrolling a heavy-duty, weighted, scrambling net. Zads, with a supine, apparently unconscious Mac, attempted to swim but failed. She could hear Clewton swearing and shouting at the crew members. She watched as the crew guys disappeared aft. Moments later, a small RIB attached to the stern davits dangled over the sea, two crew aboard, while a third operated the hydraulics, lowering her. Once the RIB broke away from the *Ponce*, she sped toward Zads and the prone Mac. As the Cox brought the RIB to a stop, the other guy helped to roll Mac's dead weight into the boat. Zads indicated that she, too, was injured and required help. The RIB sped back to the CTV with the two SEALs safely aboard.

The RIB was now once more attached to *Ponce's* davits, and Zads and Mac were helped down by the Ponce crew, Mac still unconscious. Two crewmen lifted Mac between them and dragged him inside the vessel to a cramped galley. Zads let the third guy help her, reckoning on at least four crew members. There had to be a guy at the helm. She hoped they were neutrals and not working for Clewton. That meant only the admiral and his two idiots would be a problem.

As the crew laid Mac on a galley table, unzipping his suit, Clewton and Tammes, then Graaf and Dantz, entered. Clewton nodded toward Mac. 'He going to be alright?'

Zads shrugged, making a show of being in pain when she sat down on one of the galley's luridly orange plastic chairs. 'He got in the way of the target. I think his ribs are broken or worse. Chest crushed.'

'We gotta get this guy ashore,' the blond guy said.

'Or to the rig,' Clewton said, using his admiral voice, the one that brooked no dissent. 'She's got a perfectly serviceable sickbay.' He turned to Zads. 'And you?'

'I got hitched on an unwanted ride. There was too much nitrogen. I'm still a little out of it.'

Clewton glared at her, nodding. 'Jack? Det?'

'Gone. Det got sliced by the target. The Chief, he -'

'The target,' Clewton said, leaning down into Zads' face, 'the asset, what's the -'

'*Skeeter*,' said Zads firmly. 'Jack killed Skeeter. And ... the Chief, he became entangled with – they went down together.'

'Damn shame,' said Tammes.

Ignoring Tammes, Zads looked up at Clewton. The admiral's face was a mix of emotions: anger that his billion-dollar asset had been lost and relief that Skeeter had been neutralized. Zads had noticed, too, the tiny flicker of satisfaction on Tammes' face when he heard Jack hadn't made it. From these twos' perspective, two birds with one stone—big problem solved, *and* vengeance all rolled up in the shape of Jack's death.

She knew the admiral still hadn't decided whether Zads' ignorance act was genuine. Eventually, he said, 'Alright, give me the details.'

So she told truths and half-truths. About how they were attacked by Skeeter, who, even though he was injured and was finding it hard to breathe inside the Dead Zone, was still a force to contend with. How Skeeter took out all of the blue suits. *Slaughtered* them. And then Det. Mac crushed in his pincer. But when he came for Jack, something stopped Skeeter from killing him. Whether it was because some part of Skeeter remembered his friend or because the creature was at that point dying, she didn't know. And Jack, she said, went off script. Jack shot Skeeter, and Skeeter took Jack down with him, entangled in his harpoon gun's lanyard ...

She let the tears come. It wasn't an act. Even big girls cry. And if Clewton had had doubts about her story, now, she knew, he didn't. Tammes, too.

'And ... you, you didn't see anything ... else down there, anything ...' Clewton trailed off.

Zads cleared her tears. 'I don't know, sir. As I said, it all happened quickly and was pretty murky. But, I think -'

'Yes? *Yes?*' The admiral leaned in even further, eyes blazing.

'We—I mean, all of us—thought we saw another ... team, but there was something off about their suits, their dive suits. About their suits. I've never seen a suit like that, that color, that design before—it was like the suit was a ... alive or something, like a bio-suit, maybe?'

While Zads talked about the mysterious interlopers, the admiral's face had paled, and he glanced over at Tammes, then to the usually impassive Graaf and Dantz. Their bruised faces contrasted sharply with the pallor of their skin. *They all know,* she thought, *about the green suits, the ones who'd helped them, and they're afraid of them.*

Into the silence, the admiral dismissed *Ponce's* crew. After they left, the admiral paced the room.

Dantz said, 'Sir, it could mean nothing. You know how they like to interfere, stick their noses where they shouldn't.'

The admiral stopped. 'Yes, but what if *they* know? Have you thought about that?'

'I don't see how they could know,' said Tammes.

'How do you explain their presence? On the picket line. Now *here*. There was no request for an assist. Or if there was, I didn't know about it.'

'Sir?' Zads said. 'Who's *they*?'

'Something you don't need to know about, Petty Officer.'

'But I do, don't I? I mean, know about the … other team?'

Again, Clewton stopped his nervous pacing. 'Yes, you do, don't you? In fact, Petty Officer Breaux, come to think of it, you know rather a lot about everything.'

'It comes with the territory, sir,' Zads said, bracing herself. 'Over the years, I've amassed a library's worth of so-called above top secret tittle-tattle, and I haven't loaned out one of those books once. I'm a goddamn solid bet, sir.'

Clewton rolled his eyes. 'While your service has been exemplary, Ms Breaux, we all have a shelf life, a limited usefulness span. And this is, I think, where you reach that expiration date.'

Knowing what was coming, Tammes back-stepped neatly out of the way.

As Clewton turned toward Graaf and Dantz, Zads punched Mac's arm, the one dangling off the table. Before either of Clewton's bodyguards knew what was happening, Mac had stuck his punch knife into Graaf's heart several times and was already turning on Clewton, who stood stunned, shocked at the speed of the way things had gone southerly. Dantz, meanwhile, was on his back after a sharp kick to his testicles and knee to his forehead, courtesy of Zads' feet. Zads scooped up Dantz' suppressed pistol and shot him twice in the face.

Spinning round, she saw that Mac had Clewton in a neck hold, the latter turning a satisfying shade of puce. No, scrub that – *mauve*. Zads moved smoothly over to Tammes, now raising his arms in surrender, and headbutted him on his nose, dropping him like a lead weight. She then swiveled smoothly over to Clewton and patted him down. She nodded at Mac, who shoved the already-crumpling admiral across the shiny, buffed floor. 'Tu es l'ange de la mort, Admiral. You got a lot of people dead.'

Clewton struggled to rest on his elbow, wincing, as he gingerly rubbed his throat, coughing, trying to speak, failing. Tammes was out cold.

Zads strode up to him and knelt. 'No, Admiral. No talking. No one is listening. Here's what happens now.'

CHAPTER 40

Crew Transfer Vessel *Ponce de Leon*
Tuesday, 1124 hours
Mississippi Dead Zone

Away in the distance, the unknown, modified Forrest Sherman destroyer set a course that was aimed directly at the *Ponce de Leon*. |Through the binoculars, Zads considered the now-approaching vessel. Jack's freaky ship, she thought sadly. Jack had not been kidding. Up this close, the Sherman was one screwy lady. Her physical contradictions aside, she also seemed to be affecting her immediate environment. The water surrounding the Sherman appeared slightly darker and more reflective than the surrounding ocean, creating a faint, eerie halo around the ship.

Experimental cloaking device?

Occasionally, barely visible ripples hinted at something moving beneath the surface. *The gray-green dudes?* The sky above the Sherman was mostly clear, but there were odd patches of unusually dense, small clouds. The clouds kept up with the ship, moving and swirling in a most uncloud-like fashion, casting brief, strange shadows over the ship.

More cloaking shit?

Zads lowered the skipper's binoculars, turning to Mac. 'What do you think?'

Mac shrugged. 'It's another complication we can do without. We've gotta be gone by the time she gets here – if we are her destination. She might not be approaching. She might be …'

'Picking up their guys? The gray-green guys?' Zads looked around *Ponce's* cramped bridge. Both Clewton and Tammes were hogtied with blue three-eighths thick polypropylene rope and lay on the deck against the chart table next to the destroyed radio equipment. The *Ponce* was now without comms. The captain and his three crew were huddled on the starboard side of the bridge, Mac aiming the pistol he'd taken from Graaf. He wouldn't need it anytime soon.

Addressing the crew, Zads said, 'You guys got nothing to worry about. This situation, for you, is merely an inconvenience. The only individuals on this bridge who should be fearing for their lives are these pieces of shit.' She pointed at the supine admiral, the yet-groggy Tammes, his wrecked face an explosion of blood and cartilage.

Behind his gag, Clewton's eyes bulged as he tried to speak. She turned once more to the CTV sailors. 'This old warship, here. Is she a regular in these waters?'

The captain, a short, bald fellow in his fifties, stepped forward and held out his hands, indicating the bins. 'May I?'

Zads passed him the glass, and he moved to the bridge screen window, raising the bins to his eyes. 'Hmm.'

'Hmm?'

The skipper lowered the binoculars. 'Old Forrest Sherman, right? I was in the Navy, never served on one, but I've been up close to 'em. I haven't seen this particular vessel, but there are others of a similar, ah, nature out there. Out in the Gulf.'

'Similar?'

'Yeah,' the skipper said, returning the bins to Zads. 'You know, modded up, downgraded, upgraded, whatever—a couple of old-school frigates and destroyers. I suppose I just assumed they were un-mothballing ships and recommissioning. You know, defense cuts. The Navy does what it does.'

'You got that right,' Zads agreed.

'Like God,' the *Ponce's* skipper continued, warming to his subject. 'The Navy works in mysterious ways. I learned not to ask too many questions. And to be honest, I'm not that curious a fellow.'

Zads nodded curtly to the skipper before quickly approaching Clewton, ripping the masking tape off his mouth. 'What's going on with this Forrest Sherman, these ... other ships? Are they this DESRON 13 everybody whispers about? Were those guys in the bio-suits from this ship?'

Clewton licked his lips. 'Can I have some water, please?'

'No,' Zads said firmly, also ignoring Tammes' gag-muffled protestations. 'Answer the question.'

Clewton swallowed, licking his lips again. 'Yeah, DESRON 13, it's a thing. Has been for a long time. In the days of sail, it was Flotilla 13. And when the Ironclads ruled the sea, Destroyer 13. And, yes, the combatants in the ... hi-tech suits are from the Thirteen.'

'And they're USN?'

'Oh, yes,' Clewton said. 'They're USN, alright. Unfortunately.'

'DESRON 13?' Mac said. 'Thought that was all BS.'

'You've been on enough black sails ops, McCloud,' Clewton said. 'The Thirteen's just several notches above what you're used to. It always has been and always will be.'

'But what's it for?' Mac pushed. Zads could tell he was taking the existence of DESRON 13 personally. Like her, he was sick to the teeth with all the creepy secret-ass designations, the teams within teams, the boys' clubs. It wore you out. You had in mind a clear picture of what the Navy was, what it stood for, and then the goddamn rug was pulled out from under your sweaty, flippered feet.

'Why are they here?' Zads shook her head, big-time confused, big-time pissed off. 'Is it to do with Skeeter? Is what you did to him something to do with them?'

The admiral seemed to slump. 'I don't know. Yeah, probably. We, ah, me and Lucas, that is, appropriated something of theirs we perhaps shouldn't have.'

'Zads?' Mac said, gesturing to the approaching ship. 'We've got to get out of here.'

Zads grimaced in frustration. Things were moving too quickly, and she needed help to figure out who the players were. Frustrated, she turned once more to *Ponce's* skipper. 'Okay. Launch the RIB. This is where we say goodbye, Captain.' Zads gestured to the crew. 'Bring Clewton. Tammes, too. They're coming with us.'

'No, Zads,' Mac said. 'They'll slow us the fuck down. And the Navy will want them back. They won't be as bothered about finding us sans admiral and his mad scientist bitch.'

Zads grunted, vexed, but seeing the sense of Mac's case. 'In that case, we off them now.' She took out her knife, brandishing it in Clewton's face. Clewton let out an unmanly squeal and a damp patch appeared, spreading rapidly around his crotch. 'For Jack, for Det and Cal. Harps, too. And for Skeeter.' She laid the edge of the knife on Clewton's throat, pausing.

Mac stepped into the pause, holding her arm, gently lifting it. 'Not in cold blood, Zads. It's not who we are.'

Zads willed the rage to seep out of her, taking a couple of deep breaths and letting it out slowly. Mac was right. Half right. He was a killer, not a murderer. It was a distinction that allowed him to sleep at night. Most nights. However, Zads wasn't sure about herself. The grip on the knife tightened. She could see in her mind's eye how it would go for Clewton. *A deep incision on the front of his neck. An incision that began its journey below the ear, deepening until it severed the admiral's left carotid artery. Clewton struggling for air as blood filled his trachea.*

'Can't play God, Zads,' Mac added gently.

'Pity,' she said. 'I'd do a better job. There would be more justice in the world.'

'Zads, enough.'

She nodded, rising to her feet and sheathing the knife. She looked out of the slanted bridge window. The Forrest Sherman had stopped in the

—

water about five miles away. And the ship did, indeed, look like it might be recovering something from the water. Without consulting Mac, she sliced her knife through Clewton and Tammes' bonds, both men flinching, eyes wide with terror. 'Get up.'

The admiral and the scientist rose shakily to their feet. 'Outside,' she ordered, gesturing to the starboard bridge wing. The two men, beaten and browed, silently shuffled through the door, Zads following, pushing, prodding them forward.

'Zads?' Mac said, a warning in his voice.

'Don't worry, Mac. It's only swim time.'

'But -' Clewton started.

'Hypoxic bathing, Admiral, it's all the rage, don't you know? A little bit of Dead Zone therapy – do you a world of good.'

Behind his gag, Tammes seemed to be hyperventilating.

'What's that, Doc?' Zads laughed. 'Didn't catch any of that.'

'C'mon, Zads,' Mac said. 'This isn't going to work if we don't leave now. The real Navy's going to be on asses soon, looking for these two chumps.'

Zads turned to Mac. 'That's why these two can go for a swim. Then they can be picked up by those guys.' She pointed at the incoming destroyer, the creepy-looking Forrest Sherman.

'No,' said Clewton, shaking his head. 'I can't go on there, not with them. Please, God, not with them.'

Behind his gag, Zads noticed that Tammes seemed to agree with Clewton. The man's eyes seemed to be in danger of exploding out of their sockets. 'Admiral, Dr Tammes, I have no idea why you are both taking on so. What's got you so agitated? A little swim, then picked up by your friends on yonder spooky-ass destroyer. A hot cup of coffee. What's not to like?'

For once, Clewton was speechless. Instead, he watched the destroyer – underway and approaching again - with awe and horror, slowly shaking his head.

'Zads!' barked out Mac. 'For fuck's sake!'

With one practiced move, Zads unclipped the guardrail lock, and as the rail fell away, she unceremoniously kicked Clewton and Tammes into the sea. *Ditching the garbage*, she thought.

'ZADS!' Mac shouted.

Zads offered a dainty little wave at the two men in the water. As Clewton screamed something unintelligible, she turned away. 'Okay, Mac. Let's go.' Re-entering the bridge, she looked for the skipper. Found him. 'Three things, Captain. Do not pick up the men in the water. Allow the modded Sherman *that* pleasure. Two. Don't be here when she arrives. Get the fuck away. Three. The RIB got enough fuel to get us to Texas?'

'We can give you extra cans.'

'Do it,' Zads said as Mac left the bridge with one of the *Ponce* crewmen. When Zads herself stepped out onto the tiny afterdeck, Mac was already sitting in the brow of the RIB. When they were lowered into the water, Zads sat at the hand tiller, the engine going full out. Safely away from *Ponce*, Mac shouted, 'Why the fuck Texas?'

'Not Texas!' she yelled back. 'Mississippi Delta. Swamp lands. My natural habitat. We can stay there while we figure out what to do.'

While Mac considered what to do, Zads considered the water they skimmed over—Dead Zone water. This Dead Zone, she decided, was one unsettling place. To make matters worse, their noisy forward motion aside, it was marked by an eerie stillness. It was a stillness that seemed to signal the underlying ecological imbalance existing below the surface, where Jack now rested, along with Skeeter.

The water beneath the RIB was unnaturally calm and peculiarly lifeless. The usual vibrant hues of marine life were absent, replaced by a murky, greenish-brown expanse. There were no usual ripples and movements that might indicate a thriving underwater ecosystem.

She didn't like the idea of Jack floating lifeless in such a polluted, hypoxic disaster zone. It didn't seem right. He deserved better. The reality of Jack's passing hadn't hit her yet. She knew that when it did, it would hit hard. Time was, he'd been her beau.

'What's your figuring right now?' Mac asked.

'Off the top of my head? I figure we might do a little doxing.'

'English, please? My Cajun's rusty.'

Zads laughed into the wind, the dead sea spray. 'Doxing. We're going to get Clewton's *docs* out into the public domain. A mere warmup, a revenge *entrée*. I know some hackers. They love a good dox job.'

Mac appeared to let the idea percolate. Then, 'You mean like a social media pile-on?'

Zads smiled. 'That's the one. Except we got a little role reversal up our sleeve. This time, the little people will be piling on the big people. It's officially chop-busting time. No one will want to talk to Clewton down the country club when this *merde* gets out."

'So, Chop-Buster-General, are we officially AWOL?'

'Looks that way,' Zads said, sitting up straighter, relaxing into her usual sassy, snappy comport.

'I'll be damned,' Mac mused. 'Never thought I was the AWOL type. You live and learn.'

'Hey, Mac!' Zads shouted out.

Mac turned to her.

'You can quit with the face, already. My swamp's a no-smirking zone.'

*   *   *

Unknown Forrest Sherman Class Destroyer
Time – Unknown
Position – Unknown

When Jack came to, he was in a sickbay. Or, at least, he assumed he was. The sickbay – if such it was - was divided into two distinct sections. Jack's section was mainly what you would expect, with standard Navy medical equipment, white sterile bulkheads, and bright fluorescent lighting. However, in the other part of the sickbay, the ostensibly metal bulkheads bore strange, intricate carvings and symbols reminiscent of some ancient, esoteric language. Some of these symbols glowed faintly in the dark, casting eerie shadows. The bulkhead metal also had a peculiar, almost organic quality and looked like it was subtly pulsating. And somehow, Jack knew, just *knew*, that it would feel warm to the touch. The other section was lit strangely, too - dim and inconsistent. In his section – the *human* section, he realized he'd come to think of it - the fluorescent lights maintained a steady glow. In the not-human part, the illumination seemed to come from bioluminescent algae and softly glowing crystals embedded in the bulkheads, casting a greenish-blue hue. To say that the atmosphere was unsettling was putting it mildly.

Standard medical equipment was present but interspersed with peculiar devices he failed to recognize. Some apparent surgical tools seemed to have extra, unnecessary blades or were made from unknown materials that shifted colors. Stethoscopes, syringes, and other instruments sometimes emitted faint, disturbing whispers, and everything seemed shot through with weird animism.

His section featured standard-issue Navy beds like the one he was laid up in. In the other section, the beds were somehow more organic and strangely shaped—beds designed to accommodate some unknown, unique physiology—or at least one unknown to Jack.

The sickbay air was thick and humid, carrying a scent that was a mix of antiseptic, sea brine, and an indefinable, slightly nauseating odor. The temperature fluctuated between uncomfortably cold and stiflingly warm, adding to Jack's sense of unease. Earlier, when he'd leaned out of bed to unsuccessfully reach for a glass of water on his bedside table, he'd spotted something even more disturbing. In the center of the sickbay, a prominent, circular symbol was embedded in the green-tiled deck, surrounded by intricate runes. The symbol glowed with a faint, unearthly light, pulsating in sync with the ship's movements.

Jack wondered what drugs he was on to make him see such wacky shit.

To top it off, a very curious-looking female medical corpsman entered the sick bay, looking at him with evident concern. She sported an expansive forehead, large eyes, and a snub - almost flat - nose, her short, swept-back, ash-blond hair emphasizing this. Her ears were tiny. Her lips, in contrast, were full, sensual. In the dim light, it looked like her skin had a gray-blue tint. The shirt sleeves of her working blues were neatly rolled up above the elbows, revealing colorful tattoos. Her eyes were blue and watery, and she rarely blinked. Frankly, she was one odd-looking woman.

And wrapped around her arm in a spiral was a piece of complex jewelry, austere and unembellished, wildly eccentric – kooky and visually fucking vexatious. Ill-proportioned, yet with an eerie beauty, the jewelry's aesthetic seemed based on the elliptical with many weirdly stretched circles. And while the metal looked like gold, its burnished surfaces indicated other alloys in play. Given how it hugged her skin, it was easy to confuse it with her similarly designed tattoos.

What the hell have they put me on?

According to her name tag, she was B. West, General Medical Officer, Lieutenant.

She smiled. 'How are you feeling, Mr Tarr?' Her voice was soft and lyrical.

Behind a bulkhead, something clattered in a tray, and Jack heard a quick exhalation of air and something that sounded like a curse. Whoever had spoken had sounded like they were talking with a mouthful of water. West glanced behind her, annoyed.

'What the fuck is that?' Jack asked, staring groggily at the out-there décor.

West frowned. 'What can you see, Chief?'

'All green and glowy, funny patterns, you know?'

West's eyebrows, such as they were, rose, her frown morphing into surprise. 'You can *see* that? The *other* part of the ship?'

Jack nodded. *Other part? Fuck she on about?*

The frown returned. 'Hmm. That's unexpected.'

He'd been picked up by a US warship—a destroyer judging by the size of the sickbay. But everything was way off kilter. It was like recognizing somebody, only to immediately discover they weren't the person you thought they were. The quality of light was different, darker than any ship he'd served on. He wondered if the ship was in blackout, but then red lights were used; these were green.

And what was it with the bulkheads? And the overhead? The strange patterns etched into the steel? And the crazy-crap pictures, drawings carved into the metal, the designs geometrical, yet somehow raw, brutal; the shapes seemed to imply the existence of lost knowledge; frustratingly, most of the designs defied description – apart from the vague sense that he was looking at some kind of unknown aquatic, debased version of human life – weird, creepy shit, yet powerfully primal.

I'm on the Forrest Sherman.

There was also more wood than there should have been. Where the bulkheads met the overhead, metal merged with wood like the two were organically connected.

He blinked. 'Thirsty,' he managed, trying to sit up. For some reason, he could not, and he was too groggy to figure out why. Whatever they'd given him that was causing the psychedelic visions had also turned his muscles to mush. He vaguely remembered raving about green men in green suits. Except they hadn't been green suits. But the men *had* been green. Or something.

West brought a glass of water to his lips, accompanied by a thick, fishy smell.

'Relax, Chief Tarr,' she said in her lovely sing-song voice. 'You need to rest.'

'I think I'm supposed to be dead,' Jack said earnestly. 'Didn't expect heaven to be green. Or hell, come to that. Am I in heaven or hell?'

West smiled. 'Somewhere in between.'

'So am I dead?'

West looked at him for a few moments. 'No, you're not. But from what I've heard, you came close. But you're still with us. Recovery starts now.'

'How am I not dead?'

'You were rescued. It was touch and go, as you people say. A down-to-the-wire rescue. Dramatic, apparently.'

'My team, was anybody else picked up?' *You people?*

'Not from *your* team, Mr Tarr.'

Jack leaned back into his pillow, defeated. Skeeter dead. Det, too. Probably Zads and Mac. And here he was, alive against all the odds.

Erin. I need to let her know I'm alright. Seem *to be alright.* 'Get me ship to shore comms.'

'All in good time, Chief.'

Clewton and Tammes, damn them. It was their fault. He would expose their crimes, and they would pay. Somehow, he would bring their dark deeds into the light of day. But first, he had to get off this ship.

'Where am I, West?' he said.

'You're in the sickbay.'

'Of what vessel?'

'*Innsmouth*,' she said. 'USS *Innsmouth*.'

'*Innsmouth*?' Why did that sound familiar? He was pretty sure there'd been no Forrest Sherman named *Innsmouth*.

'Yes,' West said, her eyes blazing briefly. 'And it's *Innsmouth, ma'am.*'

'I'm a goddamn civilian,' Jack shot back. '*Ma'am.*'

'No civilians on *this* ship, Chief. Only crew,' West said, smiling. 'Welcome aboard.'

The Beginning

CHECK OUT OTHER GREAT DEEP SEA THRILLERS

THE BREACH
by Edward J. McFadden III

A Category 4 hurricane punched a quarter mile hole in Fire Island, exposing the Great South Bay to the ferocity of the Atlantic Ocean, and the current pulled something terrible through the new breach. A monstrosity of the past mixed with the present has been disturbed and it's found its way into the sheltered waters of Long Island's southern sea.

Nate Tanner lives in Stones Throw, Long Island. A disgraced SCPD detective lieutenant put out to pasture in the marine division because of his Navy background and experience with aquatic crime scenes, Tanner is assigned to hunt the creeper in the bay. But he and his team soon discover they're the ones being hunted.

INFESTATION
by William Meikle

It was supposed to be a simple mission. A suspected Russian spy boat is in trouble in Canadian waters. Investigate and report are the orders.

But when Captain John Banks and his squad arrive, it is to find an empty vessel, and a scene of bloody mayhem.

Soon they are in a fight for their lives, for there are things in the icy seas off Baffin Island, scuttling, hungry things with a taste for human flesh.

They are swarming. And they are growing.

"Scotland's best Horror writer" - Ginger Nuts of Horror

"The premier storyteller of our time." - Famous Monsters of Filmland

CHECK OUT OTHER GREAT DEEP SEA THRILLERS

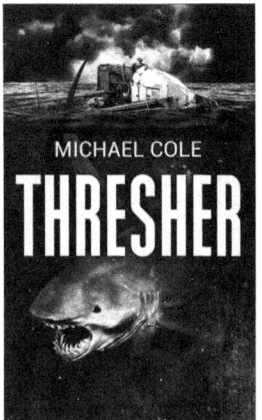

THRESHER
by Michael Cole

In the aftermath of a hurricane, a series of strange events plague the coastal waters off Florida. People go into the water and never return. Corpses of killer whales drift ashore, ravaged from enormous bite marks. A fishing trawler is found adrift, with a mysterious gash in its hull.

Transferred to the coastal town of Merit, police officer Leonard Riker uncovers the horrible reality of an enormous Thresher shark lurking off the coast. Forty feet in length, it has taken a territorial claim to the waters near the town harbor. Armed with three-inch teeth, a scythe-like caudal fin, and unmatched aggression, the beast seeks to kill anything sharing the waters.

THE GUILLOTINE
by Lucas Pederson

1,000 feet under the surface, Prehistoric Anthropologist, Ash Barrington, and his team are in the midst of a great archeological dig at the bottom of Lake Superior where they find a treasure trove of bones. Bones of dinosaurs that aren't supposed to be in this particular region. In their underwater facility, Infinity Moon, Ash and his team soon discover a series of underground tunnels. Upon exploring, they accidentally open an ice pocket, thawing the prehistoric creature trapped inside. Soon they are being attacked, the facility falling apart around them, by what Ash knows is a dunkleosteus and all those bones were from its prey. Now...Ash and his team are the prey and the creature will stop at nothing to get to them.

CHECK OUT OTHER GREAT DEEP SEA THRILLERS

SHARK: INFESTED WATERS
by P.K. Hawkins

For Simon, the trip was supposed to be a once in a lifetime gift: a journey to the Amazon River Basin, the land that he had dreamed about visiting since he was a child. His enthusiasm for the trip may be tempered by the poor conditions of the boat and their captain leading the tour, but most of the tourists think they can look the other way on it. Except things go wrong quickly. After a horrific accident, Simon and the other tourists find themselves trapped on a tiny island in the middle of the river. It's the rainy season, and the river is rising. The island is surrounded by hungry bull sharks that won't let them swim away. And worst of all, the sharks might not be the only blood-thirsty killers among them. It was supposed to be the trip of a lifetime. Instead, they'll be lucky if they make it out with their lives at all.

DARK WATERS
by Lucas Pederson

Jörmungandr is an ancient Norse sea monster. Thought to be purely a myth until a battleship is torn a part by one.

With his brother on that ship, former Navy Seal and deep-sea diver, Miles Raine, sets out on a personal vendetta against the creature and hopefully save his brother. Bringing with him his old Seal team, the Dagger Points, they embark on a mission that might very well be their last.

But what happens when the hunters become the hunted and the dark waters reveal more than a monster?